DINA NAYERI

A
Teaspoon
OF
EARTH
AND
SEA

ALLEN&UNWIN

First published in the United States in 2013 by Riverhead Books, a member of Penguin Group (USA) Inc.

First published in Great Britain in 2013 by Allen & Unwin

Allen & Unwin
c/o Atlantic Books
Ormond House
26–27 Boswell Street
London WC1N 3JZ
Phone: 020 7269 1610
Fax: 020 7430 0916
Email: UK@allenandunwin.com
Web: www.atlantic-books.co.uk

A CIP catalogue record for this book is available from the British Library.

ISBN 978 1 74331 449 4

Book design by Amanda Dewey

Printed in Great Britain by the MPG Printgroup, UK

10 9 8 7 6 5 4 3 2 1

For Philip and for Baba Hajji,

whom I once longed to see together in the same room

Part 1

UNSEEN STRAND

⁓⦿⦿⦿⁓

You and I have memories
Longer than the road that stretches out ahead.

—*The Beatles*

Prologue

This is the sum of all that Saba Hafezi remembers from the day her mother and twin sister flew away forever, maybe to America, maybe to somewhere even farther out of reach. If you asked her to recall it, she would cobble all the pieces together as muddled memories within memories, two balmy Gilan days torn out of sequence, floating somewhere in her eleventh summer, and glued back together like this:

"Where is Mahtab?" Saba asks again, and fidgets in the backseat of the car. Her father drives, while in the passenger seat her mother searches her purse for passports and plane tickets and all the papers needed to get out of Iran. Saba is dizzy. Her head hasn't stopped hurting since that night at the beach, but she doesn't remember much. She knows just this one thing: that her twin sister, Mahtab, is not here. Where is she? Why isn't she in the car when they are about to fly away and never come back?

"Do you have the birth certificates?" her father asks. His voice is sharp and quick and it makes Saba feel short of breath. *What is happening?* She has never been away from Mahtab for this long—for eleven years the Hafezi twins have been one entity. No Saba without Mahtab. But now days have passed—or is it weeks? Saba has been sick in bed and she can't remember. She hasn't been allowed to speak to her sister, and now the family is in a car headed to the airport without Mahtab. *What is happening?*

"When you get to California," her father says to her mother, "go straight to Behrooz's house. Then call me. I'll send money."

"Where is Mahtab?" Saba asks again. "Why is Mahtab not here?"

"She'll meet us there," says her mother. "Khanom Basir will drive her."

"Why?" Saba asks. She presses *stop* on her Walkman. This is all so confusing.

"Saba! Stop it!" her mother snaps, and turns back to her father. Is she wearing a green scarf? There is a spot of black over this part of the memory, but Saba remembers a green scarf. Her mother goes on. "What about security? What do I say to the *pasdars?*"

The mention of the moral police frightens Saba. For the past two years it has been a crime to be a converted Christian in Iran—or an ex-Muslim of any kind—as the Hafezis are. And it is terrifying to be a criminal in the world of brutal *pasdars* in stark uniforms, and mullahs in turbans and robes.

"There will be *pasdars* there?" she asks, her voice quivering.

"Hush," says her mother. "Go back to your music. We can't take it with us."

Saba sings an American tune that she and Mahtab learned from an illegally imported music tape, and goes over English word lists in her mind. She will be brave. She will perfect her English and not be afraid. *Abalone. Abattoir. Abbreviate.*

Her father wipes his brow. "Are you sure this is necessary?"

"We've been through this, Ehsan!" her mother snaps. "I won't have her raised in this place . . . wasting her days with village kids, stuck under a scarf memorizing Arabic and waiting to be arrested. No, thank you."

"I know it's important"—her father's voice is pleading—"but do we have to make a show of it? Is it so bad if we just *say* . . . I mean . . . it can be hidden easily."

"If you're a coward," her mother whispers. She begins to cry. "What about what happened . . . ?" she says. "They will arrest me." Saba wonders what she means.

"What is *abalone*?" She tries to distract her mother, who doesn't answer. The fighting frightens Saba, but there are more important things to worry about now. She taps her father on the shoulder. "Why is Khanom Basir bringing Mahtab? There's room in this car." It is odd that Reza's mother would drive at all. But maybe this means that Reza will come too, and Saba loves him almost as much as she loves Mahtab. In fact, if anyone asks, she is happy to claim that she will marry Reza one day.

"In a few years you'll be glad for today, Saba jan," her mother says, deciding to answer some unspoken question. "I know the neighbors call me a bad mother, risking your safety for nothing. But it's not nothing! It's more than any of them give to their children."

Soon they are in the busy Tehran airport. Her father walks ahead, taking quick, angry steps. "Look at this mess you've made of our family," he snaps. "My daughters—" He stops, clears his throat, and changes tack. Yes, this is the best way, the safest way. Yes, yes. He continues walking with the luggage. Saba feels her mother's hand squeezing hers.

Saba hasn't been to Tehran in months. When the Islamic Republic began making changes, her family moved permanently to their big house in the countryside—in Cheshmeh, a peaceful rice-farming village, where there are no protests, no angry mobs spilling into the streets, and people trust the generous Hafezis because of the family's deep local roots. Though some villages, with their terrifying mullah justice, are more dangerous for a Christian family than big cities, no one has bothered them in Cheshmeh, because the conservative, hardworking farmers and fishermen of the North don't attract close attention from the *pasdar*s, and because Saba's father is smart enough to lie, to oil the bread of curious neighbors by opening the house to mullahs and townspeople. Saba doesn't understand what they find so fascinating about her family. Reza alone is more interesting than all the Hafezis combined, and he has lived in Cheshmeh for all of his eleven years. He's taller than the other kids, with big round eyes, a village accent, and warm skin that she has touched twice. When they marry and move into a castle in California with Mahtab and her yellow-haired American husband, she will touch Reza's face every day. He has olive skin like boys from old Iranian movies, and he loves the Beatles.

At the airport, Saba sees Mahtab in the distance. "There she is!" she yells, and she pulls away from her father and runs toward her sister. "Mahtab, we're here!"

Now this is the juncture where the memory grows so foggy that it is just a dreamy patchwork of flashes. It is an accepted fact that at some point in this day her mother disappears. But Saba doesn't remember when in the confusion of security lines and baggage checks and *pasdar* interrogations this happens. She recalls only that a few minutes later, she sees her twin sister across the room—like the missing reflection in the mirror from a frightening old storybook—holding the hand of an elegant woman in a blue manteau, a heavy outer robe exactly like the one her mother was wearing. Saba waves. Mahtab waves back and turns away as if nothing were happening.

When Saba rushes toward them, her father grabs her. Yells. *Stop it! Stop it!* What is he hiding? Is he upset that Saba has made this discovery? "Stop, Saba. You're just tired and confused," he says. Lately, many people have tried to cover up things by calling her confused.

Memory plays such cruel tricks on the mind—like a movie with its tape pulled out and rolled back in, so that it shows nothing but a few garbled images. This next part feels somehow out of order. At some later point, her mother comes back—even though a minute ago she was holding Mahtab's hand. She takes Saba's face between two fingers and promises wonderful days in America. "Please just be quiet now," she says.

Then a *pasdar* in a security line asks her parents a string of questions. *Where are you going? Why? For how long? Is the whole family traveling? Where do you live?*

"My wife and daughter are going alone," Agha Hafezi says—a shocking lie. "For a short time, on vacation to see relatives. I'll stay here to wait for them."

"Mahtab's going too!" Saba blurts out. Is the *pasdar* wearing a brown hat? He can't be. *Pasdar*s don't wear the kind with a full brim. But in the memory the same brown hat always materializes.

"Who is Mahtab?" the *pasdar* barks, which is scary no matter how old you are.

Her mother lets out an uncomfortable laugh and says the most awful thing. "That is the name of her doll." Now Saba understands. Only *one* daughter is going. Do they plan to take Mahtab instead? Is that why they've kept her away all this time?

When she starts to cry, her mother leans down. "Saba jan, do you remember what I told you? About being a giant in the face of suffering? Would a giant cry in front of all these people?" Saba shakes her head. Then her mother cups her face again and says something heroic enough to redeem her. "You are Saba Hafezi, a lucky girl who reads English. Don't cry like a peasant, because you're no Match Girl."

Her mother hates that tale—a helpless street girl wasting matches to conjure up daydreams instead of building a fire to warm herself.

You are no Match Girl. This is Saba's last memory of that day. In a flash her mother disappears and there is a jumble of other images

Saba can't explain. She remembers someone's green scarf. A man with a brown hat. Her mother appearing in lines and at gates. Saba running away from her father, chasing Mahtab all the way to the window overlooking the airplanes. Each of these visions is covered by a layer of hazy uncertainty that she has learned to accept. Memory is a tricky thing. But one image is clear and certain, and no argument will convince her otherwise. And it is this: her mother in a blue manteau—after her father claimed to have lost her in the confusion of the security lines—boarding a plane to America, holding the hand of Mahtab, the lucky twin.

It's All in the Blood
(Khanom Basir)

S aba may not remember clearly, but I do. And yes, yes, I will tell
you in good time. You can't rush a storyteller. Women from the
North know how to be patient, because we wade in soggy rice fields
all day, and we're used to ignoring an itch. They talk about us all over
Iran, you know . . . us *shomali*, northern women. They call us many
good and bad things: fish-head eaters, easy women with too much
desire, *dehati*. They notice our white skin and light eyes, the way we
can dismiss their city fashions and still be the most beautiful. Everyone knows that we can do many things other women can't—change
tires, carry heavy baskets through fast rains, transplant rice in flooded
paddies, and pick through a leafy ocean of tea bushes all day long—
we are the only ones who do real work. The Caspian air gives us
strength. All that freshness—*green Shomal*, they say, *misty, rainy
Shomal*. And yes, sometimes we know to move slowly; sometimes, like
the sea, we are weighed down by unseen loads. We carry baskets of
herbs on our heads, swaying under coriander, mint, fenugreek, and
chive, and we do not rush. We wait for the harvest to saturate the air,

to fill our scattered homes with the hot, humid perfume of rice in summer, orange blossom in spring. The best things take time, like cooking a good stew, like pickling garlic or smoking fish. We are patient people, and we try to be kind and fair.

So when I say that I don't want Saba Hafezi to set hopeful eyes on my son Reza, it is not because I have a black heart. Even though Saba thinks I hate her, even though she gives all her unspent mother love to old Khanom Omidi, I've been watching out for that girl since she lost her mother. Still, just because you cook a girl dinner on Tuesdays doesn't mean you hand her your most precious son. Saba Hafezi will not do for my Reza, and it salts my stomach to think she holds on to this hope. Yes, Saba is a sweet enough girl. Yes, her father has money. God knows, that house has everything from chicken's milk to soul of man—that is to say, everything that exists and some things that don't; everything you can touch, and some things you can't. I know they are far above us. But I don't care about money or schoolbooks. I have a more useful kind of education than the women in that big house ever had, and I know that a bigger roof just means more snow.

I want my son to have a clearheaded wife, not someone who is lost in books and Tehrani ways and vague things that have nothing to do with the needs of today, here in one's own house. And what is all this foreign music she has given him? What other boy listens to this nonsense, closing his eyes and shaking his head as if he were possessed? God help me. The other boys barely know there is a place called America. . . . Look, I want Reza to have friends without jinns. And Saba has jinns. Poor girl. Her twin sister, Mahtab, is gone and her mother is gone and I don't mind saying that something troublesome is going on deep in that girl's soul. She makes a hundred knives and none have any handles—that is to say, she has learned how to lie a little too well, even for my taste. She makes wild claims about Mahtab. And why shouldn't she be troubled? Twins are like witches, the way they read each other's thoughts from far away. In a hundred black years I wouldn't have predicted their separation or the trouble it would cause.

I remember the two of them in happier days, lying on the balcony under a mosquito net their father had put up so they could sleep outside on hot nights. They would whisper to each other, poking the net with their painted pink toes and rummaging in the pockets of their indecent short shorts for hidden, half-used tubes of their mother's lipstick. This was before the revolution, of course, so it must have been many months before the family moved to Cheshmeh all year round. It was their summer holiday from their fancy school in Tehran—a chance for the city girls to pretend to live a village life, play with village children, let worshipful village boys chase them while they were young and such things were allowed. On the balcony the girls would pick at bunches of honeysuckle that grew on the outer wall of the house, suck the flowers dry like bees, read their foreign books, and scheme. They wore their purple Tehrani sunglasses, let their long black hair flow loose over bare shoulders browned by the sun, and ate foreign chocolates that are now long gone. Then Mahtab would start some mischief, the little devil. Sometimes I let Reza join them under the mosquito net. It seemed like such a sweet life, looking out from the big Hafezi house onto the narrow winding dirt roads below and the tree-covered mountains beyond, and, in the skirt of it, all our many smaller roofs of clay tiles and rice stalks, like Saba's open books facedown and scattered through the field. To be fair, the view from our window was better because we could see the Hafezi house on its hilltop at night, its pretty white paint glowing, a dozen windows, high walls, and many lights lit up for friends. Not that there is much to see these days—now that nighttime pleasures happen behind thick music-muffling curtains.

Some years after the revolution, Saba and Mahtab were put under the headscarf and we could no longer use the small differences in their haircuts or their favorite Western T-shirts to tell them apart in the streets—don't ask me why their shirts became illegal; I guess because of some foreign *chert-o-pert* written on the front. So after that, the girls would switch places and try to fool us. I think that's part of Saba's problem now—switching places. She spends too much time obsessing about Mahtab and dreaming up her life story, putting herself in Mahtab's place. Her mother used to say that all life is decided in the blood. All your abilities and tendencies and future footsteps. Saba thinks, if all of that is written in one's veins, and if twins are an exact blood match, then it follows that they should live matching lives, even if the shapes and images and sounds all around them are different—say, for argument's sake, if one was in Cheshmeh and the other was in America.

It breaks my heart. I listen to that wishful tone, lift her face, and see that dreamy expression, and the pit of my stomach burns with pity. Though she never says out loud, "I wish Mahtab was here," it's the same stew and the same bowl every day. You don't need to hear her say it, when you see well enough, her hand twitching for that missing person who used to stand to her left. Though I try to distract her and get her mind on practical things, she refuses to get off the devil's donkey, and would you want *your* son to spend his youth trying to fill such a gap?

The troubling part is that her father is so unskilled at understanding. I have never seen a man fail so repeatedly to find the way to his daughter's heart. He tries to show affection, always clumsily, and falters. So he sits at the hookah with his vague educated confusions, thinking, *Do I believe what my wife believed? Should I teach Saba to be safe or Christian?* He watches the unwashed children in Cheshmeh—the ones whose mothers tuck their colorful tunics and skirts between their legs, hike up their pants to the knee, and wade in *his* rice fields all day long—and wonders about their souls. Of course, I don't say anything to the man. No one does. Only four or five people know

that they are a family of Christ worshippers, or it would be dangerous for them in a small village. But he puts eggplant on our plates
and watermelons under our arms, so, yes, much goes unsaid about his
Saba-raising ways, his nighttime jinns, and his secret religion.

Now that the girls are separated by so much earth and sea, Saba
is letting her Hafezi brain go to waste under a scratchy village play
chador, a bright turquoise one lined with beads she got from Khanom
Omidi. She covers her tiny eleven-year-old body in it to pretend she
belongs here, wraps it tight around her chest and under her arms
the way city women like her mother never would. She doesn't realize
that every one of us wishes to be in her place. She wastes every opportunity. My son Reza tells me she makes up stories about Mahtab.
She pretends her sister writes her letters. How can her sister write
letters? I ask. Reza says the pages are in English, so I cannot know
what they really say, but let me tell you, she gets a lot of story out
of just three sheets of paper. I want to shake her out of her dream-
world sometimes. Tell her we both know those pages aren't letters—
probably just schoolwork. I know what she will say. She will mock me
for having no education. "How do you know?" she will goad. "You
don't read English."

That girl is too proud; she reads a few books and parades around
like she cut off Rostam's horns. Well, I may not know English, but
I am a storyteller and I know that pretending is no solution at all.
Yes, it soothes the burns inside, but real-life jinns have to be faced
and beaten down. We all know the truth about Mahtab, but she spins
her stories and Reza and Ponneh Alborz let her go on and on because
she needs her friends to listen—and because she's a natural storyteller. She learned that from me—how to weave a tale or a good lie,
how to choose which parts to tell and which parts to leave out.

Saba thinks everyone is conspiring to hide the truth about
Mahtab. But why would we? What reason would her father and the
holy mullahs and her surrogate mothers have for lying at such a time?

No, it isn't right. I cannot give my son to a broken dreamer with scars in her heart. What a fate that would be! My younger son twisted up in a life of nightmares and what-ifs and other worlds. Please believe me. This is a likely enough outcome . . . because Saba Hafezi carries the damage of a hundred black years.

Chapter One

SUMMER 1981

S aba sits in the front seat beside her father as he drives first through highways leading away from Tehran, then, hours later, along smaller winding roads back to Cheshmeh. The car is hot and humid, and she is sweating through her thin gray T-shirt. Her father leans across her and rolls down her window. The smell of wet grass floats in. They pass a watery rice field, a *shalizar* or, in Gilaki, a *bijâr*, and Saba leans out to watch the peasants, mostly women, in rush hats and bright, patchy garb rolled up to the knees as they slosh in the flooded paddies. Saba can see some of the workers' daub-covered houses scattered across the field near the tea and the rice. Most land-owners like Agha Hafezi don't live so close to their farms, preferring big modern cities like Tehran instead. But there is a war ravaging bor-der towns, maybe soon the big cities too, and Cheshmeh village— home to a few thousand, and an hour's drive outside the big city of Rasht—is a simple place. Dotted by water wells and fat rice barns on skinny legs like straw-hatted warlords, it is a moist, sultry northern refuge of thatched rooftops over blue-washed or natural terra-cotta houses, rice-stalk dwellings raised a little off the damp ground and clustered in *mahalles* at the foot of the Alborz Mountains. The center of Cheshmeh is marked by several paved roads that converge in a town square and a weekly bazaar (*jomeh-bazaar*, it is called, "Friday market"). Though he may be better hidden in Tehran, Agha Hafezi feels safest here, in his childhood home, where he has friends who protect him.

At the top of a big hill, just after the hand-painted wooden sign that reads CHESHMEH, Saba's father slows to let two bicyclists pass. One is a young man wearing old jeans and a large bundle on his back. The other is a fisherman in loose gray pants. His briny sea smell wafts into the car as he weaves toward the next green hill, then up and out of sight. Both faces are familiar to her. Unlike villa towns closer to the Caspian, Cheshmeh doesn't attract vacationing throngs, though some-times tourists wander into town in cars or buses to watch the harvest or buy something at the bazaar. Saba rests her forehead against the windowpane and waits for the inevitable moment when the fog gives way to a burst of trees in the distance. A doctor in an ill-fitting suit drives by in a worn-out yellow truck. He slows down beside them and waves. Agha Hafezi says a few words to him in Gilaki dialect through the open window. Saba knows that for her father, Cheshmeh is where all roads end. It has a hundred unmatched smells and sounds—the heady orange-blossom fogs, shops adorned with garlic-clove head-dresses, pickled garlic on fried eggplant, Gilaki songs, and crickets at night. He relishes the quiet of it. As they drive toward the house, Saba knows he will never try to leave again. He is a tired, too-cautious man obsessed with his secrets and with scrubbing away all outer signs of his own strength. And he is a liar.

Now, alone with her father in the front seat, Saba doesn't cry. Why would she? She's no Match Girl. No matter how big the car feels without her mother and sister, and no matter how many times her father tries to say that they're never coming back, Saba holds on to the belief that all is right in the universe. *Nothing's gonna change my world,* she sings in English all the way home, and that becomes her favorite song for the next month.

Just inside town, her father tries to feed her the first of the lies. *Mahtab is dead.* She searches for signs that he is making it up. He must be. Look at his nervous face and sweaty brow. "We didn't want to tell you while you were sick," he says, and when she doesn't respond, "Did you hear me, Saba jan? Put down those papers and listen to me."

"No," she whimpers, clutching tighter to her list of English words. "You're lying."

She vows never to speak to him again, because he must have planned all this—and Saba knows from her years as Khanom Hafezi's daughter that it's possible for just one person in a thousand to know the truth of something. She must hold on to what she saw: a woman in the terminal across the airport lounge—an elegant, stylish woman with her mother's unruly hair escaping the headscarf and her mother's navy blue manteau and her mother's hurried expression— holding the hand of a somber, obedient girl, an eerily silent child who only could have been—*was*—Mahtab.

No, she didn't die.

"Saba jan," her father says, "listen to your baba. You have your friend Ponneh. She will be like your sister. Isn't that nice?"

No, she didn't die. There is no need to find a new Mahtab.

Since there is no meal waiting at home, they eat kebabs on the roadside, staring wordlessly at the blanket of trees and fog that hides the sea. Her father buys her corn on the cob, which the vendor peels and drops into a bucket of salt so that it hisses and drips, sealing in the perfect burnt seawater taste. As she eats, the memory solidifies and the gaps fill themselves—like animals in her science books that regrow body parts, a sort of survival magic—forming a decipherable whole: the blurry outline of a tall, manteaued woman. A skinny eleven-year-old ghost of a girl in Mahtab's clothing. Is that guilt on her face? Does she feel bad for being a traitor twin? Then the hazy, colorless lounge with its hordes of faceless passengers pushing past each other to board a plane to America.

Mahtab went to America without me. The question of how she appeared in the terminal lounge is still a mystery. Probably, Khanom Basir brought her because Saba's parents didn't want her to know that they had chosen Mahtab to go to America instead of her. They wanted to spare her feelings, because they had betrayed her and because she is the less important twin. Maybe this is part of some twisted bargain for each parent to get a daughter.

For the next week Saba tries to get the spineless Cheshmeh adults to admit their lies. If Mahtab is dead, then why no funeral? And where did her mother go? Her father must have paid the neighbors to tell his lies. That's how he gets everything he wants, and so she isn't fooled by the drumbeat of death and ritual and mourning that follows. It is nothing more than an elaborate ruse concocted by the wealthy and powerful Agha Hafezi in order to give his other, more special daughter a better life—a life that Saba can observe through magazines and illegal television shows.

☙❦❧

A month after the lonely ride back from the airport, Saba tries for the third time to prove that Mahtab is alive. She runs away with Ponneh Alborz, her best friend, and Reza Basir, their shared love. Who cares that Reza's mother will scream and rail and call Saba all sorts of names reserved for wicked children? It is worth the trouble to take her friends along. She coaxes them to hitchhike with her to Rasht, where she intends to visit the post office one more time. Now that a month has passed since Mahtab left, it is reasonable to expect a letter from her—because no matter how much their parents try to cover up their treacherous plans, Mahtab will always find a way to write to Saba.

The three friends walk through the unfamiliar Rashti streets, keeping close to passing adults so they won't seem to be traveling alone. Saba consults a hand-drawn map every now and then, and straightens her blue headscarf, but mostly she watches Reza, who struts a few paces ahead, carrying his tattered football under one arm, sometimes kicking it between his feet as he runs ahead, as if to create a force field for Saba and Ponneh—because for Reza, there is no use being friends with girls if you can't be seen to protect them. He has played at this game since the Hafezis' earliest summers in Gilan. Despite her mother's insistence that she behave with the conviction that she is equal to the boys, Saba has never minded letting Reza take charge. It is one way she can fit into Reza and Ponneh's world—their peasant life of thrice-owned jeans, orange juice sucked directly from punctured rinds, mismatched bangles, provincial headscarves in red and turquoise lined with sequins, dirty hair parted in the center and peeking out from underneath. Every detail delights her. Though her father frowns at the thought of Saba entering their houses and touching the bowls in their closet-sized kitchens, he doesn't forbid it. Ponneh's and Reza's families are craftspeople: they weave rush and cloth, make jams and pickles. They have many jobs and little to spare, but they are literate and have respectable homes. Their children attend school for now, and might even go to college if they perform well on their exams. To Saba's father, they differ from the paddy workers who stop by the house in the off-season to do household work for him—though in reality all people of Cheshmeh are intertwined, with each other and with fieldwork. Who here has reached old age without transplanting rice or picking tea for a day?

Halfway down a narrow road, they hear a sharp voice. "You kids!

Come here." An officer of the moral police lingers outside a window-less store across the street. He has one knee on a stool and keeps bringing a bottle of yogurt soda to his lips. Saba freezes. *Pasdars* remind her of the airport and the one who barked *Who is Mahtab?*, tainting her last moments with her mother. She hardly notices as Reza grabs both their hands and starts to sprint behind his ball through the back alleyways, too quick for the officer to follow. He taunts the officer with the Iranian football team chant—which he has heard on the Hafezis' television—as he runs. "Doo Doorooo dood dood. IRAN!"

You're going to get in deep trouble with the police one day, Reza's mother is always telling the threesome. She says this to Saba because of her mother's underground ways and the foreign music Saba shares with Reza, and to Ponneh because she is obstinate and too beautiful to escape notice. Saba doubts that Reza pays any attention to these warnings. He is too busy playing the hero. Maybe she shouldn't have brought the two of them along.

Soon the tiny alleyways and zigzag streets in this obscure part of Rasht become familiar. Besides her trips to the post office, Saba came to this part of town once with her mother to shop for shoes. The twins were eight and the pro-hair government had not yet been over-thrown by the pro-scarf people—the street screamers that later became the political parties of the twins' fourth-grade world. That day they each bought two pairs of shoes, Saba's with slightly higher heels. Her mother arranged this on purpose because of the injustice of the centimeter's difference in the twins' heights. Saba knows be-cause she saw the scheming smile on her mother's face when Mahtab was busy adjusting her straps.

When the trio arrives at the post office, Saba puts away her home-made map, straightens her scarf as she has seen adult women do, and runs right up to Fereydoon at the counter, whose face falls as he sees her bounding toward him. Reza and Ponneh hang back, waiting for her to retrieve her prize so they can visit the ice-cream shop as Saba has promised them. She smiles politely at Fereydoon, who wipes his massive brow with a hairy hand and looks down at her from his window. "Nothing today, little Khanom."

She ignores him. "Hafezi," she says, expectant eyes on his pale face, small fingers clutching the edge of the counter between them. "Hafezi from Cheshmeh."

Fereydoon begins to mutter to himself as he feigns the motion of fumbling through a stack of mail behind him. "No, nothing for Hafezi. Look, girl, the mail will come to you in Cheshmeh. You don't have to come to us."

Saba knows that Fereydoon is tired of her. But she felt lucky today, because her friends were with her and because it has been *exactly* a month. She turns and glances at Reza and Ponneh, lingering now near an elderly man so they won't seem alone.

For a moment she is frozen—even the smile plastered to her face—and Fereydoon clears his throat several times and looks at the clock on the wall. Finally Reza runs over and takes her hand. He says, in his best imitation of city talk, "Thank you for your time, dear sir." Then, with two pathetic half-bows, he pulls Saba away.

Reza starts toward the door, but she jerks her hand out of his. She doesn't need him to intervene. Besides, they are standing in a government office, two girls and a boy alone—a recipe for trouble. When he reaches for her arm again, she pushes him away and runs out of the post office, desperate to hide the tears pooling behind her eyelids.

Ponneh and Reza follow her out of the office, down the street, and into a narrow alley that curves around to a dead end. She knows they are following, because she can hear their hushed words, muffled now and then by hands cupping each other's ears.

"Don't pick it!" Reza says to Ponneh—she must be picking the scab on his elbow again. He always protests but never stops her. "Remember about the river of blood?"

Saba remembers about the river of blood, a play on Farsi words that Mahtab used along with one of their mother's illustrated books on practical medicine to scare Ponneh. Now that Mahtab isn't around, Saba must correct the imbalance of things, rid Ponneh of her superstitions and find a new co-conspirator. For weeks Saba has had to be twice a person, encompassing Mahtab's thoughts and feelings as much as her own so that her twin will not be extinguished. If Mahtab was walking beside her, as Saba imagines her doing, she would say just the thing to conjure up all the medical terrors of picking scabs.

Saba drops down on a dirty unpaved alley walkway, crossing her legs and resting her head against a mud wall. She can feel her friends' eyes on her as she presses her face against it, expecting the scent of cooking from the adjacent house, dry dirt, and earthworms. But the wall smells like fish and wet mud and the sea. She recoils, burying her face in her sleeve. The sea is far away, but its smell is always near—that evil Caspian smell. She is not ready to welcome it back, though once she loved the scent of the sea. Maybe she will again, but now she tries to keep the water from coming. Her hands reach for her throat and her breath grows faster. She tries to expel the nightmare image of Mahtab in the water, on the day she spoke to her for the last time, the day the adults call lucky because Saba escaped unharmed. *Rescued by God's hand,* they say. Saba knows better, because she was there when *both* twins were rescued. Why was Mahtab spirited away? Why did *she* get to go to America?

And what happened in the water? She remembers that she and Mahtab sneaked out of the vacation house in the middle of the night and went for a swim. She remembers playing in the waves. Tasting the half-salty water of the Caspian Sea. Seeing a fish go by. She remembers the houses on stilts, obscured by the night fog, that drifted out of sight as she floated farther into the sea with her sister. Mahtab kept splashing and singing American songs, while Saba did the one thing she knew how to do at frightening times. She refused to leave her twin, even after she was certain she wanted to go home. She floated on her back and whispered stories to Mahtab, and Mahtab taught her four new English words she had learned that week. Four secret words that Saba didn't know. Mahtab apologized for keeping them to herself, like taking four extra pieces of candy when counting out portions one by one. *One for Mahtab. One for Saba.*

Then Saba recalls that something forced her to swallow all those mouthfuls of saltwater. A minute passed, the shoreline rising and falling, before the smelly, sandpapery hands of a fisherman lifted the two of them out of the sea. Mahtab sang silly songs all during the sleepy boat ride back to shore. Or was that another day, as the adults claim? In the memory Mahtab is wearing a yellow plastic fisherman's parka like the one she lost on last year's trip. Maybe she found it in the water. Or maybe this one belonged to the fisherman. What happened next? Flashes of people yelling at each other. Policemen peering into her face. Patches of black.

A second later she was in a hospital bed in Rasht. Where was Mahtab? Doctors and neighbors twittered around her and said, *Don't worry. Mahtab is okay.* Then, after they'd had the time to hatch their plans for America, they changed their story.

Saba catches Ponneh searching her face with her beautiful almond eyes, and she tells herself to be brave. She repeats words from her English list to calm herself.

Banal. Bandit. Bandy.

"I had a dream," she says, almost to the wall, "that my maman showed up at school and told me that I hadn't studied enough English, so I couldn't talk to Mahtab."

Ponneh scratches the tip of her dainty nose and glances at Reza. "Let's go get some cakes," she says, her voice a little uncertain.

Mahtab would have asked for every last detail of the dream.

"I think it means I'm going to see her again," says Saba, choosing to answer Mahtab's question instead, and looks up at her friends. She smiles grandly and wills them to smile back. "Mahtab too," she adds, and rests her head against the wall. She pushes her headscarf onto her shoulders and picks a loose thread from her sweater while humming an American tune from one of the illegal music tapes her father tolerates now that she is a delicate, thing to keep watchfully cupped in both palms.

"Let's play something," Ponneh suggests. When Saba doesn't respond, her face grows steely. She sits beside Saba, pulls her hand away from the loose thread, and interlaces their fingers. "You should just admit Mahtab is dead . . . like everyone says."

Mahtab would have played a hundred games of possibility before admitting such a defeat, especially without proof. How can everyone believe that Mahtab is dead without seeing her body, without putting an ear to her chest and counting the beats? Sometimes Saba wakes up in the night, her skin wet and salty again, after having seen Mahtab's body in her nightmares, drowned and fished out from the bottom of the sea. It looks just like her own and so it is doubly frightening. Maybe there is no body because Mahtab never existed. Maybe she was only Saba's reflection in the mirror. Is she trapped there now? Can Saba break the glass with her fist and pull Mahtab out?

Reza is still standing beside them, glancing at the main road now and then and chewing his lower lip raw. Ponneh keeps signaling him to sit beside Saba, to pay her some attention. This is Ponneh's way of soothing her best friend: offering up Reza as a gift; he is just a boy and good for such things. But Reza keeps his post. "Do you think the *pasdar* will find us here?" he says, and peers down the alley again. He chews his lips and gives the ball a few nervous kicks whispering, "Iran, Iran! GOAL!"

"Maybe she's not dead, though," says Saba, like she has done a hundred times in the last month. She touches her throat, rubs it with both palms, a recent tic that she knows worries her family and friends. "Maybe she went with my mother to America."

"My maman says that your maman didn't go to America," whispers Reza from above them. "And she's not coming back."

"Your maman is a lying viper," Saba shoots back. "You'll see when Mahtab finds a way to write me a letter. She's a lot smarter than both of you."

Ponneh puts on that affected look of concern that she perfected by the time she was eight. It is convincing, even comforting—Ponneh pretending to be an adult. "There aren't going to be any letters," she says: a fact as simple as the blue sea.

Reza crosses his arms and mumbles, "Why would my mother lie?"

"There are a million reasons," says Saba. "I saw them—both of them—at the airport. And besides, Baba and I drove Maman there ourselves. She had a passport and papers and everything. Ponneh, you remember that, right?"

Ponneh nods and clutches Saba's hand even harder. "Still."

"Exactly," she says, and doesn't flinch when Ponneh, who likes to pick at things when she's nervous, begins peeling the polish off Saba's fingernails. "You believe me. I saw them with my own eyes. Maybe they said she's dead to throw the *pasdar*s off my mother's tracks . . . so they'd leave us alone. Probably Baba paid everyone to lie." With her thumb, she rubs out the dirty spots from her shoes, the last pair chosen by her mother that still fits her feet. After a while she decides that all is well. Mahtab will write soon enough and the facts are unchangeable—the passport, the drive to the airport. No one can deny these things. She wipes her face, takes a last deep breath, and drags herself out from the abyss. She licks her salty upper lip and offers a distraction. "I heard Khanom Omidi has four husbands, each in a different town."

"No. Really?" Ponneh looks up, all bad things forgotten. "How do you know?"

"The Khanom Witches." Saba shrugs. "They're always talking about each other."

The Three Khanom Witches is Saba's name for the neighbors who have invited themselves into the Hafezi home since her mother left. They know how to do things that her father can't, and so they have become her surrogate family. They tell stories, cook, clean, gossip, and best of all, they betray each other in the most entertaining ways.

Khanom Omidi, the Sweet One, says, almost daily, "I have a surprise for you, Saba joon. Big surprise. Don't show the others." She lumbers over, dragging all that extra flesh in a colorful chador, a long loose garment she has worn since giving up fieldwork. It barely conceals a tinting mishap that has left her white hair a purplish brown. Sometimes the old woman Scotch-tapes her face to prevent lines. Her lazy eye searches through her stash of coins secreted away sometimes in the folds of her chador, sometimes in a cloth waistband, and she offers some to Saba, who guards these coins more vigilantly than all the wads of bills from her father.

Khanom Basir, the Evil One and Reza's mother, says just as often, "Saba, come here . . . alone." Her thin lips utter unwelcome words while her skinny, angular face scans Saba's body for signs of womanhood. "Has anything special occurred lately . . . in the hammam or the toilet?" Each time she asks this Saba hates her, because she doesn't know what Khanom Basir is looking for, and what she might be telling Reza.

The third witch, Khanom Mansoori, the Ancient One, just snores in the corners of Saba's house, once in a while tossing out some age-old truth about children to the other two women. Unlike Ponneh and Reza, who live on a narrow street below the Hafezi home in a cluster of small houses with handmade curtains of lace and cotton and some basic conveniences (small fridges, kitchen tables, gas ovens), Khanom Omidi, the Sweet One, and Khanom Mansoori, the Ancient One, live in huts made of wood, straw, and clay mixed with chopped rice. Their squat dwellings pick out from under hipped rice-stalk roofs dotting the hills just a short bumpy ride or vigorous walk past the weekly bazaar. Isolated in a wooded area, they let chickens roam near front steps strewn with discarded shoes, and they sell the eggs at the market. At one point over many years, each of them has rolled up her pant legs and stooped in the rice fields—this is how they came to know Agha Hafezi, who chose them as caregivers for his daughters.

To Saba their houses are like pieces of pottery, like art. She loves the comfort of being cocooned in tiny spaces amid thick hanging canopies that separate two musty rooms, or sitting under low ceilings in cozy corners draped with blankets that are heated by coal stoves and oil lamps. In the mornings fresh tea flows from samovars, and four-pane windows opening onto green plains, inviting in the smell of wet grass. She is drawn to the enclave of mothers in hot, cramped kitchens, squatting on tunic-wrapped haunches, building mountains of chicken and garlic skins, eyeing bubbling pots, and squeezing pomegranate juice into cups that Ponneh and Reza pass back and forth, but that Saba is not allowed to touch. Sometimes to spite her father, Saba crawls into their bed mats, intricate hand-sewn throws arranged in all four corners where families sleep together. Their bedding smells like hair oils and henna and flower petals.

To keep Saba out of their homes, Agha Hafezi allows her surrogate mothers to roam free in his house, to use his big Western kitchen and play with Saba in her bedroom, where the bed rises up off the ground and there is a writing desk for her papers.

Now Ponneh seems to be in deep thought on the matter of Khanom Omidi's secret life. "Well, I know one thing," she offers. "Omidi has a plastic leg. Once, I saw her take it off and fill it with candy and flower petals so it wouldn't stink."

"That's stupid," says Reza, who loves the ever-humming, fleshy-faced Khanom Omidi as much as Saba does. "The candy comes from inside her chador."

How does Reza know about the treasure chador? Khanom Omidi is *Saba's* Good Witch—the stand-in for *her* missing mother. "No one believes that anymore," she says. "I checked her leg when she was sleeping and it's just full of meat." Her friends give a gratifying laugh. "But the one about Khanom Basir is true. I heard she's a *real* witch."

"You're lying!" says Reza, ever quick to defend his mother.

The girls look at each other and burst into a fit of giggles. Then come the private jokes about alleged jars of fluid and dried monkey toes strung up on roofs. At first Reza ignores them; then he picks up his backpack and makes a show of preparing to leave.

"No, stay!" Ponneh puts on an affected croon. "I'll let you kiss me . . . on the lips."

Reza, still brooding on behalf of his mother, hoists his backpack on both shoulders and says, "You better think of something better than that."

Saba tries not to laugh, even though Ponneh deserves it for being so arrogant. "I'll teach you some English words," she offers. "*Abalone* means . . . um . . . money for widows."

He glances down at Saba's backpack. "What've you got in there?"

Saba tugs on the zipper because she does have something there that will keep him. Reza too devours American music, though Saba is his only source. He borrows her old tapes and tries to strum the notes on his father's *setar*, which has collected dust since his father left to be with his new family. "You probably never heard of Pink Floyd," she says.

"Yes, I have!" Reza says, his voice and fingers all anticipation. "Can I see?"

It is an obvious lie, but Saba doesn't correct him. She takes out an unmarked tape and holds it out to her friend. "You can keep it," she says. "I'm done with it anyway."

"Really?" Reza's eyes remain fixed on the tape as he drops to the ground and out of his backpack. Saba moves closer and starts to tell him all the words to her favorite Pink Floyd song, which is about bricks and teachers and rebellious kids—a song so illegal that one verse of it would be enough to make a hundred mullahs wet themselves.

"You can't accept that," says Ponneh. Reza takes his gaze off the tape for an instant; he stares at Ponneh as if pleading with her to forget their rural pride. Then his shoulders drop and Saba is forced to endure his disappointment, Ponneh's wounded glare, and the fact that she has united the two of them in their shared poverty. Maybe her friends act this way because they know that Saba would be discouraged from playing with them if any English-speaking city children lived nearby. The sole reason she isn't sent away to school in Tehran or Rasht is that her father can't bear to lose another daughter. And no matter how many ragged old jeans or unfashionable flowery headscarves she wears, or how well she fakes their accent or tries to speak Gilaki, she will always be the outsider.

"What if I pay for it?" Reza suggests, digging in his pockets for coins and counting them in his palm. He has a few tomans, not even enough for a blank tape.

"You don't have to," says Saba, wishing she knew how an adult would give a gift to someone so beloved without being accused of showing off. Then she reaches into his extended hand and chooses the smallest coin. "Just enough," she says.

They sit in the alley for two more hours. Saba and Ponneh braid each other's hair while Reza sneaks out to buy them snacks. He returns with yogurt sodas, and they talk about Saba's classes, because, even though she attends the same two-room schoolhouse as all the Cheshmeh children whose parents can spare them, she is further educated by city tutors in English, Old Persian, and all kinds of maths and sciences. Reza rifles through Saba's backpack looking for other morsels of wealthy living that seem to excite him. He pulls out a tattered, yellowing magazine and stares at the beautiful blond woman on the cover. "What's this?" he asks, and Ponneh shuffles over to have a look. Saba can see that he doesn't dare ask the question on both their faces, *Is it from England or Germany or France? Or maybe . . . America?*

"An old magazine my maman's friend gave me for practicing English," she says. "It's almost as old as I am." Then she adds, her excitement rising with theirs, "It's American." The magazine came from her mother's college friend, an elegant lady doctor named Zohreh Sadeghi, who lived far away and whispered with Maman about the new regime and the Shah. The twins used to call her Dr. Zohreh. After the night in the Caspian, she visited Saba in the hospital.

Ponneh and Reza press their heads together to pore over the fragile pages—every shadowy photo, every vibrant illustration, every detail of a mystical American life that is no longer welcome here. Saba feels guilty because dreams of such a life—dreams of betterness, otherness, of American entitlement—feel like a betrayal of her friends—of Reza, who at eleven is already a nationalist and full of Gilaki ideals, and Ponneh, who will have to become the new Mahtab. Saba translates the English words on the cover. *"Life,"* she says as she fingers the title in red-and-white block letters at the top. "January twenty-second, 1971. Fifty cents."

"How much is that?" Ponneh asks.

"A lot," she says, though she isn't sure.

"Who's the lady?" Reza asks, daring to touch the yellow hair on the brittle page. "She's probably old and gray by now."

"It says her name here," Saba says, trying hard to pronounce it, before realizing that Ponneh and Reza won't know any better. "Ta—ree—sha Nik—soon."

"Strange name," says Ponneh. "Sounds like shaving a beard . . . *reesh-tarash*."

"She's the daughter of the American Shah," says Saba, because she has read this magazine a hundred times by now, and she knows.

Reza nods gravely. "Yes, yes, I know this Niksoon. A great man."

Ponneh rolls her eyes and Saba flips to the center of the magazine, where pictures from this beautiful girl's life are displayed for millions to see. She is a princess. *Shahzadeh Nixon*. There she is in her expensive American dress (four different dresses in as many pages!), with her flirtatious American grin and her shiny American suitor—a boy so pale and handsome that he could be in the movies if he wasn't busy beaming over his shoulder at photographers and staring at the fairy girl's hands as if he were just a little bored.

"So lucky," whispers Ponneh. "Read that," she says, pointing to a headline.

"Ed Cox, a Scion of Old Money with the Instincts of a Liberal."

"That has some difficult words, but Maman translated it for me once," says Saba. "It means his money is old and his thoughts are new. Just the opposite of what you want."

Ponneh is trying not to look confused, so Saba pulls her shoulders back and says, "Old thoughts are the thoughts of philosophers, which are better than those of revolutionaries. And new money is the money you earn—like my baba did." Saba's mother never liked to mention that the Hafezi lands were inherited—now dwindled to a fraction of what the family owned under the Shah. It was an inconvenient detail to the lesson, and sad to think that rising by you sweat and wit was an impossible thing in the new Iran. No *shalizar* owner becomes wealthy on rice sales alone. There are land rentals and bribes and compound interest. Saba knows this, has studied it with her math tutors, but follows her mother's example of forgetting to mention it.

"What does this say?" Ponneh points to a caption, but Saba is no longer listening.

"This is where Mahtab lives now," she says, looking at the opulent dining room with its lush curtains, sparkling decorative branches, and tuxedoed men.

The other two grow quiet and Reza mumbles, "In the American Shah's house?"

"I don't mean exactly here," she says. She pulls out two other magazines hidden in the pockets of her backpack. She flips through the pages, every one filled with iconic images of American life—loose hair and color televisions. Roofless cars and apple pastries. Hamburgers, cigarettes, and stacks of music tapes. An expressionless statue carrying a torch. Pancake diners dedicated solely to the breakfasts of the peasant class.

Then Saba takes three handwritten pages from inside the magazine. "What if I told you that Mahtab already wrote to me?" She waves the pages in front of their faces, her eyes full of the exhilaration of knowing something they don't. "It makes sense that Maman doesn't call me," she says as her eyes fall on an advertisement for a long-distance telephone company. "She doesn't want me to hear Mahtab in the background because everyone thinks I'd be hurt that they chose *her* to go to America."

"Stop," says Ponneh, her voice shaking. "I want to go home."

"Those pages are just your English homework," says Reza, his gaze never quite meeting Saba's. "Where's the envelope? And the stamps?"

She folds the pages one at a time, tucks them together, and places them in the center of the *Life* magazine over an ad for a color television so that they will be out of Ponneh's careful sight. "Who keeps an envelope anyway? It didn't have an American postmark. It went through Turkey."

The ad reads: *You made it number one in America. . . . There's only one Chromacolor and only Zenith has it.* Number one in America must be the best anywhere. Saba tries to imagine the kind of television Mahtab watches these days. Big, hypnotic. Always in color, with ten channels, the latest shows, and no rules. No need for smuggled videotapes marked "Children's Cartoons."

"Do you know what's number one in America?" Saba says. She tries to sound playful, as if she were making up a game, and when Ponneh plays along just like Mahtab would have, Saba loves her almost as much. She realizes more and more now that replacing her sister will require an impossible balance. Ponneh is like Mahtab in all the right ways: brave, willful, in charge. But just as soon as Saba begins to forget that Ponneh is not Mahtab, Ponneh says something unguarded that Mahtab never would, or she makes a seductive face that the twins don't know how to make, and Saba breathes out, trying to release the guilt of comparing the two, of loving Ponneh too much. No, she hasn't replaced Mahtab just yet.

"What?" Ponneh reaches for one of the magazines, her too-light almond eyes sparkling with exaggerated curiosity, as if trying to make up for an earlier disloyalty.

"Harvard," Saba says, turning back to the *Life* magazine. In this one issue there are three separate mentions of the place. Shahzadeh Nixon's fairy-tale fiancé went there to study law. And a few pages later, an article about the incoming president starts with the line: *The selection of a new Harvard president ranks in gravity with the elevation of Popes and premiers.* Clearly an important university—a place magical

enough, special enough, to be the setting of *Love Story*, a film wor‑
shipped by Americans and Iranians alike, and discussed in every one
of Saba's magazines.

A place fit for Mahtab. A name most Tehranis and even some
Rashtis recognize.

"Okay," says Ponneh, putting both hands in her lap with all the
resignation of a doctor or a school headmistress. "You can tell us
about it if it helps. My mother says it's a good thing to tell stories."

"I don't know," says Reza, shaking his head. "It's getting late."

"Go ahead, Saba jan," says Ponneh, shooting Reza a warning
glance. "I'll listen."

Saba beams, but doesn't reach for the handwritten pages. "Don't
worry if you don't understand everything," she lectures importantly,
so that Ponneh giggles and shifts in place. "America is complicated.
It's better to just imagine it like a TV show."

Saba is the only one with a television, a VCR, and a whole set of
illegally dubbed and undubbed American programs on tape, which
her friends secretly watch with her, mesmerized by the cracked,
grainy images; the way people's lips rarely match the words; the
twists and turns and perfect timing of American life. Saba imag‑
ines Mahtab's life in episodes, each as vibrant and mysterious as
Shahzadeh Nixon's magazine spread, and every setback resolved
as effortlessly as in a thirty‑minute television comedy. She wipes her
face one last time, having forgotten the smell of the mud wall or the
tickle at the base of her throat. Now she has a story to tell, one that
she has memorized over countless wide‑awake nights in her bed, and
that now Ponneh wants to hear. It begins like this:

ℒ◯◯ℒ

The important thing to know about America is that over there every
citizen is at least as rich as my baba. But the key is that you have to

be a *citizen*. That's the one thing our relatives in America want most. They talk about it all the time in their letters and on the phone with Baba. My maman and Mahtab are just immigrants now, so they are probably very poor. In a few years they will get their citizenship and they will be rich again. That's the way it all works. You start off as a taxi driver or a cleaning woman, like the people in *Taxi*. Then you get your citizenship, go to a good university like Harvard, and you become a doctor like in *M*A*S*H*. Then, when you're done saving the soldiers, you might go to Washington for your medal and, if you're smart enough and get the best grades, even meet a shahzadeh and get your picture in *Life* magazine. It is all possible.

When Mahtab first arrived in America, she had to get used to the new rules, and that was probably the hardest part for her— because here, in Cheshmeh, the Hafezis are the most important family. But in America, she will have to work her way up. Don't worry, though, because Mahtab can handle a challenge better than anyone.

Now, here are some things you already know:

First, you know that going to America was a very quick decision for Maman and Mahtab. None of us saw it coming. So it's fair to say that it was full of last-minute losses: Iranian money being so worth-less (if you believe Baba), and degrees from important Iranian colleges so useless because, over there, they have Harvard. And so, in America, Maman has no job and no money. Mahtab's life is very different now. No more pocketfuls of forgotten toys and spare change. No more shelves bursting with illegal books. No more new dresses to show off to best friends. Probably no more best friends.

The second thing you already know is that in America television is free and music is free, and everyone wears cowboy hats and eats hamburgers for dinner. So even though they're poor, they have a good life, except for the hamburgers, which Maman thinks are made of garbage. They watch television together every night from their shared bed, which is probably set up in the living room of a tiny apartment—like Baba's cousins in Texas who wrote asking for money for a bigger house.

During their first week in America, when Mahtab asks Maman why their stews are full of lentils instead of lamb, why she has to join the public library for her books, why they sleep in the same bed, Maman just says, "We haven't earned anything here."

Isn't that just the sort of thing Maman would say? She used to say that to us when she took away one of our toys. *You have to earn it back.* Maman takes a break from cooking dinner to have afternoon tea. She gives a long speech about how she will get a job and Mahtab will go to school, and they will both learn very good English and save money of their own. But Mahtab doesn't like to hear this, you see. She wants to go back to Cheshmeh and live off Baba's money and be comfortable. She misses me and wants us to be together again. She doesn't like writing secret letters, and she thinks it's unfair that she was chosen to go to America when she could have done just as well in Cheshmeh.

But then Maman comes up with one of those Smart Girl Quests she used to make up for us about working hard and being self-sufficient women. "This life may seem bad, but do you want to know the best part?" she says. "The rule in America is that people get to choose how rich or poor they are. It's totally a matter of choice."

You can't blame Mahtab for being suspicious, but I'll tell you that what Maman is saying is true. According to Horatio Alger and Abraham Lincoln and the girl from *Love Story* who ended up at Harvard even though she was poor, a brainy girl like Mahtab has every good chance. And so Maman goes on: "Here, smart kids can do anything they want. If they work hard, they can be rich. And that's the simple way of everything."

Maman always talked like that. Simple rules. Black and white. I loved that about her because when she was around, I knew exactly what I was supposed to do next. Then Maman swallows a mouthful of tea so hot that Mahtab imagines her insides turning to liquid, her throat and stomach swimming in *chai*, the lump of sugar between her teeth melting like the white sediment in my science experiments. But Maman's tolerance for heat is magic and she just sighs with pleasure and keeps talking. I love that about her too.

"It's different here, Mahtab jan," she explains. "Yes, in Iran it's good to be smart, get top grades, go to college. Plenty of smart women study and get degrees. But does it matter? You still have to do some things just because you're a girl."

"What things?" Mahtab asks, even though she knows.

"Marry, cook, have babies," Maman answers. "If you want to be a lady doctor, great! As long as you have the clothes washed. The respect doesn't come from being a doctor, Mahtab jan. It comes from the washing. They pretend it's not true, but you hear it when you burn dinner because you were busy with a poem, God forbid. Not here, though . . ."

And then Maman reminds her that having her own money is the most important thing a girl can do for herself. She reminds Mahtab about sweet old Khanom Omidi, and how she spends her days tend, ing house and selling her leftover yogurt for pocket money. It's never very much, but it's important that she does it. That's what Maman told us and I've seen it myself. Khanom Omidi has hidden pockets sewn into her chadors and in her waistband—a place for her Yogurt Money. This is the name Mahtab and I gave to all secret money ever since the day we saw the old lady's stash. A name for all the unseen riyals and dollars that you earn or don't earn, but always, *always* keep hidden away.

"So if I'm the best in school and make my own money," Mahtab asks, "then everything will be how it was?" Now my sister is starting to understand how things work in America that factory garb leads to business suits. She should watch more television.

Maman thinks for a moment. Then she pulls out a copy of the

Life magazine from 1971. She shows off the pictures of the American Shah's daughter and her pale princeling and she nods. *Yes, yes, yes.* This is why every Iranian dreams of America.

"And then I'll never have to clean my room?" Mahtab asks.

"You can have a maid," Maman responds. "They give a discount to lady doctors."

"And I don't have to serve *chai* to the mullahs." Mahtab used to hate that chore.

Maman laughs, because there are no mullahs in America. No mullahs in the street. No mullahs in your house, eating your food. No mullahs whispering about you to your father so that he gets worried and buys you a new, thicker, blacker headscarf.

Then Maman ends the conversation with her usual threats: "But if you don't work hard, if you play around and get average grades, then you can always go back to Iran and marry one." Her eyes widen, as if she were telling a ghost story. "You know those mullahs, they snore. And under their turbans, they have thin, greasy hair. They like to throw their big fat arms around your neck when they sleep, and they kiss like dead fish."

Mahtab shudders. "I don't want to marry a mullah."

No one wants that.

"No one wants that," Maman says because this is how you teach girls to be independent.

Mahtab says, "I want to be rich and single with nobody telling me what to do."

And then Maman says something important. Are you listening carefully? This part is critical. She says to Mahtab, "You *will* be, because Saba is rich."

Maybe Mahtab whispers my name just then. You know, sometimes when she's bored, she reads my letters and makes up stories of our days together.

"All of life is written in the blood"—Maman leans close and taps Mahtab's nose, identical to mine down to the last bump—"and you and Saba have the same blood. It doesn't matter where you live." This is true. How much control does Mahtab really have? How much control do any of us have? It is all predestined like the old fortune-tellers say. Mahtab should know, because she was in the water that day too. And I'll tell you, she will be insulted when she hears that you crazies think she is dead!

Maman gets up to stir the no-lamb stew. Look at them: my poor mother, my sister. Look how sad they are without me. It's hard to know how much food to make for only two, or how to keep a conversation going. You need four for a full table. And look at the future that is now planted in Mahtab's mind: she will be an American shahzadeh in a magazine, with four dresses in as many photos and a quiet, light-skinned man with old money and new thoughts. She has American ambition now, the kind you see in movies about orphans. Now Mahtab is the sort of girl who worries—about money, about love, about her future. There are so many things that America has taught her to want.

The next day Mahtab goes to the library. She finds out about school courses, and entrance tests, and free money from the government, which is how the girl from *Love Story* got to go to college. She fills her mind with all sorts of facts and deadlines and admissions rules—all the same things my high school cousins in Texas have been obsessing over since they arrived there. But most important, she stamps her dreams of glamour and riches with a name. She takes her girlhood goals, her love of books, her childish need for comfort, and her twinly self-hate and wraps them up in a neat little package, sealed tight and sizzling with an iron brand. A name that even the greasy, cumin-scented Iranian man at the gas station will recognize: Harvard.

✉☙☯☙✉

"See?" says Saba, getting up and dusting off the dirt of the alleyway from the back of her pants. "How's that for a good story? A hundred times better than TV."

"That's it?" Reza asks. "That's all there is? Does she go to Harvard or what?"

Saba tries to contain her anger. "We're eleven," she says. "Obviously her letter doesn't say whether she got in. What do you think this is, your mother's story time?"

"I thought—" Reza mumbles. "I'm sorry."

"Saba just means that a good storyteller doesn't give everything away at once," says Ponneh with a seriousness that makes Saba smile. Ponneh is always adding weight to the things Saba says just by agreeing with her.

"Exactly," says Saba. "It's like *Little House*. One problem per episode."

Ponneh and Saba follow arm in arm as Reza leads the way back to the main road—because he claims to know how to handle policemen with his masterful command of big-city ways. There they will find a phone to call Saba's house, where all their panicked parents and the Khanom Witches are likely gathered. Reza doesn't seem very worried. Ponneh picks at some dry skin on her elbow and says, "Too bad we never bought any sweets, since we won't be allowed any for the next ten years."

Saba unlinks her arm from Ponneh's and takes out a wad of bills from her pocket. "We should save the money for something better," she says, thinking of Khanom Omidi's hidden coins and the fact that Ponneh will never have her own private wealth, no matter how small. There live too many older sisters with needs greater than Ponneh's in the Alborz home. "Let's start a dowry for you, for when you're older."

When Ponneh's face darkens and she starts to object, Saba says, "Our secret. We'll take care of ourselves."

Khanom Basir says that Ponneh will need a dowry to escape the moral police. In five or six years she will be a woman. According to the adults, beautiful single women often find that they've broken some rule. So who knows what will happen to someone who dares to have a face like Ponneh's.

Sun and Moon Man
(Khanom Basir)

S aba thinks I don't like her, but she's too young to remember
everything. When the girls were seven I started to notice that
one of them was the *real* trouble. Mahtab used to watch us cook,
and she used to concentrate so hard that I would get nervous
and send her away. She obeyed, but I knew better than to let that
girl put a fool's hat on my head. Saba may have been loud, but
Mahtab was always quietly doing something bad, and I knew every
time Saba got into trouble that the onion had been hanging with
the fruit. Saba blamed her sister each time they were caught and I
believed her.

It is a mother's job to teach a girl to be crafty. But Bahareh Hafezi
didn't pay attention to village ways. She was too young and she
thought being a good mother meant being strict with the small rules,
the ones about candy and *pesar-bazi* (playing with boys), and *kalak-bazi*
(playing tricks), and *gherty-bazi* (playing at vanity), while teaching the
girls to rebel against impossibly big ones. She didn't bother to teach

them how to make ordinary moments turn their way. But Mahtab already knew how. Saba never learned.

One day we were cooking smoky rice in their kitchen—do you know this rice? It is the best in the world. So rare and produced only here in Gilan—and the girls were hanging about under our skirts. Their mother said that if they behaved they could join us for tea, so they sat still and whispered, Mahtab feeding Saba some crazy story (*kalak-bazi!*).

The girls had a lot of books, but their favorite stories were the kind you hear in the village square from the hundred-year-old tooth-less goats with long water pipes and tiny stools. Those men talk all day about jinns and *paris* and how to bring good luck. They tell old stories like Leyli and Majnoon, Rostam, or Zahhak, with the snakes growing out of his shoulders. I recognized the story Mahtab was tell-ing Saba because it came from one of these old men, but I assumed Mahtab didn't believe it.

"What are you telling your sister, Mahtab jan?" I asked.

"Don't interrupt me," she said. "I'm behaving!"

So I just listened as Mahtab told Saba about the Sun and Moon Man, who takes down the sun every night and puts up the moon. Saba played with a teaspoon she had stolen from a bowl of honey-comb, while Mahtab lectured on and on. "He takes longer in the summer to do it, because he likes to play outside," Mahtab said, and Saba believed her. And some small creature in my belly said that Mahtab was playing at something.

Then they changed topics for twenty minutes until Saba brought up yesterday's hiking trip in the mountains—the one Saba had missed because she had been too sick to travel. "I saw the Sun and Moon Man there, you know," Mahtab said with a careless, fox-eyed look. Saba didn't interrupt as Mahtab talked about having seen him and his yellow shirt and yellow pants and yellow basket where he kept the sun and moon. She only licked honey off her teaspoon, and Mahtab talked about the Sun and Moon Man's office, with its pulleys and buttons and levers, a big teapot and papers everywhere. Then Mahtab taught Saba the song you have to sing to him to get him to work fast, "*Hey, Mr. Sun and Moon Man, put up the sun for me.*" She sang it to the music of a foreign song that their mother said was called "Tambourine Man," which was one of their favorites.

The little devil. All that spinning, just to make her sister jealous.

I guess that's what you get when you're lucky enough to learn English and listen to English songs and have a foreign education. Devilry disguised as cleverness. Mahtab liked playing these naughty cat-dance games with her sister. She liked being the smart one, and she had a big imagination and a wicked little heart. Sometimes I too blame Mahtab for abandoning Saba, who was so much more the dependent one. I just can't help it—may God forgive me—but without her sister, Saba has lost her magic. I remember all this now that the distance between them isn't measured by tiny fingers or by gossiping lips to eager ears, but by so much earth and water. How much earth, Saba asked me once after the big loss of half her family. *How many scoops of my teaspoon would get me all the way from here to there?* She held that spoon poised against the earth as if she were ready to start digging to her sister. She knew just how to break my heart.

"He isn't paid enough," Mahtab said that day about the Sun and Moon Man. "The sun is hot, especially to carry by hand." And Saba knew it was true, because at the end of every tale, the storyteller is required to do the truth-and-lies poem, the one that rhymes "yogurt" and "yogurt soda" (*maast* and *doogh*) with "truth" and "lies" (*raast* and *doroogh*).

> *Up we went and there was* maast,
> *Down we came and there was* doogh.
> *And our story was* doroogh *(lie!).*

Or:

Up we went and there was doogh,
Down we came and there was maast,
And our story was raast *(truth!).*

We mothers know to respect this poem, and so when we tell made-up stories like Leyli and Majnoon, or the city mouse and village mouse, we do the first version, and when we tell the history of the Prophet Muhammad or King Xerxes we do the second. After telling her story about the hiking trip and the Sun and Moon Man, Mahtab did the second version, and so she said her story was true. That's why Mahtab wasn't a real storyteller, little rule-breaking rat. Now Saba has learned her sister's lies, because Reza told me that after her Mahtab story in the alley in Rasht, Saba did the second version too.

Chapter Two

The autumns of Saba's adolescence are spent battling the Gilan sky. She is ever suspicious of the wet, insatiable months after most of Iran's rice crop is harvested from lush fields. These dewy *shalizar* mornings have a way of distracting from truth—everything bursting out in eerie contrast and forcing the people to crave the fresh and the new, to pretend nothing has been lost since the last harvest. In the fall, leaves in a hundred shades of orange and red break into little pieces and mix with airborne drops of the Caspian. They create a vapor that slithers into noses and invades bodies, causing people to forget all but the sea and its fruits. It makes them ravenous for fish and rice. It erases the memory of last year's sorrows and faraway relatives. But not for Saba, who has been in the deep parts of the water. The constant rainfall frightens her. She is baffled by the white nimbus of mist that hangs just below the top of the Alborz Mountains and above the sea (at the point where the two seem to crash into each other), and by the stilt houses disappearing in both directions, their tops and bottoms lost in water and in cloud.

Every year the vision of her mother in the airport lounge holding
Mahtab's hand grows hazier. Was she standing by the gate or in the
security line? Saba used to be sure that it was at the gate, but now she
knows that it couldn't have been, because Saba and her father didn't
make it past security after she ran off to chase Mahtab. And what
was her mother wearing? A manteau? A scarf? She used to think that
it was her favorite green one, but a few months ago Saba found the
fading scarf in the back of a storage closet. Then, just as she was on
the verge of releasing the vision to the chasm of forgotten daydreams
and spotty memories, she stumbled on a copy of her mother's visa to
America. *Proof.* But of what? Saba conjures the airport image often
and the faces never blur. Her mother and sister rushing toward the
plane and floating away into an oblivion filled with magazines and
rock music and movies of men and women in love.

Now at fourteen, Ponneh and Saba spend their free days watching
workers in the rice fields or videotapes at Saba's house. Today, in the
Hafezis' enormous hilltop home, they busy themselves with Madonna
and Metallica, *Time* and *Life* magazines, *Little House on the Prairie*,
Three's Company, and the Three Khanom Witches. The girls tiptoe
through a sort of recovery, because two days ago, they had their biggest fight.

It started when Saba sat in her pantry with Reza—a secret place
where only she and Ponneh used to meet—with her Walkman, listening to a bizarrely named band called The Police. She was whispering
the lyrics into his free ear when Ponneh appeared, surprised and
angry. She was in the pantry for only five minutes, doing a poor job
of feigning interest, when she cut her hand on the sharp edge of a
tomato can lid.

"Reza, help!" she cried. And this was the biggest injustice, because
the last thing Ponneh needed was rescuing. But nowadays, when
Reza is around—and especially when he is listening to Saba's music,
or humming American tunes, or asking what this or that lyric

means—Ponneh is always getting hurt toes and scratched fingers and holes in her shirts. Then she uses every Band-Aid that Reza fetches and every pencil lead he squeezes out of her forearm as proof of his devotion. But Saba knows that none of these are signs of love. Her mother has said that *real* love is based on shared interests—like Western music.

But after Ponneh cut her hand that day, Reza sat beside her and sang bits of a French song that Saba had shown him a few days before. "Le Mendiant de l'Amour" became popular in Iran because of its easy-to-mimic chorus and manic Persian-sounding melody. "See," he said to Ponneh, "it's about a girl named Donneh, which is almost like Ponneh." He started to tap his hands on his knees and tried to sing the lyrics with his thick, uneducated accent: *Donneh, Donneh, Do-donneh* . . .

"That's not what it means," shot Saba, feeling personally injured by Reza's blatant mistranslation, by his awful accent, and his lovely voice. "*Donnez* means 'Give me.' It's French. I told you already." She wanted to repeat her point, but didn't want to be accused of showing off again. Reza didn't respond. He studied Saba's face. Then he hummed the verses he didn't know and kicked Ponneh's legs to get her to cheer up.

Before he left, he whispered to Saba, "Are you missing Mahtab?" For three years Reza has asked this—a placeholder for all the emotions he cannot yet diagnose. Whether Saba is sad or angry or jealous, he asks her the same question, putting on a concerned tone. Saba replies with shy smiles and nods. It is their private routine.

Later, Ponneh accused Saba of excluding her again, revealing their secret pantry, and showing off in English. Saba accused Ponneh of cutting her hand on purpose, not truly caring about the music, and stealing her song. But in a world without Mahtab, Saba can't last long without a best friend. Soon more important things distracted them. Ponneh discovered that with the right color chalk, she could draw entire scenes on the inside of an old white chador. They spent the next two days cocooned in *hijab*, decorating the secret parts of the tattered cloth with images from storybooks and American magazines. They sat cross-legged with the fabric pulled low over their eyes, trying to see the drawings from inside. When it didn't work—only made the cloth itchier—they moved on to standing bare-legged over a portable fan laid on its side so the chador would blow up around them like bat wings, baring their newly rounded legs like Marilyn Monroe's.

Today they run around Saba's house, belting out a song from a 1960s Iranian movie called *Sultan of Hearts.* *"One heart tells me to go, to go. Another tells me to stay, to stay."* Saba has the better singing voice, so she serenades a giggling Ponneh with elaborate and dramatic bows and gallant gestures.

"Saba, bring me my sack," says Khanom Mansoori, the Ancient One, who has been left in charge of the girls while the other women run their own household errands. Saba's father trusts the old villager to teach his daughter respectable, womanly ways. But even at nearly ninety years old she projects a childlike mischief. Saba thinks it's the combination of her deceptively tiny body and all the trouble she must be dreaming up in the hours she spends pretending to sleep. She pulls her shrunken face into a wrinkled scowl and—desperate for amusement and suffering from failing ears—pretend whispers to an eager Saba, "I have a new you-know-what! Bring Ponneh and get rid of the *adults*."

This is Saba's favorite sort of summons, because it means an afternoon with the only Iranian magazine she likes to read: the prerevolution copies of *Zanerooz. Today's Woman.* Though the magazine covers serious topics now, such as women's rights, in the Shah's time it focused mostly on fashion, hair, and gossip. Each issue contained one tantalizing story called "Fork in the Road" about love triangles, or estranged husbands, or the midnight creeping of lecherous stepfathers who assumed girls didn't talk, followed by a good revenge. Pages of delicious scandal and temptingly forbidden descriptions.

Ancient and bored, Khanom Mansoori likes the cheap thrill of racy stories she cannot read with her own fading, untrained eyes. Who can blame her for enlisting a pair of curious fourteen-year-olds as co-conspirators when she is left unsupervised with them, and when her equally ancient husband isn't around to entertain her?

On this September afternoon, when Saba is trying hard not to let the autumnal Caspian vapors erase her memories of Mahtab, she reads Ponneh and Khanom Mansoori a story about a young man with two lovers. One is beautiful, the other charming. One is quiet, the other exuberant. One makes him want to go on adventures around the world, the other makes him dizzy with romance and content-ment. The story enraptures Saba, by the strange contrasts and the rivalry. Whom will he choose? She glances at Ponneh, who rolls on her back and settles against a wall of colorful pillows.

"Khanom Mansoori," Ponneh wonders aloud, "which do you think the boy should choose?" Saba places a finger between the pages and closes the magazine. She too wants to know, but she would never have asked.

Khanom Mansoori nods her small roundish head and says, "What does it matter what I think?" She smacks her lips together and her eyes begin to close.

"I think it matters," says Saba. "Come on, pick!"

"Well," Ponneh interrupts, "I think he shouldn't choose. I think the girls should decide for him. He should marry neither or both. That way they can still be friends."

Saba considers this for a moment. She decides not to let Ponneh finish and returns to the article. These stories always end with an unsolved dilemma. *What would* you *do?* the author goads. When they reach the end, old Khanom Mansoori tells Ponneh and Saba her own love story of a husband who has doted on her for seventy years. In return, the girls tell Khanom Mansoori about the unfairness of being fourteen and loveless.

Beautiful Ponneh with her almond eyes laments over being forced to tolerate a budding unibrow until she is married or, by some miracle, allowed to pluck early. Saba complains silently, never aloud, that her Persian nose has grown unwieldy and her body is starting to curve. She has pockets of fat, so graceless, and she is sprouting—becoming tall—while Ponneh is dainty. She too wishes she could pluck the tiny hairs around her eyes and lips, and that she wasn't so dark, with her black eyes, black hair, and olive skin. Ponneh's skin is the color of porcelain and her eyes an impossible shade of hazelnut.

And then the old lady, though half asleep, says something to make them both sit up. Like a prophet she opens her mouth and infects the room with awed silence. "I wonder if Mahtab is growing a big backside like you."

Ponneh glances at Saba and begins to object. "What are you—"

"Oh, hush, hush, Ponneh jan," says Khanom Mansoori, waving a hand in Ponneh's direction. "Saba knows what I mean. Don't you, child?"

Saba licks her dry lips and squints at Khanom Mansoori as if trying to peer through a crack in a wall. "Mahtab's dead," Saba mutters, because she has been told that this is the truth. Ponneh beams with pride and nods, which helps Saba with the guilt of having told a kind of lie, and of growing up and surrendering to the slow, bleak workings of adult logic. Saying the words aloud brings on a flutter of panic, like admitting out loud that there is no God after a lifetime of faith. A voice whispers, *I saw them get on a plane.*

But Khanom Mansoori is shaking her head, making her scarf slip and revealing henna-colored tufts. "*Hmmm* . . . They said you were smart, full of book-reading and intuition. And here you are, believing everything they tell you to believe. You don't know what's true"—she shakes a finger at Saba and glares—"*ultimate* truth, *real* truth like most people don't see. You can't even unlock the magic of being a twin."

Saba is bursting with the hundred responses that bubble up all at once, but before she can choose, Ponneh jumps to her feet. "Come, Saba," she says. "We need lunch."

Saba doesn't move. She looks into the unfocused gaze of this tiny old-world fortune-teller who, through her curtain of cataracts, has seen more of Saba than her own father has. "Mahtab's dead," she repeats, her voice betraying a hint of encouragement.

Khanom Mansoori leans in. "What about that letter?" she whispers.

Saba stares wide-eyed at Ponneh, her best friend, who looks both disapproving and ashamed—because who else would have told old Mansoori about the letter? She tries to remember if she ever asked Ponneh not to tell. Is this a betrayal? Will Ponneh be angry if Saba considers it so? Finally she decides.

"I'm too old for those stories," she says, her voice all confidence and maturity. She knows what Khanom Mansoori is trying to do. She is close to the end of her life and she enjoys this abstract talk, the kind of what-ifs that take away the sting and foreverness of death. Maybe she wants Mahtab to be alive as much as Saba does. Or just to know that even if Mahtab is dead, someone keeps her memory fresh. Regardless, Ponneh's opinion is much more vital to Saba's happiness—and Ponneh is a realist.

"Too old for your own sister?" Khanom Mansoori tuts. "Not good."

"The letter was only make-believe," Saba offers for Ponneh's sake. Then she adds, because it sounds so adult to say the words, "I was a kid. It was a way of coping."

Khanom Mansoori chuckles. "Make-believe? Well, I don't believe you," she says, laying her head against the wall and slipping into sleep even as she speaks. "Come back when you're older and not too grown-up. . . . Go on, both of you. I need a nap."

Saba wishes Khanom Mansoori wouldn't fall asleep. She wants to reach out and shake her awake. But Ponneh takes both her hands and pulls her up with all her strength, so that the momentum launches them into a manic run toward the kitchen. As they rush off, Saba hears the old woman's faint snores, a last chuckle, and the mumbled words: "See me when the kid and the coping come back for a visit. They always come back when you think you're grown . . . always, always."

৩◉৩

Agha Hafezi attempts to leave lunch—or at least hints of what to do for lunch—for Saba almost every day when he is busy in his office and his rice fields. On his worst days he leaves cash, or a note for Saba to deliver to one of the *khanom*s. Usually it says something like: "May I trouble you to cook lunch for my daughter? And tomorrow please come to the house and we will have a feast with our friends." This translates to a bargain: Feed Saba today and tomorrow you can use our well-stocked kitchen and invite whomever you wish—two chores, but well worth a social event funded by the Hafezis. On his best days he leaves a plastic container of Saba's favorite stews, left over from one of these parties. Today Saba spots an enormous white fish thawing in a bucket in the sink, with a note. "Saba joon, do you know how to cook this yet? If not, fetch Ponneh."

She eyes the plastic bag Ponneh pulls out from her backpack— white rice and smoked carp, a simple money-saving dish. She moves toward the fridge, but Ponneh is already taking two spoons from the drawer. "Don't worry. I brought enough for both of us."

"Thanks." Saba takes a spoon. She nods to the bucket and the expensive white fish flopped inside. "You can maybe take that to your mother."

Ponneh's face darkens. "I can afford to share one stupid lunch."

"Sorry," says Saba, as they settle on the ground at the center of the cavernous Hafezi kitchen. The room is full of contrasts, with its old-world *tanoor* from Ardabil—left over from the time of her grandfather who loved bread more than rice, though he didn't make a show of it in Gilan—next to an industrial refrigerator and burlap sacks of home-grown rice in a corner beside a restaurant-quality oven and a huge rectangular sink. To make up for her mistake, Saba makes sure to eat out of Ponneh's bowl—though her father has told her not to share food so intimately with any of the villagers. She takes a bite of smoky fish and buttery rice so plump and light, the grains float off the spoon and melt in her mouth. She tries to think of a way to restore Ponneh's pride and says through a mouthful of underspiced food, "What if I just eat all this myself and you go on a diet?"

Saba heaps another spoonful, knowing that this will please Ponneh, that she will tell her mother and they will both feel proud. In Cheshmeh the quality of your food determines the quality of your family, and this is something Saba can give to Ponneh that no one else can, because the Hafezi stamp is hers. Maybe it will help make up for all the times that Ponneh offered Saba these intangible gifts—like during the first big rainfall after Mahtab left, when Saba wouldn't get out of bed and Ponneh blindfolded her and forced her into the kitchen pantry for a surprise. After a few moments in the dark, Saba felt some-one's soupy breath on her face and heard a familiar whisper, "I don't want to," followed by a cry of pain. Saba yanked off the blindfold and saw Ponneh twisting Reza's ear and scolding him until he ran off. "I'm sorry," she said to Saba, her tone irritated, "I was going to get you your first kiss, so you can be happy again."

Now a sad look passes over Ponneh's eyes and she says, "You want me to diet so I can be a stick. Then you can win Reza for yourself and leave me out . . . like in the 'Fork in the Road' story, where one girl gets left out."

Saba stares at Ponneh and tries to work out what game they're playing now. She searches for a response. "That's different! You can't be in love with two people."

Ponneh shrugs. "Who says? You don't like it because you want a big Western-magazine love story that doesn't happen in real life. And you like to fight. You and Mahtab were always competing for things. Now you're trying to compete with me."

The mention of Mahtab sparks a heat in her chest that Saba wishes she could rub out with her fingers. How dare Ponneh say that? Who does she think she is to mention Mahtab's flaws? "We didn't compete," Saba snaps. "I just don't think your way works."

"It could," says Ponneh. "And Reza agrees with me. His baba left to be with a new family when he could have brought them back here. They could have all stuck together. It's better to have good friends for life than to win one stupid love contest."

"It's not a contest. . . ." Saba wants her friend to understand, but Ponneh has always been one of many—never part of a pair.

Ponneh interrupts. "I say three is always better than two. In the end, it's your friends who help you. Look at Khanom Omidi and Khanom Basir and all those women. They do more for each other than they do for any husbands."

"That's peasant talk," says Saba. "It says so in the Bible and every place."

Ponneh looks thoughtful. "Maybe . . . But I think it'll be the three of us forever. You, me, and Reza. Even if we get married to other people, or if you go to America."

"Okay," Saba mutters. Her stomach hurts. "Whatever you want."

Ponneh continues. "Maybe we can *all* run off to America and dye our hair yellow. And you and I can wear red, red lipstick all day outside like in *Life* magazine!"

"Fine." Saba drops her spoon and gets up to leave. She is still angry because Ponneh hasn't apologized for speaking badly of Mahtab. And her back aches.

Saba stomps out of the kitchen. As she heads to the living room she hears Ponneh's scream follow her down the hall: "Oh my God! What is *that*?"

Khanom Mansoori stirs on the floor pillows. "What is all this noise?" she hums, smacking her lips several times before opening her eyes. Saba turns to see Ponneh now standing behind her, mouth agape. Khanom Mansoori is snickering. "Oh, for God's sake, I'm too old for these girl-*bazi* things."

Ponneh runs to Saba and says, "Don't worry! I'll go get my mother and we'll take you to a hospital in Rasht. You just wait right here."

Saba follows Ponneh's gaze over her own shoulder and down to the seat of her pants. She lets out a shriek when she sees the blood. She is covered with it, and now both girls are screaming. Khanom Mansoori is trying to hoist her child-sized body up, muttering, "Aieee . . . No need for hospital. Stop the screeching and the drama-*bazi*, *khodaya*. Let me just get my thoughts together." The bewildered look on a face lined with years of experience makes Saba panic even more. It must be cancer. Or a burst tumor. Or internal bleeding. The old woman drones on. "Ponneh jan, you better call Khanom Omidi or Khanom Basir, or somebody else . . ."

It takes Khanom Omidi and Khanom Basir only ten minutes to arrive, and when they do, they are laughing and gossiping as if nothing were wrong. Saba wants to scream at them. This is her death, and they could at least muster as much concern as they showed when they all faked Mahtab's death and sent her off to America.

"Let me see how to say this," Khanom Omidi says, as she chews on a piece of basil. She must have been caught in the middle of a meal. She adjusts her girth and pats Saba's trembling hand as she tries to explain. "In the old days, we would have to tell the whole town . . . and there is this story . . . let me see." She moves to sit and, never forgetting her lazy eye—visible only when she looks up or down—pulls Saba into her line of vision. "There was a girl named Hava. And God decreed that the price of sin—"

Khanom Omidi is mumbling, looking for bits of wisdom in her memory. It is her habit to dole out advice generously on all things (whether or not she knows anything about them) like coins and dried mulberries from the thousand little pockets sewn in the folds of her fabric coverings. This indulgent woman reminds Saba of the Victorian doll on her desk, the one with dusty pockets sewn all over her dress for hiding jewelry where no one will expect. Sometimes Saba tucks coins in the hems of her own clothes to bring on the sheltered feeling of having a secret plan. She could use a secret plan today.

She strains to recall a section about blood and womanhood in one of her mother's medical books, something about cycles and hormones. And did a calamity like this happen in a novel? Usually in books, if a passage seems odd, she blames her English and moves on. Now Khanom Basir, the Evil One, takes Saba's hand. Saba tries to pull away, but raising two sons has given the awful woman a strong grip—and an expression like a snake preparing to strike, all beady eyes, sunken cheeks, and crafty, lipless smirk.

"Enough now," Khanom Basir snaps at the other women, snickering behind their hands. "Laughing at a girl in her first messy state, it's like poking at a sleeping camel."

Saba and Khanom Basir spend the next half hour alone in the dim toilet past the living room. "You are not dying," she tells Saba in her no-nonsense tone. Then she explains it all—almost as scientifically as Saba's mother would have. "It's not the worst as far as curses go. We bleed once a month and in return men have to toil and suffer until they die. They smell. They grow hair everywhere. Their bodies are shameful to look at—everything splayed out on the outside like that. . . . I'll tell you, Saba jan, I love my sons, God knows they're perfect, but . . . On your wedding night, when you see it, you'll know what I mean and you'll thank God for what he gave you."

Afterward Saba thinks that none of the other women could have done a better job of revealing the mysteries of womanhood without fuss or embarrassment. Of course, had Reza's mother realized that Saba was imagining all these wedding-night discoveries with one of her own precious sons, the cunning woman would have been much more careful with her words. Still, Saba wants to please her. She relishes Khanom Basir's rare kindness, her attempt to make her comfortable with her body. Maybe her mother would have done the same. Only it would have been just the two of them, and Mahtab.

"Should I call my mother?" Saba asks. "I want to call her."

Khanom Basir's body seems to tense. "She can't get calls where she is."

"Why not?" Saba asks—maybe now that she is a woman, she is entitled to some truth. "I know she's in America. I want to call her. Why can't I call her?"

"Oh, God help us. . . . She's not in America," Khanom Basir says coldly. "And it's your father's decision when to tell you everything. So don't use this as an excuse to create yet another Saba drama. Okay? Part of being a woman is accepting things that happen and not making your pain the center of everything. Do you understand?"

"Yes," she mutters. If her mother was here, Saba would tell her that her back hurts. She would tell her the definition of all the words she has looked up in the dictionary. She would show her the lists she has made since the separation—lists of her favorite songs, of English words she knows, of movies she has watched, and of books she has read. On the day they meet again, her mother will want to know these things.

Back in the living room, Ponneh jumps up and cheers. Apparently, she too has had an explanation. "Good job, Saba! You're a woman now."

"Hush, child," says Khanom Omidi, tossing some dried jasmine from her chador in the air around Saba. "Do you want the whole world to know her dirty, dirty business?"

But Ponneh ignores them. She steps aside and waves at a tea tray on the floor with so much flourish that one would expect a Norooz feast instead of the tea, *kouluche* pastries, and chickpea cookies that Ponneh seems to have found in the back of Saba's pantry. "I made you a becoming-a-woman snack. So you don't faint or freeze from blood loss."

She gives Khanom Mansoori an eager look, and the ancient woman nods her hennaed head slowly, her heavy eyelids half closed with sleep and erudition, as if to say, *Yes, Ponneh jan, you have learned the science of it.*

A few minutes later, Reza shows up at the door with his muddy football and a stack of blank tapes he hopes to fill with Saba's music and is shooed away by the women making the most embarrassing fuss. "Go away, go away. None of your business!"

Saba wonders if Mahtab too experienced this milestone today—because aren't they identical and tied together by shared blood? If her mother was here, Saba would tell her that she actually *feels* older. Maybe Maman would reply that, yes, she certainly looks grown-up. But then Saba considers that it might be ungrateful to focus on her mother now—when these other women made such a show of tending to her and even endured the shame of discussing topics that every self-respecting Persian knows to push under a rug.

"I'm sorry I yelled," she says to Ponneh, and takes a becoming-a-woman chickpea cookie directly from her best friend's unwashed fingers.

The Storyteller
(Khanom Basir)

Every woman has a talent, and if you ask me, every talent is worthwhile and important. But as always, Bahareh Hafezi didn't agree with me. She told her daughters: If you don't prove yourself smart enough to heal bodies alongside men or design heaven-on-earth structures like the thirty-three arches or write beautiful verses like the *Rubaiyat*, then the world might decide that you will be the lady who makes the best cakes or the most savory stews or the best opium pipe for her husband. That will be your role.

"A sad fate! Worthless work!" she said, when she wanted the girls to read a book.

What crazy-*bazi*! The woman was as one-sided as a mullah's coin. After all, Khanom Omidi's talent was cooking, and if she had chosen to be a brain surgeon, who would make the perfect saffron rice pudding, exactly thick enough, full of almonds, never clumpy? The girls used to watch her make the pudding, patiently grinding the long fiery tendrils of saffron with a fist-sized mortar and pestle, the *scratch scratch* of pollen against rock, releasing the aroma of both a heavy feast and a soft perfume, and staining her fat, already yellow fingers a deeper orange. Like a magician, she had so many tools she wouldn't let me borrow. A cherry pitter. A flower-shaped mold on a long stick for Window Bread. The tiny mortar and pestle.

That woman was the Sorceress of Saffron.

And this was the reason she was happy and still healthy at such an old age, because as everyone knows, saffron makes you laugh. When the sun sets at the end of each day, all the women in the soggy rice fields in the North go home tired, with their pants rolled up and their legs soaking and diseased, a bright triangular cloth, the *chador-shab*, tied securely around their waists to protect their backs and carry this and that. Elsewhere, women who work in the rose fields of Qamsar or the tea fields here in Gilan go home smelling of roses and tea, their skirts full of the leaves and petals they have spent all day pulling. But in other parts of Iran, still, women in saffron fields arrive home in tight, jolly clusters, crazy with laughter, and they continue on like this, well into the night.

The Hafezi girls were told that their talents lay in their brains, and that this would make them different. They would continue the family tradition of success and moneymaking. This expectation was there in every word, every gesture, every promise.

"Can we go to the beach?" they would ask their father.

"My daughters, I will take you to the sea and dry you with hundred-dollar bills," he would say, because that was a sign of his love and commitment.

Later, after the day their plans went wrong and he was left with Saba only, he said to her, "Saba jan, you don't need to go to America. You are brilliant and you have fine taste." And that meant that Saba would still shine here in her baba's eyes.

Talents, the Hafezis believed, transcended location and circumstance.

You know, I too have a gift—the best one, a power over words,

over legends, truth, and lies. For money I weave rush into baskets
and hats and small rugs, but for my friends I can weave a tale so subtly, so beautifully, with such rises and falls, such whispers, that children and adults are lulled like snakes in a pot. They sway with me,
allow me to carry them away. Then when I'm finished, they wait
eagerly to hear: *Up we went and there was . . . which one? Yogurt or yogurt
soda? Maast? Doogh? Truth? Lies?* Under the *korsi* blanket draped over
a hot stove, where feet are warmed and stories are told, I reign
supreme. Though . . . they say that the *korsi* is the birthplace of all lies.

I was the one who first told Saba about her body, about marriage,
because her mother hadn't. Okay, so I didn't tell the full story. I gave
it the usual flourishes of the storyteller, jinns and diseases, untimely
deaths and the smallish possibility of some vague fulfillment. But
most of all, I told her this: books kill a woman's sexual energy, the
allure you're born with. It can be snuffed out, you know. And Saba
and Mahtab were doomed from the age of three, far too educated to
ever understand how to appeal to any man. Sure, they could get into
trouble like anyone else, but could they lure with their eyes like Ponneh can? Girls who can read books cannot read men.

Their mother is the one who gave them this fate, with her note-
books and her ideas and her fears. She used to watch the girls and
chew her lips raw because she wanted them to have grand storybook
destinies; and when you have a task like that, you can't sit around
bonding over tea, plucking each other's eyebrows. You have to stamp
out the distractions. That was her kind of mother-love. Grand,
useless.

She ruined those girls. Deep inside where no one could see, something was stunted. Their father didn't help the matter either—
because, tell me, how can a girl who has been told to dry herself with
hundred-dollar bills ever be a good wife to anyone?

Chapter Three

AUTUMN 1988

By eighteen, Saba has collected five hundred pages of simple and fancy English words, not only to someday show her mother—though after seven years without a word, hope is waning—but also because the word lists have become a part of her life. Having studied the language since early childhood with an intensity unheard of in Gilan, Saba feels a tingle of pride each time she catches herself thinking in English.

Vile. Vagrant. Vapid.

Saba glances at a trio of aimless girls in the alley behind a local store—an impossibly small square box that somehow has everything for sale, not just eggs and sugar, but milk in plastic bags with snip-off tops to drop into a jug, a dozen kinds of pickles, saffron, soap, piles of pencil erasers, toy watches, dried fruit, olives, and nuts. Every corner is crammed full—loosely categorized stacks one behind another, stretching deep beyond the inner walls, burlap sacks of rice around the register, garlic cloves hanging over the door. Saba clutches her rush basket, now full of tea and sugar, and turns away from the girls crouching close together in the far corner of the alley. Though they hide it well, Saba is expert enough to know what they are doing. It is an intimate act, a shared risk, smoking together in public. She smiles at the fumes wafting subtly out of the front folds of one girl's blue chador, an unnecessary extra covering since her colorful, layered Gilaki garb is modest enough. But chadors are ideal for hiding things. The girl has pulled hers up high over a tight scarf and a long skirt of greens and reds not because she is pious. No, this girl is just bored, playing games, as Saba does with her friends in her pantry.

Up above, a crow calls out from its perch on a phone line.

It is autumn again. The ground is covered with trampled wild berries, pieces of orange rinds, and crushed cans. Cool breezes carry plastic bags into treetops. Wet and dry, red and yellow leaves drift over the streets. The air smells like rain, like a fistful of wet morning grass held up to the nose. Saba feels trapped here, with the blissful poor, in a world made up of the scattered parts of many different eras. A group of older women passes by her. Over their long-skirted, brightly mismatched village dresses, they have draped the austere black of city women. They are probably headed to catch a bus to Rasht or to a holy shrine, where they will be black crows pecking and preening in a line. She takes the time to notice the parts of them most unlike her mother, with her elegant clothes, her illegal books and her defiant red nails. The village women flap their fabric wings and cluster together. One of them has double-wrapped her chador tightly around her chest and tied it in front—rural practicality, very unfashionable. Saba looks at their sizable hooked noses and the way another one clutches the loose cloth with her teeth so her hands can be free to hold bags. Her lips disappear behind mouthfuls of black and suddenly she has a bird beak. Is Saba more like Bahareh Hafezi or this woman?

She nods hello and continues on. Minutes later, she turns toward a small dirt road at the edge of the town center and lingers. She shouldn't be here alone. Her father doesn't like it when Saba makes herself a target, as he puts it. But this is where the Tehrani promised to meet her, so this is where she will wait. He appears after fifteen minutes, an oily, opium-addicted twenty-year-old with uneven stubble, yellow teeth, and a premature bald spot in the middle of his too-long hair. He waves a black plastic bag in her face.

"A thousand tomans," he says. No greeting, as usual. Saba doesn't even know the Tehrani's first name. Just that he's someone's cousin's cousin, and that he comes from Tehran carrying illegal treasures for sale. Most video men are cleaner, more careful with their dress. But Saba prefers this one because he knows his material. No bumbling analysis of movies he hasn't seen, no worthless advice. ("Yes, *India Jones*," one of the video men recommended once, "a very nice Hindi romance.") The Tehrani is a connoisseur.

She reaches into her pocket and hands him some bills. He chuckles.

"*Each,*" he says. "I brought good things. All arrived this month." He glances around the corner. "The price covers the trip and the special order. I do it only for you."

"It's still expensive. Let me look first," she says, and when he hesitates, she adds, "What, you think I'll run off with it?" He smirks and hands over the bag. Saba peers inside. She tries not to gasp for fear that the price will jump—because inside the bag there are six magazines, half of them fashion issues, none of them more than a year old, two videotapes, and five audiocassettes. At the bottom of the bag she digs up a tattered novel with no cover. "Oh my God," she whispers.

The Tehrani smiles. His shoulders tense as Saba looks behind her and throws an arm around his sweaty neck. "Okay, okay," he says, "I told you I'd get it, didn't I?"

She picks up the book again. *The Satanic Verses*, by Salman Rushdie. Saba has never read a novel in the same year it was published. Let alone one that could get her killed.

"That book is more . . . as we agreed," says the Tehrani, but Saba doesn't care, though this is one volume she will have to read and burn. She turns one of the tapes over in her hand. "It's just what you asked for," the Tehrani says proudly. "My man in America taped the Top Forty off the radio, plus the usual: Beatles, Marley, Dylan, Redding, U2, even Michael Jackson, the devil's mouthpiece himself. The videos are TV shows from *this* year. Clear sound this time, hardly any white lines or shaking. Trust me, you'll like."

Saba thrusts a wad of bills into the Tehrani's hand. He counts them and says, "I have a surprise from America for my best customer." He pulls out a yellow bottle—a treasure that Saba has hunted for daily since the revolution, along with many other foreign things she used to love. "Neutrogena, all yours," he says. "Go make your friends jealous."

Saba opens it and breathes in. "You're the only good soul left in Tehran."

He coughs and says, "How about a kiss, then?" tapping his cheek. Saba raises an eyebrow, wishes him a safe trip, and moves quickly to her own end of the village.

A few paces outside the house, she hears voices pouring from the open windows of their large sitting room. First the high-pitched whines of the *khanom*s, strained and out of breath, followed by the low drones of village men, meandering slowly, struggling to do so wisely. None of them her father's voice.

Someone lets out a low-pitched belly laugh. Someone else says, "I swear I'm not exaggerating. May God strike me dead right now . . ."

Saba enters through a back door that leads into the hallway next to her bedroom. She tosses her basket onto the bed, tucking the bag of Western contraband under her mattress. She stares into the mirror. Tufts of reddish-orange have escaped the headscarf loosely draped in an urban style over her shoulder. Last month she let a seventy-year-old woman with a secret salon in her living room color her hair—a costly mistake.

Someone calls from the living room, "Saba. Saba, come and join us, child."

She grabs a cloth and wipes her face clean of makeup while straining to make out the individual voices. Is Reza among them? What about Ponneh? She tries to decipher the conversation to see if her friends are already establishing the alibi the three of them will use in an hour or two to escape—but the buzz of voices doesn't include theirs. She pulls her scarf behind her neck: if she can't let her hair fall free, she favors the traditional Gilaki way of wrapping the fabric around her neck and tying it in back, taking care to show off a finger of center-parted hair. Before she leaves, she eyes her pile of English textbooks, the only Western books she can keep in plain sight without fear of fines, arrest, or at least a long fatherly scolding. At the top of the pile, a science book is open, revealing a photograph of a flower in a delicious shade of orange. The caption says: "California Panther Lily."

Vibrant, Saba thinks, repeating the list of English v-words she memorized today. She says the words to herself over and over as she checks the room one last time. *Verdant*. If her mother was here, Saba would use *verdant* in a sentence. If Mahtab really *did* go to America, how many good English words would she know by now? Probably all of them—more than a person can learn from smuggled novels and magazines, or from browsing a tattered children's dictionary, or even from the best Iranian tutors. But Saba is eighteen now and she knows the world of adults. She doesn't talk about Mahtab in this way because girls who are supposed to be dead can't learn English. Still, the mystery of her mother's departure keeps Mahtab alive—one day Saba will know the whole truth.

In the hall, she almost collides with her father, who likes to walk and think about four different things at once. He isn't a large man, but he has solid, imposing features that remind Saba of a wrestler. There are dark lines above his cheeks and his jowls are speckled with gray. His watery eyes, sad even when he's smiling, give him an air of kind-ness. He doesn't talk much, likes to keep his thoughts and expla-nations short. But he is firm in his opinions, one of which is that he'd rather be safe than express them. He likes fine things, which is why, he often tells her, he married a woman with a master's degree and had daughters who studied English for fun before they could ride a bike.

"Saba jan, come and help. Mullah Ali brought some people . . ." His gray mustache bounces, sweeping his slack cheeks as he chews. Saba smells honey. "I saw the tapes," he adds. "A collection that size will bring trouble. What if your cousin Kasem sees it?"

"Is he coming? He's not going in my room!" She shudders. "I hate him . . . always looking at me that way. Worshipping Mullah Ali." She sticks out her tongue in disgust.

Her father warns her with a glance. "He's my sister's son. Be kind. And show some respect to Mullah Ali. He's a decent man, a helpful man. I don't want trouble."

Saba begins to storm off, mumbling, "All mullahs are pigs, even decent ones."

"Watch your tongue," he whispers. Then he softens. "Yes, I know . . . but please, Saba, you used to be sensible. Drop this May Ziade act." His attempt to placate her falls apart at the mention of the obscure Arab feminist whose last name happens to mean "too much" in Persian. Her father loves to use this otherwise random woman in his lectures. "The name says it all!" he exclaims. "What-ever your views, learn restraint." Often he adds, as if to entice her to behave, "You know, keeping silent, not expressing opinions, is a talent of the finest people in the Western world. It shows a mastery of self."

May is a good name, Saba thinks, and crosses her arms, maybe to invite his anger.

"What?" Her father sighs. "Tell me. What is it that you're so desperate to say?"

She snaps, "It's not fair that you talk to me like I'm some delin-quent. When have I ever caused problems?" This is a kind of truth—she has become an expert at fulfilling her illegal desires without attracting trouble.

Her father glances back toward the living area. He is still whis-pering, but his tone is as loud as ever. "*When?* I'll tell you *when.* Every other day I have to cover for you to someone. Oh no, Khanom Alborz, that wasn't my daughter barefoot with red toenails in the street. No, no, she didn't mean anything by that remark, Mullah Khan. No, Khanom Basir, that wasn't my daughter making inappro-priate advances toward your son. What are you thinking, Saba? This isn't Tehran. Everyone knows everyone!"

The last remark stings. She has tried hard to keep her feelings for Reza a secret. She has pulled away each time he has touched her hand, looked away, face burning, from his knowing smiles. Even in the pantry, when his bare foot creeps too close to hers, she has tried not to give in, to exercise restraint. "I didn't do anything . . ."

But her father is only getting started. He paces, picking at the paint on the wall as if he can't control his hands. "What's the matter? Help me understand! Are you unhappy? You have the best tutors and more foreign books than anyone, and all these women to take care of you. Why do you want to jeopardize your future?" He pulls a lock of red hair from the front of her headscarf and flips it aside. Saba wishes he would just see how careful she is, how sensible, maybe even shrewd. And doesn't *he* take risks for *his* many dangerous habits? "You won't even get rid of that music! I don't know . . . I wish—"

A bewildered look passes over her father's withered face.

"You wish what?" Saba whispers. *That I was Mahtab? That she was the one left behind?* When the twins were born, they were often told, Saba had a cord wrapped around her neck. Mahtab waited patiently, pink and beautiful, never shedding a tear while her twin was blue and near death from impatience. Once at a party Saba heard a distant aunt wonder if this impatience as a baby had caused damage to her brain. After all, wasn't Mahtab the smarter one? The twin better suited for America. When her sister was around, Saba used to giggle at this sort of talk, because Mahtab was the other half of her and it didn't matter which half was considered good and which wicked.

Her father shakes his head. "It's time to find you a husband."

"That's not what you were about to say," she goods. Her father is a progressive man. This isn't about marriage. "You wish I were Mahtab." It would be grotesque to cry in front of her father, so she tries to seem more adult, hard-hearted and above girlish blubber.

Her father's eyes widen. "What . . . ?" He seems agitated and confused. "Yes, I do wish for her sometimes," he says. "Can you blame me? If I had done things differently—"

He looks away. What is he thinking? Is that guilt making his jowls shiver? Regret? Though she has never asked, Saba imagines that her father has nightmares, that he doesn't tell her where her mother went because he was there and couldn't change any of it. How daunting to be the one in charge of a caravan when so many pieces are breaking apart one after another. At what point do you simply let go of the reins and give yourself up to falling? Who do you call to rescue you?

She touches her lips with two wandering fingers. "I'm sorry," he says. "I didn't mean—" Saba shrugs. Agha Hafezi sighs loudly. "I meant that life would be simpler if I could have been a better father, so you could both be here . . . but everyone knows that twins are the same. You and Mahtab, God keep her, are just the same to me."

Everyone knows that twins are the same. This is her parents' philoso-phy. All fate is determined by the laws of blood and DNA, and two genetically identical girls will always live the same life, they will always provide the same comfort to their parents—whether they are at home or in a faraway place.

"Baba," she says, and clears her throat, "please tell me where Maman went."

Her father rubs the corners of his eyes, a ploy to avoid her gaze. Finally he looks at her with a weak smile. "When you were small, Khanom Basir told me everything about you." He laughs, and Saba wonders what this has to do with her mother. "She told me you made up a letter from Mahtab to entertain your friends. She called it stress."

What is he trying to accomplish? She wonders if her father has been at the hookah. He touches her shoulder with a massive hand. "I like your way of dealing with impossible things," he says, "the way you make a perfect world for yourself and say to everyone *that's that*. . . . Makes life simple . . . So, for the sake of killing the bad memories, let's just say your mother's in America . . . just until I'm sure of a few things myself."

A part of her wants to press on, to insist again that she *saw* her mother and sister get on that plane, and that he can stop running away from the murkier, more enigmatic possibilities. She wants to force her father to finally tell her. *What happened? Why can't I speak to her on the phone?* But her father looks like a lost child, and he too is without a mother, or wife, or sister. She remembers the days after the separation when he spent sixteen hours a day on the phone in his office. No meals, no visitors, just call after call to agencies and bureau-crats and mullahs—even some whispered conversations with her mother's friends and members of the underground Christian commu-nity, people whom Saba recognized as her father's real friends, though they never came over for dinners like the mullahs so often do. They whispered to her father that all would be well, that he should keep faith and pray to Jesus to banish his doubts. Did he keep faith? Maybe . . . but he also kept a suitcase under his desk—a toothbrush, a flask of water, pajamas—in case his God failed him and he was arrested without warning. Saba prays to Jesus sometimes. Though she is unsure, it is enough that her mother believed—that it would make her proud. She decides that her father has been through enough for now. He is trying so hard to keep a smile. Better to be kind, to conspire with him. Though he is only humoring her, she will be generous and play along. "Okay," she offers, "that's what we'll tell them."

"No," he says, his expression suddenly cautious. "These are all private things." With that the moment is lost, as is Saba's chance to be good to her father—*a stupid thing to try,* she thinks.

⁊ֱֶ◉ֶ֯ל

Saba moves quietly to the back of the sitting room, the one decorated in Persian style with old rugs, rush mats, and pillows around a floor cloth, a *sofreh,* in place of a table and chairs. This is the only room, in which her father entertains villagers. The Western dining room with the Nain rugs and carved chairs, remains mostly unused, except when Saba's tutors visit from Rasht. She likes to study there because it has a big window and photos of her mother and Mahtab. In summers when they were small and the carpets were being aired and checked for mold, she and Mahtab used to lie facedown on the tile floor of the Western room in their underwear to cool their bellies. Now in the casual sitting room, she places herself just behind the Three Khanom Witches and Ponneh's mother, Khanom Alborz, who is often a reluctant addition to the party. Saba remembers her father's words. Do they all know about Reza? Are they mocking her? Her head spins.

Vertigo, she thinks it's called in English.

For the sake of the clerics, the women are draped halfheartedly in house chadors—white ones with big purple blossoms, or polka-dot ones with rows of pink roses and curlicues—from the cloth bundle kept stocked for guests near the door, next to the pile of everyone's shoes. For Saba's father, this practice shows off his piety to the mul-lahs; but around Tehran where black coverings are the norm, it is a welcoming gesture to offer a guest a bright house chador. *Please change your chador*, they say, *get comfortable, stay awhile*. It is an invitation to slough off crowish exteriors, to display one's natural colors, to engage in the chirping talk of Persian mothers, which is the same in every region.

Why? How? What?

Chera? Chetor? Chee?

Chirp. Chirp. Chirp.

Saba knows that it is a popular joke now to call Iranian women crows because of the black chadors worn in cities or solemn places, but in his early hashish moments, when he is most reflective, her father scolds her for it. He says Persian women are more like the terns of the Caspian that hover and glide over the foggy sea, not like crows at all. Don't be fooled, he says. They are terns in crows' clothing. You see, the Caspian tern started out here, but exists now all over the world, in every continent. It is a fierce water bird, with a deep red bill, a sharp, blood-red mouth. And while the body of the tern is white, its head is covered in black. It watches with coal-black eyes and attacks without pause, bloodying anyone who disturbs its nest. "Just like your mother," he says, breathing out the comforting smoke. "The tern has a wild and angry spirit living inside."

What a wonderful way to describe someone—even her rage made into poetry.

Around the *sofreh*, three men are lounging on a thickly stacked row of large, colorful pillows. They wear the clerical robes of mullahs, and turbans wrapped around their heads like crowns of white rope. Saba hates Mullah Ali, the oldest one with the white beard, whom her father credits with keeping the family safe despite her mother's too-loud Christianity and flagrant activism. She hates his robes and his mealtime speeches, his reverent attitude toward old women, and the way he has taken her witless cousin Kasem under his wing. Most of all she hates him for being a mullah, a symbol of a bleak new Iran. The constant intrusion of a mullah in one's home is a strange thing in the quiet, unassuming North. So his presence, however friendly, is a sort of blackmail, alms for all the secrets he keeps for her parents. She wonders how her father first broached such topics with the mullah, how he knew the subtle language of it. It is her habit to reject or ignore every kindness offered by this man.

Now he is telling a story about his recent dental surgery. "I'm serious as the grave!" he says, through bites of watermelon. "He pulled out a tooth so long, my left arm shrank. See? You see how it doesn't match?" He holds both arms to the side of his body and the men roar with laughter. One of the women tries to top him. "I once had a tooth that went as deep as my jaw. There's still a hole where I hide jewelry from thieves."

Her father sits quietly in a corner, not eating, only reflecting, taking no part in the conversation. Is he thinking of his wife and other daughter? Does he know the truth about them? He must. Wherever she is, Maman would need his help. They say that children have an intuitive sense for what is true, and Saba has always felt a certain truth in the shadowy mother and daughter at the airport, rushing for a plane to America. Once, though, she dreamed that a faceless *pasdar* held a knife to her throat and ordered her to stake her life on Mahtab's whereabouts. She woke with a tight aching in her stomach and the words *bottom of the sea* new and salty on her lips. Or was it *across the sea*?

Her father leans back, showing little need to entertain. These guests come every few days unannounced, cook for themselves and for him, expect none of the politeness and cheery hospitality they would feel entitled to if he had a wife, only raw materials and a place to practice their conversational arts. Most of them have never been invited into another home like the Hafezis'. Saba imagines that privately they feel sorry for her father and like to assure themselves they are helping—that these parties are good for *his* spirit.

"Agha Hafezi." Mullah Ali addresses her father, but looks over at Saba the way a cunning parent looks at a small child about to be tricked into being good. "How would the lady of the house like to bring us some fresh bread and yogurt?" He asks this with a flourish, as if he expects her to be honored by her role. A better, smarter girl would have gotten up right then. But she ignores him and goes back to eavesdropping on her adopted mothers. Her father sighs loudly and glares. She can almost hear him thinking, *May Ziade*.

The mullah clears his throat, embarrassed. "Oh, were you talking to *me*, Agha?" she says dryly, and her father turns white. Mullah Ali chuckles and shakes his finger at her. Luckily he has been at Agha Hafezi's pipe. He takes a sip of his tea—which the other mullahs will swear was the only pleasure of the evening. No alcohol, no crude stories, no women present, young or old. Mullah Ali leans on his side and takes a puff of the water pipe, breathing in opium from Khanom Omidi's stash. Saba knows where to find the rest, tiny brown balls buried deep in a jar of turmeric-cumin mix. Why does she bother to hide her indulgences? Opium is cheap and she's a harmless old woman.

"This is just a light tobacco, yes?" the mullah asks Agha Hafezi, who nods twice.

Convenient, Saba thinks, how opium and hashish—which sedate the masses—are so easy to find in this new pious Iran, and alcohol—mutinous and unpredictable—has to be consumed in shame and secret, hunted and bargained for from trustworthy sources, or brewed in tubs in the bathroom where a mistake in its strength could kill (and has). For a few after-dinner drops, Agha Hafezi must travel to back alleys and transport cheap sludge in unmarked containers to his storage room. Meanwhile, his hookah is always uncovered in a corner. Though, if he isn't discreet, either habit could get him jailed or killed. Saba recalls the early days after the revolution, before his trust in Mullah Ali was fully cemented, when her father would invite friends and business partners to the house. He was a jovial man then, hopeful of maintaining his prerevolutionary lifestyle. He used code over the telephone to indicate what he had procured. Each drink had its own name: whiskey was Agha Vafa. Gin was Agha Jamsheed, and so on. He would say, "Come over, my friend. Agha Vafa and Agha Jamsheed have both arrived. Come and talk with us."

In the family's vast but dim kitchen, Saba takes some *lavash* bread out of the oven, along with newly picked parsley, mint, and a bowl of yogurt, and returns to the sitting room. She places the food on the *sofreh* and gives her father a cold, wet cloth. He smiles his thanks as he places it on his forehead and leans into the soft crimson pillows. When Mullah Ali praises her for the *sofreh*, she picks a dead bee from the bowl of honeycomb and dumps it on a used plate between him and the food. Her father glares at her, but the mullah doesn't notice. He leans over the bee and takes a spoonful of fresh cream.

In moments like this, she daydreams about America, promising herself that she will go one day. She has outlearned most of her tutors, yet her father never mentions college. She knows he is afraid to let her go, that he thinks she is too fragile, though all her Tehran friends are preparing for it now. Saba has never pressed the subject because if she goes to university in Iran, she will have chosen *this* life. She knows what happens to Iranian doctors and engineers in America. They drive taxis. No, she won't go to college here. She will read novels and speak flawless English, and she will save herself. One day she will wear jeans and hairclips to class. Brazenly polish her nails in the middle of a lecture like she saw once in a movie. She will be a journalist and she will find her mother.

Soon Reza arrives. Saba sits up and thinks of all the ways to escape with him. If Ponneh were here, the three of them could sneak off together and Reza wouldn't suspect Saba of loving him. At eighteen, Reza is unusually tall for an Iranian man, and a target of jealous jokes. He has dark hair, longer than the devout men wear theirs. It's silky and straight and falls neatly around his face. It reminds her of the French tourists, college boys who came to visit once when she was eight. Saba likes his Western clothes, his refusal to grow more than a millimeter of facial hair, his accent, and his love of music. She likes that he thanks her when she brings out the tea, unlike his older brother, who doesn't even look at his wife when she brings him something. She even likes the worshipful way he listens to his mother and defends old Gilaki traditions without a thought.

Flushed from playing football, he pushes back his sweaty black hair. His shoulders are relaxed, his smile full of recent victory. From her bedroom window, Saba has seen him score hundreds of effortless goals in sandaled feet. He must know that she watches him, because he plays in the same spot every day, then knocks on her window to see if she has any new music. He still has that same ball from when they were children.

"Agha Hafezi, when are you giving your daughter for marriage?" one of the black-bearded mullahs asks in a grandfatherly tone, despite the fact that he is much younger than her father. She flinches and glances at Reza, who shows no reaction at first and then gives the pitying half-smile he uses when the adults discuss her marriage prospects. She looks at Khanom Omidi for help, but she is busy digging into the spaces between her yellowing teeth with a long fingernail.

"She's only eighteen," her father says.

"Too old, I'd say," says the mullah, whose oafish lounging is making Saba livid—one leg spread out, another tucked in so that his knee is to his belly, and a hand clutching bread hangs off the edge of his knee.

Vultures. Vipers. Vermin.

Reza catches the look on her face and gives a reassuring shake of the head. "Leave her alone, Agha jan," he says to the young mullah. "Smart girls should study." At first Saba isn't sure if she likes this comment, though later she decides that she does.

From across the *sofreh*, Khanom Basir is keeping an eye on her son. She nibbles on a piece of mint as Reza settles on a pillow. He accepts the cup of tea Saba offers him, stirs in two cubes of sugar, and places a third between his teeth, pouring the hot liquid in over it. Saba pushes a plate of *ghotab* bread toward him. This is another morsel that she has added to her stores: Reza has a sweet tooth. He hates mornings and he loves the Beatles.

"Saba, can you come here a moment?" Khanom Basir calls, an unlikely sweet smile stretching her face. "Saba jan, I say this in place of your poor mother, who isn't here to tell you herself. But that skirt is bad for mixed company." She takes Saba's hand and pulls her close like a confidante, while Saba struggles not to crave her approval. "We have full view of your ankles. Go and fix yourself. Find a chador in the bundle, my good girl."

"But I have my scarf." Saba straightens her headscarf and smooths her skirt. She doesn't want to drape herself like an old woman. She glances at Reza, her lifelong friend, wishing that he would listen and help her in these underhanded moments with his mother.

There is a knock. "Reza, go and get the door," Khanom Basir orders. "Do you think it's Ponneh? Now, *there* is a girl who doesn't need to show skin to be beautiful. No fancy-*bazi*. No trouble to her mother." Khanom Basir sighs at Ponneh's endless virtue, looks at her son for a reaction, and mumbles, "If only she was allowed to marry."

Reza gets up and follows Saba out of the living room and down a few steps. One of the mullahs shouts behind him, "Watch out, don't knock your head on the ceiling."

In the hallway, Saba is afraid to look back at him, afraid to smile.

She wonders if he too knows the things her father claims everyone knows. She walks down the hall feeling his presence behind her, unable to turn until he takes her hand.

"Stop rushing off, Saba Khanom," he almost whispers, in his beautiful rural way. He interlaces two fingers with two of hers and she feels a heat bursting from her chest and crawling up through her blouse, creeping past her shoulders to her temples. It scorches her layers of fabric and leaves her naked. She tries to focus on his imperfections, his village accent and the awkward way he calls her Miss Saba. His voice is far too smooth and throaty, a ruttish eighteen-year-old who has learned to woo women from Western television he half understands. Saba knows this and she wants him more—because of this stupid attempt at touching her and because of the warm sweat on his hand and because of the way he's trying to mask his height by stooping just a little.

They are standing a few feet from the door now and Saba tries to think of something to say. But before she can respond, she hears the demure clearing of a familiar throat, and Ponneh, having let herself in, stands watching them, the heart shape of her face outlined in a baby blue scarf knotted like a flower behind her neck, her almond eyes fixed on their fingers, which are intertwined for only a second more.

Reza drops Saba's hand and shrugs, as if he knows what Ponneh is thinking. After a moment Saba mutters, "Are we going in?"

"Nice hostessing job," says Ponneh, hanging her outer jacket on a nail by the door. "I had to let myself in. Oh no, no. Don't kill so many sheep on *my* account."

Saba waves her hand at Ponneh's remark. "Don't start the guest-*bazi*," she says. "I have no patience for it today." Ponneh laughs and takes Saba's arm, because she loves being reminded that she needs no welcome here. For years she has let herself in, has even sneaked into windows at night and raided the kitchen with Saba.

Reza, looking embarrassed and annoyed, wanders back into the living room. Likely he has already forgotten whatever impulse she ignited in him.

"What was that about?" Ponneh whispers, her lips almost touching Saba's ear.

"I don't know. What?" Saba shrugs. "Guess what? I got us some Neutrogena." Ponneh gets American products only when they are offered by Saba, not just because she is poor but also because of her mother, the widow, who seems to enjoy suffering. Khanom Alborz has always been pleasant to Saba. But she is methodical, traditional in the bizarrest ways. She battles her fear of the unknown with arbitrary rules that she imposes on her five daughters, including the sick, bedridden one. If she found Ponneh with an unearned luxury, she would give it to her oldest daughter.

Back at the *sofreh* Saba leans her head on Khanom Omidi's shoulder and the old woman pulls her close. She tries to avoid the pudgy gaze of her lumbering, oversolicitous cousin Kasem, who seems to have arrived via the back door. As she brings a hot cup to her lips, Saba hears more of Mullah Ali's wisdom. It seems that the mullah has had too much of the pipe, maybe even a drink. Usually he refuses alcohol, except when he is alone with Agha Hafezi or when he is given the drink "accidentally," without his consent. *Who's hiding the bottle this time?* Saba glances around. There is something hard under Khanom Omidi's skirt. When she tries to touch it, the old woman slaps her hand. The mullah is shaking his head at her father. "I'm not talking about their baby-age. What I'm talking about is their minds." He taps his head with his finger. "It is a well-known fact that women who are not otherwise occupied . . . physically . . . get unhealthy notions. It's well documented . . . and then, even if you do marry them off, they never respect their husbands. They question and nag . . ."

Khanom Basir sighs dramatically. "For God's sake."

"What about Kasem?" Mullah Ali hums and pats Kasem's thick neck, as if expecting everyone to have followed his thoughts. "A fine boy. Saba should marry him."

Saba sits up. She blurts out, "But he's my cousin." Beside the mullah, Kasem looks down and smiles through a deep, feminine shade of red.

Vomit!

Kasem is shorter than Saba and strangely proportioned. He isn't overweight, but he has a surprisingly protuberant backside. He looks soft—in his physique, in his face; Saba imagines he is a bit soft even in his bones.

"Let the men talk, child." Mullah Ali closes his eyes and addresses Saba with a hushed, almost weary voice, as if he is tired of repeating himself.

"You're lucky your daughter hasn't been to England or America," the other mullah interjects. "You escaped a curse. America would have corrupted her."

Saba imagines again Mahtab's life in America, a less compliant coming-of-age. Is she happy there? Is she in love with an exuberant American? At the very least she would have a much larger pool of men to choose from. In Cheshmeh, though talk of marriage is a constant pastime, the war with Iraq has left few men her age—and none like Reza.

"He's her cousin," her father says, with finality. "She can't marry her cousin."

"The boy is my student. A fine choice. And you know cousins are a match ordained by God and the heavens." Mullah Ali sits up, offended, determined to win.

Saba sees that her father is annoyed, that he wants to say something about genetics and chromosomes. Like the educated Westerners he admires, he holds his tongue. She knows that he won't insult his nephew, who has been faithful to the family, kept their secrets, and spoken well of them to Mullah Ali.

Her father clears his throat. "In any case, they're too young." He waves away the topic like a lone mosquito, too small to merit much effort, too bothersome to ignore.

Victory, Saba thinks in English, silently congratulating her father.

"You know who is a good choice for Saba?" says Khanom Basir. "Agha Abbas. Yes, he's old, but he is rich and kind."

Saba begins to object. Agha Abbas is the oldest bachelor they know, a widower even older than her father. "Saba and I will decide this later." Agha Hafezi is quick to preempt.

She leans on a cushion and observes her father's kind eyes, the way he doesn't share food with the villagers and waves away their rural wisdom. Should she show him that she is thankful? No, he won't understand what she means by it. He will probably pity her. She eyes the snaking blue lines on Mullah Ali's ankles as he leans across the *sofreh.*

Varicose veins, she thinks they are called.

She watches the clerics, and she waits for the darkest early hours when matchmaking will be safely out of every mind and an unmarried girl with too much spirit might have a moment of pleasure.

❧⦿❧

Since Mahtab left, Saba and her friends have hidden in the dark food closet of her kitchen during parties. They always find a moment to get away, even if for only ten minutes. Now they sit in a circle in the pantry. Ponneh produces a small soda bottle of clear liquid. Reza's eyes light up and he reaches into his pocket. A half-smoked hashish joint.

"Where did you get *that*?" Ponneh asks.

Reza feigns nonchalance. "One of the men in the square." Saba doubts that's true. Even the Tehrani won't meet her right out in the town square, certainly not with drugs.

Ponneh checks the door again. "Right here in the pantry? What about the smell?"

"Please," says Reza. "This whole house smells funny. If they catch us, we'll say we found it in Agha Hafezi's bedroom."

"That's a lot better," mutters Saba.

"So Mustafa proposed again today," Ponneh offers. "He thinks that *pasdar* uniform is attractive. I'd rather die." Saba giggles. Reza scoffs and lights the joint.

They sit there together for half an hour, consuming their stolen treasures, glancing at the door every few seconds. Saba relishes the intimacy of it, smoking together in the dark. It's an indulgence that only the best of friends share nowadays. She lets a fat curl of smoke escape her open mouth and breathes it back in through her nose. Ponneh takes dainty puffs. She brings the tiny joint to her lips, locks eyes with Reza, and looks away. She passes the stub to him and leans back against a shelf full of cans.

When Saba and Ponneh return to the living room ten minutes after Reza, they find the adults occupied in similar ways. Telling bawdy jokes. Letting scarves fall onto shoulders. They sit on a carpet near a pile of pillows. Ponneh loosens her scarf around her neck and pushes it back farther, showing off four or five centimeters of silky brown tufts parted loosely just off the center. She does it with such a flourish. Saba tells herself that it's the hashish making her paranoid. She smells her fingers, that delicious earthy dust. Saba too wants to cast off her *hijab*, but she has to wait longer. Saba is taller, shapelier—beautiful in sinful ways that make other women shake with furious piety, while Ponneh radiates an innocent loveliness they worship.

Saba busies herself by bringing more water with mint and lemon. When she returns, she hears her friends whispering, feigning casual talk.

"But why not?" Reza pleads. "We're both eighteen. We're old enough."

"You know I can't," Ponneh whispers back. "You know Maman's rule."

"I've never heard anyone else with a rule like that," he says.

"Well, there it is. I have three older sisters, and none of them are married. So that's that."

"And the sick one? She can barely stand up. We both know she'll never—"

"That's cruel," she snaps. "You sound like Mustafa with his ridiculous *suffering.*"

There is some mumbling. He is whispering something in her ear. He is trying to comfort her, convince her. No one is listening to them and Saba too decides not to hear this. Reza is only a man and men are weak. Who knows what he would be saying if she was the one sitting beside him now. Saba knows Reza is confused. He believes in the old ways, yet he is obsessed with Western culture. He recites the oldest poetry and convinces himself that he can live in a world where men have enough love for four women and romance is a series of storybook snippets full of longing and revelation. He doesn't understand politics, hates religion, and has never dreamed of anyplace outside Gilan. He follows Saba's father because he imagines that one day he too will be a landowner in Cheshmeh and that he will be a hero to his family—that a dozen old women holding babies will sit in front of the house and watch him kick his old football between two trash cans, and he will reward them with songs as they squat in his tiny but well-stocked kitchen and cook him his favorite dinner. He lives in a world of women. To be deprived of any of them—Saba or Ponneh or his mother—would be unfathomable to him.

Later the younger mullahs leave and she is left with her father, her two best friends, the women, and Mullah Ali. When the cleric is nodding off and the others are free to have a sip—the small soda bottle holding the homemade liquor is now in plain sight instead of hidden under Khanom Omidi's skirts—and Saba's father has had a few puffs as well, the women laugh loudly and Saba crumples her scarf under a pillow. Even Khanom Basir has an indulgent look, having forgotten Saba's inappropriate skirt. Then the requests begin. "Saba jan, please dance for us," says Khanom Omidi.

"Yes, Saba, you have to dance," Ponneh says, and starts to clap.

Her father laughs with real mirth, the way he once did. "My daughter is good at many things. She is like her mother. A creative soul."

Mullah Ali nods sleepily. "Yes, yes."

Still they wait till he has fallen into deep sleep. Since the revolution, no one dares to dance or sing in front of anyone but the most intimate friends. And though Agha Hafezi has received much protection from the mullah, Saba's father is already tempting fate by having a party with unmarried men and women in the same room.

But soon the cleric is asleep and suddenly it is no longer this year, or this solitary season of life. Suddenly Saba is a girl from many decades ago, in an old Iran that may never have existed. Was it only an invention? Tall tales from her parents' generation? Oh, but it must have existed because in those days Saba's mother, despite her education and Western ideals, was known for indulging her untamed self, dancing immodestly in public, displaying her naked bliss or sorrow on *sofreh*s long cleared of food and tea.

Reza is already getting up to retrieve the guitar hidden in the closet behind Saba's father. He settles across from Ponneh and the older women. Khanom Basir and Khanom Omidi clear the *sofreh* and Saba moves barefoot to the center of the carpet. Reza begins an old Farsi tune, slow and meandering, full of long, somber notes on which Saba's arms and legs can linger. His fingers rouse the strings with the same miraculous ease with which his sandaled toes kick a football. She lifts her arms so they become a winding halo around her face and torso. She bends her head back and lets her long hair fall, knowing that in this hazy secret hour no one disapproves. No one will claim to remember. She is loved though she teeters on the edge of danger—a mullah sleeping just there in the midst of so much crime. How intoxicating! Despite the risks, her throat doesn't constrict. She is alive— no sea waiting to swallow her, no Mahtab in the mirror.

Reza has closed his eyes and is moving his head to the music. Just before the end of the song, she turns and catches his melancholy look across the room to where Ponneh is leaning against a pillow. He fumbles a few notes and mouths, *I'm sorry*, but no matter how she replays the words in her mind, Saba can't decide if they were meant for her.

She banishes the question. This is too rare a moment to waste. Her hair flutters over her arms and cheeks, awakening a hundred sleeping sensations. Her fingers reach for each note as if chasing feathers in the wind. They hover over her body and face, the body and face of a newly grown-up Mahtab across the sea, and she spins on the faded carpet to Reza's song until all propriety is gone and she is herself again.

Marriage Proposal
(Khanom Basir)

Y ou might say the girls were raised here, by a great many of us. Before the revolution, they came only in summers, danced around in pink dresses without sleeves sent from big London stores, and the other children followed them, mesmerized. They picked oranges and lounged under trees reading their English stories. They went to mixed gender beaches with their parents. They let their hair fly on the backs of motorcycles and watched workers in fields. They loved the moist air of the North, the endless green of Shomal. But the Shomal that Tehranis knew was a different world from ours. It still is.

You see, half an hour's drive in one direction leads to the Caspian Sea and to well dressed English and French speaking tourists with foreign degrees doing who knows what in Western villas. Half an hour's drive in another direction leads into the dirt roads of the mountain. If you ever come to Shomal, *this* is the sight to see: donkeys and horses carrying men in skullcaps and women in bejangled, color ful clothes into the forest, to their unpainted baked mud or clay houses all grainy with hay. And the straw jutting from walls and covering their low, low roofs. I like these peaceful parts of the mountain, the wildflowers and jackal songs, the water wells and feather-paved coops.

Before the revolution, Tehranis came to escape a world of loud music, Western television, fashionable parties, and clothes measured by a hundred tailors. And what did they find here? Just us villagers in our Gilaki coverings, farming rice. Now they come to escape *pasdar*s everywhere and riots and secret living. And what do they find here? Just us villagers in our Gilaki coverings, farming rice. In Cheshmeh, where we believed in modesty before 1979, and where we refused to go to extremes after, there are days when you might forget the world has changed—unless you are a Hafezi.

In the old days, the Hafezi girls ran in and out of our houses and we fed them from our kitchens, warmed by how little they knew of the differences between us. Of course, there were rules. The Hafezis made it so we could never treat the girls as our own. *Proper Farsi only,* Agha Hafezi said. *No Gilaki with the girls.* He demanded this, though he spoke our dialect to the workers in his rice paddies. Saba eventually learned to switch between Farsi and Gilaki (*Khuda daneh,* she would drone constantly like an old woman). Mahtab never spoke anything but Farsi and English. This was one easy way to tell them apart.

I saw back then that Saba was the twin who had inherited her father's Gilaki spirit instead of her mother's crazy foreign one. There was an incident when she was seven, when she proposed marriage to my son. Sweet, yes, yes. She wanted to be one of us. But it salted my stomach with worry. The twins spent all day putting together a *khastegari* present, full of pastries and coins they had saved, and—my favorite because it was a token good only for your distant aunt—a picture of their mother as a young woman to prove how beautiful

Saba would be. They stole some makeup and painted her seven shades of blues and reds. It was a spectacle. They even bought a piece of lace for the veil.

Outside my house there is a winding dirt road that leads around the hills. And if you stand at the window you can see the Hafezi house in the distance. It rests higher on a hill by itself, on a bigger road. So I saw them coming from far off, one sister watching from behind a tree nearby as the other sister knocked on my door. I answered. "And which are you?" I said, even though I knew. I wanted to spare Saba the embarrassment, with that ridiculous veil. And then out comes Reza, showing up at the door in his underwear, not putting the clues together, poor boy. How is he to know what goes on in the minds of girls who read too much?

When I tried to send Saba away, Mahtab ran out from her hiding place, put her little hands on her hips, and said to me, "You're a mean old lady. We saved all our money for this *khastegari*. We even went through Khanom Omidi's treasure chador!"

Hah! You see, when you leave girls to their own minds, they grow a tongue—not to mention a long, sneaking hand that'll surely land them in hell.

Being smart girls, they knew I would call their parents. So apparently they spent the afternoon hiding out, messing around with that donkey-brained cousin of theirs. They used to spend a lot of time making up stories for him, because Kasem was ready to believe anything. One of the biggest mysteries of this world is how a boy like him can be worshipped and waited on like a pasha, when he's so clearly a fool. But that's how it is with boys. Don't think I don't see it just because I have sons. I know what girls suffer. I may not be one of those big-city feminists, but I'm not blind. My heart broke when I saw their father praise Kasem or pull him onto his lap while Saba and Mahtab watched like hungry orphans in overpriced dresses.

Every day I watched from my window as their father left for work and the girls followed him down the road, trying to see who could hold his attention longer. And when we were all at their *sofreh* for dinner and the house was buzzing and no one was listening to the girls, I heard them competing over who would get to walk on his aching back or bring him his tea later. And they argued over which was better: the time Agha Hafezi went to their school to demand that some filthy boy Mahtab "loved" be forced to play with her, or the time he came home full of celebration—a new piece of land—and picked up Saba only and danced and danced around the room until she pretended to faint.

Still, it isn't Agha Hafezi's fault that the girls were starving for his love. He didn't know any other way. He was a happy, hard man. He had Bahareh to take care of the girls' daily needs. His job was to provide, to protect them. What man without troubles spends time thinking of how to bond with his young daughters? They are not simple like boys.

But he did worry and work hard for them—that I will swear is true—rolling up his pant legs and walking through the sodden fields with the workers. I have never seen another landowner do this. He grew up here, you know. His father built the big house and the son has grown attached to it despite his city wife. He is Gilaki at heart, like Saba. Sometimes you see him with a fancy raincoat and a long umbrella, inspecting this or that. Sometimes he is in breezy cotton work pants and a knit cap in the local coffee shop, smoking with the old men. Once I heard him say a few words of Gilaki to Ponneh when she came to play with his daughters. He said to her, "How's school? I'll give you a new dress for every year you finish." But Ponneh was too proud even then—and now she can sew her own clothes from old patterns or new ones she copies from tourist women.

Lately Agha Hafezi has taken to bad habits. He failed to protect his family, and Saba is the only one he has left. He is softer, full of mourning, obsessed with questions of the spirit. He feels her value and he keeps trying to mend things, but how can he know the way? He never learned her heart when she was young and willing.

Maybe it's too late for the two of them. Maybe Saba should abandon these games with my son and get a husband who can also replace her father . . . someone older, stronger. But she will never admit this. She is the kind of girl who wants both the dates and the donkey, never compromising. But she will *have* to compromise. My son is already in love. As for Saba, I am thinking Abbas Hossein Abbas is the perfect choice for her.

Chapter Four

AUTUMN 1988

Having Khanom Mansoori and her husband over to the house is like having no guests at all. Saba calls Khanom Mansoori the Ancient One not only because she is twenty years older than the other caregivers in her life but because she is always either dozing or talking to herself. She requires no company, no hostessing, no effort. When her husband accompanies her on a visit, Saba and her father feel no obligation to remain in the room. The old couple will talk to each other for a while, eat something, drink tea, and eventually one of them will notice something off—a pillow in a color she doesn't like or the telephone or a picture of Saba's mother in the corner—and they will realize that this is someone else's house and leave. Agha Mansoori likes to make a show of caring for his wife, and Saba knows that in order to avoid insulting the old man, she must bring out a tray of apples and cucumbers and place them in front of him, never his wife. He will then take twenty minutes to scrape out the insides of the fruits into a bowl and serve them to her himself. Saba wonders if he has always done this, or if it's his way of feeling useful in his later years—because when the women gather alone, his wife seems perfectly capable of eating solid apple slices with her healthy back teeth.

Today the couple has stayed longer than usual and Saba has decided to watch a video instead of listening to their discussion about whether the big rainstorm that destroyed their first house happened in the fourth or sixth year of their marriage. She sits on the floor of the living room and switches on the television and VCR. She chooses a tape containing random episodes of a number of popular American television shows she has asked the Tehrani to record for her. The sound is a little scratchy, the dialogue hard to understand but, aside from a few lines of impossible American slang, it's decipherable for someone with Saba's excellent English. A few seconds into the first sitcom, the music catches the couple's attention. First Khanom Mansoori nudges her husband and then he too is captivated. "What in God's name are they doing there?" he shouts.

It's the opening credits of an American show called *Family Ties.* "Why are they all hugging there?" Agha Mansoori asks. Then when he sees TV-husband Agha Keaton kissing Khanom Keaton, his eyes grow wide. "*Vai*, did you see that, Khanom?"

"It's an American show," Saba says, amused. "Do you want me to explain it?"

The old man waves for her to be quiet as the first scene opens. He moves closer to the television as if he can understand the fast-paced, crackling English words.

In the show, Khanom Keaton hangs up the telephone and Agha Keaton scolds her. "*Ei vai*," says Agha Mansoori, mesmerized. "Look at that. They're fighting now."

Khanom Mansoori chuckles, probably at the urgency in his tone.

"They're not fighting," says Saba. "He's only saying—"

"Hush, Saba jan," says Agha Mansoori. And then he throws his hands up in the air. "*Vai*, look what they are showing there! No shame . . ." Khanom Keaton sits on her husband's lap. Kisses his lips, his neck, and murmurs soothing words. Agha Mansoori slaps the top of one hand with the other. "God help us . . ."

Saba has seen this episode twice already. It's yet another one in which Alex P. Keaton tells his laid-back American parents that he must, must, must go to Princeton. *What is this Princeton?* Saba mused the last time, because as far as she knew, only one college was worth mentioning in America, and that college was called Harvard. Sort of like Tehran University—a core academic hub surrounded by village institutions. But now Saba is well informed. She has researched this Princeton—a place that also educated Sondra Huxtable of *The Cosby Show* even though she is no pale princeling—and all the colleges like it with names unfamiliar even to the highly educated in Iran.

Saba relates to Alex's struggle with his parents. Like ambitious Alex, she is a capitalist. But this is Gilan, the birthplace of the Communist Party of Iran, the land of Mirza Kuchik Khan and his socialist Jangali movement that fought for the downtrodden and the peasant class in Gilan's forests back when the Mansooris were very young. If the old couple understood English, they would agree with Alex's hippie parents.

But Agha and Khanom Mansoori ignore all of Saba's attempts to explain the plot. When she tells them that Alex P. Keaton is visiting the Princeton dorms, Khanom Mansoori says, "No, no, that boy there must be his cousin. They look exactly alike." When Saba explains a line of dialogue, Agha Mansoori ignores her and touches the screen just over the orange-and-blue bedspread. "We had a blanket like that one. Do you remember, Khanom? The day Hasan brought it and we spilled the tea?" To which his wife responds, "It was soup. Where is that old thing now? Was it really an *American* blanket?"

When it seems that the two are distracted by memories—she talking about old days and he nodding and shelling pistachios into a bowl—Saba moves to turn off the television, but Agha Mansoori objects loudly. *"Aieee.* Wait. We are watching the story there. It's shameful, Khanom . . . shameful." Then he leans over and drops a handful of naked pistachios into Saba's hand. He waits for her to eat them, as if they were medicine.

In seventy years maybe Saba's own husband will call her "Mrs." instead of her first name. Maybe he will have a sweet, gummy smile, shell nuts for her, and worry about how many she eats. If she married Reza, she is sure he would do all these things.

They watch for three hours, never skipping the commercials, until the tape cycles through six episodes, including an episode of *Growing Pains* and half an episode of *The Wonder Years.* Saba likes American high schools. She wonders what it would be like to go to one every day—to have a locker for her banned books, to have a boy occupy the locker next to hers. She takes in the details of the shows— the slightly uncomfortable look of suburbia, the layout of kitchens, women's haircuts, the ubiquitous pancake diner. She misses her sister. At the same time, she wants to be alone. Funny thing about television shows, she thinks. They cover so many worries and crises and hurts. Yet somehow they wrap them all up in thirty minutes or less. What a beautiful world where all of life's aches are wiped away with one group hug after exactly 22.5 minutes of visual storytelling. Saba wants to live in that world. She imagines that her sister already does.

The sky outside grows dark and Khanom Mansoori has fallen asleep. Her husband continues to sit ten centimeters from the television and comment to no one. Then something jolts the old lady and she sits up and calls out, "Saba, come here."

Saba moves to the other side of the room, sits on the carpet beside Khanom Mansoori. She adjusts the pillows behind the old woman so she can be more comfortable.

"Saba jan, what happened to all that business about Mahtab and America?"

Usually a mention of her sister makes Saba's throat constrict. But something in the old woman's tone makes Saba lean closer. Is Khanom Mansoori dreaming? Has she confused the year? But then her withered lips whisper something that Saba knows is not a dream. "Are you still too grown-up for stories? You remember . . . the kid and the coping?"

Saba smiles, recalling the day they read *Zanerooz* magazine with Ponneh. It is impressive that Khanom Mansoori remembers a conversation from so long ago. Saba smooths back the strands of henna hair that have escaped the old woman's scarf. "I'm not too old anymore," she whispers, and rests her head on Khanom Mansoori's shoulder.

"Tell me a story then. Something Mahtab wrote in a letter."

"There was no letter," she says, hoping that someone will challenge the lies she has learned to tell about Mahtab. *Across the sea,* she whispers over and over in her dreams to *pasdar*s holding knives to throats and forcing truths out of reluctant lips.

Khanom Mansoori shakes her head. "Don't tease an old woman," she says, her voice birdlike. "At my age, you learn that true things are different from things your eyes can see. I want to know what's in the letter before I judge that it's not true."

Saba lets out a laugh because she doesn't know what to say to such a request. She appeals to the old woman's husband. "Agha Mansoori, can you help me, please?"

There is a moment of silence, and she thinks Agha Mansoori didn't hear her. But he says without looking away from the television, "What help? Just tell her the stories or the letters or what have you so she can tell you if they're true. What's the difficulty?"

Saba sighs, "But there *are* no—" She stops because it is useless to argue with them. Besides, why is she fighting? She saw Mahtab get on a plane to *somewhere*. There is no denying that. And she hasn't told a story about Mahtab—except to herself alone in bed, or a few details to Baba—since that day in the alley behind the Rashti post office.

The Mansooris won't judge her. They are creative with the truth, not only because they are Iranian and realize that good stories must be embellished, and words of praise must be exaggerated, and half of all invitations must be lies, but also because they are old, and it seems to Saba that this is what happens at the end of life, as in the beginning. People enter and leave this world trying to understand what everything means, how easily the costliest possessions can break, and what is theirs to keep. When they discover the bitter truth that everything is fragile and eventually gone, they make up a new reality in which the best of what is lost waits for them somewhere they are too busy to go. *Where is Uncle Koorosh? you ask. He moved to France* (died). *The beautiful neighbor boy? He is in college* (jail).

"All right," Saba says, and takes a breath. Why not honor Mahtab in this way? Besides, unlike all the rest, Mahtab's story *could* be true by some magic available only to twins. Didn't Khanom Mansoori herself say that the bond between twins is unbreakable? That each will always know the truth about the other's days? She is the one person who will understand all the possibilities following that day at the airport, and all the promise of the elegant mother in the terminal holding the hand of a girl with Saba's own face.

"Good girl," Khanom Mansoori sighs.

Here is how this will work. You both must promise that you will tell no one about Mahtab's life. I will tell you her stories as on a television show, and each episode in the series will be about a day when she released one of the bondages of being an immigrant. You see, if there is one thing I have learned from books, television, and friends in exile, it is that the American way of life is so overwhelming, so grand, that outsiders are infected with a whole set of Immigrant Worries. In time, Mahtab will overcome the greatest of these fears, one by one. I know this because I know my sister; and in America, problems are solved in small bite-sized increments—just like you see on television.

Taken together, these episodes will be the story of Mahtab's life. I have some of them hidden away on paper—maybe, as you say, these are my sister's secret letters to me. *Immigrant Worries*: the narrative of how she releases her old life and leaves me to mine. By the end, she will no longer be an immigrant and she will no longer be a twin.

To begin, you should know that, like Alex P. Keaton and both my parents, Mahtab is obsessed with university. She wants to go to Harvard because that is the best one, the only one Iranians know. It's a Friday afternoon in April—the one that just passed—and Mahtab sits on the curb next to her mailbox in California, waiting. She watches the panther lilies—because, you see, panther lilies grow in California, and they are *verdant* and *vibrant*, if you care to describe them in English. A fly buzzes around her face. A *pari*, a pretty, luck-bearing fairy, the kind that ignores all but faithful drinkers of old lore, sits atop the peeling fence post, unnoticed by passersby, her faint buzzing mistaken for a bee.

"Ah, a pari! That means good fortune," says Khanom Mansoori.

"I saw a pari *once,"* says Agha Mansoori. *"On the very day my mother died."*

Mahtab is aware that she has been very lucky, with her fine life and her strokes of good fortune. She tries not to think about Saba, her unlucky twin, because why remind the *pari* about the unfairness of it all? Fortune isn't always so black-and-white, after all, and blessings can sour. Maybe one lucky day at the age of eleven can consume her life's allowance of fortune. Maybe she is standing at a peak and it's time to tumble down.

"Hmm," says Khanom Mansoori, *"is that what she worries about now? Sad."*

As a precaution, she appeases the immigrant gods with hard work and sweat, toiling at a pancake diner every day after school. On slow afternoons she talks to José, the middle-aged dishwasher, who she suspects is an illegal immigrant from Mexico—that's in the South. Instead of talking, José passes the days with songs. He sings along to Otis Redding tapes in the kitchen, which is how Mahtab can tell that he speaks English. She likes José. He has unruly salt-and-pepper hair and kind eyes. He is never clean-shaven and he has thick black sideburns that peek out from beneath a dingy baseball cap. He peels carrots and makes sandwiches for her, leaving them on the counter after work. In return, she tells him her secrets when she's bored or anxious—that she has Harvard-sized dreams, that she loves martial-arts movies and has seen *American Ninja* three times.

Today she's late for work again, waiting next to her suburban curb as she has done all week. Finally she spots the mail truck in the distance. It drives past the Changs', the Hortons', the Kerinskis', and the Stephanpouloses'—because American streets are filled with names like these—until it arrives next to a peeling fence post and a lazy *pari*. It pulls up in front of the Hafezi house and a disembodied hand reaches out the window. Like a mail-truck genie, the hand stuffs her mailbox with five thick envelopes and four thin ones.

"Is that a good thing? These thick and thin envelopes?" says Agha Mansoori.

Oh, yes. You see, in America, people like to sue. And so universities try to mitigate admissions-related heart attacks by hinting at their decision with the thickness of their envelopes. It is very much like the thickness of a stew—hefty ones signal success.

Later in life, when Mahtab tells the story of the college-acceptance genie, no American believes her. She doesn't mind. Even now she knows not to get technical with Americans. They are a logical race, these Westerners. They don't have spirits and body parts floating around in everyday life. They will never understand Mahtab because they are used to happy blond princesses like Shahzadeh

Nixon who keep their fingers out of the garlic and their hands folded in their laps.

"Way to go, kiddo!" a voice from inside the mail truck shouts at her—because that is what American genies call children whose names they don't remember. "Good schools!" Mahtab can barely feel her legs beneath her. She lifts her feet, kicks off her sandals, and swims through the thick haze to her mailbox, now crammed full of thick and thin, knocking the lounging *pari* off her pedestal with one flail of her soaring limbs.

Before we open the envelope from Harvard, I must be sure you understand. You see, Khanom and Agha Mansoori, this isn't only about education. Mahtab needs a father. Can you imagine how much she must miss Baba? Maybe as much as I miss Maman. But unlike me, Mahtab fills the holes in her own heart through the strength of her will. She is clever, and she doesn't sit around and suffer. So, as she tears open the envelope, she is imagining herself in the warm, secure arms of Baba Harvard—the world's perfect father, with his deep pockets and endless erudition and mild discipline and visionary philosophy. She turns it over in her hand, examines the Cambridge postmark, runs her fingers over her own address. It's neither thick nor thin. She rips it open, hands shaking, and scans. Sadly, I don't have the knowledge to re-create this letter for you, but it says basically this:

Dear Ms. Hafezi,
Something something . . . WAITING LIST . . . Some other things.
Sincerely,
Harvard College

"Well, I don't believe this!" says Khanom Mansoori with a huff. "Who is this Agha Harvard who thinks he can make our Mahtab wait? Does he know she can chatter all day in English? *She must know a thousand big words!"*

Yes, thousands! Well, by the time Maman comes home, Mahtab

is already immersed in the mourning process: hair rumpled, pajamas askew. Mahtab never does anything without conviction—so she doesn't notice all the wonders of having a mother who returns home every night to witness her tragedies. Look at our maman sitting by my sister's bed, the way she smooths her hair, the way they look so alike now that Mahtab is grown. They are no longer the woman and child at the terminal. Now Maman's elegance has been worn away by exhaustion and factory work, and her bob is full of gray. But see how Mahtab and I have inherited her dark looks? Jet-black hair. Sleepy eyes. Tall, curvy bodies. Are Mahtab and I still identical? Maybe not for long. She has been begging for a nose job, a rite of passage for many Persian girls in our circle—for the ones in Iran, because the headscarf leaves them no outer beauty but the circle it draws around their face; and for the ones in America, because of so many lonely Immigrant Worries.

By May, when no new letter comes from Harvard, Maman begins to feel a strange fear—a special breed of exile panic that comes from standing at too many borders with dangerously thin piles of paperwork. Mahtab is inconsolable. She spends her days alone in her room, misses school, flies into rages. She rants about becoming a postal worker, or a professional gardener, or a middle-class wife, like the women in TV shows. Maybe she will have to go back to Iran and marry a mullah, she says.

Despite her own fears, Maman begins to consider the surgery as a way of appeasing Mahtab. What else can she do? She has been through too much on her own. She has worked her way up from factory laborer to factory management, has delivered her daughter from a meager apartment to a modest house. She has already lost one girl, and has built calluses in her heart where that daughter used to live. Though she loathes change in all forms—though she doesn't want her own mark to be removed from her child's face—she relents for the sake of Mahtab's happiness.

Of course, I can only guess at her thoughts. I know my mother must be different now—because people change, so slowly that they are blind to it, in the same way that yellowing teeth go unnoticed until one day ten years have passed and you remember that it's been a long time since anyone complimented your smile. I imagine that my mother misses her old life, her old friends. She is probably the lonelier of the two by far. Unlike Mahtab's, her losses are impossible to overcome. Her immigrant curse is a tangible, breathing thing. It lives and eats with them, like an unwanted stepparent.

Afraid for her daughter's future, which has already cost her so much, she takes out a loan to pay for the new nose. See how she helps my sister discard me? I can still picture her standing in the airport, holding Mahtab's hand, refusing to look back when I called to them both. Even though I was screaming their names, they boarded that plane without even a good-bye. And now they abandon me again and again, in new and more imaginative ways every day.

"Don't be sad, Saba jan. I'm quite sure noses grow back with age."

But maybe it has all been for the best, because look there:

On a doubly lucky morning in late May, Mahtab wakes up from surgery to find the good-luck *pari* lounging at the foot of her bed. A blurry three-headed version of her mother is waving a letter and jumping up and down. "You're off the waiting list! You're going to Harvard, Mahtab joon!" And so she is transformed. A Harvard girl with a sleek nose, long and thin with a slight upturn.

Before she leaves for university, Mahtab dyes her hair auburn. I would never choose that color. And later, at Harvard, when she changes her name to "May," she won't even think of me. With each deviation from her original looks, she feels a bit freer, a bit less bound to us—to our twin world. No one will ever stop her in the streets and say, "Hey, you, I just saw you in some village in Iran. You don't belong here."

When Mahtab still was in that village, when that village was the only place she belonged, she used to listen to you, my dear Khanom Mansoori, explain how carpets are made and how to judge them. The three base colors, the quality of the fibers, the number of knots, the neatness of the fringe. One day you gathered the two of us into your lap and showed us the back of a carpet. "You see how messy it looks? All those strands in the back? You don't see them because it's their job to be invisible, but really they are holding it all together." There is an Unseen Strand that holds together sisters across the world. No matter where they travel and how much earth and water come between them, even if one of them leaves this world altogether. And though you can't see it, it's the reason that you can never really run away, just like the right side of a carpet can't cover the living room if the left side is in the hall. "And twins," you said to us on that day, "see how the pattern in the carpet has perfect symmetry? Both sides exactly the same? How can you possibly separate the two halves? People would always know that a piece is missing."

Ever since Mahtab moved to California, the Unseen Strand has felt like a noose around her neck. And now, with each physical change, she feels it loosen so she can breathe. As she looks at herself in the mirror at night, she feels sad for her sister, with her Persian nose and unshaven legs, with her Gilaki headscarf and village-girl chores.

A week before she leaves for Harvard, Mahtab craves some company—feels that she should say good-bye to someone. Maybe she regrets never saying it to me. Maybe that's why, when she can't think of anyone to talk to, she goes back to the diner and sits in a corner, watching her classmates eat pancakes and tease each other with private jokes.

How will she ever make friends at Harvard?

But Mahtab never approaches. She just sits and waits. None of them is the person she wants to speak to. She spies on them for an hour and then, as her classmates finish their food, gather their backpacks, and drop green bills on the table, Mahtab thinks maybe no person will fill the void. Maybe in this new world she will have to toil and wait for me to join her—like a sort of purgatory. Maybe she will have to sweat to appease the gods who dole out luck—the ones who choose one sister over another though they are exactly the same in their blood—because she has already had more than her fair share.

Still, she is desperate to belong here. Will she ever be like them anything? Will Baba Harvard be all that he promised to be? Will he reject her because of her foreignness?

If her real father were here, Mahtab thinks, she wouldn't need to fit in. She wouldn't want to change the features she shares with him. She would bring him her grades every semester and wait for that slow smile that spreads like a thick dye over his face and reveals his cream-colored teeth one by one. She would never rebel or date boys he didn't like. She wouldn't ask to drive or wear short skirts, and she would make him tea in the afternoons—watch him sip it through a sugar cube between his teeth.

The diner is nearly empty. She hears Otis Redding—do you know Otis Redding? He makes beautiful music—wafting into the dining room from the kitchen. *Sittin' on the dock of the bay*. José's distinctive voice hums along with the melody. She follows it into the kitchen, thinking maybe he is lonely in there.

"*Mija*," he says, which is what his people call beloved girls. "I thought you quit."

She walks up to him and mumbles something about being bored. She wanders closer to the sink until she is standing next to him, watching his hands and forearms disappear into a pillowy mound of dish foam. Then, without meaning to, she rests her head on José's shoulder. She knows it's strange. She can tell because he has suddenly stopped scrubbing, his body rigid. But she doesn't care. It has been a long time since she felt the twists and knobs of a fatherly shoulder against her cheek.

"Good-bye, José," she mumbles into his scratchy flannel shirt. "I'll miss you."

He smooths Mahtab's hair with his wet foamy hand. Maybe he too misses the softness of a daughterly cheek on his shoulder. He says, "You take care, *mija.*"

There. She has said her good-byes . . . to *someone*. Not to me. The thread that holds sisters together across the world is broken and there is no more symmetry between us. But I see now that it has been just about twenty-two minutes and, according to the rules of American television, a problem must now be solved. It is time for Mahtab to purge the first of her Immigrant Worries. Do you want to hear what it is? The first worry is the same for everyone. From now on, Mahtab of the auburn hair and pointy nose and fine education, adopted daughter of Baba Harvard, stops fearing her Persian roots. But don't be sad. That face, it still exists somewhere—except now it isn't part of a pair.

☙‥◐◑‥☙

Khanom Mansoori is fully awake now and she takes Saba's hand, touches her face, and says, "You know you're like my own grand-daughter."

Saba nods, as does Agha Mansoori. "Yes, yes," he's saying, "our own granddaughter."

His wife continues. "Mahtab or no Mahtab. Letter or no letter, that story is truth."

Though she wants to linger in her surrogate grandmother's arms, to cry a little and ask her why she thinks this is so, she only kisses Khanom Mansoori's papery cheek and gets up to make dinner. The Mansooris have stayed too late, and so they will spend the night with the Hafezis. Saba tries to push the old woman's words out of her mind, because there is no time to linger on sad things. She doesn't want to be the kind of girl who is lost in her own thoughts and day-dreams. She has to find some bedding for her guests now. But Kha-nom Mansoori calls after her to wait a moment. "It doesn't matter where something happens, as long as it *happens*. If I told you the story of the first time I kissed Agha here . . . on our wedding day or in the yard when we were twelve. Who really cares about all that? The details you can change. The where and the when. It's the *what* and the *how* that make it truth or lies."

Agha Mansoori turns red at the memory and mumbles to himself.

"Khanom Basir said that it's unhealthy for a grown woman to dwell," says Saba, "or to tell stories about people who aren't with us."

"Please," says Khanom Mansoori, as she reaches for her glass. She makes an exaggerated gesture of swatting away Khanom Basir's com-ment. "What's healthy for a little girl is healthy for a grown woman. Grown women just need bigger portions."

"That's a very nice thought," says Saba. The nicest she's heard in a long time.

"Go on, then," says Khanom Mansoori. "Finish your story, so we know it's true."

Saba gives an obliging nod and finishes. *"Up we went and there was doogh . . ."*

The Truth of It
(Khanom Mansoori—
The Ancient One)

A gha, did you hear the things she said? Were you listening carefully? You didn't say much so I think you weren't listening.
She's not like our granddaughter, Niloo. Saba is a book type and she
knows how to hide her meaning. You need sharp ears, Agha jan. By
the time she finished, you could see that her color had flown away.
You could hear her missing Mahtab. You couldn't? Oh, listen to you,
Agha. You see camel, you don't see camel. You are a little boy yourself. That's why I like you so much.

I don't like sleeping at that house. I'm still tired. But it was good
that we stayed. I don't know how she doesn't get scared in that big
house at night.

Ai, my poor girl.

Do you want to hear the real meaning of that story? Yes, I have it
figured out—help me sit down, will you?—all that business about
Baba Harvard and saying good-bye to the kind dishwasher man from
South Mexico . . . sad, sad thing . . . it's not about missing parents and
broken families. It's about that crazy, crazy man sitting in the big

house and watching his daughter run around trying to get his attention. What's wrong with him? If you knew how many hours she spends
alone, you'd grow horns from shock.

No, don't tell me he has tried. I never see them together outside
the house.

Agha, next time you go over there, maybe take her a little present, or ask about this or that. Compliment something small, like her
wrist bangles, or if she is not wearing any, the whiteness of her skin.
Fatherly things, so she's not so thirsty for it . . . And don't look so
scared. She's a young girl, not a garden snake. I saw you gawking at
the television, so you have plenty to talk about. Maybe let her explain
the stories without interrupting so much—yes, you did interrupt. I
managed to understand some of it, though . . . some Keaton-Meaton
crazy-*bazi* . . . A useless story. No head or tail to it at all.

Aah, that's nice. Scratch just there. Thank you, Agha jan.

Do you think all the gossip is right? Some say that Abbas would
be a good choice for our Saba because he is old and rich like her
father. Others say that her cousin Kasem is a good choice because he
is already family. It makes me sad because I always wished she would
find what you and I had. Young love . . . love that is not all about
enduring. Maybe some fun. Remember when we were her age . . . the
mornings behind the house?

Yes, yes, I know it's improper. I won't talk about it.

I'm not talking about it . . . Why have you stopped scratching?

What was I saying before? I'm tired, Agha. I haven't slept well. All
this death everywhere gives me bad dreams. Help me lie down . . .
Days are so strange now, when all our real friends are dead and we're
living in the world of their children. I'm afraid of dying. It's a depress-
ing business.

What do you think, Agha jan? Maybe Saba has figured out something through her twin-sense. I think there are many sorts of truths to
this story and the biggest one is that Mahtab is still alive somewhere.

Chapter Five

On a wintry white Friday afternoon, Saba walks the open mar‐
ket, the *jomeh-bazaar*, and thinks she should become a better
liar. It must be easy in America, where people say what they mean. In
Iran, you have to be backhanded, to convey your wants by seeming
to seek the opposite. She wishes she had lied less convincingly to
Reza.

Lately he visits her house more often, asking to play the guitar
hidden in the sitting‐room closet. He places his fingers on the strings,
comparing the sound with his father's *setar* or the bigger, rounder oud.
"Baba can play any string instrument," he brags. They have been in
her pantry only once without Ponneh. It was awkward, the two of
them, alone in the dark—nothing like the natural, uninhibited feel‐
ing of their threesome, always joking and flirting, making fun of
Kasem. Instead Saba and Reza sat nervously and listened to a cassette
player. He lit her cigarette and watched her take a drag. When there
was a lull, he fiddled with the matchbox. "Saba Khanom," he said,

"are you—" and he stopped. She thought he was about to ask if she was missing Mahtab, as he always did.

"*Vai,*" she sighed. "Don't start with the Saba Khanom stuff."

Then he plucked her cigarette from her mouth. "Can I kiss you then? Just one time?"

She was caught unprepared and said no, though she wanted to say yes. He didn't ask again. Now she worries that she has insulted him. Maybe he thinks she doesn't want to kiss a villager. The problem, Saba decides, is that she hasn't learned to lie and still convey the truth—like when her father tells the mullah there is no opium in the pipe.

She can smell opium now, as she passes an elderly man in a skullcap. The bazaar, which is the main livelihood of many of its merchants, is situated in the town square, along with a handful of stores, a kebabi and fish restaurant with tables outside, and a coffeehouse that serves only tea and water pipes on deep red reclining rugs. There is a bench and chairs where old men sit under trees. The marketplace is where the bus stops and where friends and strangers congregate. On busy days, a *pasdar* or two loiter in a jeep, keeping their eyes on the sinful young. The market is open all year, even on winter days when a wet chill descends from the mountains, making the air thin and painful. Saba wraps herself tighter in her layers of scarves and thick coat. A heavy breeze blusters through the tunnels formed by tarps and roofs of plastic sheets. There are few vegetables today, only basics like onions and potatoes. Usually baskets with every kind of green herb are arranged in rows, piles of mint, parsley, and coriander, but today the merchants are selling from preserved supplies. Huge wreaths of dried herbs hang above their stalls. At the baker's stand, Saba spots Ponneh holding a paper bag with the telltale syrup stains of *baghlava* at the bottom. Ponneh reaches for some coins to pay.

The baker says, "Please, Khanom, I am your servant." Saba takes the time to watch this game of *tarof*, pretend generosity, and marvels at the ridiculousness of it.

Ponneh says, "Really, I insist."

The baker looks down and cocks his head humbly. "Please, they are yours."

Ponneh repeats one more time, "I insist."

And then the game is over. The baker accepts, and the *tarof* dance comes to an elegant end. Saba smiles at the thought of what would have happened if Ponneh had accepted the "free" pastries. The baker might have chased her down the street or started a tab. This is the way of things. Social laws aren't reserved for social settings. Butchers must offer free meat. Barbers must pretend to cut hair for their own pleasure.

Lying well is crucial in Iran. Everyone practices at least the two most basic arts: *tarof* ("Come, sir! Eat, drink. Take my daughter!") and *maast-mali* ("covering with yogurt"), the art of pretend innocence. ("Oh, it was nothing! A dent? It was barely a scratch. In fact, I wasn't even in the country that day!")

Ponneh reaches a pretty hand into the bag and pulls out a hot, dripping pastry.

"Saba jan!" She runs over and gives Saba a hug with her forearms and elbows since both hands are occupied. "Reza was here earlier buying tea," she says. "I ran into him and he said he can come to the pantry at six." She holds out a pastry to Saba. "Here, try this." She glances at the baker, who gives her a gummy smile. "If that man weren't toothless and a hundred years old, I'd marry him and spend my life getting fat."

Saba takes a layer of the pastry, relieved that Reza has invited himself to her house. He must not be too insulted, after all. Maybe one day he'll ask to kiss her again.

"Just a bite?" says Ponneh. "Don't *tarof*. Maman gave me the money."

They walk together toward the colorful pyramids of spices and nuts—cumin, turmeric, walnuts, and almonds—arranged on tables like the hills of a distant planet. A crowd has formed next to the fisher men's coolers of fresh catch and beside a butcher selling lamb shanks. The shoppers don't form a line, except for the first two, and then they explode into a cluster of shoving, peering, and shouting.

Hours later, their baskets full of vegetables, tea leaves, rice, fish, and a jumble of staples, their purses depleted of ration coupons and money, they head home as the hum of the afternoon call to prayer, the *azan*, wafts from the local mosque and the sun begins its descent, washing the mountains beyond in new colors. They pick up their pace. Soon nightfall will make it difficult for young women to be out without risking questioning.

Just outside the bazaar, Saba hesitates. "Look who's there," she whispers.

Mustafa, a young officer of the moral police, is watching them. He has claimed to love Ponneh for years, and she has always refused. Now that he wears the *pasdar* uniform, he takes pleasure in torturing them, forcing them to abstain from the few discreet freedoms most villagers still enjoy. Saba tucks some loose hair into her scarf.

Mustafa strides toward them, straightening his olive colored uni form, his eyes fixed ahead. Saba quickens her step, recalling the day an airport *pasdar* barked at her mother. Then, just as they are about to turn a corner, she hears a snap. Ponneh stumbles.

"Damn, I broke my heel." She curses as she reaches under her manteau and floor length skirt to pull off the shoe, a shiny red thing with a heel the length of a finger.

"Why are you wearing those to the market?" Saba stares at the shoes.

"I like them! And no one can see."

Saba doesn't find this strange. Ponneh has always done what she wanted, and after the revolution, a pair of red shoes is a brave thing, not superficial or vain. Saba too has experimented with this form of rebellion. Many of her friends have.

Mustafa catches up with them. His voice is like a whip, and he pretends he doesn't know them, a game he expects them to play. "You there," he says, probably thinking his unkempt beard hides his age and identity. "What are you doing? It's getting dark."

Saba feigns a respectful tone. "We're just going home. Good day, Agha."

"Let me see your papers," he says. Ponneh rolls her eyes, balancing on one shoe.

Saba tries not to scoff. She slips into a rural accent. "We were just buying food."

Mustafa shakes his head. "Where is your home?"

Saba stifles a shocked laugh. "Are you serious? Mustafa, you know us—"

Mustafa's eyes dart to Ponneh. Saba holds her breath, watching him recall Ponneh's beauty as he looks her up and down with that same grotesque, leering look that she associates with Kasem. And then she sees something that looks like hatred.

Ponneh fixes her gaze to the ground, trying to hide her annoyance. *No need to worry,* Saba thinks. Ponneh's scarf is perfect. She is wearing loose layers and no makeup. Only the red tip of a shoe peeks out from underneath her clothes. Mustafa has nothing on them. His eyes flit from her face to the shoe. "What's this?" he says as he kicks aside the hem of her skirt. "Those shoes are indecent," he spits.

"They're under my clothes," says Ponneh, teeth gritted, eyes disdainful. "Go away."

"Such high heels are shameful and improper," he says.

Ponneh raises her voice. "What business is it of yours? Is this some kind of fun for you?"

Saba gasps, but Mustafa ignores the remark. "Decent Muslim women know to be modest," he says flatly. Now Saba too is annoyed, as with a child who won't stop playing an obnoxious game. There is nothing Ponneh could have done to avoid this, short of wearing a burkah. Even then, Mustafa would target her. "Come with me."

Saba mumbles in disbelief as they follow Mustafa toward the thatched-roof house that serves as the local headquarters of the moral police, the *komiteh*. Ponneh carries her shoes in one hand. A few paces from the bazaar, on a quiet road with a high wall made of mud and hay, she stops. "Mustafa, that's enough. You've made your point."

Mustafa turns, his face red. He clearly expected her to obey, to submit and give him some satisfaction after countless rejections and humiliations, all his wasted pining. He puts a hand on his baton and steps closer to Ponneh. "Walk," he commands.

Saba puts an arm around her friend, but Ponneh shakes it off. Her willful expression is frightening. She lets out a small, scathing laugh. Hazelnut eyes widen, as they did during so many childhood fights when something inside Ponneh snapped, causing her to give up everything just to prove her point—always belligerence over tact. *Please, Ponneh, don't be stubborn now.*

"No," Ponneh says, her voice cracking a little. "I'm going home."

"You'll get a hundred lashes," Mustafa warns, hovering close. "Just wait."

Saba freezes. Can a pair of red shoes get Ponneh lashed? Certainly not here. What lies does Mustafa plan to tell when they reach the *komiteh* office? He could say anything. The law is a fluid thing in Iran. Saba remembers that early after the revolution, *pasdar*s would go around smelling houses to see if anyone had been eating sturgeon, forbidden because of its lack of scales. That was a crime that could earn a few lashes—based on the proof of a *pasdar*'s nose—until later Khomeini declared the valuable caviar fish halal.

Mustafa grabs Ponneh's arm. A sour taste fills Saba's mouth.

Ponneh pulls her arm away hard, and he stumbles back.

He takes her face in one hand, a gesture that for a second seems tender, his thumb moving in a tiny circle against her cheek. Then he squeezes her mouth open and whispers, "Whore."

It is the familiar reckless flash in Ponneh's eyes that makes Saba move. She drops one of the bags. Oranges and tea spread across the gravel street. "Don't!" she shouts.

But Ponneh has already done it. It is far too late now. By the time Saba can restrain her friend, she has slapped a *pasdar* hard across the face.

Then Mustafa's baton is out and Saba can barely distinguish her friend's body from his. He strikes her on the back, and she crumbles. She screams. He tucks the baton under his arm and pushes her to the ground. In another second Ponneh's mouth is pressed against the dirt. Mustafa falls to his knees beside her, breathing into her ear while pressing the baton into her back. He mutters something as he lifts her chin toward a tiny alley hidden by the dark. He waits, but she gives him a repulsed look and twists her head out of his grasp.

Ponneh huddles by the hay-spattered wall and tries to kick him away. Mustafa raises his baton and slams it hard into the wall just above her ear. Clumps of dried mud rain down on her, and her hands fly up and clutch her neck. He does it again, as if to exhibit his strength. Ponneh jumps each time the baton cuts the air just past her face.

Saba pleads, suddenly recalling something Khanom Basir used to say: *A beautiful girl always manages to break some rule.*

"Go to hell," Ponneh breathes. "I'd rather be with a dog."

Mustafa raises his baton and brings it down hard on her back.

Saba screams and throws herself on Mustafa, but he flings her away with little effort. She tries to breathe, her hands stroking her neck as she pushes away thoughts of drowning. She tries begging him in Gilaki, but Mustafa isn't listening. Two women in dark clothes pass by the small street. They stop and peer down the road at them.

Is Mustafa relishing the opportunity to beat a pretty girl like this? It confirms something Saba has known for a long time: that the moral police don't hate indecency as much as their own urges. Every day they think of some new cruelty—mystifying rules and grisly homegrown tortures and murders in the night—that makes Saba want to run away, to abandon Iran altogether, to wash her hands of the stench of the Caspian and be finished. Iran is finished. When Mustafa is an old man, will he remember that he once beat a girl just because she retained her loveliness despite him? *What a joke. A damn pair of shoes.*

Ponneh is sobbing. "Wait," she pants. "I'll go with you—"

But Mustafa doesn't stop. He is huddled over her, striking without control. Sometimes, when his rage weakens his aim, he hits the ground or the wall. Did he hear Ponneh? Regardless, Saba heard and she knows the regret Ponneh will have to endure later. But now the pretty look is gone from her eyes and she is just a scared animal, the loss of dignity nothing compared with the physical pain. If Mahtab was under Mustafa's baton now, Saba would suffer no less for her.

Past simple shock, Saba becomes absurd, picking up a discarded bag of tea as she watches her friend cower and sink lower with each blow.

The two women rush over, shrieking, "Hey there! Hey! What do you think you're doing?" They seem unafraid of the *pasdar*. This isn't Tehran, after all. Everyone knows everyone here.

As they draw closer, Saba manages a deep breath, relieved at the sight of Khanom Omidi and Khanom Basir. Reza's mother calls out, "Oh my God, Ponneh joon!"

Khanom Omidi lumbers over, huffing as she tries to pull Mustafa off. Khanom Basir thrashes him with her basket until he stops, dazed.

"Shame on you! You dog!" Khanom Basir screams. "Are you crazy?"

He straightens up, eyes wide at the sight of the older women. Like a child, he puffs out his chest and attempts to recollect his own version of things. He puts his baton back in his belt and wipes his sweaty brow as Saba rushes to help Ponneh to her feet. Suddenly she is embarrassed that she saw any power in Mustafa's uniform and that she didn't stop him. Now that he has expelled his anger, Mustafa looks stunned because they can all see his true purpose, what he really wanted from Ponneh.

"You're all coming with me to the *komiteh*." He is short of breath, trying to calm down, to seem authoritative. "You have so much to answer for."

Khanom Omidi gives him a hateful smile. When it comes to *maast-mali*, no one is a match for this old woman. It's ridiculous that Mustafa should try. "Good idea," she says. "Let's call Mullah Ali and tell him what a good job you're doing."

"You can make your calls at the office," says Mustafa. "Let's go."

"Good, good," says Khanom Omidi, pretending to follow. She clutches her back and sighs, as if thinking aloud. "And we must remember to send for Fatimeh too."

Mustafa goes pale at the mention of his sick, doting grandmother. There is a moment of silence when it seems that he might be ashamed. He turns to Ponneh. "You're lucky. I'll let you go with a warning. But if I ever see such indecent behavior again . . ."

Khanom Omidi nods, *yes, yes, yes*. "Let's get you two home," she says. The mistress of *maast-mali*—how smoothly she does it. She raises it to the level of craft—the way one might learn to hold a paintbrush or properly age a jar of garlic pickle.

A small crowd has gathered at the end of the road. Mustafa pushes through them and disappears. Saba spots a familiar woman, a thin, angular woman around her mother's age with scholarly glasses and a regretful expression. She blends into the crowd and no one talks to her. *Who is she?* Saba is sure she has seen her before, maybe spoken to her.

Ponneh has to be carried home on Khanom Omidi's ample arm. Her bruises are already purpling her arms and lower neck. Saba doesn't want to imagine the state of her body under her clothes. A relentless stream of mucus and tears pours from Ponneh's nose and eyes, and Saba feels obliged to wipe them, to share in the filth. Ponneh mumbles incoherent nothings, coughs, and once in a while chastises herself for having offered herself to Mustafa, a regret she will surely endure for a long time.

"That *kesafat* . . . that dirty piece of shit," says Khanom Omidi, who always enjoys a good swear or two, but this time she doesn't stop cursing the entire way home. She sings it like a dirge. "That son-of-a-dog, that *beesharaf*, that sloppy elephant's cunt." She shakes her head in exaggerated mourning then perks up. "*Shhh*, Ponneh jan. I'll make you something to take away the pain. I just have to get my special spice jar. How'd you like that?" Saba wonders how Khanom Omidi can possibly risk opium at a time like this, but this is her way; life is about small pleasures. Besides, Ponneh will need the release when she realizes no justice is coming, that no one will fight for it. All this thanks to a broken high heel.

After taking Ponneh home, Khanom Omidi and Khanom Basir head to the Hafezi house to prepare dinner. Saba stays. In a tiny bedroom, she inspects Ponneh's back. Her bruises are gruesome, ranging from a sickly yellow to deep purple. Ponneh is determined to hide them. Saba rubs an ointment on her back, helps her slip into a soft shirt under a thick, protective sweater. Ponneh crouches on the floor in the corner of her bed mat like a frightened cat, careful not to lean her mutilated back against the wall. Her face is all ash and bitter lines and sorrowful red patches. When Saba tries to comfort her, Ponneh pushes her hand away. "I can't believe I gave the bastard the satisfaction."

"He'll never try again," Saba says. "You did nothing wrong."

Later Reza sneaks in through a small window in Ponneh's room, the one that faces the forest instead of the road. His mother has told him everything. He sits on the mat and inches toward Ponneh; he holds her head to his chest, careful not to touch her bruises. He sings a children's song and Ponneh smiles and looks up into his face. "Remember the extra part we made up?" he teases, and moves closer so their noses almost touch and Saba can see his hair falling on Ponneh's face. "No more bazaar for a while. I'll take care of your shopping." Then he adds, "And don't worry about Mustafa. I'll handle him."

Saba sits on Ponneh's other side and tells her that she and Reza will take care of things. She watches them, tries not to be selfish or focus on her own pain at such a time. But she thinks that Khanom Basir might have been right all these years. Maybe Saba's friends are in love. Look at the way he touches her hair. Look how he doesn't weigh each word to see if it's proper or pretend he can recite English lyrics. Look how a force pulls their faces in, and they have no control at all. He has probably never asked Ponneh if he can kiss her. He probably never had to. They belong to the same world, a rural place without fathers where sturdy-armed mothers rule. They understand each other. There are no big houses, or acres of Hafezi lands, or the possibility of America between them. But then Ponneh reaches for Saba's hand. "Look, it's the three of us together always," she says, as if she needs them both, and Saba thinks she might be wrong.

They decide that it would be good for Ponneh to have dinner at the Hafezi home—to be among women who worship her face, who would never have her beaten for it. Reza leaves first, and Saba stays to help Ponneh get ready. "Do you remember when we were fourteen and you hurt your hand?" she says. "Reza sang you that French song."

"*Donneh, Donneh, Do-Donneh,*" she sings. "Just like Ponneh."

Saba nods. "Exactly! You remember?"

"You said it meant something else," says Ponneh.

"I lied," says Saba, as she braids Ponneh's hair like she used to do when they were children. "It's the name of a beautiful girl. Do you want me to teach it to you?"

Saba sits with Ponneh for another hour, singing "Le Mendiant de l'Amour," telling her stories, and coaxing her to dream about a day when they will both be married. Or a day when they will own a store in Tehran. Or a day when Saba will win the ear of the president of America and they will use the dowry money she has secreted away to run off and live in Washington, in the president's big white palace, where Mahtab can visit them.

✥✥✥

Ponneh jan, don't be sad. We all know you would never have gone with Mustafa. Everyone lies. Everyone has secrets. Do you remember the day I told Khanom Mansoori that I was too grown-up for Mahtab? I lied. Do you want to hear a story about her? I can tell you a good one, from a letter about Harvard and a day when she too breaks a high heel. Like you, she wants to fix it; and that leads her to a stupid boy, like Mustafa, and Reza, and every confused man who doesn't know what to do with his desires. But unlike you and me, Mahtab is lucky and brave and American. So when her broken shoe takes her to this boy, she can maneuver things so that it is *he* who ends up firmly underfoot. Isn't that wonderful, Ponneh jan? Just wait till you hear the rest. . . .

Ponneh, why are you crying now? Don't cry. I thought it would help.

All right, no stories. Forget the story now. I will save it for another day, for other ears. . . . Let's go to my house. I bet if no one is watching, Reza will do all his football tricks for us in the front yard. Or we can go to the pantry and smoke, just the three of us like always. We will convince him to bring his father's old *setar* and sit in a circle with our bare feet touching his and watch him pretend he isn't excited by it. Admit it, Ponneh jan, don't you love the feel of his bare skin, though it is only a foot and nothing else? Afterward, when it's just the two of us, we can spend all night talking about the blue veins running to his toes and wondering when we might see and touch them again, on the hands or feet of any man. We can get high from his plastic bag of herbs and he can strum the notes of his song—the one about home fading away—his fingers barely touching the strings so no one else can hear the small sparks of music between our huddled shoulders.

Rice, Money, Scarves
(Khanom Basir)

Mahtab and Saba were very good at lying. They learned it as children, from the storytellers and the exaggerators and the *tarof*-givers around town. Just look at all this Mahtab-in-America pretend-*bazi* nonsense. Saba knows she's lying, but she claims she has this source or that source, just to vex me. But who can blame the girl? Lying is a necessary skill now. We must hide every good thing—music, drink, excess joy, and pretty clothes.

In houses all over Iran (especially in places like Hamadan, where the father of both my sons, Reza and Peyman, grew up, where the winters are bitter cold and all you have for warmth is your friends and your water pipe and your music), the place to tell lies is under the *korsi* blanket. That is where you go to hear stories—a very Persian pastime, because afterward, you can rub yogurt all over the lies, *pretend innocence*, or you can say a little rhyme about *maast* and *doogh*, and make it all white as milk again. And how can you resist? The Caspian air fuels the creative mind, the artist, and it doesn't matter if you're only some nameless village woman. It doesn't matter if your own story has long become stale. There, under the blanket, you are goaded by the spirits of the night, all those curious eyes across the *korsi*, the hookah changing your thoughts, tempting you to weave a good tale. *Korsi*s are where great lies are born. I know. Telling good stories is my vocation.

When the girls were small, they liked to pretend, and often I was their victim. Mahtab especially believed she could kill me with her eyes. Once I made the mistake of saying that lately it was easier telling them apart because one of them had grown a belly. Yes, yes, I know. Don't blame me. I didn't see quickly enough that being different was frightening to them. Before I saw the mistake the damage was done. Oh, the curses brought down on my head, the hexes from every region muttered around child-sized bonfires. Oh, the venom poured into batches of precious smoky rice, cooked outside on a makeshift stove and overseasoned with salt and sand, presented to me as a neighborly gift. Surely they hoped that when I ate it, I would feel their anger and be sorry. Well, I am able to admit that it hurt my feelings, that sandy rice. The thought that they dreamed of me retching into a putrid hole in the ground, begging the gods for forgiveness. The gods refusing to forgive. Toilet jinns pouring out of the hole and ripping my head clean off. Yes, I heard all this backyard fantasizing. They didn't think I heard, but I did. It's hard not to believe it when a child calls you a monster. But I had my own boys who loved me.

The next day their mother gave them a lecture about stealing things and wasting things because the smoky rice was for a special occasion. Afterward Saba told me that she wished she had money of her own so she could just say to her mother, "Here, take this for the rice," and casually toss bills on the table like men in movies. She said she wanted to have a big powerful job, like a foreign journalist. What a thing to say! That is why I predict a logical marriage for Saba, a husband who is either rich or distracted. She needs ease; her mother taught her to toil only for vague ideas. She doesn't have the strength and will to marry for love, to fight all the cruelties that await lovers in these harsh times.

Soon after that, everything changed. It was 1979 and time for the revolution. Out went the Shah and in came the clerics. There were protests in Tehran about women and their hair, and a while later it was all decided and done. From then on, girls went to separate schools, they covered their bodies from head to toe, they learned to be afraid of streets. And Saba added three things to the list of things she hated: men with long beards, murals of bloody fists growing out of flower beds, and every kind of scarf.

Chapter Six

AUTUMN–WINTER 1989

E ver since Saba and Ponneh arrived exhausted to dinner, the sound of bawdy laughter has filled the Hafezi house—mullah and *khanom*s in hysterics over sacred Islamic law.

"I have your answer!" Mullah Ali muses as he slurps his tea. The dinner is finished and a few remaining guests are lounging on cush⁄ions around a *sofreh* laden with pastries and several carafes of hot tea on warmers. There is *naan panjereh*, fried dough in the shape of stars dipped in powdered sugar; *baghlava*; halva; and cream puffs. The mullah is holding a chunky metal pipe, which he heats over the gas stove. "I have your answer, Khanom Alborz! Listen . . ." He puts up his hands, unleashes that Cheshire grin, and the other guests are engrossed. "The boy cannot be allowed to be alone with your daughter, which makes it difficult to employ him as her caregiver, correct?"

Ponneh's mother nods. Old Khanom Omidi shifts in her house chador and nudges her friend Khanom Basir. At this point in the dinner, the two of them are cooking up dirty jokes by the tens and twenties, and Saba wonders how this can possibly be acceptable in front of a cleric. But Mullah Ali is a rare breed. If Saba made any of these jokes, she would be reprimanded by every authority figure within earshot, but somehow, being middle-aged, being married, being a dinner guest at the Hafezi home gives you license to push your headscarf back half an inch, to let your toes peek out from under your skirt despite chipped nail polish (Khanom Basir's quirky indulgence, her own private fancy-*bazi*), to lean back on the pillows and make testicle jokes, even to poke fun at the *new* Iran. It doesn't matter that men and women are mixed like this. They are older. This is private. And there are no young *pasdar*s and junior clerics watching.

"Not a *caregiver*," responds Agha Hafezi, the evening's host, "he's a doctor, willing to stay in Cheshmeh. A licensed specialist who has studied scoliosis and her other ailments. I say we forget the rules and just call it an exception."

"No, no, Agha." Mullah Ali taps his forehead. "The exercise enlarges the mind."

Agha Hafezi shrugs at Saba, who raises both eye brows. Ponneh winces. How can Khanom Alborz tolerate this?

The mullah continues. "There are ways to make a man *mahram*, so that he is allowed to visit her room." The guests stare at him, transfixed. When Mullah Ali has found a solution to a problem, however big or small, he is as warm and entertaining as a teahouse story-teller. He holds the people's attention with wide eyes and puffed-out cheeks. He scans the room with a raised forefinger, daring everyone to guess.

"The man will never *marry* her," says Khanom Basir. She eyes Khanom Alborz, the mother she has just insulted. "Sorry, but it's true. It's not that she isn't beautiful like her sisters . . . she's just . . . too sick."

"I know! A brother is *mahram*!" Kasem pipes up excitedly, casting a furtive glance at Saba that makes her turn with revulsion. It is obvious to everyone that Kasem is the only person taking this discussion seriously. *Am I related to this fool?* Saba thinks. If he had paper, he would probably be taking notes. Mullah Ali chuckles and takes Kasem's pudgy face in both hands. Agha Hafezi puts a protective arm around his nephew's shoulder. Saba wants to scream at the unfairness of it. Instead, she strings together c-words from her list: *coward, cretin, creepy-crawly cactus creature.* She congratulates herself on her near fluency. Mahtab would be proud, maybe a little jealous because Saba has managed this feat not in an American school but on her own in Cheshmeh.

"That's right, my boy. And how do we *make* him her brother?" Mullah Ali sips his tea. "They must be fed from the same breast. Then they will be brother and sister."

Everyone obliges the mullah with at least some laughter. Khanom Alborz spills her tea on her mint-green tunic and reaches for a cloth. Khanom Omidi, always conscious of her lazy eye, pulls Saba into her line of vision and holds her against her enormous body. Her fleshy neck smells like jasmine, and Saba joins in the laughter when the cheery old woman says loudly, "See, child? I told you. Every candidate has to demonstrate a certain level of brain damage to be accepted to mullah school."

The mullah says in a kind voice reserved for the elderly, "Ah, but dear mother, if we didn't have creative minds, how would anyone get anything done around here?"

Khanom Omidi adjusts her back pillow. "Too much creativity."

Khanom Basir, the storyteller, takes center stage now. She moves her pillow closer to the *sofreh*, sits with her back straight, her legs crossed under her haunches, her skirt pulled tight across her knees. She tells the old story of Leyli and Majnoon, and the doomed lovers come alive. They are present not just in her words but in her arms, which cross sadly over her heart; in her fingers that dance in a thousand varied gestures; in her eyebrows that arch and fall and pull together again; in the sad lyricism of her voice. Her eyes rest mostly on Reza, as if she is telling this story only for him, imagining some grand love story for him. And maybe she remembers a little of her own losses.

Soon Saba notices that Ponneh is growing agitated and impatient with the party. She must be thinking of Mustafa and her aching back. The bitter look never leaves her face, and halfway through the story, she hobbles to her feet and quietly slips out toward Saba's bedroom. Khanom Basir watches her son's eyes rove after her. She finishes her story and accepts the applause of her neighbors. She doesn't rush through this gracious last part—when others might shrug off the attention—probably because this one skill, this ability to capture their emotions with her storytelling, is the reason that she, an uneducated, sometimes mean-spirited woman, is so beloved and sought after. It is the reason that her house is always full and that she is invited to every gathering. The reason that girls like Saba, girls without mothers, go to so much trouble to win her love and attention.

When the story is over, Khanom Basir takes the opportunity, for the umpteenth time, to question Khanom Alborz about the pair. "So, Khanom," she teases, "when can we come for a *khastegari*? I'm telling you, those two belong together."

Khanom Alborz tenses. "My friend, I've told you already. Until her older sisters get married, she can't be married. It would be an insult to them."

"The healthy ones, yes, but the sick one too? And in such troubled times?" She stops there. Khanom Alborz has been away all day and doesn't know yet about Mustafa.

"No. I said no." Khanom Alborz puts up her hands and shakes her head. This is the one issue on which her conviction overrides her fear of Khanom Basir. "Her sister can't help being sick. Why should she suffer alone? We've all suffered since their father died. And this is the way he would want it. Everyone has to pay a price."

Rarely does Saba see the proud Khanom Basir look genuine, pained, even humble. She whispers, "But Khanom, they love each other."

Saba tries to ignore this. Why should she let the talk of two older women cause her pain? Still, it seems that the world wants Reza to choose Ponneh and leave her alone.

"They will all make good marriages eventually. They're so young," says Khanom Alborz. "But if you insist on matchmaking, you could find someone for Agha Abbas. He needs the help and doesn't have much time."

"Why should he need help?" Kasem asks, his tone resentful. "He's rich."

Abbas Hossein Abbas, at sixty-five, is one of the oldest bachelors in Cheshmeh. A widower with no living children or grandchildren, he has recently made it known that he is lonely and ready to marry again—though everyone believes he only wants one last chance to revive his bloodline. Saba knows him from afar, since Abbas hasn't been to her father's home in years. Khanom Omidi says that he avoids large social gatherings and stays in his house or in the town square, smoking and talking with other idle old men.

Reza starts to get up to follow Ponneh, but her mother's fiery stare keeps him bound to the cushions. Finally, when Ponneh returns for a cup of tea, Reza slumps off through the kitchen. Saba gathers up a few dishes and begins to walk away too. But then Khanom Basir says, "What about Saba?" Saba feels Khanom Basir's serpent tongue whip around her like a rope pulling her back into the room.

"That would be a very nice match," says Mullah Ali in a wise tone. "He is a devout Muslim. He gives generously to our mosque. He deserves a young wife."

Saba gives her father a pleading look. Agha Hafezi only nods, glances into his teacup, and says, "He has spoken to me."

Saba stumbles, collects herself, and says, in a barely audible whisper, "Why?"

"He is considering it . . . coming for a *khastegari*. To ask for your hand." When he finally catches her eye, he smiles faintly. "I haven't said anything. Anyone can ask. It doesn't matter till we decide." Saba wonders why her father has chosen this moment to tell her this, in front of all these people. Maybe it's easier for him. Her hands tremble and she drops a spoon from the top of her dish pile.

"Don't worry," her father reassures. "We will choose someone you like. Someone your own age."

"We?" The mullah shakes his head. "You're letting the child have a say in it?"

Agha Hafezi nods. "It doesn't hurt to have another perspective."

"Do you remember that time when Saba was seven?" Khanom Alborz laughs.

"Oh, please, don't bring that up." Khanom Basir shakes her head, but Saba can see the amused look on her face. On any other day she would be mortified by the story that she knows is forthcoming. But now maybe it will remind her father of her desires.

"She was seven years old and she went on a *khastegari* to ask for Reza's hand. Do you remember? It was the funniest thing."

"Please don't remind me," says Khanom Basir with a long sigh. "She was crying and making a big show. That's what you get when you let a young girl run wild." Then she leans over and whispers to Khanom Alborz, "That girl has a thousand jinns. . . ."

A thousand jinns. How unfair that Mahtab, who instigated that marriage proposal when they were seven, is now far away in another world, leaving Saba here all alone to deal with the accusations and marriage schemes.

She takes the dishes into the kitchen, puts them in the sink. She glances at herself in a window and pushes her canary-yellow scarf back until a shiny lock of hair bounces free and rests across her eyes. She goes outside, only half admitting to herself that she is looking for Reza. He is leaning against the trash cans, drinking from a paper bag. He wipes his face with the back of his hand. He asks, "Any chance of the pantry today?"

"Not yet. Ponneh's already had a lot. The bruises aren't so terrible, though."

"She'll be okay," he says, giving the paper bag a quick shake. She hears the liquid sloshing back and forth in the bottle. Then he tilts his head toward the house and says sadly, "You know how many lashes we could get for this? The opium and the alcohol?"

Saba nods. "Don't worry," she says. "Even in Tehran, everyone does this. And in case you haven't noticed, the mullah is an addict. He can't afford to lose his ready *sofreh*."

They stand there for a few minutes, leaning against the trash cans, side by side, not saying a word. Reza sighs and shakes his head. "Strange day," he says.

"Yes."

"I talked to Mullah Ali about Mustafa," says Reza. "Something will happen to him. I'm sure." But Reza doesn't look so sure. "I wish I could kill him myself."

Saba nods. "It was scary how much he hated her." She thinks about something that her mother told her before she left Iran. How the mullahs took all the Western art from the Queen's private collection and shut it up in a basement so no one could look at it. All those beautiful pieces. Warhol. Picasso. Rivera. *That's what this regime does,* her mother said. *They shut up beautiful things in dark places, so no one can see.*

Reza begins to hum a slow, familiar tune. Is he trying to soothe her with this droning American melody? Does he even know the words? Reza believes the only important part of a song is the music; but this isn't true. For Saba, the words are everything and the music only secondary. She sings in a whisper. *"You got a fast car. But is it fast enough so we can fly away."*

"Huh?" Reza turns. He gives her a puzzled look.

"It's the song you were humming," she offers, hoping he will continue along with her.

But Reza's face turns cold, and he says, "Not now, Saba." Then he adds, "I just like the tune," and she remembers his innocent belief in music, a crime now like so many beautiful things.

He looks at her and she tries to seem happy but fails. She wishes she hadn't said anything. Again she has insulted him, reminded him that he is a villager. She lets her expression fall where it wants. "You're missing Mahtab," he says. She chuckles at their old routine. "Have a drink." He holds out the paper bag and she takes a long, throat-burning swig.

"Do *you* miss Mahtab?" she asks.

"I liked Mahtab very much," he teases. "She had a beautiful face . . . and pretty fingers." He touches the tip of Saba's finger. She pulls away only a little, and he smiles.

When they were small, before the revolution and puberty, they were allowed to play together in the street. It is likely that Reza knew Mahtab just as well as anyone outside their twinly universe. Saba looks up at the sky and takes another drink. The heat of the liquid opens up her throat and makes her braver, happier. "Mahtab liked you very much."

"I'm lucky," he says, and they pass the bottle between them again, in memory of Mahtab. Reza adjusts his angle against the wall, so that his legs go farther out and his body shifts down to Saba's height. "I used to think you two were princesses," he says. "I thought you would marry the American prince from the magazine and leave us all to pine for you."

"Both of us?" she says. The air is freezing, but Saba's cheeks grow warm. She knows what Reza is doing. His days of playing football and guitar for worshipful audiences have given him the cruel male instinct to lay a trap for any woman who seems a willing target. To amass possibilities so that in his old age he can brag in the town square, *I could have had her . . . and her . . . and, yes, that one too.*

She wonders if Reza dreams of America; he has no notions of it outside the TV set. Would Mahtab love him too? Reza has a Gilaki soul, like her father. Though he's interested in agriculture and asks Agha Hafezi about it sometimes, he doesn't mind the odd jobs and the boxy stand near the seaside where he sells his mother's rush baskets, loofahs, brooms, pickles, and preserves. He hates big cities and the new Iran. He longs for a good, slow hookah afternoon in the Iran of his childhood the way Saba longs for America. He despises change, showy tourists, religion, and his reluctant spot in the back of the mosque beside the discarded sandals. He loves his father's *setar* and the Beatles.

"No man should have to choose," he says. "And twins . . . imagine the sight you would have been." He touches the lock of hair coming out of her scarf. "Maybe God took her away to save you from people like Mustafa." Saba nods, trying to keep the lump from growing in her throat. He says, "You know, once I saw a man get flogged for kissing a woman on the cheek in his own house. There was a *pasdar* passing by the window."

"That can't be," she says. "Not in Shomal. I saw a couple kiss on the lips once in the market."

"And because you saw someone get away with kissing on the lips, then I can't have seen someone get flogged for kissing on the cheek?" Saba shrugs. She is a little bleary now. "That couple you saw in the market, were they over eighty or under six?"

"Funny." Saba mocks him. She hates it when he pretends he's older. So transparent.

"You don't know much, do you?" he says. "You think there's a ladder of kisses. Cheeks, then lips, and so on. That's what small children think."

"So?" She folds her arms and tries not to scoff at his arrogance. Talking with Reza about kissing is like standing in a baker's kitchen, holding a warm cake and only smelling.

"So, Khanom, a kiss on the cheek can be a lot more serious than a kiss on the lips."

"Ah, so much expert-*bazi*. What do *you* know?" Saba pulls herself up and starts to walk away, but Reza takes her arm, pulls her to him.

He squeezes her face tightly in both hands and says in the shrill, accented dialect of the old men in the square, "Come here, child, stop struggling and give us a kiss." Saba tries to pull away but is overcome by a fit of laughter.

"Oh, wait," Reza says. "Forgot to remove my teeth." Then he smacks his lips and lands hard on the right half of her mouth. *"Bah, bah,"* he sighs. "Who'd want to flog an innocent old *hajji* for that?"

Saba makes a show of wiping her mouth. "Okay, you made your point." She smiles despite a pang of regret. Her first kiss wasted. Has Mahtab had her first kiss by now? Saba wonders. Was it worthy of television? Maybe she is having it now, somewhere in the American Northeast—or Holland or England or France.

"Khanom," he says, "I'm not nearly done making my point."

He puts the paper bag aside. She glances past him. Whenever Reza watches her like this, in the bazaar or pantry or even in dreams, she always looks away, never brave enough. Her hands are tucked behind each thigh, but he finds them, interlaces her fingers with his. He hums a little, and she smells the alcohol on his breath as he rests his cheek on hers. He is clean-shaven, his skin warm and sandpapery. She wonders if he can hear her blood speed up, gurgling like a treacherous stomach, or if he feels her cheek catch fire against his skin. She struggles not to move or even swallow too hard, afraid of embarrassing herself. Despite the effort, she can hear her own breath as she takes in the sandalwood smell of his soap and wonders why the simple act of being alive has to be so loud. But Reza isn't listening. His lips brush against her cheek and linger there. "See?" he murmurs in her ear, as he reaches for the bottle, one finger carelessly stroking the skin around her wrist. "Try getting away with that in the market." Then his lips brush past hers as she inches toward him.

In the next second Reza jumps clear of her, his face ashen.

Kasem is there, staring openly. A curious grin and an angry flash pass across his face at once. Reza takes a few steps toward him, but then Kasem turns and dashes into the house, Reza taking off at full speed behind him. "Kasem, stop! Stop!"

The back door slams as Reza rushes to catch up with Kasem. Saba's hands shake. She scrambles to hide Reza's alcohol. Her skin is like ice—except for a tiny spot in the middle of her right cheek, still warm and flushed, where the last vestiges of fire have not yet died down.

A few moments later Reza returns. "I didn't follow him in," he says. Her scarf has fallen onto her shoulders and he pulls it up with both hands. He glances back at the house. "It would look worse, me trying to shut him up. Go find Ponneh. Say you've been in your room all night. She'll vouch for you."

"Are you sure?"

"Of course. Ponneh would never get us into trouble. Now go."

Saba hurries back to her room through the side door. She finds Ponneh resting on her bed. She is sitting up, holding two of Saba's English novels in her lap. Uncomprehendingly, she runs a finger over the title of the thicker book, *The Joy Luck Club*. Ponneh doesn't read English. She stares at the cover of Golding's *Lord of the Flies* and mumbles in Gilaki. Saba, who buys or trades half a dozen novels every month, eyes her newest acquisitions, recently printed paper-backs that she bought from the Tehrani at ten times the right price. Ponneh is bending the spines, but Saba doesn't care. She drops onto the edge of the bed, trembling, clutching her scarf tightly around her neck.

"What's wrong?" Ponneh struggles to sit up. She touches Saba's back, rubbing a little as Saba sits shivering at the edge of the bed.

"I . . . am . . . in so much . . . trouble," Saba whispers. She grabs her throat, the heavy sensation of the water rushing back. She doesn't care that Ponneh is watching.

Ponneh stashes the books under a pillow, manages to shift all the way to Saba's side, wincing with every movement, and says, "What? What did you do?"

"Nothing. But Kasem thinks he saw us . . . Oh God, I'm in so much trouble."

"Calm down," Ponneh says, almost unsympathetically, as if to imply that this is nothing compared with her own ordeal. The indif-ference in Ponneh's voice unnerves Saba. "Tell me. What were you doing?"

Saba stares into her friend's curious face. "He only kissed me on the cheek. It was just a kiss on the cheek. That's not bad, right? We do that all the time."

Ponneh sighs. "I can't believe you, taking risks on a day like this."

"It was nothing!"

Ponneh's eyebrows pull together and her face looks even whiter. She takes Saba's hand—only two fingers really. "You can't just sit still for *one* day? Hasn't today been bad enough?" Saba can tell Ponneh is still punishing herself for her weakness.

"If Kasem tries to say something—"

"Do you want me to say you were here the whole night?" Ponneh interrupts.

Saba nods. She strains to hear what is going on in the living room now. She hears voices. Kasem, Mullah Ali, the synchronized cawing of the ladies. She doesn't hear her father. A few moments pass, and Khanom Omidi pokes her head in the bedroom door. "My poor Saba, what has happened?" She waddles to Saba and sits on her bed, puts Saba's head on her ample lap.

"Is Baba coming? What did Kasem say?"

"You are lucky for now, my girl. Your baba went to the caretaker's to get more firewood just after you left. He'll only be ten minutes. He doesn't know anything yet. But why were you out playing around with Reza? You are a smart girl! Always careful!"

"I didn't do anything, I swear. We just ran into each other. He kissed me on the cheek, and then Kasem saw and took it the wrong way."

"Kasem told Mullah Ali that you were doing more than that," says Khanom Omidi. "Anyway, I *hope* you did more than that, Saba jan, or it will be a very expensive nothing." She gives a sad chuckle and lets it fade. Unlike other mothers, this indulgent old woman has never advised the girls to forgo any pleasures—only to keep them hidden. She seems disappointed that Saba doesn't have lurid tidbits to offer.

"What a waste," Saba whispers. She imagines all the punishments Mullah Ali might concoct—that she be flogged or married off to Kasem. Worse, she conjures the flash in Khanom Basir's eyes as she bans Reza from Saba's house forever.

Khanom Omidi frees Saba from her scarf and strokes her hair. She kisses her temple and rubs her cheeks with creased, briny fingers. Saba wishes she hadn't woken up today. Everything is differ-ent now, and she despises the world that has sprung up around her. It's like a tentacled plant that has been growing quietly, taking care to go unseen until it's too late to keep its fingers from choking her. She wants to escape. Maybe she will wake up one night and flee to Reza's house . . . convince him to run away to America—exit visas be damned. They can swim. *How many scoops of a teaspoon,* she wonders, *from this side of the world to that?* After some minutes with no one bursting in, Saba goes to the door and peeks out into the hallway. In a far corner, she sees Khanom Basir leaning against a wall.

"Promise me," his mother begs Reza, "promise that you aren't get-ting involved."

Slouching in the corner, her usually stern face bewildered, Kha-nom Basir looks weak, even helpless. Saba can't decide if she feels bad for her, or if she is just sad that the thought of her involvement with Reza is so revolting to his mother. Saba tries to read Reza's lips as he whispers, *It was nothing.* Is he appeasing his mother? She can't help but think that this is very cowardly of him. But then again, maybe it *was* nothing. Maybe he just doesn't know what to do. He holds his moth-er's head against his chest and kisses her henna-stained hair. Then he helps her fix her headscarf as he did with Saba minutes ago. Saba tries to catch his gaze, but he looks up only once. His eyes are filled with bafflement, as if he had been bitten by a caged snake. He shakes his head at Saba and mouths, *I'm sorry,* and Saba is reminded of the day he whispered those same words across the *sofreh* when she was da-ncing and couldn't be sure why he was saying them. She ducks back into the room.

"He's denying it," she mutters.

"He's just a boy," says Khanom Omidi, "young and confused. Look at what he's dealing with. Such a big, big need to rescue every-one. That's how young men are."

More *maast-mali* where there is no innocence.

Ponneh snorts, almost bitterly—but maybe it's the pain or Kha-nom Omidi's opium taking effect. "He's not so confused. Men are men." Seeing the scowl on Saba's face, she adds, "You're too good for someone that weak. And all men are weak."

More *tarof* where there is no generosity.

When Saba's father returns home, he is given the full story. Mullah Ali explains. Saba was seen playing around with Reza Basir. Outside. Without her *hijab*. She was seen in a very compromising position. If Kasem had not stopped them, it would have been much worse. Khanom Basir interjects, reminding Agha Hafezi over and over again that his daughter is out of control and needs a husband, and that her son Reza is not a candidate. But do not worry, Agha Hafezi, a proper course of action has been discussed by your benevolent guests. This need not damage your daughter. Why should you worry about her with such careful guardians to think of her interests? Do not worry, dear sir. For you do not parent alone. Just remember that your daughter's reputation is at stake, and think of all the evils to which this small infraction could lead.

Saba, who is listening to all of this with her ear pressed against the bedroom door, considers once or twice escaping through the window—because the worst scenario, the most dreaded possibility, is the very thing they are now discussing: a marriage. *Please, God, take Kasem on some clerical errand to Mashhad or Qom.*

She hears Khanom Basir loudly worrying about Saba's reputation to her father.

"I hope you're noticing that no one's blaming Reza," Saba says. "How is that fair?"

"That's how it is," mumbles Ponneh. She seems relaxed now, sleepy from the "spice."

"Do *you* blame me?" Saba asks, sniffing Khanom Omidi's discarded cumin jar.

"Look, kiss him all you want," says Ponneh, her words slurring a little, her head slumping against the wall as she lets *The Joy Luck Club* drop from her hands. "Just don't risk this good thing we have . . . the three of us . . ."

"Good, good, let her sleep," says Khanom Omidi, her voice thick and low as she leans over Ponneh and feels her face. "And don't listen to the talk."

There is a knock on the bedroom door and Saba's father enters. He is alone and she wonders for just a second where Reza has gone.

"Saba," her father says, tired resignation shading his face. She watches him wipe his damp forehead with the back of his hand and prays for a swift Kasem-free kind of justice. He plays with his finger where his wedding ring used to rest, a habit from older days. "It's time for a change. Maybe time to get married."

Here it is. The worst. She thinks of Mahtab, who doesn't have to submit to such threats. Mahtab, who always does whatever she wants. "I'm not getting married."

"I've called Agha Abbas," Agha Hafezi says, without looking at his daughter. "He will come for *khastegari* tomorrow. I think you should accept."

Agha Abbas? The old man? Saba tries to adjust to this new information. They are asking her to marry an old man? Is that better or worse than marrying her insipid cousin? Somehow answering this question seems of utmost importance just now. It takes only a moment's thought. "Well, you can just forget about that."

"Let your father finish," Khanom Omidi says, her tone soothing. "Maybe there is some good in this. Abbas is very rich. You might be happy."

· "I can't believe you'd think I'd go along with this," says Saba.

"There is one other way," her father offers, almost unwillingly. "Your mother would want me to provide this option for you. You can go to college in Rasht. But these are your only two choices, Saba jan. Marry or go to school. No more of this . . ."

"In Rasht?" she mutters. Not Harvard. Not even a small American college. Not even Tehran University—after the thousands of hours spent perfecting her English, reading every available book, learning multivariable calculus and chemistry and physics. It seems a defeat. She isn't even twenty yet. Shouldn't she hold out for something more? In America, you can go to college at any age.

"Or Tehran," her father says. He pauses. "Your mother would have wanted you to go to Tehran at least. But I hope you will stay here." He sounds weak, miserable. "I know it's selfish. But you're all that's left of us. Of me." He reaches for her hand. Suddenly he seems old to her. His hands are cold, the skin loose and veiny.

Her father rarely mentions all that they have lost. He has never really seemed to need her. She has often wished to hear him say it—that he is afraid of losing her—though she knows it is the reason he never mentions college. Now that he has admitted it, it makes her want to stay, to be with her remaining family, and wait for her chance. She imagines herself as a young widow: free. Now she asks herself another question: Does she want to save herself for an American university or to save herself for Reza? The time has come when she can do only one of these things. Which has she truly longed for? Which dream keeps her awake at night? Which possibility will she keep? "You think marriage is better?"

Agha Hafezi rubs the sweat from his forehead. "Yes, this is best. The man is old. He's richer than you know. And life is much easier for a widow than an unmarried girl. People won't watch your every step. You'll own lots of property. What if all *my* lands are taken away and you have nothing? He is Muslim enough." He looks away, embarrassed. "I advise you to avoid the solitary, lifelong burden of a child by this man. Be smart, be patient, and one day your turn will come. Then you'll have the wisdom of a few years, your family nearby, and your own money too. You can use the lands as collateral and go not just to Tehran but abroad. Visas are easier for married women, you know."

"I thought you wanted me to stay nearby," she says, though she knows her father is right. Visas *are* easier for those with a spouse in Iran. And once married, she will leave the restricted world of single women with its guilty cheek-kisses and endless modesty. She can make dirty jokes and laugh out loud and drink secret juice without hiding in the pantry. Would Mahtab see this side of it? And is she actually *considering* this marriage?

"For a while, yes, but I can't keep you forever." He takes her hand. "You're a smart girl. Think of what a wise move this is. College isn't fun or liberated like it was in my day—you can't say two words to the boys. And you've already read more books than their graduates. It's all Islamic education now, barely any professors. Plus, we have money. You can get a degree in a few years." He coughs into his hand. "I heard what happened today to Ponneh. Your mother's friend Dr. Zohreh was there."

Saba remembers the familiar woman in the crowd. Khanom Omidi utters, *"Ei vai,"* and waves her hands as if trying to disperse a bad smell. So much shame in one day.

"Things like that happen all the time to single girls," says Agha Hafezi. "If you were married, you would have protection. You would have more freedom—the man is old and half blind. He won't care what you do all day. He's the best choice. Reza isn't right for you. He's just a boy. He's weak, has no education, no resources. Does he even *want* to marry you? Please, Saba jan, if you do this, I can stop worrying all the time."

"Or, *you* could protect me," Saba mumbles, and watches her father's nostrils flare. They both know that he has already tried. His face softens and he doesn't argue. She feels defeated. "I want to stay with you . . . but college seems less like a punishment." *Maybe,* she thinks, *it would be more like something Mahtab would do.* Or would it? Maybe Mahtab would convince Reza to run away to America. Maybe she would marry the old man and save herself for better days, better offers in thicker envelopes from faraway places. "Khanom Basir will think she's won."

"Not at all . . . This isn't some big, big tragedy," Khanom Omidi insists, always the grandmaster of *maast-mali*. "We will cover it with just a little bit of yogurt. Later on, no one will bother to know the timing of things or who did what when."

"This is what you must do," her father says. "He is a good man."

Saba mulls over her options. As she sits on her bed, turning the offer in her mind, she thumbs through years of collected records and tapes. The Beatles. Bob Dylan. Paul Simon. Johnny Cash. Elvis. She puts a tape into her timeworn Walkman. The man named Otis with a golden-tea-and-cardamom voice sings about the sun, and a dock, and ships rolling away. He sings about loneliness and a place called Georgia. She wonders if Mahtab has been there. Saba has looked up every word of this song—as she has done with every favorite song—in her English dictionary. She lingers over the tape for a few moments before deciding to hide it in a safer place, away from the rest of her treasure.

If she marries Abbas, she will move from her father's hilltop home—a solitary white house at the foot of a tree-covered mountain overlooking the thatched roofs of Cheshmeh—to her new husband's equally grand house in a busier village a short drive away. The house, she has been told, is less remote, on a small street where there are neighbors and open courtyards with benches, fruit trees and fountains behind high walls, and covered walkways, fashioned in the style of Tehran neighborhoods rather than the Gilaki open-façade homes. Since it is closer to the sea, tourists pass through sometimes and buses run more often. Abbas's town has better amenities, clinics and stores, and two underground home salons where women drink tea and crack sunflower seeds instead of sipping water and eyeing each other's bodies in an outdated hammam. But there are fewer open wells to steal a drink from and longer lines at the thrice-weekly bazaar where she may have to jostle for her share of eggs, milk, and other staples. Her father has said that if she misses her friends, she can come home and receive visitors here.

Later her father knocks on her door. "I have something to show you," he says. "It will help you make a reasoned decision." He pulls out a letter and holds it tentatively out to her. She resents the way he uses the word "reasoned," as if she isn't capable of it on her own. "Do you see now, my dear? Marriage and love, they're separate. Marriage is about logic. And in the privacy of your heart, you can love anyone you want."

He continues talking, but Saba doesn't hear anything as her eyes scan the envelope. She stares at the label, her first clue in years. *I knew it.* She has always believed that her father has known things that he did not tell her for fear that she would leave him. The letter has been returned unread, passed from hand to hand, both their names left off to guard against unfriendly eyes, but originally, when he held hope that his wife might read his words, her father addressed it to her mother in Evin Prison.

⋯

October 28, 1981

I'm not sure this letter will ever reach you. They've given me no clue about your situation and all the post is being checked. I've been on the phone every day since we separated trying to get some answers. I've spent so much time and money, and still no word. Don't worry. Saba is fine. They are watching our house. Since I saw you last, they have been a constant intrusion in our lives. They send mullahs and pasdars to watch us, but luckily Mullah Ali is kind. He carries this letter to you and assures our privacy.

You can't imagine how Saba has changed. She's still stubborn, but learning to be cautious around adults. I don't think she is handling the situation well. She's developed a tic in her throat that disturbs me (a motion like she's choking). My dear, my thoughts are always with you and the hope that our family will be together again one day. There's so much to know with a young girl. I make mistakes daily. She cries and cries and sometimes I think nothing will calm her. She still conjures Mahtab, and even talks to her in her sleep. I think I'm failing her. I don't think any of us really understand about twins.

Yesterday our friend Kian was killed in Tehran for preaching the New Testament in his home. They tossed him into the street like a dog. No blindfold. No ceremony. He was shot five times. Bahareh jan, I think he saw me there. He looked right at me, right into my eyes, just before the first shot. I couldn't move. I couldn't go to help him. There were others there too—all helpless. But that is not the worst of it. I've had to do an awful thing. Though I love you, I was forced to file for divorce. After Kian, I had to prove to them that I wasn't involved, and there is Saba to think about. For her, I paid a lot of people, abandoned my friends, and hung a picture of Khomeini in my office. And now the law separates me from you. I realize it may seem like you're all alone. But in the privacy of our hearts we are free to love whomever we want. Marriage and love aren't connected in this new world. I wonder if they ever were.

Until next time, God (Allah or Jesus or whomever you prefer) be with you.

෧◑◑๑

Evin Prison. She repeats the name to herself until it sounds like gibberish.

Why was the letter returned unread? Was her mother ever there?

Is she there now? What about Mahtab? By the next day Saba has read the letter a dozen times, noting her father's every word, every wavering line, every small clue to his heartbreak. After she has stayed up all night speaking with him and Khanom Omidi, going over her options and changing her mind twice, reasoning and thinking and planning, she finally agrees.

"Okay," she says, "okay, I'll do it." And it is done. Saba Hafezi will be married. Afterward she gives herself up to a strange relief. She is not enrolled in an Iranian college, which would mean tying herself forever to this new country she has come to hate. She is saving herself for America, the one reluctant suitor for whom she is willing to wait. She has read the letters from distant cousins in Texas and California, heard stories from the Tehrani tourists who rent seaside villas here, all of them confirming that an Iranian degree means nothing in the world of pale princelings and American shahzadehs. Only Baba Harvard can keep his children from driving a taxi or collecting garbage. She will wait for him and, in the meantime, stay here with the baba who needs her.

Her father places a call to Abbas. The old man comes to the Hafezi house to pay his respects and put his dignity on the line, even though he knows what the answer will be. Ponneh and Khanom Omidi, who are constantly by Saba's side, have assembled a large *sofreh*. Since the decision was made so quickly, the engagement is a lonely occasion, with Ponneh and Khanom Omidi in the kitchen, and no one but Agha Hafezi, Kasem, and his mother—and, of course, Mullah Ali—to witness the engagement. As for Abbas's family, he has no one. In a sad attempt to conceal his age, he says that his mother would have come, but she has a cough. Agha Hafezi smiles, well aware that the mother is ninety-five and bedridden. Saba notices none of the activity around her. Is her own mother dead? Jailed? Has she escaped to America? If she was taken to Evin, could she have gotten on that plane with Mahtab? Maybe she could have a few weeks later, but not on the day Saba remembers—the day of the green scarf and the brown hat.

The ceremony starts without Saba, who lies in her bed, trembling, until she is called. But in the end, she keeps her resolve. She knows now, after reading her father's letter, that there is no grand tragedy, no death and ashes, in the practical separation of love from marriage. It is a mundane thing that leads only to more of the same daily life. Marriage is unrelated to the restless grief of being near Reza. So she will be smart and savvy like Mahtab. She will make a decision that will provide some freedoms and keep her only family and beloved village mothers nearby. She recalls the words her father wrote to her mother. *Marriage and love aren't connected in this new world.*

Finally Khanom Omidi comes to escort her to her future.

She sits in the corner of the room watching intently as her father and Agha Abbas discuss terms. Abbas offers rugs, gold, jewelry, and a small fortune in cash in case of divorce. Her father offers a tenth of the sum as a dowry and demands that Saba be Abbas's final wife, that he take no other wives, legal or de facto, while she is alive. Abbas bows his head. He understands what is asked of him. He has no children, no remaining wives or heirs. Agha Hafezi is asking that he leave his daughter a rich woman, with no other claimants to add complexity to her widowhood. Besides that, he wants to put property and cash in Saba's own name. He creates a marriage document with every loophole plugged as tightly as they are in any other of his business dealings.

Agha Abbas raises his hands, palms up. "What's mine is yours. . . . Ehsan jan, when you're my age, you will know the price a man will pay for happiness in his final years."

Agha Hafezi nods when he is satisfied with the terms. Saba breathes out. This moment doesn't seem so ugly or frightening now that she has a firm grip on her future. This is the act of a logical and forward-thinking woman—an American scholar or businesswoman entirely unlike her adolescent self. From now on, Saba Hafezi will behave a little less like Ponneh, beaten for her beauty, waiting help-lessly for change, and a little more like the sister conquering the world so many scoops of a teaspoon away.

Later, when Reza comes to congratulate her, Saba smiles icily. With her eyes she accuses him of so many things. He has been weak, no hero at all. Who cares that she may never again touch Reza's warm, prickly skin? Marrying him would be worse. There is no romance in self-sabotage. From now on, Saba will sweep her heart of useless longings. She will be in control of her own emotions and make this old man her world. She will see the good in him and block her every disappointment. She will protect herself against pregnancy; children would bind her permanently to Iran and make it hard ever to marry again. There will be happy days ahead, and afterward she will make new dreams.

The icy smile stays on her face for days, even as the women pre-pare her for her wedding with gold jewelry and henna and *noghl* candy, and as she sits in her wedding dress under a canopy with Abbas, she submits to a frenzy of Persian arts and ministrations and tries to look older, self-assured. *Beautiful girls always find that they've broken some rule*, Khanom Basir once said. Silently Saba replies, *But smart girls make their own rules*; and she watches Abbas as Khanom Alborz and Kha-nom Basir rain sweetness on her marriage by rubbing two large cones of sugar over her head for what seems like an hour.

Journal Notes
(Dr. Zohreh)

When my friend Bahareh called, I rushed to examine her daughter in the Rashti hospital even though childhood trauma isn't within my specific field. This was in the early days after the revolution and the war . . . I believe sometime in 1981.

As I expected, Saba hadn't been informed of her sister's death and continually asked for her. I told Bahareh that she must tell her daughter the truth soon, but my friend was in a state of denial. She said that it might be best to keep Saba in the dark until the two of them could start anew in America, an idea that I found preposterous because it would only lead to a double dose of stress. Saba was already suffering from delirium and she likely knew on *some* level. But Bahareh said that she wanted to keep things simple, that it would help Saba to imagine her life in two parts, to sever all ties at once.

I must admit that I felt a deep sorrow for my friend, who was beginning to show a certain obsession. She said in a confused, almost manic voice, "This must be God's plan. Saba will do wonderful things with her life. My job is only to deliver her there." Bahareh was always fanatical about her children's purpose in the world and had been planning for some time to educate them in the U.S. It was her great‹ est strength. She was willing to die in a stampede just to lift her daughters' heads one inch higher than the horde.

Later Saba asked me if I believed in heaven and hell and I said that no one really knows. Then she asked if I believed in America and I responded that, yes, *that* is a real enough place. She seemed pleased with the answer. I do wish I knew exactly what happened to Bahareh on the day they tried to leave. Her husband has forbidden me from contacting Saba because of the dangers involved. But I will continue to search for my friend. I see all the most likely answers, of course, but that is no substitute for knowing.

Chapter Seven

AUTUMN–WINTER 1989

S aba slaps the top of the VCR until it comes to life under her hand and images flicker across the screen. She leans back on a cushion in her father's living room. She is still wearing her wedding dress and the room is a mess from celebrating. She won't be delivered to her husband's house until tomorrow, when a group of friends will help move her possessions. She finds it strange that Abbas didn't insist that she spend their wedding night with him—but that's a blessing she doesn't question. She has so many other things to worry about now. Did she make a monumental mistake? What is this panic in her chest and how can she drive it out? She is watching a movie she has read about in American magazines ever since she was a child. The Tehrani has finally managed to get her a copy. *Love Story*. Set in Harvard University, full of wonderful Harvard details that she can drink in. A building that Mahtab would admire. A corridor Mahtab could have passed through. A chair she might have sat in, in a class she might have taken. She watches the movie all the way through, even though she finds the story too sickening and sweet. Love doesn't work like that. If Mahtab fell in love at Harvard, it definitely wouldn't work like that.

She hears a noise outside and Khanom Mansoori, the Ancient One, shuffles in. "Why aren't you sleeping?" She lowers herself onto a cushion and pushes away some plates of half-eaten pastries. She caresses Saba's cheek, brings Saba's face closer to hers like she's going to kiss it, but doesn't.

"Khanom Mansoori," Saba whispers as she buries her head in the old woman's shoulder. "What have I done?" Will being married to a rich Muslim really protect her any more than being the daughter of a rich Christian? Is his money any safer? Will this plan help her to find freedom or someday to reach America? Should she have gone to Tehran?

Khanom Mansoori offers no answers. She hums a song. When she is finished, she mutters, "Has Agha been to see you? He had a gift for you."

Saba holds out her wrist to show the bracelet that Agha Mansoori gave to her that afternoon. "You have the nicest husband," she says to the old woman. Saba wishes she could see a photo of the couple when they were her age, but maybe that would ruin the fantasy. She sus-pects that, even when young, they weren't particularly beautiful. They are both so petite that they give the impression of miniature people. Agha Mansoori has a small head, even for his size, and Kha-nom Mansoori's eyes are too wide apart. But somehow, when Saba imagines them at twenty, they morph into a statuesque movie couple with waves of jet-black hair and brooding eyes. She thinks of the lov-ers from *Sultan of Hearts*—an old Persian film in which the heroine sings mournfully in the town square—and imagines herself in love, or even involved in a dramatic affair.

Khanom Mansoori nods and grins gummily. "You are like a granddaughter to us. And now Abbas will be like our grandson." Saba chuckles, and Khanom Mansoori responds, "All right, maybe more like a son or a cousin."

Tonight a layer of gray fog hangs over the village. A hard rain began half an hour ago. *Love Story* plays on the screen and Saba explains the plot to Khanom Mansoori. She doesn't recall how or when the story transforms into a tale of Mahtab's American life. At some point the sights and sounds of Harvard, all the details she has devoured from books, magazines, and movies, gel into a clear and inevitable picture of her sister.

"It's the twin sense." Khanom Mansoori nods with certainty. This is the effect the old woman has on the world. Somehow she forces the murkier truths to emerge from nothing. It isn't like the art of *maast-mali*, which is about distorting truth, but its complete opposite, like chiseling out the delicate bird that has been hiding inside a shapeless rock.

ဢ๛ၜၑ

Please don't start thinking that my sister has forgotten about me just because there has been no news from her for a while. I have so many stories of her, but this is the next one I'm choosing to share with you because, well, I was right. She *did* manage to purge another big Immi-grant Worry. She accomplished something that I couldn't: she reached out and grabbed for herself the power to say no, the strength to do and be anything—ultimate success, endless possibility. And this is how she did it:

Mahtab strolls through Harvard Yard—which from a bird's-eye view looks like the most scholarly place on earth—her black winter coat wrapped tightly around her body, her boot heels clicking tenta-tively as they avoid potholes and cracks in the brick sidewalk. To her classmates, Mahtab is a puzzle. At first glance she is the vision of a typical American girl. Auburn hair. Elegant clothes. Even her skin seems paler, no olive peeking out from under porcelain powder. Yet she is somehow unavailable to them. In fact, Mahtab feels more foreign than ever at Harvard. She is bad at making friends, which is the trouble with twins. She hasn't called Maman in weeks.

"I don't like this part," says Khanom Mansoori. *"Why must she be so alone?"*

You're right. And she does begin to feel the need for something—but not affection or love. Though she is ready for her own *Love Story*, my sister doesn't want to replace me. It's a new kind of accomplishment that she wants. Someone to stamp her as eligible for this world—complete and free from all things Cheshmeh. She finds that someone in the winter of another college year—thanks to a pair of broken high heels.

Yes, yes, it's *just* like that other pair of broken high heels. I tried to tell this story to Ponneh, and she would not hear it. But *you* know that there are mystical ties between twins. Remember what you told us about the Unseen Strand?

Now, let us get to the scenery of Mahtab's new life. It is very different from Cheshmeh. She is in her first or second year, I have lost track of the cycles and semesters, but I do know that she lives in a tiny attic room with a round window overlooking the Charles River and a foggy, hazy bridge with streetlamps. The room sits atop a famous library, the one that houses signatures of almost every U.S. president and a book signed by T. S. Eliot. And no, I am not exaggerating. I've read about this library in a travel guide. Imagine a Saturday night—the night of the week when American college students socialize. Mahtab prepares to go to the library instead. She wants to be the best. To be special to Baba Harvard, her new father. Isn't that *just* like her?

Tonight, as she puts on her shoes, a fateful heel snaps off in her hand.

She knocks on her neighbor's door. Clara, an overly feminine girl from the American Northeast, answers the door. She calls my sister "May," and when she cocks her head, a whole row of light brown curls falls to one side. Have you ever seen *real* American curls, like the ones on Shirley Temple or that girl they call a Steel Magnolia? I have seen her only in a photo, but the Tehrani has promised that when this movie is finally on video, he will get it for me. Mahtab holds up the shoe and asks if Clara has any glue. From inside she hears several voices and the sound of clicking heels on a hardwood floor. Someone laughs and stumbles out of the room wearing a thin dress but no shoes.

"Hey! Look who it is. It's *Mahtab* from next door." Simone, a malcontented New York princess, doesn't care what Mahtab wants to be called. She says Mahtab's name as often as she can, with emphasis, like an accusation. She lets the name fly unexpectedly, pointing and shooting with amazing accuracy. She changes its meaning, turns it into a weapon. *You're a fraud,* she says. "Are you here to go out with us?" She eyes the broken shoe with an upper-class American disdain that can't be explained without a full lesson on the history of her people. The head and tail of it is that they don't really have any history. Age is one thing America lacks, so certain Americans compensate for it with scorn.

"Leave her alone. Muslims don't drink," says a third roommate—the one with clicking heels—as she applies lipstick in the hallway mirror.

"I'm . . . not Muslim, actually," Mahtab says.

The third roommate smiles sweetly. "Yeah, but *culturally*, right?"

Khanom Mansoori chuckles, because mocking educated Americans is so satisfying. "You made that part up to amuse me."

All right, maybe I heard it on TV.

Having failed to find glue, Clara returns holding several pairs of high heels, some black, some blood red like Mahtab's. "You can borrow one of mine," she says, because Clara, like most American girls, has thousands of shoes that she throws away like corncob skins the moment they are off her feet. She is even more shoe-crazy than our own Ponneh, though I defy you to find an American girl who has been beaten for her heels.

Mahtab thanks her. "Where are you all going?"

Clara says—and let me make sure to get all these words just right—"I'm going to see *Lord of the Flies*, and these girls are going whoring at the Fox."

Hah! What a thing to say! I do wish you understood the snappi-ness of the word *whore* used as a verb. Once I saw it in print, and it doesn't sound quite as ugly as it does in a vile mouth like Mustafa's. These Americans have the most wonderful phrases.

"I did not understand any of that," says Khanom Mansoori. "Do you want tea? I want tea."

Fine, fine, I will explain. *Lord of the Flies* is an old black-and-white movie about a book on the evils of boys left in a world without female goodness. The Fox is an exclusive men-only private club at Harvard that dares to exist even in the eighties. It is a place where they smoke and drink and sleep with desperate women. There are other clubs too, with strange names like Fly and Porc. . . . I learned that from a juicy article in *Harvard Magazine*, which the Tehrani charged me twice his fee to procure, even though he has a cousin who owns an Italian restaurant in Harvard Square, and the ads were ripped out in case of border inspections, and the pages were covered in dried red sauce.

Now, here's something I know for sure. Mahtab isn't one of those girls who lobby against the Harvard men's clubs. She has always found them intriguing. They remind her of the Harvard she's seen in movies from the 1950s. Mahtab usually rages at anything that even hints at sexism. But somehow the all-male clubs have escaped her rage. Let them have their club. As long as the women aren't serving drinks, it doesn't offend her. Mahtab is more bothered by the concept of a cookie-baking, dinner-at-six housewife than the idea of being excluded by any man. She would rather be left out than boxed in. Until now she has refused to line up outside and be judged for entry. Despite the blatantly sexual nature of this act, for Mahtab it bears a strange resemblance to Iran. When she passes a club on a Saturday night, sometimes she stops and watches. The blazer-clad golden boy at the door leers at the first girl in line, probably a first-year student. He looks her up and down, stops just past her hemline. Suddenly a white scarf flies off someone's neck. It turns and weaves and makes its way through the line of scantily dressed girls. It wraps around the boy's head. Now he is wearing a turban. Now he's growing a black mustache and unruly beard. The expression on his face doesn't change. Mahtab always leaves right then.

But today, after three of these same boys—all members of this Fox Club—arrive in Clara's room, Mahtab is tempted to stay. They lounge in the corner. One of them, James, squeezes beside her on the couch. "You smell nice," he says and eyes her from head to toe, and starts talking to his friends before she has a chance to introduce herself.

James plays something called *lacrosse*, a bizarre sport. He is tall like Reza, rough-chinned and athletic. He wears his sandy brown hair long and shaggy, has freckles on his pinkish tan arms and short blond hairs that run from his wrist to his elbow. He is a big American, hard to overlook.

"Ooooh ho ho, Saba jan," says Khanom Mansoori. *"You'll have to keep your blond-man fantasies in check now that you're married . . . but no harm in a little storytelling. I met a blond man too once. A Dutch man with yellow hair like wheat."*

Mahtab eyes his white polo shirt, his khaki pants. She stares at the golden fuzz on his arms. She is attracted to his whiteness, to his New England banality. It's promising. Not at all threatening. Nothing bad ever comes from a man with white baby fuzz on his forearms.

She has never seen white baby fuzz raised up over a woman's head, can't imagine it surviving in a rice field. She considers this and acknowledges it, is aware of it. She decides it's a good first criterion— as good as any. She's always known that she would never be with a Persian man. She would sooner die a virgin.

"*Saba, why say such a horrible thing?*"

Don't blame me. These are Mahtab's words. For as long as she lives, Mahtab will never welcome a Persian man into her bed. But who knows, maybe she will change her mind. American girls are allowed that and so much more.

"Do you want to come out with us?" James asks Mahtab. Simone raises an eyebrow at one of the boys. Mahtab sits on the edge of the couch, waiting for the eyebrow to shoot off her head and fly away. James makes a pleading face and mouths *Please?* and Mahtab finds that her feet are tapping out an eager rhythm of their own—what a beautiful surprise. Oh, how I love telling you about my sister's ela-tion, her happiest moments.

"Why not?" she mutters—an American way of saying *God, yes!*— a reverse *tarof.*

Two weeks pass and Mahtab has a boyfriend. James has phoned every day since the night at the Fox, when he walked with her all the way to the club, stayed with her the entire evening, brought her drinks, even took her out for food when she got hungry in the early morning. He commented on her careful walk, the color of her hair, her pretty feet. Once he touched her neck with his rough lacrosse hands and told her she was very soft, even for a girl. "A girl like you should never set foot in a gym," he said. "It would ruin you." The shy, uncertain compliment was an unexpected delight that made her unconsciously caress her own neck now and then for the rest of the day.

"Where are you from?" he asked one day early in their cautious romance.

"California," she said.

"And 'May,' that's just a nickname, right?" he said. "You don't look like a May."

"No? Okay, June then. My name is June." James laughed, so she told him the story of her mother sending her a birthday cake to Harvard. *Happy Birthday, Mahtab Joon,* the frosting read. And the delivery boy, not realizing that *joon* meant 'dear,' told her she had a cake from a person called Joon.

Mahtab Joon. May June.

They played a game where he tried to guess her country, and even her city. Then he kissed her in the street and she thought of how easy it was. She made careful note of his warm, tomatoey breath, his thin lower lip, and the way he kept his hands away from the parts of her she knew he was desperate to touch.

"Saba jan," says Khanom Mansoori, "how do you know about such things? Maybe we should talk about what comes after a wedding . . . or better yet, let us call Khanom Omidi! She will tell you stories that will make you grow horns from shock, though, from what I hear, no man ever complained with that one. Yes, you'll need to learn these things now that you're married."

What's the matter? Do you think I know nothing? I don't believe people need lessons the way you think they do. Take Mahtab, for instance. She wonders how she understands this or that. Who taught her what to do with James at such a time? I don't have to experience it myself, Khanom Mansoori. I can pretend. God knows, when my time with the old man comes, I will be shutting off every such instinct, imagining myself in another place, another time. I have already prepared the story I will play in my mind and the song that will transport me there. But I don't need lessons. I know a lot of things. I have read a thousand books, a sea of magazines, and I watch American television.

Two weeks later Mahtab sits in a café, waiting for James to bring her coffee. She wonders what people in Cheshmeh would think of *that*: a preppy American boy bringing her coffee. She watches him stop by the sugar station, pouring exactly the right amount of milk and brown sugar into her drink. The elation rises and pops inside her chest, like a soap bubble from a television ad, clearing out so much of the bitter heaps that are lodged there. She has the feeling that she is important now, because someone like James knows how to make her coffee, knows what she likes for breakfast and that she eats with spoons instead of forks, that she is never full until she's had rice. These small corners of James's mental space are tangible places that she owns and occupies; they somehow make her more real. Rare now are the moments when she imagines herself hanging on the edge of every scene, pulling and struggling to stay put while someone far away holds her by a taut rope. You see, like any immigrant who has been offered the best of a new world, Mahtab is costantly afraid that it will be taken away. It is how I too would feel—that fear of doing something wrong, of losing it all. She has always harbored the dread that at any moment the person holding the rope will give it a good yank and pull her away. But now, when she is with James, her very own pale prince, she sometimes forgets about that invisible thread pulling her toward her other self.

"My Saba, those parts make me very sad."

Don't be sad. I have made my bed. I will be happy even if it was a mistake. What are the chances, after all, that a perfect man like James will ever find me here? I cannot have what Mahtab has. But who knows, Khanom Mansoori, it *is* possible that Mahtab will aban‹don him for other things. Can you imagine it? An Iranian girl reject‹ing such a man when I was forced to accept one who is so much less? I like the idea . . . but let us see.

Mahtab often wonders what more James will do for her. She asks him for little things, small favors she doesn't really need. He brings her ice cream on his way to her room. He Super Glues her broken high heels. Each time, that confident sensation grows and becomes more addictive. Sometimes she thinks it's a little like that day she got into Harvard. It gives her a feeling of accomplishment. *Harvard wouldn't take just any girl. James wouldn't pick up just any girl's dry cleaning.* Until now, Mahtab has felt out of place at Harvard, as if someone left the windows open in the admissions office and some benevolent wind picked up her application from the trash and placed it onto the "yes" pile. But James's gestures do more to eradicate such thoughts than all the good grades from Baba Harvard. See what power I have over this man who isn't ordinary at all—who, in fact, may rule the world one day? See what power I carry in my small body, in my blood, and therefore in the blood of my sister? Because fate, and every personal triumph and talent, is not a matter of location but is carried in the veins.

Over coffee, James holds her hand and tells her that his mother has come to visit. He invites Mahtab to meet her. But James knows nothing about Iranian manners. He insults her by giving her a gift— a leather handbag to carry to the meeting, one that looks exactly like the one Mahtab already owns. At first she is confused. "It's just like mine."

"Well, it's not *just* like yours. This one's leather."

"Mine is leather."

James gives her an aren't-you-delightful smile. "Yours is not leather."

Khanom Mansoori nods. "Yes. They say Americans judge each other this way."

Annoyed, Mahtab makes a face. "Yes it is. The man at the flea market—"

"Will you just carry it for my sake?" he asks, and Mahtab thinks that this must be the kind of thing that impresses his mother.

"Fine." She smiles. "But I bet yours doesn't have a clasp shaped like a shoe."

"Made of solid gold, right?" He winks. He isn't funny.

"Exactly," Mahtab says, unable to decide if she is mocking herself or James. She doesn't care right now. She is only just discovering her power. And as you know, Khanom Mansoori, no outcome is certain until 22.5 minutes of an episode have passed.

You also know this: Mahtab tends to overthink things and place herself into all sorts of made-up situations. Well, she spends the entire week anticipating what James's mother will be like. She imagines— hopes even—that she is a stereotypical society maven, an underfed, sour-faced, racist woman who will pretend to be nice to her while advising her to stay away from her son. She is hoping for an experi- ence similar to the picnic scene between Rose and her boyfriend's so-white mother in *The Joy Luck Club*, which is a book I promise to tell you about later. She imagines herself standing up to her nemesis, pulling her shoulders back, and towering over her, saying that she didn't leave a country full of *pasdar*s and *akhound*s and mullahs only to bow down to a middle-aged princess. She giggles as she sees herself storming off triumphant, with James as her prize.

Despite her bravado, Mahtab practices what she will say. She is ashamed of her life before Harvard—at least the American portion of it, which includes her mother's factory job and their unsophisti- cated house. She decides to leave that part out. In Iran, her family is educated. In Iran, Hafezis are rich and respected. It will take too long to explain that doctors and engineers and scholars there rarely achieve the same heights in America—not with degrees from Iranian colleges. It will be too frustrating to make this woman under- stand that, instead of learning French, Spanish, and business, they signal their mental power by quoting Ferdowsi, Khayyam, and Hafez. They swallow up volume after volume of impossibly complex verse. They learn it so well that it comes out on its own when they are drunk, slurred and incoherent, but correct to the last word. And so these proud academics come to America and drive taxis. It isn't their fault. Because what other American job makes such good use of ancient Iranian prose, hour after hour, day after day, in a muggy cab with strangers, force-feeling them poetry in all its feverish singsong melancholy?

As it turns out, Mahtab gets no opportunity to champion her people, no satisfying and dramatic win to add to her credit. James's mother seems to share her son's fascination with the exotic.

"I absolutely love the rugs, dear," she says as she touches Mahtab's arm. She is shorter than Mahtab expected, but thin, with a Diane Sawyer haircut and three strands of pearls. "We have four in our house. The Nain ones are best. Have you been to Nain?"

Mahtab shakes her head, then changes her mind and nods. She wants to say something about exploited child workers, but she isn't sure if that happens in Iran. This woman is nothing like the mothers she has known—neither the California teachers nor the Khanom Basirs and Hafezis of the world. James's mother is dainty, kind, probably hiding something. Maybe she is striking from some unknown angle. Mahtab prepares herself, recalling the voracious guile of Persian women who can carry on four conversations at once, keeping a lulling ebb and flow while digging into your unsuspecting soul with garlic-covered fists and yanking out the slimy secret parts of your carefully crafted story. For later. They tuck it away in their apron pockets. They dry their hands and ask more questions.

Once she described the women of Cheshmeh to José from the diner where she used to work, but he nodded and said, "That is *all* women, *mija*." He had no idea.

"This diner man sounds very wise," says Khanom Mansoori, then drones to herself, remembering, "diner man from South Mexico . . . hmmm, yes, go on."

In any case, Mahtab doesn't blame the women. It is the sea that does it to them, the malice of the Caspian. Mahtab hates the sea. She hates to swim and she doesn't like the smell of algae and fish. The women from home wade through this wicked water and it gets into their bodies. It floats through the air, a spiteful milky fog. They drink it, breathe it, and cook their food in it. But Mahtab isn't scared. She believes now that if she put all the evil inherited from her fore-mothers to good use, she could do many impossible things: stir mischievous jinns, wake sleeping ghosts, govern hordes of unwilling men. She wants dominion over a boy like James—and over his spoiled, white-pearls mother.

James's mother continues. "I love everything about Persia. Do you prefer calling it Persia or Iran?" Mahtab shrugs. "I'm sure you've read Ferdowsi and Rumi and Hafez. I read them all in college"—she names a second-rate one—"I brought you the *Rubaiyat*." She hands her the famous FitzGerald translation, which Mahtab knows is the best.

Mahtab is a little disappointed. She loves a good challenge. She was hoping for just a bit of racism. Just the faintest amount of class superiority. She feels cheated. James's mother, Mrs. Scarret, contin-ues. "I have a Persian cat, you know."

Okay, that does it. Another self-important connoisseur with a handful of random facts. The Persian-cat, Persian-carpet variety are the most grating. "Actually, Persian cats aren't from Iran," she says. At least she's never seen one there.

James's mother taps her chin. "Oh, yes they are, dear. They origin-ate in some plateau . . . around the Hindu Kush Mountains, which is technically Afghanistan, but of course, we know that that was all part of Persia at one point, don't we, dear?" She finishes her sentences with long sighs that start with a high-pitched expulsion of air and settle into a soft buzz, like an airplane starting up. *"Hmmm . . ."*

Now Mahtab feels foolish. She plays with the boring, no-frills clasp of her leather bag. James is smiling reassuringly. But that's not the kind of assurance she wants just now.

"James, can you get me a cup of tea?" she asks, trying to get back some control.

James, who has been thumbing through one of Mahtab's books, looks up.

Mahtab doesn't notice the color leave his face. Doesn't see him first glance at his mother, who raises an eyebrow and begins to examine a nail, then at the long line in the tiny coffee shop, then at the full cup of tea in front of Mahtab. He gets out of his chair and throws an embarrassed look at his mother.

"James?" Mahtab says, distracted. When he looks back, she adds, "And two sugars, please?" He gets in line without a word.

I'm sure you don't know yet what Mahtab has done wrong, Khanom Mansoori, because your own husband lives to serve you. Reza too is a man who likes to rush to the rescue and will do whatever we ask of him. I wonder what Abbas will be like in this regard. Will he be chivalrous or brutish? Mahtab's Harvard athlete is neither of these. He doesn't live to serve. He hasn't been raised on a diet of romantic folklore and tragedy.

This will be trouble for Mahtab. And we must concede that in every life—even the best magazine lives—there are obstacles and issues to face. Even Shahzadeh Nixon has troubles to her name, if the news media are to be trusted. What big scandals a girl with a thousand dresses can have! Well, Mahtab's first-ever boyfriend is about to discover that Persian women aren't easy to handle compared with the rest. I have heard it over and over from tourists who pass through my father's house, and this is why our men have created a new world that keeps us firmly under their feet. In America, though, an Iranian girl can rail and rant and make demands. She can be selfish in her choices. She can fling every hated garment to the wind and discard men like flyers in the street. She can unleash the wild creature within for just one day and be forgiven.

Have you ever wanted that, Khanom Mansoori? To give yourself up to madness in front of the world and have it forgotten? I read a book called *The Bell Jar*, in which a girl does the most unspeakable things, toys with a man who loves her, sleeps with a stranger who makes her bleed, refuses to follow any rule at all, and moves on with no consequences. She is even allowed back into college! How it fills my entire body with longing to run—far away, or up into the mountain, or into the sea.

Oh, but to see Mahtab so free! A part of me wants to witness this perfect American boy unhinged for sport. Don't laugh, Khanom Mansoori. You know my meaning well.

Mahtab and James don't see each other the next day. She doesn't worry. She isn't the kind of girl who wastes precious time fretting about men. Secretly she wonders if she should not have corrected his mother. Maybe it would have been more respectable to have her facts straight. On Saturday night she decides to go for a walk by herself—all night if she wishes, because there is no curfew. Just before ten o'clock, she wanders into a pub near her dormitory. It is perfectly normal for a girl to enter a bar alone on a Saturday night.

In three hours she samples all of the following movie drinks you can't find in Baba's pantry: a Dutch beer, a whiskey sour, an old-fashioned, a sidecar, and a martini. She doesn't finish them, of course. She is in full control of herself—though if she wanted to, Mahtab could get drunk and vomit in the street with no more than a slap on the wrist and a headache the next day. The bartender doesn't say no. You see, Western bartenders are permissive, slick-haired ex-medical students who specialize in the subconscious mind of beautiful women. They have crooked half-smiles and rolled-up shirtsleeves where they stash cigarettes, and they respect Mahtab's right to do what she wishes. That's the rule. Trust me. They know not to toy with the rules. Bartenders are good, reasonable people.

When some time has passed and happiness returns, she notices James sitting in a booth with someone. She slips from her stool and walks over. Caught off guard, he stumbles through a greeting before glancing at his drinking companion—it is Simone, the unhappy New York princess. She wears a long white nylon coat that looks like a plastic bathrobe. Mahtab finds it bland and ugly, but she compliments it all the same, because this is one custom the women of the world share.

"Hey there," says Simone. "I don't think James wants a big discussion tonight."

"Then what are *you* doing here?" Mahtab asks.

Simone takes her hand lovingly. Mahtab cringes. "Look, *Mahtab*, I know this is your first relationship, if you want to call it that. But sometimes men just need to talk to someone who isn't the 'girlfriend,' you know?"

"What a wicked girl," drones Khanom Mansoori. *"From what diseased womb does a snake like that spring up?"*

Yes, indeed, women like her exist everywhere. But don't worry, James doesn't want her. She is just the kind who likes to be involved.

He looks tired, a bit disheveled. He sips from his oversized beer mug and gives Simone a cruel look. "What are you doing, Simone? I told you to stay out of it." Mahtab has never heard him speak that way. It seems cowardly, the way he snaps. She has never seen him ugly with drink, his face scrunched up in confusion and annoyance.

She drops into the booth beside them. The smell of his breath is overwhelming, and she wonders if she likes this boy after all. Simone shrinks into her corner of the booth, folds her legs under her, and wraps up tighter in the coat. James waits and watches Mahtab with an increasingly miserable expression.

"What's going on?" she asks. "You're ignoring me. Did something happen with your mother?"

James lets out a bitter laugh. "Look, May, I'm not your bitch." Another good American word that I can't fully explain. It's like saying, *I'm not your foot towel.* Mahtab is speechless. He continues.

"I don't have to call whenever you say. I don't have to tell you who I'm friends with, and, even if I called, you'd just give me a list of chores to do."

"But I never . . . You offer to do those things. I thought you wanted to . . ."

"Yeah, the first time. But when did you ever offer to do something for me?"

Confusion envelopes Mahtab like a filthy white coat, wet and heavy on her shoulders. She struggles to shake it off, break free. When she can't, she slumps her shoulders and begins to chew her nails. James leans toward her and tries to take her hand so that it's only he and Mahtab in the conversation now, a barrier of arms and glasses between them and Simone.

"Look, May, I know about you and Iran and all the issues with men but—"

"Men always think they know," Khanom Mansoori sighs. *"Always, always."*

"I don't have any issues with men," she snaps.

"Fine, but this is not working for me. It's emasculating, getting your dry cleaning and having you boss me around. You do it in front of everyone. And with my mom . . ."

"I didn't mean to correct her."

"What? No . . . you told me to get your drink right in front of her. You could have made an effort. Hell, you could have gotten *me* coffee. . . . It was embarrassing, okay?"

Mahtab's face grows hot. Is he asking her to serve him? Is that what he wants? She's not sure if she's embarrassed or angry. She rubs her tired eyes with her thumbs and waits for him to continue. He fumbles for a while, and Mahtab becomes certain that she is no longer interested in this conversation. She moves to leave. "Think whatever you want. I'm done here," she says. "I have papers to write."

Oh, how many papers she has written by now, covering a universe of wonderful topics!

But James grabs her hand. "Maybe we can start over," he offers. He backtracks, afraid of losing her, and launches into a speech about her beauty and all that he admires about her. She is reminded of an Iranian *khastegari,* where the man, sincerely or not, goes on and on about the girl's rare virtues, even threatens suicide. Now she is transported to Cheshmeh, where dozens of expectant eyes are watching her, waiting for her to accept the proposal from a seemingly perfect man. Oh, and she *must* accept. She *will* accept. This is what is planned and desired for her. She tries to shake off the image, but fails—especially after a Dutch beer, a whiskey sour, an old-fashioned, a sidecar, and a martini.

Just then Simone leans forward on the table and slips an arm through James's. She whispers, "I'm hungry. Let's order some food."

Mahtab's cheeks burn. She starts to get up, but before she has a chance, James untangles himself and gives Simone's shoulder a shove. It isn't much of a push. He is just drunk and wants her hands off him. But this is not what Mahtab observes. You see, Khanom Mansoori, it is an American girl's prerogative to perceive what she wants, even if it is not the truth. She can have her own version, and it doesn't count as only half a testimony, as it would here. In America, the woman's version of events is often the one that sticks. It counts exactly as much as she wants it to count. And here is what she chooses to see now: white baby-fuzz arms flinging a woman across a table. Hard. Simone rubs her arm and slides down the booth. Does her head hit a wall? Mahtab tells herself that it does. James's unfocused gaze flits between Mahtab and Simone. Oblivious to what he has just done, he mutters, "I told you to stay out of it."

Mahtab gets up. "I'm going home." She doesn't raise her voice. No need to.

"Why?" James pleads wide-eyed. "Stay for a while. It's not a big deal."

But Mahtab is busy watching something else. The white nylon coat slides off Simone's body and floats to James as he lounges in his comfortable booth. It covers his trembling shoulders in its validating embrace. Now he is wearing a caftan. Now he is a cleric. Now he lifts his head higher and everything he has done is okay. He may not think this, but there it is. Mahtab has seen it. The robe has covered him and he is lost, become one with the ranks of every hateful male Mahtab has ever known or imagined—like the *pasdar*s and clerics, or Mustafa, who held the baton over Ponneh, or Reza, who cannot stand up to his mother. James can never cast off this robe or convince her of his own fears, because Mahtab doesn't forgive the little things—not when it comes to men and their unearned power. *He is weak, weak, weak.* She is much like me in such thoughts. Harmless? No. Without intention? Never. *There* are *no little things.*

"You are too harsh, Saba jan . . . with Reza and your father and every-one. Forgive, dear girl. Reza is your friend. Your baba is your baba. Weak-ness isn't a sin."

Yes, but Mahtab, the lucky twin, doesn't *have* to forgive or settle. That's the point. She has the ultimate power to reject, to refuse for-giveness. She has abilities that I—as I sat and listened to a suitor for my own hand—would have given a fortune to possess.

"I don't want you," she says to her blond prince and his white baby-fuzz arms. "There are thousands of men at Harvard." James is weak, afraid, ruled by his so-daunting mother. She cuts him out of her heart, as I too have done once before.

As she walks away, Simone calls after her, "I heard you wanted to carry a plastic purse to meet his mother." Then she smirks as one would do at a village idiot.

Mahtab recoils. She goes to the slick-haired bartender and asks for a grocery bag. As she empties the contents of her leather purse into the bag, a feeling of nobility, of sacrifice, overtakes her. She doesn't consider this action trivial, as other girls might. Instead she credits herself with much more. Over the next few days, the events of tonight will grow bigger and bigger in her eyes until she has defined herself by them. Even though she may realize later in life that James is just a confused, inexperienced boy without much temper, she chooses to see it as a vindication. Most likely she will never forgive James for unknowingly stumbling into the vicinity of her fears. And how do I know this? Because I know my sister better than anyone. Mahtab ties the plastic bag with a jerk, returns to the table, and tosses the leather bag into Simone's lap. It is an exquisite perform-ance, like a good television-style slap of the face.

Back in her room, she calls Maman. She pulls her dormitory pil-low close to her and tells her mother all her worries. In return, Maman tells her a secret—the facts of her time in Evin Prison, which are still unknown to me. Do *you* know them, Khanom Mansoori? No? One day, I swear, I'll gather all the details.

Before hanging up, Maman informs her about my upcoming mar-riage to Abbas and the fact that now I will be forever joined to some-one other than my twin. I do wish I could see her face when she hears this news. Though I know all her usual expressions, her face in this moment is a blank to me. In all the years, neither of us ever bothered to imagine it—the moment of finding out that the other is lost.

Are you surprised, my friend? Yes, Mahtab thinks of me, even though she is busy with her student life. We are sisters. We are one blood. And of course Baba would have informed her of my marriage. Somewhere far west, Mahtab and Maman must know that I am married.

Khanom Mansoori, do you believe that she got out of Evin? They say that inside those walls they torture and execute hundreds every year. But then, many get out, forever changed, forever fearful. Those are the ones who run off to America, the ones who cut Iran out of their hearts. If Maman got out of Evin, she would surely run. I wish someone would tell me the truth. Obviously Baba knew more than he told me. Maybe there is still more he is hiding. Lately in my dreams when the *pasdar* holds that knife to my throat and tells me to stake my life on Mahtab's whereabouts, I find that my mouth is sealed shut, that I can't help but let him cut me, because I have no answer.

"Don't cry, sweet girl. What if I sing you a song?"

No, no, I'm sorry. Let us focus on the happy part. This is the story of how Mahtab overcomes another Immigrant Worry. News of my marriage has made her realize something important: she may be from an Iranian village, and James a northeastern boy of platinum and gold, but today she wielded all authority. There must be something in her small body that can summon the world to move. Her broken-high-heel story didn't get her beaten like our Ponneh, but it brought her here, to a place where it is *her* foot pressing on some man's back. After accidentally unhinging the unattainable James Scarret, Mahtab will never again fret about having the strength or power to succeed at anything. I may be married to an old man, but my sister said no. *No. I don't want you.* Just as simple and final as that. *No.* A final word that no one can question. Mahtab gets to continue her search. She is free and has only begun to conquer the throngs of pale-faced magazine-cover princelings who rule us all from their private clubs.

Good for you, Mahtab joon. You are a better woman than I.

Part 2

YOGURT MONEY

Some people got hopes and dreams,
Some people got ways and means.

—Bob Marley

Fever for You
(Khanom Basir)

Do I feel bad for Saba? Yes, I feel very sad. But should I put dirt on my head? She is married to a rich man. Yes, there's the Mahtab business, but that is no reason for pity. She is doing it to herself, hashing, rehashing. You know, the other day Khanom Mansoori said that in Saba's stories there is never much talk of Mahtab pining for Saba. Curious, I thought at first. Then, after some thinking, my two cents dropped, as they say, and I understood. Mahtab is free and Saba knows it. Mahtab doesn't long for anything. Saba can't admit the truth of her sister's release, so she makes up stories that hover around it. If you ask me, a seasoned storyteller, I would say freedom is such a powerful thing that no amount of denial can cover the smell of it, so it comes through in the stories. Mahtab doing this, Mahtab doing that. All that adventure and studying, her bread in oil.

It is *just* like Saba to pine for someone who never thinks of her.

She pines for my son too. She should know better, since she has seen what real love looks like. In winters, old Khanom and Agha Mansoori would visit the Hafezis and throw a *korsi* blanket over a table and a stove. We would huddle together, our bare feet tucked under, drink tea, and listen to the bubbling water pipe and Khanom Mansoori's sweet, girlish voice, like an overplucked *setar* string, singing ancient songs. Then her husband would hobble over, carrying a bowl of the gum-friendly foods they liked to share—apple or cucumber mush, or pomegranate seeds with salt, or orange slices covered in hogweed powder. "Khanom," he would say, "I've seeded a whole pomegranate for you."

I'd nudge Saba and tell her an old saying. *Only die for someone who at least has a fever for you.* She would pretend she didn't understand, but she did. She still does. Now if only she'd see that there is a difference between just youthful fever and fever *for you.*

Chapter Eight

Six months after marrying Abbas, Saba finds herself in a kind of ease—a stable not-unhappiness that keeps her pleasantly occupied. She isn't a girl who can be married anymore, and so, in many ways, she is free. Yet she is often bored, in food lines, at underground beauty salons, listening to Abbas. Should she have gone to college? No, she assures herself, and buys more books. What's the use of studying Western literature in Iran, where half the books are banned and college entrance depends on knowledge of Islam? For now she has the Tehrani, purveyor of the very best education. Later on she will have her full and challenging life. Maybe she will fall in love. Maybe she will solve the mystery of her mother, who, despite the letter, could be anywhere. After all, according to every office Saba has phoned, her mother is no longer in Evin. She might very well have escaped with Mahtab on a different day. So for a little while longer, until Saba can find her own way out, Mahtab has to live richly for both of them. Meanwhile, Saba has uncovered secrets that have given her dominion over her limited world.

As a married woman, she can come and go more freely. Often she accompanies Ponneh or one of her village mothers through winding, tree-lined roads to small shops and markets, stopping to collect the ration coupons of the others. They visit the stores that are said to hold staples on this day or that, following rumors from shop to shop, collecting the most essential items, each supplied daily by a different store out of fairness. *Agha Maziar has eggs today. Iraj Khan got all the week's chicken.*

When possible, Saba doesn't chase mass-produced rationed foods. She can afford to buy more expensive organic eggs or chicken directly from local farmers. Some things she gets from the black market. But there is still the sugar, cooking oil, butter, and imported items to buy the usual way. Before the war ended, store owners with the good fortune to acquire exclusive access to something vital would illegally bundle that item with unsellable junk they wished to unload. *Eggs can be bought only with the purchase of a flyswatter. Milk is available when you buy drain cleaner. A toilet bucket with your sugar today, Khanom? Only a suggestion* . . . Some shopkeepers still try this, and Saba piles the useless items in her cavernous storage room. Abbas detests household clutter.

In the first days of their marriage, she hated Abbas for failing to be as blind as her father promised he would be. He tossed out what he thought was all of her American music. He meticulously searched through her clothes for loud or colorful garments. He even examined her personal hygiene items, scrutinizing each article and throwing away anything that didn't meet his obsessive standards. Unlike her strict mother, who years before had searched Saba's room for signs of vanity, Abbas wasn't looking for forbidden razors, but unclean ones; he wasn't hunting for frivolous tweezers, but frowning at the tiniest hair stuck inside them. He had a thousand ridiculous demands. Khanom Omidi called it *vasvas*, the Persian word for that streak of obsessive compulsion that runs through all people. He complained that his dinners weren't warm enough, that his yogurt wasn't thick enough, that there was pulp in his bowl of pomegranate seeds. He was used to his ways. Why would Saba begrudge him a few eccentricities in his old age? And why would she leave the house without wiping that spot behind the oven?

But on the night Abbas first visited her bedroom, two months after their wedding, Saba forgave him all his peculiarities. Two months and he had never once asked to share her bed. Never once tried to touch her. Never even implied as much. He gave her a small bed-room across from his own, with a bed, side table, and lamp. It was a guest room. Like the rest of the house, it was decorated in the Western style, with chairs and beds instead of mats. He asked that she keep her clothing in his room, as was the marital custom. He asked that she leave no sign of herself in the guest room—in case of snooping visitors or a wandering kitchen maid. Every night, as they retired to their separate rooms, he mumbled in a tired voice, "Good night, child. Sleep well." On those early-marriage nights, she asked herself, *Does he expect me to go to him?* And she decided that she never would.

Two months after their wedding, as Saba was beginning to fall asleep, she heard her doorknob turn, and there he was—standing in his long shirt and old pajama pants, looking even smaller and frailer than he did during the daytime. She panicked, thinking of what was to come. Now, when she recalls that night, she remembers three sensations overtaking her in achingly slow succession. The first was stomach-turning regret—*Why didn't I go to Tehran? Any other girl would have gone to Tehran.* She remembers pressing her lips together and peering out of half-closed eyes to see what he would do, then hearing his footsteps as he approached her bed and hating herself for making the logical choice. She recalls Abbas climbing into her bed, and her revulsion when his pajamas slid up his leg and she saw his veiny, wrin-kled ankles in the dark.

Does he know I'm awake? she wondered, and pretended to sleep, still clutching her blanket for protection. In what she hoped resembled a natural fit of sleep, she rolled over to face the wall. And then it happened. Abbas moved close to her and placed his head next to hers on the pillow. He stretched out and pulled her covers over himself. She held her breath as he reached out with one bony finger to stroke her uncovered hair. He buried his beard in her neck and fell asleep almost instantly, sighing at what must have been the day's aches and pains, then snoring gently into her hair.

Saba remained frozen that night, keeping a constant vigil over her body. She planned how she might delay the inevitable nightmare with lies and promises and clever tricks. Soon she too fell asleep, and when she woke, only three hours later, she found Abbas still asleep, his bushy chin still buried in her neck. That was when the second sensation washed over Saba: sweet relief. She carefully removed herself from under Abbas's frail arm, sneaked into his bedroom, and retrieved some of her day clothes. She changed quickly and headed to the kitchen to make breakfast. There, in the kitchen, she experienced the third distinct sensation of that strange night: the thrill of possibility. Could it be that Abbas is too old for . . . that? Maybe she'd never have to do any more than *this*.

The next night Saba waited to see if the previous evening's visit would repeat itself. Abbas hadn't mentioned anything to Saba all day long. But he seemed happier than usual. He complained only once about the yogurt, and when his tea was too hot, he mumbled and blew on it until it cooled. Saba began to fear that last night was only a groundbreaking and that Abbas would expect more tonight. But the old man stole into the room with barely a noise, slipped under the covers, and buried his tired head on Saba's shoulders, falling asleep almost instantly.

Sixteen nights and nothing changed in Saba's bed except for a few small demands. Some nights he would pull her close to him and wrap a thin arm around her torso. On other nights he would complain of the cold and grumble that she shouldn't turn her back to him. Frequently he asked her to scratch his shoulders and back, a task that revolted Saba, given the volume of dry skin and scraggly hairs on his body. Afterward he always said, "Thank you, child," in a strangely apologetic way. After a while he came to her room before she went to bed and performed his lengthy bedtime rituals alongside her, asking her to mix his cup of medicine with sour-cherry syrup and ice water. Every night he clipped his nails to exactly a millimeter, cut his arm hairs with tiny scissors, and folded his dirty socks into perfect squares before putting them in an ordered pile to be washed. "Always someone is watching," he said, "and it's good for them to know I'm clean and neat."

Soon, Saba's fears began to subside. Abbas seemed to have no intention of consummating the marriage, at least not with anything more than the torturous intimacy of watching him groom himself. Each night she watched him and counted all the mental diseases that go untreated in this small town. Each day she told herself to relax. He was old. He obviously wanted a wife only for the sake of image—to prove his youth, his efforts to build a family. She was no more than a pair of perfectly folded socks and therefore had nothing to fear. But something inside her wanted to make sure, to put an end to this nightly dread. One morning she decided to say something.

He had just asked how she had slept. "Fine," she said. "Abbas . . ."

"What is it?" he said. They were sitting at the small wooden table in the kitchen.

She hesitated. She wanted him to know, without being insulted, that she preferred to keep their current arrangement unchanged. Finally she blurted out, "I can't give you children." The words hurled from her mouth without grace, like garbage thrown out the window of a fast-moving car. She immediately winced at the stupidity of the lie.

Abbas looked up from his breakfast. His jowls bounced as he chewed. Saba could see in his eyes that he knew why she said this. He chuckled softly. "Yes." He swallowed. "At my age, a man only wants a few small comforts. . . . I'm past that time in my life."

Saba felt sorry for him just then. She wanted to pay him a compliment, so she said, "You're not so old." And then she regretted it, thinking it might be taken as an invitation.

Abbas looked sad. "No, there will be no children," he said, as if he were speaking to his lap. Then he raised his head and added, "But you'll die a rich woman. It's no loss for you."

She put another slice of cheese on his plate. "I don't want children," she said.

"Is that so?" He seemed to awaken. "Is it because you want to be a scholar?"

"Yes." She smiled. A baby would tie her to Iran. No sneaking off in the night or easy American visas unless she left the child behind, as her mother had done.

"Are you happy then," he asked, "with just us two in this big empty house?"

"Yes," Saba said, though a part of her was already mourning a loss. How long would this last? She would never have to sleep with an old man, a relief, but would she never feel the joy of being with someone she might love? When would she be allowed an awakening? How long before she could run away? She mixed his morning medicines into a perfect sour-cherry cocktail with plenty of ice and syrup. He smiled as he took a sip.

"You know, my last wife was very fat," Abbas said, puffing out his cheeks. Saba laughed through a mouthful of tea. "It's true. It's true. She was a *khepel*. But I was always warm at night. When she died, that was the first thing I noticed. This house gets so cold and drafty, doesn't it?" Saba nodded. "The second thing I noticed was no more pickle smell. She used to pickle everything, sweet woman." He sighed and took another bite before getting up to go for his morning walk through the lush, dewy villages. At the door, he turned and said, "Saba jan, as long as we live our lives the way we like, there's no rea' son for anyone else to know . . . about our private business."

"Of course," she said, reveling in her newfound freedom and fail' ing to fully understand Abbas's apprehension, the potential threat to his reputation and pride.

"Good day, child," he said. "Don't read too much. You'll wear out your eyes."

And so, months later, Saba finds herself happy. Sometimes, when she is alone and can't keep the thoughts away, her skin remembers touching bare feet in the pantry or clammy hands slipping into hers. The fantasies show no face, and she pretends she is dreaming of a younger version of her own husband, of an adolescent love broken across decades. There is a certain romance to that. She will be loyal to her kind husband, she decides, and summon joy—late-night fevers be damned.

She spends most days at her father's home because she is comfort' able there in the house where she has a hundred secret places to hide music or books or magazines, which she still purchases from the Teh' rani. Abbas doesn't insist on going with her; he likes to spend his days out, smoking, playing backgammon, and telling stories with other men in the town square. Besides, her father enjoys having her com' pany, and she helps with the burden of his constant guests. Lately Khanom Omidi and the elderly Khanom and Agha Mansoori visit her father's house often, and Saba spends countless slow, lingering afternoons in their company—hearing stories, scraping cucumbers, sweetening tea. She watches the elderly couple feed each other an array of mush—apple pulp crushed in a bowl, melon scrapings in a glass with ice, sweetened saffron rice pudding with rosewater but no almonds—and she begins to imagine herself in old age, not a widow, but a beloved wife. In seventy years, maybe her own husband will scrape food for her. She has so many years beyond Abbas, she real-izes. There are so many ways for this story to end.

A spring chill hangs in the air, so she prepares a foot stove for the trio, which she places under the thick *korsi* blanket at their feet. They compliment her, claiming that her marriage has made her extra sweet, extra sensitive to the needs of her elders. A *korsi* is a treat in balmy Shomal, where a space heater is enough. May God bless her, they pray.

"Saba jan, you are needed at Khanom Basir's house." Her father comes out wearing a thin shirt and loose pants. He joins the elderly couple under the *korsi* and puffs on his hookah, sending his regards to the women in Saba's life through rings of smoke.

Agha Mansoori is halfway through seeding a pomegranate. He grabs clumps of seeds with his blue-veined fists and tosses them into a bowl. The seeds bounce this way and that, leaving blood-red streaks on the sides of the porcelain. They come to rest in a neat pile, a sea of ruby-red gems. His wife takes notice and shakily reaches for one. "Not now, Khanom. Wait till the bowl is full, so you can have them twenty at a time with a spoon." She puts the seed back, and a guilty look passes over his face. "No, no. You start. At our age, what if we don't make it to see the end?"

So much sentiment over a pomegranate seed. Sometimes in gloomy moments Saba considers what she might be missing. She has lived without so many kinds of affection. As she gets up to leave, she hears Khanom Mansoori's fragile voice, high and shaky like old violin strings. "Who has a good story for us?"

⁓◉⁓

It has been months since Saba, Reza, and Ponneh sat in a circle in her father's pantry. It has been months since they smoked and drank together, told stories, and laughed at the oblivious adults. And in that time she has wondered daily, *Where is he now?* Is he in Ponneh's arms, in some alley somewhere? Is he waiting for her in some secret place? While Ponneh has always protected their threesome, she has few choices for marriage other than Reza. The war with Iraq has taken so many men. Saba wonders how Reza has escaped it—some medical loophole or maybe just sheer luck—since he has no money for bribes. She has never asked because it is an unlucky and unwelcome topic with the men. Though the war is over now, she still has nervous dreams that he is sent off to some unknown battle zone or that he is attacked in the night by thieves or the moral police. After every dream, she wakes up in a guilty sweat because her mother taught her not to pine after men, not to tie her happiness to them, and to find her joy in work and study. She obeys her mother's voice and casts Reza off until he is gone, until the young and adventurous companion of her dream universe is nameless again.

He could have stood by her when they were caught. He could have rushed to her rescue. But he was weak and did nothing, and now she will not want him.

But in this small town avoiding past loves is a luxury. And now that Saba is married, Khanom Basir feels no qualms about calling on her with requests, gossipy inquiries, and attempts to pry into her personal life. She has not once apologized for the role she played in arranging Saba's marriage. Instead she employed a healthy dose of *maast-mali* to cover her actions and considers Saba indebted to her. Today Saba has offered to shop for the Basir, Alborz, and Mansoori families. Yesterday she picked up their money—for meat, bread, eggs, vegetables, and possibly some mandatory mop, old soap, or pumice stone—and now she must stand in line for the sake of everyone's dinner. She checks her purse for the extra ration stamps that her father buys from the black market—unused coupons from addicts or people with recently dead relatives whose IDs still work—and distributes to their friends.

Hours later, appearing at the Basirs' door, laden with fresh fish and other supplies, Saba pushes aside the kitchen drapery and finds Ponneh and her mother chopping vegetables with Khanoms Basir and Omidi, the older women squatting on the floor with skirts wrapped tightly around their thighs, and Ponneh on a small stool, halfheartedly skinning a carrot, dropping orange curlicues all around her feet.

"Did you separate it already?" Khanom Basir says without looking up.

"Not yet," Saba says, and greets everyone, kissing Ponneh on both cheeks.

"Never mind, I'll do it myself." Then Khanom Basir looks up and adds, "God keep you."

"How are you, Saba jan?" Khanom Alborz asks. "We haven't seen you recently."

"Well, she is still a newlywed," Khanom Basir says with a suggestive little grin that makes Saba shudder. "Why would she have time for us?"

"I've been at Baba's house a lot lately. I'm sorry we haven't seen you there," Saba says to Khanom Alborz.

"Oh yes, well, my daughter takes up so much of my time," Khanom Alborz responds, dropping her head in exaggerated sadness. "She keeps getting worse. You should thank God for your health, girls."

"Yes, yes," Khanom Basir chimes in again. "You two are the picture of health and beauty. Tell me, Saba, are you keeping your husband happy?" The coy grin returns, and Saba turns toward Ponneh, who makes a face and looks away.

Saba moves closer to Ponneh. Khanom Basir, taking her eyes off her cutting board for a moment, walks over and takes Saba's chin in her hand. She gazes at her, almost lovingly, and Saba breaks into a shy, nervous smile.

"Your husband lets you wear makeup?" Khanom Basir asks. A blue-and-violet-checkered scarf is draped loosely around her neck. Saba remembers that the scarf once belonged to Khanom Alborz and wonders how Khanom Basir got it. It is old—left on a beach by a tourist—but it has a famous French name. Now Khanom Basir wipes her brow with it, as if to say she's above it. "Well, you're married now," she says in a tone that Saba admits is almost kind. Then she reaches into the pocket of her long dress and takes out a crumpled piece of paper. "I found the recipe to wash your big win-dows. Here."

The recipe is a simple three-ingredient mixture of mostly vine-gar. It is written in a scrawled, uneven hand. Saba thanks the older woman, who has made unnatural efforts at teaching her every house-hold skill—her way of showing that they can be friends now that the marriage question is settled. Shortly after her wedding, when all her surrogate mothers came to her new home and showed her how to store her spices, and bone her fish, and every other mundane thing they could think of, it was Khanom Basir who taught Saba how to make her own favorite dish, the perfect *gheimeh*, even though it was too heavy for Abbas's stomach. And two days after her wedding, it was Khanom Basir who brought over a hearty *âsh* stew to "give her strength." And now she holds out Saba's portion of fish, neatly sealed in plastic wrapping. "Would you like to take it now or come back for it after your errands?"

"I'll come back, thanks," she says. These gestures remind Saba of the day she started to bleed and Khanom Basir explained woman-hood in the toilet. Now she is one of them, a married woman with a certain dignity—though in her heart she is no older, no wiser, no less consumed by selfish desires, and given a choice she would rather squander every afternoon smoking with her single friends in the pantry.

Ponneh walks her out, linking her arm through Saba's. "Next time I'll give you a warning signal and you can leave the fish outside."

"I'm sure they'll love that," Saba says. "I see your mother gave Khanom Basir her nice scarf. Isn't that the foreign one she got from the tourist?"

"It was a reconciliation gift after another one of their fights." Ponneh tucks some loose hairs back into her headscarf and picks a stray strand off her tongue. "About my sister's illness and how I'm not allowed to marry yet. How I'll die a pickled old maid."

"Don't be dramatic," says Saba. "How is Reza?"

With her mischievous almond eyes, Ponneh says, *Don't ask.* Saba giggles. She feels sorry for her friend. Her mother's rules leave her no outlet other than clothes to express herself. Recently she has attempted Tehrani styles, wearing fewer bright colors and tossing her scarf loosely over one shoulder, pushing it far back to reveal puffed-up hair over her chiseled face. Saba lowers her voice to a whisper. "Really, Ponneh jan, look at you. You *must* have a lover. . . ." Ponneh glances up with a half-smile but Saba continues. "I have trouble believing you've gone all this time without . . . *someone.*"

Ponneh pulls at the sleeve of her pink cotton blouse. "I have enough friends."

"That's not what I meant," says Saba.

"I know what you meant." Ponneh looks up. "I miss the three of us. Reza does too." When Saba starts to ask again, Ponneh interrupts. "Don't worry so much. We'd never leave you out." Saba takes her friend's hand. She knows that Ponneh is only trying to spare her pain—that surely she and Reza see each other often. She can see it in the way Ponneh avoids the question, the reflective way she picks at her nails and looks away for just a second. Now Ponneh switches to a whisper, her eyes sparkling as she leans in. "I'll tell you a secret. I have a new *friend*, someone I met at—" Then she stops and Saba wonders why Ponneh doesn't want to tell her where she has been.

"Yes?" Saba searches Ponneh's face.

Ponneh rolls her eyes. "Her name is Farnaz." Khanom Omidi passes by them on her way out. She kisses them both good-bye and smiles her oblivious smile. When she's gone, Ponneh whispers, "Some-times, it's more fun with another *girl*."

"What are you two talking about?" Khanom Basir shouts at them from inside.

Saba turns back to Ponneh. "What *are* we talking about?"

"Don't get me wrong," says Ponneh. "This is just practice. She'll be married soon. Maybe I will too one day. But for now . . ." Ponneh raises an eyebrow proudly, like a child caught being fantastically bad. Saba can't contain herself. She reaches for Ponneh's arm, and they double over in quiet laughter.

She wants so much to tell Ponneh about her arrangement with Abbas. To declare that she isn't sleeping with an old man and that she too needs a little practice. There is a comfort in joking with Ponneh about intimate things again. But she decides to keep her secret. She promised Abbas. *It's always best to reveal less,* her mother used to say, and it seems wise to follow this advice now. "I miss it too," she says. "All of us together in the pantry."

Ponneh wipes some kohl from the corner of her eye. "Do you think Abbas would want to join in?" And they burst into another fit of giggles like they used to do when they were little girls.

"I better go—" Saba starts to say good-bye. She leans over to kiss Ponneh.

Ponneh cuts her off. "Look, I have some news."

"What is it?"

"Do you remember that woman who saw us . . . that day? Your mother's friend?" The light tones are gone from Ponneh's voice and she wears the same serious, heavy-hearted expression she wore for the first few months after the incident with Mustafa.

Saba nods. "Dr. Zohreh? I didn't think you saw her."

"I didn't," says Ponneh. "She asked for my name around town and she found me."

"Why didn't you tell me?" Saba demands.

Ponneh shrugs. "It was my secret." Then she says, much more bitterly, "I'm the one it happened to, not you. Besides, you were busy being married."

Saba starts to apologize, but vague memories of her mother's friend grip her.

"Dr. Zohreh wanted me to ask you to come and see her. She said there's something your mother wanted you to know." A tightness spreads across Saba's chest. Ponneh crosses her arms. "I'm considering joining their group. Your mother's group. Sheerzan." *Lioness.* She laughs, leans in, and adds, "You'll have to forgive them the awful name. They're doctors and engineers, not poets."

"Why would *you* join?" Saba asks. She hasn't heard the name *Sheerzan* in what seems like a hundred years, and even then, only in passing, in whispered conversations between her parents. But she can conjure enough memories to realize that Ponneh, a village girl who quit school after eighth grade, doesn't belong with them. Her mother's friends were college students and daughters of important men. Why would the doctor approach Ponneh and not her? Despite her indignance, Saba knows she wouldn't risk her future the way Ponneh might—it would be cruel to cause her father more worry. She wonders what her mother would think now if she saw Saba and her friends at the age of twenty. Reza still idling away the days with football. Saba married to an old man, and Ponneh an activist. She would grow horns from the irony of it. How much does Dr. Zohreh know about the mystery of Bahareh Hafezi? "What did Maman tell her?"

"That's all I know." Ponneh shrugs. She raises that seductive eye-brow again and adds, "That's where I met Farnaz." Saba has the feel-ing that Ponneh is trying to change the subject. Maybe she doesn't want to share her new confidante. Stuck in a poor household packed with sisters, Ponneh rarely gets her own private joys. Saba kisses her friend good-bye, and they promise to meet in the pantry on Friday with Reza because it would be a shame to let their greatest childhood happiness die.

On Friday afternoon Saba tells Abbas that she will be at her father's for the rest of the day. She will be back before dinner, so he won't have to eat alone. But when will she have time to cook dinner? he wor-ries. She reassures him that she made tonight's dinner this morning. But it won't be fresh then, he predicts gravely—doesn't Saba know that fish has to be eaten right away? Oh, but not to worry, Saba prom-ises, because the meal is made with lamb. Evidently Saba has forgot-ten that Abbas requested fish for dinner. After much haggling, Abbas is satisfied with a promise of fish for tomorrow and leaves the house. Saba, who plans to leave half an hour later, returns to the guest room, uncovers her hidden stash of makeup, and applies the faintest layer. She plays Paul Simon songs, disguised in piles of English language instructional tapes, and reads *The Captive*, a book of poetry by the renowned Persian poet Forough Farrokhzad, a woman whose works are banned and who, like Saba, cut her education short and married young. *O stars*, she writes about a lost love, *what happened that he did not want me?*

Saba lingers on that line, a momentary indulgence. *What happened?*

When she is sure Abbas is gone, she leaves through the back and goes to her father's home. From the far side of the house, Agha

Hafezi's music drifts toward the kitchen as she enters. Soft notes seep into the thin walls and lightly touch her ears. He is playing a tape of French songs. Saba immediately recognizes her father's favorite, "Le Temps des Cerises." He plays it when he's in another world, leaning against his cushions, wishing for another time, his eyes tired black slits that penetrate the smoke-filled room with their unfulfilled hopes. He doesn't understand the words of the song, but he understands *something* about it. The melancholy. The memory.

She finds Ponneh and Reza already waiting inside the pantry. She hasn't looked at Reza up close for six months. He seems somewhat changed. His chin is a little rounder and covered with a thicker layer of stubble. His skin is paler. It suits him.

"Long time since I saw you," Reza says awkwardly, and leans forward to kiss her on both cheeks. Stray thoughts of that other kiss warm her skin, and she hopes Reza doesn't notice. She tries to expel the memories, tells herself they are worthless, that he failed her, and there is no point in dredging up new hope from old disappointments.

"What are you listening to these days?" she asks, realizing that her efforts at feeling nothing are doomed. Reza's face brightens and he lists some songs—nothing new.

"I learned how to play 'Fast Car' on the *setar*," says Reza with a grin. Saba's chest constricts at this reminder of the day they were caught together. She wants badly to hear him play the song. He has a talent for making every tune sound a thousand years old.

It takes only a moment to unpack the contents of their coats and purses—a bottle of homemade wine, three hashish joints (a luxury compared with opium, signaling that her friends consider this a special occasion), and a small box of sweet *ghotab* bread.

"So," says Reza, and waits. Neither of the girls speaks. Ponneh takes a drag and blows the smoke into a drain in the floor strategically positioned between their crossed legs. "How's . . . being married?"

"Don't be an idiot," says Ponneh, taking another hit. "You know the situation."

Reza looks at her with eyes narrowed. "Do you plan to finish that by yourself?" Ponneh passes him the joint. None of them mentions Saba's marriage again.

"I'm going to call Dr. Zohreh about my mother," Saba says.

Ponneh perks up. "I've been thinking maybe that's a bad idea," she says. "I really shouldn't have said anything before."

"Who's Dr. Zohreh?" Reza says.

"Look, Saba jan," says Ponneh, "she couldn't have any new infor‹ mation. If she did, if your mother had contacted her, she would have called your father, right? I told you everything already, and it's not good to dwell on things your mother said years ago."

"You *didn't* tell me everything, though," says Saba. "Like what exactly is the group doing, anyway?" She tries to place Dr. Zohreh in her memories and vaguely remembers her mother rushing off for days at a time to meet with people Saba didn't know. She thinks Dr. Zohreh might have visited her once in the hospital and tries to remember the days surrounding that night at the beach. But what's the point? This talk is like fixating on a broken music tape or a misplaced list. She knows every word of the lost information, but she has an obsessive need to look and look for something she might have missed.

"Who's Dr. Zohreh?" Reza asks again, louder this time. Ponneh takes a deep breath. She glares at him and scratches a well‹tweezed black eyebrow with the tip of her barely peach fingernail—a subtle challenge to the moral police and the strength of their eyesight.

"I didn't join anything yet," Ponneh says. "It's called Sheerzan . . . Saba's mother and Dr. Zohreh started it after the revolution."

"What's the group for?" Reza asks.

"For women, what else?" Ponneh laughs, as if this was obvious.

"I don't like this," says Reza, shaking his head. "You'll get into more trouble."

Saba plays with the lighter. "Reza's right. You should leave it alone."

Ponneh scoffs. "What do you know? You weren't the ones—" She stops and picks something off her tongue. Then, after a moment, she shrugs and says, "They have a shack in the mountains, right above the sea. It's beautiful." Her bloodshot eyes soften and she leans back against the shelves.

"You've *been* there?" Reza asks. "I can't believe this!"

Ponneh ignores him. "They're *amazing*. They told me that Persian women are made of fire inside." She taps her chest with her free hand. "These mullahs and *pasdar*s know that. And what do you do when you want to douse a fire? You throw a big, heavy cloth over it, deprive it of oxygen. And that's what they've done to us. Isn't that poetic?"

Saba's mother used to say similar things when she first had to put headscarves on her daughters a year or two after the revolution of 1979 and when she saw the rows of amorphous, shrouded, black figures in the streets for the first time. Rows and rows of crows in a line. Rows and rows of fires doused. Did this group have something to do with her disappearance? Did she go to prison because of them? What crime did she commit that her husband wasn't equally guilty of as a fellow Christian convert? The memories are too jumbled and she resents her mother for leaving her with so little help.

"What do they do?" Reza asks. "Is it illegal?"

Ponneh takes half a piece of *ghotab* bread. "Like I said, they have a shack in the mountains by the sea. And they find tragedies against women all over the country. They document them—write about them, secretly photograph them for American newspapers."

Saba considers the timing of Dr. Zohreh's message about her mother, her motives for reaching out to her now. Dr. Zohreh wouldn't think much of Saba if she knew what she had done, how she had given up college to marry a rich old man, a Muslim who might cover up the religion her mother flaunted. Deep down, Saba knows that she is no longer a rebel despite her music, that she traded her mother's teachings for her safe plans.

Trust me, Saba used to say to her mother when she was only five years old. *I know a lot of things*. Her mother would laugh at this, and Saba imagines that she would take these words no more seriously now. If she had her mother's address in America, she would scream the words into a tape recorder and mail it to her. *Just trust me. I know a lot of things!* Except Saba doesn't even know if America is where her mother has gone. Maybe she's in a cell. All she has is the nimbus of a woman and a girl in an airport terminal—a hazy Mahtab looking at her with the guilt and embarrassment of leaving her behind. Is it a false memory? Lately her nightmares of the knife-wielding *pasdar* have eased. She doesn't have to stake her life on any truth yet. She has begun looking for her mother and has written two letters to Evin Prison in Abbas's name, keeping it hidden for her father's sake.

Reza's eyes are wide now and he has forgotten about the hashish and alcohol. "That's so much worse than I thought," he says, scratching through his longish hair.

Saba sighs. This is going nowhere. "What kind of tragedies?" she mumbles, trying to picture the seaside shack among the villas or in the tree-covered mountains.

"They have boxes hidden all over the shack," Ponneh continues. "Pamphlets, pictures, typed and handwritten letters. All going to America, England, Australia, France—but also to Rasht, Tabriz, Tehran, Isfahan. They send the material to newspapers and television. People who should know these things but don't. And they send pamphlets inside Iran too, to women who might join. It's really something."

Ponneh pulls a photo from her pocket. A picture of a woman with a shaved head and scars from a recent lashing marring her beautiful back. Below the picture is a caption: "Crime: Unruly scarf slipped off in the wind." Saba notices the beauty of the woman's half-turned face and glances at Ponneh, who is chewing her nails. She can see Ponneh's hesitation in sharing this secret, these friends, with her, because after all, Ponneh has experienced something that Saba hasn't. The woman in the picture, like Ponneh, probably could never have been pious enough. Never obedient enough. Because her crime was all over her lovely face. "Isn't it grotesque?" Ponneh says, her tone hard and dry.

"Don't be so vain, Ponneh jan," Reza says, as if reacting to something entirely different, some private exchange from another day.

"Well, this is just the reaction Dr. Zohreh wants," Ponneh says. "Outrage. I think it's grotesque that the poor girl . . . no . . . that *I* have to carry these marks on me forever. What if I get married?" Her voice breaks and she squirms in her clothes, as if she can feel the bruises. According to Khanom Omidi, they aren't healing and parts of Ponneh's skin are permanently numb and discolored. Nerve damage. But she is lucky her spine is okay.

Reza nods. "Ponneh, you're beautiful," he says, as if he can feel the bruises too.

Saba blows a lungful of smoke into the drain. "The *most* beautiful," she says, and squeezes Ponneh's shoulder. "Don't be sad. Not in the Pantry of Earthly Delights."

Ponneh smiles weakly. For a few more minutes she describes the ugly things that have happened not so far away, while Saba considers her own life, her luck, the fortune she has engineered for herself. Something about Dr. Zohreh's group feels off to Saba—not so much like fighting as adapting. Not leaving this doomed country but squirming until the present situation is comfortable enough. She prefers her own way, her immensely more logical way of lying low until she can break free. She has a marriage that allows her to come and go and plan her future unnoticed, while Dr. Zohreh is sending pictures to faceless allies abroad—politicians and reporters who may never respond. Screaming into the Western void to friends who may not even exist.

When Ponneh is finished, they sit in silence. They should feel awkward, but they are used to this bizarre threesome they have created—each of them craving it in some way. "Please don't join," Reza says. "It isn't right. It's not how things are done. Be patient and one day you'll find you're happy. Like our mothers. If you think they don't matter in the world, you're a fool. You both need to stop trying to be so grand." Ponneh huffs and looks away. He begs again, "Please don't."

"Don't worry, I haven't," says Ponneh, and passes the bottle to Saba.

They spend another hour with the alcohol and pastries, talking over Reza's faint humming. If they were alone, Saba would ask him to sing something. They would listen to her music, her Walkman's metal headpiece stretched to fit over both their ears, as was their habit when they were children. When Ponneh goes to the bathroom, Reza reaches over and touches Saba's hand and whispers, "Do you forgive me for that day? I'm sorry I didn't try harder." She nods and looks away. He moves to whisper in her ear. "When the old man dies, you will have just reached the prime of beauty."

She pushes him away, distracts herself by making a mental list of all the ways to approach Dr. Zohreh. She wants to do it alone, without Ponneh. "Don't play these games with me again," she says. "We're not kids. It's insulting."

Only die for someone who at least has a fever for you, Khanom Basir said once.

He looks bewildered. "I'm not playing," he says. "You're my friend,

Saba jan. Do you think I can just replace my friends like they never existed? Your place is empty here." He takes her hand and puts it on his chest, but she pulls away. "I brought you an apology gift, the best I could afford. I went all the way to Rasht for it." He takes an old book with a broken spine out of his jacket. "American stories," he says proudly, and she holds it to her chest and decides never to reveal that the book is in either German or Dutch. He says, "I even tried to befriend the old man, your Abbas Agha, so I could visit you. He was in the square and I asked him his favorite poet, offered to run errands. I did everything. The pompous old thing thought I wanted money and shooed me away."

This makes Saba laugh, and she pushes him away again just as Ponneh returns. "What's so funny? I need a good joke." She relights a cigarette and sits cross-legged in her corner.

Then the pantry door bursts open and Ponneh scrambles to toss the half-smoked butts down the drain. The bottle is empty, but Reza drops it and it rolls through the dark, clanking against food cans as it goes. Saba's mind rushes through all the possible excuses and settles on *I'm married and free to do what I want.* But before she can speak, she glimpses her father, white-faced, almost hunched in the doorway, his eyes red, his gaze so out of focus that he can't have noticed the contraband.

"Kids, we have to go," he says in a quiet tone. "Saba jan, come, my dear."

Already Saba senses the hole in the world. Something precious is gone, and in a few seconds her father will tell her what is lost. She reaches for her throat and begins to cough. Reza rushes to hold her, a habit from a far-off past, but he steps back when her father reaches her first. She swallows hard, but the water is so deep and she can't climb out.

"What happened?" whispers Ponneh.

"It's Khanom Mansoori," says her father, and trails off. Saba can see him changing his mind, altering the words he had planned to say probably from the time he closed the door on whoever delivered the news. He looks with worry at her hand around her throat and Saba removes it. "Agha Mansoori is all alone now. He'll need your help."

The journey from the pantry to Agha Mansoori's house is a blur. Her father tells them the story. Khanom Mansoori died in her sleep, cradled in the arms of her husband of nearly seventy years. Saba tries to picture it and it's easy to do. "Agha jan," she whispers to him softly as she falls asleep, "my mouth feels dry," and he hobbles off their floor mattress to get her some water. When he comes back, she is breathing gently, and he places the water next to the bedding on the floor. Maybe he lights an oil lamp. He holds her in his arms. When he wakes, her skin is cold and ashen. The water is untouched. And he cries out and calls for Agha Hafezi to come and take him away.

Saba can't decide what all this will mean. Khanom Mansoori never took center stage, but she was somehow a necessary part of life in Cheshmeh. She was a listener, a patter of hands, a giver of assurances, a sleeper. How will life continue without her? Who will beg for stories of Mahtab? On whose eager ears will Mahtab's legacy fall?

For a full day Agha Mansoori refuses to let her be buried. "I promised Khanom that we would be buried together in the same ground." He stands alone, looking naked and finished, and the memory he stirs in Saba is of the day the couple watched *Family Ties* with her—American TV people in their glittery world. He said *Shame, shame*, while refusing to let Saba turn off the television. She wonders if there will ever be a person who could be buried alongside her— someone other than Mahtab. Someone who wasn't born by her side but found a place there.

"But Grand-baba, be reasonable," Agha Mansoori's granddaughter, Niloo, pleads. A group of neighbors are standing in Agha Hafezi's dry storeroom, the only place large and cool enough to place a body. "We have to bury her *now*. It's Islamic law."

"Please," the old man implores in a raspy voice, "just give me ten days to die."

Saba grabs Ponneh's arm and is relieved that she's not the only one shaking.

"Dear Agha Mansoori!" says Saba's father. "Don't say such things."

"After she is buried, we can't disturb her again. But if we wait . . . I'm sure she would want to wait for me." He nods to himself, certain of his decision, but when he looks up, all eyes are averted. He looks about wildly, unable to make sense of the world. To his left, Khanom Omidi is weeping into a handkerchief. He turns to find Saba in a corner, her head lowered in prayer. "Saba Khanom." He looks at her with large, imploring eyes. "I beg you. Convince them. You're good with words, child. Tell them we can't send her into the dark place alone. Tell them to wait ten days to put her in the ground. Go on, dear." With that, Agha Mansoori buries his head in his hands, cries noisily. Agha Hafezi turns and looks at Saba, wide-eyed and unable to decide.

"I . . ." Saba begins.

"All this death talk," Abbas says. He sounds frail, so obsessed with his mortality. Saba is disgusted with her choice. He excuses himself to go home and doesn't return.

"You children," says Agha Mansoori. "I may be old and ignorant, but I know my own wife." He wipes his face and fixes it into a prophetic scowl. He gathers up all the foreboding in his body and flings it with a small voice. "She will haunt you all."

Saba goes to him and puts an arm around his shoulder. He sniffs, and wags his prescient forefinger in their faces. Agha Hafezi sighs as he launches into pleas, assurances, grand and eloquent speeches about life, death, and eternity. The old man sobs quietly throughout the speech. Afterward, in the drawn-out silence filled with the collective worry and expectation of the families, he coughs into a graying handkerchief and reveals that he hasn't been listening at all. "Ten days isn't good for much. But I'm tired, Agha jan. I don't think I'll last very long."

"I don't know what to do." Agha Hafezi, frustrated, speaks to no one in particular. Somehow everyone knows that Agha Hafezi, not the Mansoori family, will make the decision. He rubs his eyes with his thumb and forefinger, exhausted. The old man takes Saba's arm for support.

"Ehsan jan, I promise to stop troubling you in ten days' time," he says.

Saba remembers the day her mother and Khanom Mansoori taught her how to lay dough inside the walls of her grandfather's *tanoor* in their kitchen. How many days before the airport incident was it? Did her mother disappear a week later? A month later? On that day Khanom Mansoori said the same phrase to Saba's mother— because no one else had a *tanoor* and she wanted to make bread for her brother who came from the South and wasn't used to rice for every meal. *I promise to stop troubling you in a few days' time.*

"This is insanity. We're not leaving you to do *that* to yourself," says Agha Hafezi.

"Nothing to be done, Agha jan. I'm old. And I haven't slept well in a long time."

And so they wait. Khanom Mansoori is washed, shrouded, and kept in Agha Hafezi's cavelike storage room, just a short walk from the house with its Western kitchen and bags of rice, old-world *tanoor* from out of town, and Saba's beloved pantry.

The next day Mullah Ali visits. When he hears of the plan, he is livid. "I won't allow it. It's wrong, and goes against Islamic law. She must be buried immediately."

Saba has never hated the mullah more. Look at all the other laws he has overlooked for his own pleasure. What about the parties?

What about Mustafa, who went unpunished? Surely this is not the time to be strict. "What do you suggest?" she says coldly.

The mullah thinks for a moment and turns to Agha Hafezi. "We will bury her now and tell him she is still in the storeroom—just while he's in the worst of the suffering. Then we will order the tombstone with both of their names to satisfy him. Of course, we will need a real one too. I'm sure he'll relent after a while, and we can quietly mark her tomb with her own stone," he adds in Gilaki. "Hafezi, can you oblige us?"

"Of course," says Saba's father, happy to pay for whatever will get the body out of his storeroom. It is a good solution, full of convenient half-truths and *maast-mali*.

For days Saba keeps a constant watch over the grieving widower, making sure he does no harm to himself. She tells him stories, plays him all her favorite television shows, tries to entice him to eat. She goes along with the lies—that Khanom Mansoori is waiting for him in the storeroom and that he can't visit her because she has to be kept cool and dry. *Oh yes, everything's fine,* she mutters, as if she were lying about a relative in jail. Soon she realizes that she shouldn't worry about suicide since Agha Mansoori considers it a sin. What's more worrisome is that the old man is determined to die a natural death so that he can join his wife. He does everything possible to fool the fates. He casually peels the labels off his medications so that Saba has to make sure they are in their correct bottles after every use (they never are), "forgets" to turn off ovens and lamps, invites the chilly air and jackals in through the constantly open windows of his tiny wood-and-rice-straw home. On a good day, when he engages in conversation, she learns that he has eaten the same thing every week for fifty years: his wife's *baghaleh ghatogh* with rice. Saba has seen him eat this dish before, always with a side of pickled garlic and piles of white rice, without utensils, using the tips of his thumb and two fingers to smash the individual grains into a buttery ball. Saba marvels at the impressive morsels he can pick up with just those three fingers. Maybe she will try to make him Khanom Mansoori's famous dish. After all, it's her job to keep him alive.

For a few days she forgets about Dr. Zohreh and all the injustices against women and dedicates herself to this one feeble man instead. For days, as Saba attempts to prepare his wife's dish, Agha Mansoori gives a sad and noncommittal string of commentary. "A bit more garlic, child. No, no, less dill . . . well, doesn't matter, I'll die soon anyway." He cowers just beyond Saba's shoulder, his body protesting the act of standing upright—as well as eating and breathing—his eyes resolutely following her hand. She soaks the lima beans and peels them. Agha Mansoori watches as she fries them using the exact amount of garlic, dill, turmeric, and eggs that he instructs. She pours the mixture over a fluffy bed of white rice, not sparing the butter in any step of the process. In the end, he takes a bite and says, "You tried, Saba jan. You tried. But I just can't taste her hand."

"Will you eat it anyway?" she begs, and when he does, she feels gratified, as if he has done her a great favor.

On the seventh day after his wife's death, Agha Mansoori oversees the preparations of halva and dates to be given out to the mourners. "We have to have plenty, Saba jan, because if we sweeten the mouths of our neighbors, they will pray for her soul, which is essential if we're going to be together in a few days."

"I'm sure she's in heaven now," Saba says, certain that even a Christian God would take Khanom Mansoori for himself. She counts the halva anyway, just in case.

He mumbles as if frightened. "Better to be safe." Then he requests that, when he dies, she match the amount of halva and dates exactly.

As he makes his way through town, passing out the halva with Saba, Agha Mansoori sings adoringly of his wife. Like a young lover, he crows about how beautiful she was on their wedding day, how sweetly she took care of their family, how lovingly she decorated their home. He goes on about his wife's "delicious hand," and Saba promises herself that she *will* have this, even if she has to wait a hundred years and outlive everyone. Maybe she will have it with Reza, or maybe she will find her lover many decades from now. She will be his nurse when they are both old and frail and there is no one left to care for either of them.

Eight days pass and Saba grows concerned. She watches the wrinkles in Agha Mansoori's brown face grow into trenches, engulfing his beady hazel eyes in their folds. She sees his jowls reach for the earth while the bend in his back urgently makes for the sky. What will happen when the deadline passes? How will this poor old man go on? She shares her fears with her own husband, who has experienced the pain of losing a wife.

"He will go on," Abbas says plainly. "He will move past it."

"He seems so weak," she says. "He's determined to die."

"Don't worry, child," is Abbas's only response.

Saba look at her husband and is emboldened by the peaceful expression on his face. She remembers the tender way Agha Mansoori looked at his wife as he made her fruit mush and blew on her tea, and the way she once felt about Reza. Such things are possible still, even here. She feels a deep courage, a desire to make an effort on her own behalf, an awareness of her own dying body. And Abbas's.

"Abbas," she begins timidly. "Can I ask you for something?"

"Anything, *azizam.*"

"I've been very happy with you, I hope you realize." Abbas smiles deeply, and Saba is encouraged to go on. "But we're so far apart . . . in age."

She can see that Abbas assumes—like all men do—that she is already mourning the possibility of his death. "We have many years left together," he reassures her.

"Yes, but after . . ." Saba looks down. *I'll still be a virgin.* They haven't discussed their arrangement since that morning a few months ago. Abbas is silent, so she continues. "Would you want me to marry again?" She wonders if she should assure him that she hasn't told anyone about his private failures, that she never will. The smile has fallen from his face, and she fears she has already said too much. He can't possibly enjoy having her youth and the possibilities that await her after his death flaunted before him.

"What is this about?" His voice becomes gruff.

What Saba wants to ask, the thing she hopes for the most, is that he will testify to the nonconsummation of their marriage in a letter intended only for a future husband. Surely this can't cause any harm. Surely he must realize that it is in her best interest to conceal the truth so that she can inherit his fortune. So, Saba reasons, he must have no fears of her speaking out publicly. And in any case, why wouldn't he help her in this small way? If it causes him no embarrassment, why wouldn't he give her this small insurance policy against a second loveless marriage in the event that she never makes it to America? Is she being greedy? Saba braces herself. She has to ask him for this one thing. Otherwise who would ever believe she is a virgin? She would never have a chance with a man her own age, one whom she might love more than even Mahtab.

"I was just thinking," she begins carefully, "how well-suited we are for each other." She gathers together every ounce of sincerity she can muster into a tight ball that she flings at Abbas with each calculated word. "I would never say anything to hurt you." Confusion colors Abbas's face. "But would you want me to marry again?"

His expression darkens. "I don't think I'd have much say then."

She sighs. "You could write a letter. I would never show it to anyone. Write down our secret, and I promise to protect it for us." Her voice shakes with desperation, and she is ashamed now at having entered this conversation. She touches his hand.

"*Azizam*," he says, "if I write it down, your inheritance would be in danger."

"That's why you can trust me. It's something we can do for each other."

Abbas laughs at her cunning. "My smart little wife," he says, and taps her hand listlessly. Then, without answering, he gets up to go to bed. "I don't want to talk about death anymore," he mumbles over his shoulder as he makes his way through the house.

On the ninth night, in a fit of bad sleep likely caused by the impending funeral and their soon-to-be-permanent separation, Agha Mansoori takes a last breath and joins his wife. Afraid of what she will find, Saba doesn't return to his house to check his medicines. She doesn't smell the air or browse for guilty purchases. She says good-bye and promises to be his witness before God that he never harmed himself. She passes out the exact amount of halva that was offered during his wife's mourning period.

Saba and her father help the family shroud Agha Mansoori in the storeroom and carry him out to be buried beside his wife under the double tombstone. Father and daughter stand side by side, each saying a silent prayer. Each missing a lost other self. Saba wonders to which God her confused father is praying now. Probably to the God of his wife, whom he followed devotedly all the time he was with her. His breathing is shallow and pained, his eyes bloodshot. Long after the family leaves with the clerics, Saba and her father remain in the cavelike hollow built into the hillside, silently watching, thinking. How much has changed since her mother left . . . *to go where?*

"Baba, tell me what happened to Maman?" Her voice echoes through the dark length of the open storeroom. It is a long, tubelike structure that narrows toward an invisible end, its walls of mud and rock rough-hewn, its deep crevices unexplored. Saba wraps her arms around her shivering body and glances at the cartons of food, the black-market products bought at steep prices, the foreign luxuries—

digestive biscuits, La Vache Qui Rit soft cheese, Johnson's baby shampoo, Canada Dry, nothing all that perishable—hidden in the deepest clefts.

Agha Hafezi takes a tired breath. "I'm sorry," he says, "I can't give you what you want, Saba jan. I have my theories. I've looked. You saw how my letter was returned, and they never told me anything. I had to divorce her or risk losing you and our life."

Saba tries not to fidget. "But what about America? When did she go to jail?"

Her father shakes his head. "The airport was chaos. You ran away and I had to chase you. And then I turned around and she was gone. I saw the *pasdar*s and then I couldn't find her again. I spent days calling people." He sounds weak. He fixes his gaze beyond her shoulder. "Later someone told me they saw her in the prison, but I said it can't be. She can't have gone there, because my Saba saw her get on the plane and it must be so. It must be so, because my daughter is so smart. She sees everything and she doesn't lie."

For years Saba has imagined the moment when her father would admit that her mother is in America. His words, she dreamed, would be the plank that would keep her afloat. But now, on hearing that her own foggy perception has been her father's plank, all support disappears beneath her, plunging her into the icy water. How reliable is this single scrap of memory that she has worn out over the years like a fading photograph? For an instant the picture of the elegant lady in the blue manteau and green scarf becomes clear again. Her mother steps out of the hazy terminal and smiles at Saba. She clutches Mahtab's hand and steps easily past the crowds onto the plane.

A dozen questions fight for space. *Did Maman call from America? Can Mullah Ali help? Why did the* pasdars *arrest her? If she never made the flight, where is Mahtab?*

"She never contacted me again," her father says with painful finality. She watches his throat move as he swallows hard, and she thinks

that her Mahtab stories have hurt him, kept him from moving forward because he is too afraid to force her to accept his truth. When
she starts to speak, he says, "Enough," his voice taut and pitchy. He
crosses the storeroom to return to his memories, leaving Saba to the
numbing consolation of her music and movies, unaware of the dis-
tress in which she has left her unhappy husband, who, after months
of marriage, has finally opened his eyes to his own disposability.

String-Fingered Dallak
(Khanom Basir)

The Hafezis were book types and strange; there was so much they didn't teach those girls. Once, when they were nine years old, they got into trouble for shaving their legs to the knee and plucking three hairs from the space between their eyebrows. Three hairs. I wanted to ask Bahareh why she was so strict with woman things, but you know how it is—ask the camel why it's pissing backward and it says, "When did I ever do anything like anyone else?" Bahareh thought she was teaching her girls to be important.

They weren't allowed to shave anything, or perfume anything, or pluck anything. She didn't want them to grow up too soon or become women before *she* was ready. The only grooming they were allowed was to rub the bottom of their feet with a pumice stone—because soft feet were the sign that they were Hafezi daughters and not one of their field-workers: important. Their mother checked their legs every day, especially after the revolution, to make sure they weren't breaking her rules. *Be strict with the small rules, and teach them to risk their necks breaking the big ones.* Such craziness! Sometimes I thought I was the only sane person in twenty kilometers.

What pointless rules! Northern girls are hard workers and not at all plagued by vanity. When Gilaki women talk about indulgences, we mostly mean food. But then one day Bahareh told her daughters to avoid riding bikes, which is necessary with all our hilly roads. Most normal children ride because they have to earn a living. "You're young women," she said. "You will tear your curtain." Even with her modern ways, her Western clothes, Bahareh followed the old when it came to sex and raising girls.

"What curtain?" Saba asked, and her mother said to stop asking questions. Apparently some stupid girl had used the bike story on her wedding night, and the Hafezis didn't want their daughters to have any excuses. Ridiculous. Girls will always have excuses. A fox will always have his tail as a witness.

Even with all her medical books, their mother didn't tell them about men and women and such things. On the day Saba began to bleed, it was I who had to tell her she wasn't dying. You see, Bahareh was afraid that they would discover boys and turn their backs on her grand Western dreams. She wanted her twins to stay young and untouched forever. Bookish, full of plans and ambitions, forever belonging only to her.

And so they grew up strangely, with almost no information about their own bodies. I wonder how Saba is managing now that she's married. Probably the old man doesn't have many needs that require womanly skill or scrutiny. You see, they are a good match.

One day Bahareh and I were in the private hammam in the Hafezi house while she was getting her string treatment, her preferred method since she hated the smell of the pastes. We didn't hear Saba searching the house for us. Then she just appeared there. Bahareh sat up and pulled a towel over her chest, but Saba had already seen everything. It was a dry treatment—no steam and fog to disappear in. Imagine how it must have looked to the girl. Try to see it through her innocent eyes. Above her mother, hovered a huge washer-woman, like a *dallak* from the hammams, the kind who wash you with a rough sack over their hands. She was wearing a *lungi* cloth around her waist, her fingers tangled in a web of string.

She bent over Bahareh, pulling out hair after hair from her most private places with fleshy hands twisted up in the thread, one end of it in her teeth. The web moved almost on its own, unseen strands all tangled up, taking her fingers and pieces of Bahareh with it. The woman looked at Saba, her crooked teeth biting a string, and the poor child ran out as fast as her legs could carry her.

Chapter Nine

LATE SPRING 1990

Saba walks home from her father's storeroom by narrow mountain roads, forgoing the bus for the freedom of climbing up and down the dirt paths leading to the next village. The trees, bursting with blossoms a few weeks ago, are now lush with new fruit, but she is transfixed by thoughts of prisons and halva and double tombstones. Rebellious mothers with photo cameras screaming into the Western void. Legal testaments to virginity and unwilling husbands. Younger men and the happy memory of a not-so-innocent kiss on the cheek. She wonders if Ponneh is longing for such things. Her oldest sister lingers but is getting sicker. Khanom Alborz's rules have turned the poor girl into a relic, a village curiosity. All anyone can think is, *When will she die and free her trapped sisters?*

Saba grasps the doorknob. She calls out to Abbas. The house looks empty, and she wanders through the kitchen, dropping her bag on a low stool near the window. She leans across the table to inspect the bowl of fruit—delivered this morning by a local gardener Abbas favors—stems still intact, skin glistening and bruised from the humid

Gilan air and the ride in the back of the merchant's rickety truck. She rearranges a few pieces according to color and picks out a cucumber—a staple of the Persian fruit bowl—slices it lengthwise and sprinkles salt onto the flesh. Even as an adult, Saba never skips the childish step of rubbing the halves together to create a salty foam. She brushes the wet tip of her nose as she makes her way through the house, calling out Abbas's name in every room, not because she needs him but to confirm that she is alone. Finally she finds herself outside her room, the room where she sleeps but has yet to keep any of her clothes. Certain now that no one is home, Saba sloughs off her headscarf and jacket, leaving on only a thin blouse and a gray skirt. She opens the door, ready to toss the garments onto her bed, and then she stops.

Abbas is standing against the end table. There are strangers in her bedroom with him.

She greets the two unfamiliar women who are sitting on her bed, amorphous in urban chadors, sprawling with a maternal ease. They look like Basij Sisters, the blackclad Islamic women of the volunteer Basij militia who help impose postrevolutionary rules on fellow Iranians. Why are they here? Women such as these are rarely seen in small northern villages. They are both covered to their eyebrows— not a single strand of hair visible, but so much dizzying black. They speak to Abbas in hushed tones. At first Saba doesn't fear their presence, marveling only at their bulk, the way they fill her room like black clouds. Like vultures clad in raven dress. But then she sees one of them break into a lipless grin, the kind that sinks deep into the face and overtakes the eyes with its severity, and she thinks she has seen her before. Isn't this the *dallak* she saw once when she wandered past an open door and spied her mother under a handful of thread? *Throwing bands* was their term for it. Isn't she the one who hunched over her mother's lower half, two fingers of each hand entangled in a mesh of shiny string, plucking away like a hunchbacked musician? In the old days, *dallak*s, usually men, used to do everything in bathhouses, scrubbing, massaging, even performing circumcisions. Their female counterparts, with their loofahs and pumice stones, are largely out of work now that most public hammams are closed because of indoor plumbing. They have moved on to other work— underground salons, tailoring, housecleaning. Maybe this one has become a Basiji. Many poor women have. Saba can see that neither woman is local, at least not anymore. She eyes these foreign creatures, so different from her mother, the scholaractivist in London blouses, and from her colorful surrogate mothers with hennaed hair, bejeweled scarves, and manyhued skirts worn two or three at a time.

"Shut the door, Saba," says Abbas. Saba complies.

He takes her hand and pulls her inside with a certain resolve that she doesn't associate with him. He nods for her to sit on the bed. The women make room for Saba between them, greeting her with excessive formality. The thought occurs that maybe someone else has died. *Oh God, not another death so soon.* The former thread artist puts a hand on her leg. Abbas kneels down and looks in her face, as if at a wayward child. "Saba," he begins. "It is my job to look after you and our best interest. To protect us from harm. Even if that means protecting you from yourself."

She wrinkles her brow, failing to understand him.

Abbas pulls himself up, straightens his pants, and smooths his shaggy hair nervously. He nods to the women and says, "I'll be waiting outside with payment."

Saba hears him mutter something as he slams the door. *The bargains of women.*

Now a primal fear takes over. A banshee wakes inside, sensing danger, and lunges toward freedom, pressing its weight against the inner wall of her chest, crushing her heart in its panicked fist and making her ribs ache. *What is this?*

When she thinks of this moment over the coming years, she

always remembers this: a thick hand grasping her from behind. The painful recoil and the nausea as she is yanked backward by a forearm around the stomach. A giantess pulling her writhing, screaming body onto the bed, pinning it with the weight of her sizable arms and chest, which are now planted squarely on Saba's torso.

"Get the bag," she says in a thick *dehati* accent from somewhere in the South, a peasant accent with the unmistakable tones of field-workers, hammam attendants, and housecleaners, women with no steady income, no ties to families like hers. Most likely these two are stricken with a deeper poverty than any of the mothers who have passed through Saba's house and won her father's trust. She has heard that many desperate women—former prostitutes, destitute mothers—join the Basij Sisters and that it is possible to hire them for unthinkable things, dirty acts that must be hushed up. The Basij have never been above such things, especially if they can tie it by the thinnest fiber to God and Islamic law. *What has Abbas paid them to do? How did he find them? Did he ask around the old bathhouse?* In a fit of calculation, Saba considers telling the familiar one who her mother is. Will she care? Will she even recall her former life? Now the memory intensifies, and for a single blink the woman reaching for her bag isn't covered in black but is bare-breasted, a *lungi* around her waist as it was on the day Saba last saw her.

She frees her right arm and lands a desperate punch to her captor's nose. She hears a crunch and the woman shrieks, spitting curses in all directions as she clutches her face and loses her grip on Saba just long enough for her to dash to the door. As Saba reaches for the doorknob, she turns to see the woman bent over the carpet, barely able to contain the cascade of blood escaping through her interlaced fingers. The sight makes Saba pause; in any case, the door is locked. Realizing that she is trapped, she feigns bravado. "Do you want more?" she shouts at the bleeding Basij or whatever she is. "I swear if you touch me, I'll have you killed in your sleep."

The second woman, her mother's former thread artist, takes her by the waist and lifts her off the ground. She tosses her onto the bed.

"Just hold her. We'll put your nose right after," she says.

As the thread artist pries open a gray, pyramid-shaped handbag, Saba manages to raise her head just enough to see a sliver of movement beyond the blurry folds of the blanket and discarded chador that are now covering half her face. In the sack, she sees rags. They fly in every direction as the woman rummages through the bag. Saba sees something shiny. It reflects the light from the window, and for a moment it blinds her with its glare. She turns her head and makes one more attempt to break free.

"What do you want?" she shouts. "Do you want to be arrested?"

And then the instrument is above her and Saba can see that it is just the broken head of an ordinary metal fire poker—or at least that's Saba's best guess. The uninjured peasant woman, the one who was once as close as this to her mother, pushes Saba's skirt over her knees and makes a crude joke. Something about needing her threading services. She takes the fire poker and, her breath reeking of stale milk and garlic, her body lumbering and strange, holds it with the casual precision of a doctor.

Saba tries again to dissuade them. "You're both going to jail if you touch me."

They ignore her. *"Yala. Yala."* The injured one tells the other to hurry. She is bleeding all over Saba's bed. Her companion obeys, reaches beneath Saba's skirt as the bleeding woman on top of her tears her legs apart, and then Saba understands.

"Please," she begs, blurting out whatever comes to her mind through mucus and tears. "Are you Basij? You can still go to jail. My father . . . he's . . . Do you need money? I have money." They seem determined not to hear her so she closes her eyes and turns her head, thinking that at least she isn't being murdered, a fear that had briefly entered her mind. She says a prayer, hoping for some miracle, and when she knows it won't come, she prays that the fire iron has been cleaned.

Then the sharp head of the crude instrument is in. She feels its hard, metal point prick a little at first, then with an excruciating twist as it makes its way all the way inside. She screams. She dreams up images of how she will make these women suffer later when her father knows what has been done.

She tries to leave this place, to shut off her mind and conjure a low, crooning voice from America that once reminded her of tea and cardamom. She imagines herself far away from here, somewhere inside the song.

By the sea. In a place called Georgia.

Sitting on the dock of the bay.

She is humiliated by the hot stream of angry tears falling down her cheeks. The injured woman puts her hand on Saba's forehead as if to reassure her. She wipes the sweat from Saba's brow and shushes her with singsong humming. Saba wants so much to hurt this woman who seems to believe she knows her best interest—or why soothe her as a nurse soothes a child afraid of a needle?

How funny that Abbas hired a former *dallak* for this, a purveyor of feminine allure, an artist suddenly turned against beauty. It's probably all the same to Abbas, this particular line of work. Who else does every wife call when she needs to tend to some dark female nuisance? This is just another distasteful, lavatorial task, like scrubbing off old skin in a hammam. She pushes the woman's hand away. "Don't touch me, you dirty *dehati*. Wait till I tell my father."

The woman snickers. "You're so smart. . . . What will your father do? Tell the judge your husband is no man and have you disinherited?" She turns to her partner. "Is it done? Check and let's go." Through the space between her legs, Saba sees the uninjured woman's head disappear behind her trembling knees. A funny smell rises from the sheets and mixes with the sour stench of the peasant woman's breath and clotting nasal blood. Saba feels something warm and sticky as she forces her thighs together. A pair of cold hands releases her knees, and they snap shut, causing her to roll over onto the soaking sheets, dark with her own blood and her captor's, like an abandoned battleground at dusk.

"Yes," says the Basij's muffled voice. "Let's go."

The duo, their faces now fixed in her mind, strip her sheets for payment and rush to the door without another word. She watches them go, a weight in her chest moving painfully when one of them turns back to look at her. She tosses Saba a pitiful glance, her own version of female kinship. Outside they bark something to Abbas before collecting their fee and leaving the house in a dark, looming silence that is to be Saba's home for . . . how long? Maybe forever. Maybe a hundred black years.

For days Saba lies in her bed, alternately weeping and feeling like a fool for her tears. Is she no longer a virgin? Was this her very own twisted wedding night? Should she remember it always? *The bargains of women.* Abbas is right. She was a fool to try to bargain with him. She was a fool to ignore his fears and focus only on her own, to think she could marry and abandon him for an easy visa. What an idiotic plan. She was stupid enough to deserve this. And now she is here and married—for how long? She remembers the day she comforted Ponneh after the encounter with Mustafa. If only Mahtab were here to comfort her. She laughs at herself for judging Dr. Zohreh and her friends, thinking that they were yelling out into a faceless void in the West, while she was in complete control. She curses the vanity of her so-called logic. Now she reconsiders telling her father, because what is there to say? The peasant woman was right. He cannot seek justice without endangering her fortune. Beyond that, as a Christian convert he has to be discreet. Inviting legal battles or drawing the attention of the Basij would put them both at risk. The law frightens Saba. What if she told her father anyway, even though he can't act on it?

The information would make him suffer and he would behave even more strangely toward her. No, she decides, telling him would be a mistake.

She replays the event in her mind over and over, but is unable to pinpoint what has happened to her. Was it a crime? Does such a crime exist between husband and wife? Would it be wise to try for justice on her own? Ponneh never got any. What about leaving Abbas, moving to Tehran, and staying with a relative? Right away she rejects the idea. Things have changed. The worst has happened. It is no longer enough to slink off to America, become a taxi-driving, factory-working immigrant like the kind her cousins have described in letters. She wants much more for her sacrifice. *I'm not leaving without the money.* This isn't, after all, her father's vulnerable wealth that might be taken away by a whim of the government, but safe Muslim Widow Money that she has earned. One day she will flee Iran, find her mother, but she will take no steps that will leave her disinherited. Now is the time to be strong and rational. She forbids herself to betray Abbas's secret out of revenge or anger. Unlike Mahtab, she cannot say no and walk away without loss. She will *maast-mali* the matter and collect her Yogurt Money, like the coins Khanom Omidi squirrels away from her yogurt sales. This kind of reward is her only consolation now that she is a wounded thing. It is her only means of freedom.

"Bésame Mucho"
(Khanom Basir)

Lately I have been thinking about good-byes. In the year after the loss of Mahtab and her mother, Saba began to rebel in school and so her father sent her less and less, calling more often on tutors, men and women from Rasht who had once lived in America. They didn't just teach her from books, but also explained all the slang from her TV programs and how to have a fast ear in English. Sometimes she would go to school when there was a test, and even then she caused trouble—wearing a brown *maghnaeh* (the ugly triangle-shaped school scarf) instead of a gray one as required, or wearing it backward, leaving the neck and ears exposed, or drawing fake tattoos with red marker on her own skin. She would come home and hide the angry letters from teachers. I told her, It's no use riding a camel bent over. That is to say, if it's obvious what you're doing, don't make a pathetic effort to hide it.

She was so lost then. One day, from the Hafezis' kitchen, I over-heard Saba crying in the sitting room because of some small thing, a program that no longer aired because of the new government. She grumbled and chewed her nails over it, adding so much meaning. What was left for her now? So many of her favorite things slipping away with each passing day. As I peered around the corner, I could see on her blotchy face that she was thinking of Mahtab, all the dreams they had together. Look at them now, the Hafezi twins. What has become of them and their grand future . . . their mother's plans?

When her father got home, Saba had fallen asleep on a cushion in the corner of the room, tears dried to her face. He looked bewildered. He took off his jacket and put on a very famous song by Vigen. I can see that to this day, Saba has a special love for Vigen, this handsome Christian artist who brought western guitar music to Iran and whose first song was called "Mahtab." The song Agha Hafezi played that day was "Mara Beboos," or "Give Me a Kiss." If you ask anyone around here what the two most beloved Iranian songs are, they will name that one, along with "Sultan of Hearts." There's a story that says the words of "Mara Beboos" were written by one of the Shah's prisoners as a father's good-bye to his daughter just before he was executed.

Kiss me for the last time, the doomed man says, *may God keep you for all time.*

Saba told me once, when she was a few years older, that this is just another pretty Iranian lie, because the song is exactly like a Spanish tune with the same name.

Some time later Saba began to wake. She must have heard her father singing this haunting, wistful melody over and over to himself. He was sitting on the cushions around the living room floor, staring at nothing, thinking. I peeked in every now and then—there was no bottle or hookah around, but he was in another world. Then Saba crawled over to him and he pulled her onto his lap. He sang the words in her ear, and they sat together for a long time, her head on his chest, humming a father-daughter song.

My spring has passed. All pasts have passed. Now I will go toward the fates.

Afterward her father told her the story behind the song. "This is how all fathers feel about their daughters, and only their daughters. It is the same across time and the universe, and no mothers or sons or cousins or any other pair can replicate the hopes that lie beneath it."

Isn't it funny how some memories are lost until one day they decide on their own to come back? I remember now that it was on that day that I first heard Saba tell a story about Mahtab—just a few words that made Agha Hafezi chuckle, about Mahtab's plane ride to America. She did it for her father, to give his lost other daughter back to him.

"I'm taking you out of that school," he said. "It's a waste, all the Arabic lessons; better to focus on making you fluent in English. I'll take you to say good-bye tomorrow."

Good-byes are such luxuries. Some people pine for them for entire lifetimes.

Chapter Ten

AUTUMN 1990

S aba bleeds more often than once a month now. She has back pain, sometimes a small aching in her stomach. It is a punishment, she tells herself. After the two women left, Saba bled for two days. She didn't tell anyone because, after all, there was a secret to keep. Besides, didn't Khanom Omidi once tell her that women bleed their first time? Her cycles were erratic after that. Each month they lasted twice as long as before, and she often found dark red patches on her underwear and bedsheets in between cycles. She didn't tell anyone. Maybe the bleeding was God's judgment for failing to guard herself in this frightening new Iran and for believing she had so much figured out. When she and Mahtab were children, their mother used to say that God always punishes the proud because "pride can ruin you, and Saba jan, your brain is your greatest vanity."

"Isn't that Mahtab's vanity too?" Saba would ask.

Her mother would shake her raven head with its five gray hairs and whisper that Mahtab's vanity was worse because she didn't stop at trusting her own mind but believed herself capable of manipulating the world. "But you focus on the plank in your own eye," she would advise Saba, referring to some Bible verse. "And I'll deal with your sister."

Now, when preoccupied with the practicality of her own choices, Saba remembers that there is always someone savvier, always someone with a better plan. And what can a girl do when she has been outwitted? Her only weapon against Abbas is his loneliness, which she takes cruel pleasure in amplifying—denying him entry into her room, accepting social invitations without him, making dinners for one. What can he do to stop her? Her inheritance is protected by an airtight contract. And he knows that if he was to harm her physically in a way that she could show to the world, she certainly would.

Day after day he silently begs for understanding. He tiptoes around the house, looking for her here and there, leaving her small presents of fresh unskinned almonds and peaches. Sometimes he wastes an entire bag of apricots, cracking open the pits one by one because he knows she likes the juicy nut at the core. But his sins are too unforgivable for Saba. Let him die of loneliness. Let his last nights be empty and cold and let him wither, knowing he will never again be comforted by the touch of another human.

She retreats into lonely corners of her home, gobbles up Western media like a starving beast. The Tehrani, her constant friend though they barely speak, brings her his most popular items—the things he trades from house to house with the highest turnover—everything from Michael Jackson videos to Indian films to exercise tapes, but Saba only craves more American movies. After *Love Story* opened her eyes to the magic of Harvard, she promised the Tehrani twice his usual price if he would bring her more movies and television shows set there. His first attempt was a disaster. A hodgepodge of garbage set in Hartford, a few episodes of *Cheers*, and a movie called *The Paper Chase* that wasn't actually filmed there. Though there is a fascinating moment at the end when the main character, a the law student, a makes a paper airplane out of his report card and tosses it into the ocean. What a thing! He doesn't even look at it. There are many papers—marriage contracts and Iranian passports and letters to Evin Prison—that she wishes she could release into the sea, where Mahtab could catch them and sort through them for her.

Now she is watching the Tehrani's latest acquisition, an independent college film that she likes despite its poor quality. It depicts the right sort of place for her sister. She memorizes the names of the streets and buildings in the film. She watches the way women speak, the way men move, the shocking way one of them spies on his beautiful friend as she undresses. What a bizarre and wonderful world.

Soon Khanom Omidi comes in and sits beside her. She rests her head on the old woman's lap. As she rocks and hums and strokes Saba's hair, her folksy tunes mingle with the sophisticated English words emanating from the television, creating what Saba imagines is the music of her sister's immigrant world. To her own disgust, she begins to cry again. Lately the weeping has become impossible to control like a tic.

"What's the matter? Oh no, Saba jan," Khanom Omidi coos, "don't be sad, child. You can be happy if you try."

On the screen, students wear jeans and sweatshirts in a lecture hall. They go to a party in their pajamas. They linger around dining tables with red wine and thesis pages.

Saba doesn't respond. She sobs into her surrogate mother's ample skirt and wishes for her sister. Khanom Omidi seems to have a vague idea that something has happened to Saba. She hums her song, takes Saba's face in both hands, and tilts it toward her. "I know you've been hurt," she says, her tone full of quiet gravity. "But marriage is an uncut watermelon. You can't see inside before you decide."

Saba lets out a snort. "That saying is for naïve girls. It doesn't cover *everything.*"

"Maybe not," Khanom Omidi says, and goes back to her rocking and humming. "Saba jan, just tell me what happened." After a long silence, she whispers, almost to herself, "The good thing about old people is that they die. Soon we all die."

Saba hugs Khanom Omidi's waist with both arms. She can see that the old woman feels guilty about encouraging the marriage. "You can never die. I won't let you."

Khanom Omidi makes a clucking sound with her tongue and pinches Saba's chin. Saba thinks about dying, and blood, and how, according to her mother's theories on destiny and DNA, everything would have been the same even if she had moved to America. All fate is written in the blood. So what is Mahtab, her perfect blood match, doing now? Lately Saba has been practicing her English word lists again, in case her mother wants to hear them one day. "I miss Khanom Mansoori," she muses. "She used to ask for stories of Mahtab in America."

"That sounds like her." Khanom Omidi brushes some hairs out of Saba's face. "You can tell *me* one if you want."

"Maybe I'm too old now to play games like that," Saba says.

"Never too old. When a person is too old for stories, he might as well be buried. Storytelling is how we get back the people who are far away from us." Khanom Omidi hoists herself up from the small carpet she likes best and brings Saba a small glass of clear liquid from the pantry. "Drink this," she says. "We won't tell anyone."

Saba situates her head in the space between Khanom Omidi's thick arm and her soft, comforting lap, and looks up. She can see the old woman's crossed eyes and feels an even deeper affection for her. "Okay, Khanom Omidi," she says. "I'll tell you the story of my marriage . . . but in my own way. Since it's a secret, you'll have to settle for Mahtab's version. She's my twin and her fate always follows mine in some way. I think you especially will like this one because it's about *maast-mali* and something else you know better than anyone . . . getting and keeping Yogurt Money from cruel men."

Every story must have a resolution and, as on a television series, every resolution must fit a theme—Immigrant Worries are the signposts of Mahtab's life. This story is about money. You can imagine it, can't you? You don't have to travel to faraway places to know that immigrants worry about money because their own wealth is lost in another land. This story is also about a dilemma. Should she take it, she wonders, this money that belongs to a rich Persian man with a bruised ego and a fear for his reputation?

In her third year of college, Mahtab begins to wonder what she should do with her life. She wants to be a journalist, a storyteller for a big respected magazine—it is what we both wanted as children. So she travels to Boston and New York for interviews, wearing black pantsuits with multicolored shirts and playful sheaths peeking out from under stern woolen collars. She gets French manicures, highlights her hair, and waits for someone to offer her a place in the world. In the lobbies of publishing giants, she sits across from similarly dressed twentysomething men and women all in black. Crows in a line.

Since James, she hasn't had time for men or relationships. She spends her nights reading her books and selling tickets at a local theater for extra money.

It's lunchtime. Mahtab and Clara, of the broken-high-heel day, eat salads on the lawn outside Harvard's famous Widener Library—wait, is there a lawn outside Widener Library? Yes, I'm certain there is. Mahtab lies on the grass, her hands behind her head. She adjusts her sunglasses on her nose and picks at her food. She doesn't notice the dark, smiling boy with the inquisitive expression standing over her. He's young, no older than Mahtab, possibly in his last year, poorly shaven, tall, and dressed in expensive jeans. "Are you Iranian?" he asks. "I have good radar, but I wasn't sure about you."

"It's because I had my nose done," Mahtab says in a matter-of-fact, almost bored way. His beauty doesn't faze her in the least. She is accustomed to exquisite men.

"That's usually the first sign," he says. His adolescent smile makes her laugh.

His name is Cameron. He pronounces it the Western way, not like the Persian Kamran. Cameron Aryanpur. *Aryan Poor.* She likes his name.

"So, *May.*" Cameron says her name with skepticism, like a placeholder, like a *We'll see.* "Do you have time to go out with a poor Aryan?"

"How poor?" she says, and accepts before he can answer.

Cameron is the first Persian man Mahtab has ever dated, or even considered dating. In many ways, their lives have paralleled, though Cameron's family left Iran long before the revolution, ensuring the safety of their fortune in European currencies and American real estate. As the school year rolls along, Mahtab finds herself always near him. They spend evenings in his dorm room, watching movies, talking in Farsi, reheating classic dishes that his mother has brought from Westchester. Tomato and eggplant with lamb. Fenugreek, parsley, and coriander with lamb. Split peas and potatoes with lamb.

They talk about food, music, books—all they have retained of their culture. They flirt in English and Farsi, a miraculous middle language that is oddly sensual. They leave notes for each other on their dorm-room message boards in English using Farsi letters, like a grade school secret code. Since no one else can read the notes, they write the most scandalous things. You see, Khanom Omidi, they can do this in plain daylight and no one will stop them. To her delight, Mahtab finds that she is much tawdrier than she ever imagined. She takes hours composing these cheap messages to him. Cameron too seems enraptured by their shared blood, and she wonders if they are acting in some ethnic play. Their private theater continues for a long time. It consumes her like a good movie.

They sit together in lecture halls, wearing jeans and sweatshirts. They go to a party in their pajamas. They linger around dining tables with red wine and thesis pages.

Sometimes he tries lines on her, calling her his favorite Persian dish or his Shomali Shahzadeh, and she rolls her almond eyes, think, ing he is training to navigate his way around all Persian women. She's never met someone so confident in his own charm, yet so obviously learning. He exudes youth, like Abbas exudes death. But the poor Aryan isn't only a princeling of sorts, a fellow child of Baba Harvard, he is also a poet, afflicted with the same immigrant puzzles that per, plex Mahtab. She tells him she hates her theater job and that she wants to be a journalist. He tells her that he wants to go back to Iran, to become involved in some sort of resistance, to pursue a new regime. He is enamored with the idea of an underground movement—and all things underground: movies, music, books—of rediscovering "our homeland." He uses Farsi words deliberately in his English: *roosari*, not "scarf"; *khiar-shoor*, not "pickles."

"He's like you, Saba jan," says Khanom Omidi, "mixing English into your talk."

Like every American child of foreign parents, Cameron likes to analyze and categorize his people until the riddles feel solved. It makes Mahtab feel a sad empathy.

You may not know this, Khanom Omidi, but like us, American Persians can feel the loss of old Iran, of beautiful Iran, the Iran that was full of romance. Maybe America is empty for them, so they make Iran into a heaven that no longer exists. Like Agha Thomas Wolfe says in a book I just bought from the Tehrani: *You can't go home again* Home is never the same. Mahtab and Cameron know this. Even I, who have never left, know this. I see my home changing.

Every month I read the ghostly misery of those so-lucky immigrants in letters from distant cousins. They are a wandering people, and they gravitate to each other like lost mongrels who know each other's smell.

"Show some respect to the ancestors," Cameron says one day when Mahtab sacrifices rice for fear of an unforgiving dress. "You can't just decide to change a thousand-year-old dish. There should be rules for being a *real* Persian, wherever you live." He smiles at Mahtab with gleaming white teeth set off by shiny-black bohemian hair that clashes with his chic clothes and pretty stubble manicured in a distinctly un-Islamic way.

"Reza has stubble like that. Is that what this Cameron looks like? Like Reza?"

Oh no, no, even Reza doesn't have magazine teeth like these. You get them in America, along with your fancy degree. There are some bridges we can never cross all the way from this village, Khanom Omidi. But Mahtab can. She too has white teeth all in a row, arranged for her by dentists when she was twelve or thirteen. She has that perfect postsurgery nose too. They are such a pair—chosen by nature, like twins.

Her wealthy Iranian is very different from my old decrepit one.

Cameron's comment leads to an analysis of every dish, every custom and ritual. Is this a hard rule? Is that truly Persian or just Arabic? Don't they do this differently in the South? In one night they create a set of commandments scribbled out on the back of an old history exam. They try to write it in Farsi, but neither remembers how to spell the big words and they end up stumbling through at a fourth-grade level before switching to English. They laugh easily at themselves, and neither is particularly embarrassed.

Do you want to hear it, Khanom Omidi? My friend the Tehrani confirmed this for me, and let me tell you, American Iranians have a bizarre sense of what makes them Persian. It makes me wonder if my information about Americans is as cartoonish, because in their quest to find an old, forgotten Iran, they have turned us into soft-bellied muses in garden-side sketches and warriors carved in the ruins of Persepolis. We are no more than smoky figures wafting out of poetry books. The Tehrani tells me that the ones who have been away the longest worship the dirtiest *shalizar* worker like homesick disciples.. Cameron and Mahtab too lose hours scribbling their so-called rules:

To achieve Persian authenticity, you order pickled garlic with dinner. In a Western restaurant, where no garlic sits stewing in brine for ten years, you order yogurt and raw onions, or raw radishes, mint, and basil to eat with your food. You consider an appetizer the product of Western foolishness, because what pansy appetite needs to be coaxed awake? You eat with a spoon, never a fork and knife, because what horrible cook leaves meat so tough that it would require anything but a spoon? You add a raw egg yolk and butter to your rice, skipping this step only for a rich sauce. You never stop at two or three cups of tea, and you eat something made with honey for dessert. You lie back afterward on a mound of pillows—you are inevitably sitting on a hand-crafted rug on the floor—smoke too much, drink more tea.

You never whisper when a scream will do; never reveal truth when a lie will do.

Oh, the miracle of being born below the Caspian. You may be endowed with a shrieking, matricidal, six-horse jinn of a temper. You may be granted the most unfortunate crow's beak of a nose. And, unless you're a dehati *with no roots, or a half-breed, you almost certainly have a history of poetic lunacy in the family. But it's all worth the ability to metabolize a small deer overnight.*

"Oh, Saba jan, that is so true! Even worse than that, if you ask me."
They laugh loudly and spill their drinks as Cameron, in his politi-cian's voice, proclaims their work finished and Mahtab cheers and

decides to be in love. What a strange world. My Mahtab, so many scoops of a teaspoon away, still manages to fall in love with a Persian man. Should I warn her? If I only knew how to reach her.

In this blissful time before he is tested, Cameron seems beautiful to her.

Before Abbas became a monster, he too seemed fragile and gentle, and I loved him in a different way. He was a sort of father to me, when my own was unavailable. But Mahtab doesn't need a father now. She has Baba Harvard. And so, before his transformation into Abbas, Cameron is his own unique self, his natural self, a wandering, displaced male Mahtab. An exile and a perfect fit.

She doesn't know that her ideal Iranian other self—though he stands just there, brushing his teeth while she watches him in the bathroom mirror—doesn't exist.

She wants to touch him, to hold him, to throw away her reservations and crawl into his clothes with him. Why does he not want that too? Sometimes when he's asleep on his back with all his limbs spread out, she lies on top of him in the exact same formation, so that every centimeter of her is touching him, from the tips of her toes on his ankles to the top of her head just below his chin, with every finger perfectly aligned to his. She listens to his slow heartbeat and wishes they could freeze in this pose, like two halves of a starfish.

Though they've lost count now of all the nights they've spent together like this, Mahtab senses something off in the way Cameron holds her hand. The way he kisses her. The way he gets up just before the end of every movie and cuts off their numerous but short-lived tangles on the couch. He is traditional, she thinks. His reaction to her causes a deep lingering frustration in her belly, in her limbs as they hover over him. Has Mahtab slept with a man before? This I don't know. Do American girls sleep with men before they are engaged? On television they do, but maybe Mahtab would not. She doesn't have to. One day she will marry the man of her choice, and she will have it all.

Once she kisses his stomach and he pulls away. He holds her hands behind her and jokes, "I thought this was an Islamic relationship." She laughs and decides he is shy.

Sometimes at the theater she reads Forough Farrokhzad. *O stars, what happened that he did not want me?* Then, like a good Persian, she lies to herself.

She makes the mistake of telling her mother about Cameron. Maman immediately becomes nervous. "Don't get involved with an Iranian man, Mahtab jan." She doesn't say why and Mahtab doesn't ask, because her mother too has her private fears.

Two months into their romance, they arrange to drive down to New York for dinner at the Aryanpur home. As the day draws closer, Cameron grows agitated. "They're very traditional Very faithful Muslims," he says. "Please watch what you say. Don't talk about Iran or politics, and don't mention you're a Christian." He plays with his cuticles. "There's one more thing." He looks past her. Seeing him so nervous makes Mahtab curious. "My mother," he mutters. "She wears *hijab.*"

Mahtab laughs, relieved. "That's okay. I've seen *hijab* before. I did *live* in Iran."

"No, just listen," he says, taking her hand in both of his. "I would be forever grateful if you would please consider wearing a headscarf to dinner."

Mahtab can feel the blood draining from her face. She opens her mouth, but nothing comes out. He says "Please" one more time, and her speech returns, galloping with the fury of a herd of wild horses. "No way in hell. Don't ask me again."

Mahtab leaves Cameron's dorm room in such a frenzy that she expects never to see him again. She slams every door between his

room and hers, raging from hallway to street and back to her room.
The following days are marked by confusion, a constant obsession
with Cameron's words and intentions. He must not know her at all,
after so many nights together. Because there is one thing that's certain in Mahtab's world, and that is the unchangeable fact that she
will never, *never* wear *hijab*. Why then is she standing now in front of
a store called Hermès—or is it House of Hermès? I don't know which
name is on the door—examining that expensive blue-and-violet-
checkered scarf in the window? Why is she considering it with such
care, such mixed feelings, as if staring at evidence of a lifetime of her
own crimes? Why does she, on a Friday morning before class, arrive
unannounced at Cameron's door, holding the orange Hermès box—
like the ones you see vacationers from Tehran carrying around their
seaside villas to show off their foreign shopping—and a filled-up
credit card, her head wrapped fashionably (only halfway) in a perfect
imitation of Jackie Kennedy, complete with oversized glasses?

"The way the chic-chic Tehrani girls wear it," says Khanom Omidi,
"very nice."

As she stands waiting, the Mahtab who never sacrifices her
dignity struggles to break free, to force her feet to run away. In a
deeper corner of her stomach, a wild being, a selfish thing that doesn't
bother with principles, battling instead to satisfy her every hunger,
pins her feet to the ground. Reminds her that it's only a piece of cloth.
Makes her aware of a frantic physical longing for Cameron.

When Cameron answers the door, she says, "This is the best
I can do."

He takes her in his arms, kisses her cheek. "I knew you wouldn't
let me down."

"How could I say no?" she says, pushing past him as she presses
the orange box, empty except for a receipt, into his chest. "Look at
the pretty scarf you bought me."

Before you ask, let me explain that in America people don't buy things with cash. They have cards that record every purchase, and later they pay for everything all at once. So Mahtab hasn't actually paid yet, and Cameron reimburses her discreetly by slipping cash into her purse. It is all very subtle, very well whitewashed. This way no one can ask what he has just bought.

"*This is strange business. Where does the money go, you say?*"

I will explain later. But for now, they set off to New York.

And yes, Khanom Omidi, I know the blue-and-violet scarf sounds exactly like Khanom Basir's. That's because it too is a guilty scarf—one she doesn't deserve.

As Mahtab expects, the Aryanpurs are wealthy and gaudy in the way only American Iranians know how to be—the way Baba's cousins were when they spent a summer in Shomal. They greet her effusively, praising her fine balance of piety and fashion sense. They kiss their son on both cheeks and Mr. Aryanpur frowns at Cameron's shirt. "Button up," he grumbles, eyeing his son's hairless chest. "Shameful habit." Mahtab likes Cameron's metropolitan grooming rituals. She finds hairiness the first sign of "too much Iran," remembering her own struggle to get her mother to allow shaving. After much research, Khanom Omidi, I believe that Iranians have a relationship with body hair that is unique and, to be honest, doesn't make much sense. What is all the fuss, really?

The Aryanpur home is simultaneously solemn and garish. On the walls hang several round panels of Islamic calligraphy, written in beautiful Nastaleeq script, next to depictions of scenes from Nezami and Ferdowsi. On the shelves, volumes of the Koran are respectfully kept away from other books. The family's wealth is dripping from every corner. In the dining room, a thick tablecloth of maroon and gold covers a cherry table large enough to seat twelve. Far too many things are made of solid gold.

"Your given name is Mahtab, yes?" Mrs. Aryanpur asks. Cameron's mother is a living embodiment of her surroundings. Though covered from head to toe, she wears a thick layer of makeup and long red nails. Though she avoids the fashionable style of leaving several centimeters of hair uncovered, a stray strand tells Mahtab that, yes, her hair is that distinct Los Angeles orange—like the showy California Persians you see in photos.

"Yes. But I use May now, to simplify things," says Mahtab.

Mr. Aryanpur releases a deep sigh that seems to have been waiting inside. "That's too bad. You shouldn't abandon your Persian name. It means 'moonlight,' you know."

"Yes, I know." She notices that Mr. Aryanpur too is no stranger to boxed dye. His impossibly black mustache is a stark contrast to his salt-and-pepper hair.

"Very nice," he mutters, and meanders away from the door.

There is something familiar as they sit down to dinner—a sort of awkwardness to the pace and flow of the evening. I have seen it myself in the home videos that arrive from Baba's cousins in California—these meals are a bizarre, otherworldly hybrid of ours and the ones you see on American television. The Aryanpurs, like Maman and every other immigrant family in this world, are in limbo, caught between two vastly different sets of rituals. Not knowing whether to start at six o'clock or ten, they nibble on nuts and dried fruits until they are almost full and they start dinner at nine. Unsure whether to respect the Iranian custom of bringing all the food to the table at once or the American one of eating in courses, they serve green salads as an appetizer, hurrying through them like a chore—a mandatory homage to their new country—before parading the meat courses, each cooked in a combination of at least five spices. The conversation is always easy, though. They begin with poetry and literature, they recite and counter and correct, reminiscing about Isfahan, Persepolis, and the Caspian, and then, hours later, move on to the most basic inquiries about each other. They are much like the families who come for one season to the villas by the sea, peers of my own parents in education and interests. Though in America, they are free to indulge in whatever pastimes and conversations they wish.

From then on, the Aryanpurs spend most of the evening gathering information about Mahtab's parents, background, and education.

"So you're in your third year at Harvard," Mr. Aryanpur says, while struggling to adapt to the American place setting. He is becoming visibly angry as the grains of buttery basmati rice flutter through the fork and land back on his plate. When he thinks Mahtab is not looking, he reaches for his dessert spoon. The sight of him piling grains onto this minuscule spoon, hands shaking all the way to his mouth, reminds Mahtab of her own father—though she's not sure why. She thinks of José from the diner and considers that maybe this man reminds her of all fathers. There is a pain there, in the empty space where Mahtab stores fatherly longings. She wants to reach out and touch Mr. Aryanpur's hand, to refill his tea and show that she is no trouble at all, to count all the ways Cameron looks like him. She has the feeling that he spends much of the day in the house, probably because he has no fields to watch over. "We keep telling Cameron to marry a smart girl," Mr. Aryanpur says in his low, dull voice.

"Baba!" Cameron snaps.

"Well, it's true, isn't it?" Cameron's father looks shocked. "Why should you be embarrassed by the truth of marriage? Why should you waste your life?" Mr. Aryanpur continues as if Cameron had not interrupted at all. "But it isn't Cameron's fault. We discouraged dating until he was settled in college."

And then, as if only just now reminded of it, Mrs. Aryanpur says, "Our son is top of his class, you know? Did you know that?" She looks eagerly at Mahtab.

"Yes, I did." She laughs, and turns to Cameron's father, who has begun speaking again.

"I think you would make a very nice candidate. What do your parents do?"

Just as Cameron is about to object, his father turns to him and snaps so loudly that Mahtab almost jumps. "I've told you not to sit like that." Immediately Cameron uncrosses his legs and turns a deep shade of red. Whatever reaction he would have shown to his father's marriage comment is gone now, and Mahtab wishes she knew what it would have been. Cameron avoids his father's gaze, smiles lovingly at his mother, who takes his hand. Mr. Aryanpur continues on about Iran and education and the significance of each of their wall hang-ings. He seems older, more set in his ways, than his wife. She drinks her tea from a cup, whereas he pours his into the saucer to cool, holds a sugar cube in his teeth, then brings the saucer to his lips with both hands—the way we were served tea as children so we wouldn't burn our mouths.

Mahtab likes this man. By the end of the evening, she comes to believe that she might soon join the array of beautiful fixtures in the Aryanpurs' life.

Cameron spends the drive to campus thanking Mahtab and apol-ogizing for his parents. Even after Mahtab tells him what a wonderful time she had, he continues to act tense, restless. She makes nothing of it, assuming that he will be himself by the morning.

She tries to call the next day, but he doesn't answer the phone. Days pass with no sign of him. When they run into each other one afternoon, he says that he is busy with his research on Iran and that his adviser is going to help with his grand plans to return.

"You aren't tired of me now that you've appeased the parents?" she jokes.

He laughs and says that he could never be. But is he telling the truth, this young, elegant Persian? Has he tired of her?

Over the next week Mahtab busies herself with work. She's always short on money and she spends her evenings selling tickets at the theater. She has a vague, nagging feeling about Cameron, a low-grade nuisance like a blister or an insect, but she is too busy to act on it—until one night when work ends early and she decides to visit him.

She sails past the library and the campus center. In a small shop window, she reapplies her makeup before entering his dorm. She finds Cameron's door unlocked and slides in, calling his name as she flings her purse on the couch. There is a noise in the bathroom. She rushes toward the bedroom, sloughing off her coat and thinking of dinner. Cameron is there—a flash of skin as he pulls on a sweater, a sad expression on his face.

Next to him on his rumpled blue bedsheets sits a waifish beauty, blond, barely eighteen, fidgeting like a child. But he isn't a child. He is a man, half dressed, and clearly too young and confused to have ever encountered this complication.

Despite the lack of understanding in Mahtab's smile, Cameron is far too smart to attempt to hide his indiscretions, and so he has already begun scrambling to contain the damage. Oh, the damage. He runs his hand through his hair. How many problems might this create? Surely he will lose his girlfriend. But what more? Remember, Khanom Omidi, that the poor Aryan wants to work in Iran. Oh, what bad business this is.

"Poor boy," says Khanom Omidi. "Mahtab will move on. But he will have such troubles."

Well, maybe he is only experimenting, like Ponneh does with her friend Farnaz—don't look shocked; I know she told you—or maybe this is his truth and he will grow up suffering for it. Mahtab stands there, still unsure, watching Cameron with tired, black-lined eyes now wide with disbelief. Is the stranger a student? A delivery boy? Gradually the details make themselves visible to her and overtake the bigger picture. The red-faced boy squirming on the bed. A button on his jeans missed in haste. The musky odor hanging low overhead. Clothes tossed in every direction. Condoms on the dresser.

When the truth reflects back at him through Mahtab's eyes, Cameron doesn't apologize. He pulls her into the living room and shuts the door. In a too-calm voice he tells his girlfriend that their wishful romance is over.

"I don't understand," she says. "You like men now?"

"Not *now* . . ." He looks offended and drops his eyes. "I *have* been . . . I *am* . . . yes."

"But we were . . ." Mahtab wants to mention the late nights on his couch but, in the face of the guilty scene now embedded in her memory, her own romps with him seem laughable and innocent—a few kisses here and there, a wandering hand that knows just where *not* to go. And so she grasps at something else. Something that triggers a new, more intense hatred of him. "You made me meet your parents. You made me wear *hijab!*" Suddenly his crime is magnified a hundredfold.

"Come on, was that such a big deal?" he says. "You got a nice present out of it."

Somewhere inside a banshee wakes, eyes his limbs, and tries to choose which to tear off first.

"You're such a . . .!" Now I can't complete her sentence for ignorance of the best English curses, but you can imagine. She ranks and burns, furious at that guilty piece of silk.

He starts to beg, apologizes, calls her his best friend. "Please understand," he says. "I *do* love you, but I had so much pressure. You met my father. I *can't* tell them . . ."

The banshee looks for some turmeric in which to marinate his pieces when this is over.

"Why not?" demands Mahtab. In a flash of calm she remembers details from the dinner and adds, "You *do* realize that your father already suspects?"

"He doesn't!" Cameron runs his hand through his hair again, his eyes fixed on her forehead. "And I want to work in Iran, remember? Mahtab, they *hang* people for this."

"*Yes, they do.*" *Khanom Omidi shakes her head.* "*Our best days are gone.*"

But Mahtab doesn't notice the fear in his voice. She doesn't stop to admire him for wanting to go to their shared homeland despite the dangers. She only hears the angry screams emanating from deep within herself. She curses him again and storms out.

Cameron follows. "Mahtab, you cannot tell anyone about this," he says, and grabs her arm. "You have to keep it a secret." Her chest throbs at this one final touch.

"Why should I do that?"

"Because! Nobody can know. I can't have them thinking I'm . . . *like that.*"

Mahtab laughs. "Are you stupid or looking for drama? You're not going to get hanged. Plenty of people are gay in Iran. Gay is fine. Just be sure to find a wife first." Then, remembering that this is exactly what he was doing with *her*, she tries to pull away toward the landing at the top of the stairs.

Because, Khanom Omidi, this is exactly what all Persian men do when they fear their manhood might be in question. They find a wife. They protect their secret. They rub out the evidence. This is the part where my heart aches most for my sister. We fall into all the same traps. And like me, Mahtab makes the mistake of goading the beast. Through the fog of humiliation, shock, and an ocean of hurt, a mocking smile creeps onto Mahtab's lips and she taunts him, though she wants to drop into his arms and cry and cry and see if he will be revolted. "I wonder if there's a number for the moral police in Tehran."

Maybe he wants to hurt her now. Maybe he wants to hire a former *dallak* to prove his manhood for him. But this is America, and in America men can't get away with such violent ways. There money is the only weapon worth having, and desiring this or that kind or person isn't such a frightening thing.

When Cameron doesn't respond, she shouts, "Let go of me," and frees herself from his grasp. She doesn't cry—not till later. She just walks away marveling at the never-ending ego of Persian men . . . or maybe all men. Because right now more than anything else, Cameron is worried for his reputation, afraid that she will broadcast his secrets into an echoing, cavernous hammam of angry women, assembled there to confirm his repeated failure to consummate the affair. And the reason? Because he's . . . *like that.*

And now we come to the moment when Cameron, the poor Aryan, solves Mahtab's next Immigrant Worry and joins all the other thirty-minute anecdotes that make up her perfect TV life. The following week Mahtab avoids Cameron's calls, though he phones several times a day. He isn't trying to rekindle their relationship, or even their friendship. He is calling to beg for her silence. Yes, Mahtab plans to keep quiet, but does she tell him so? She would never consider giving him such satisfaction. Until one day she gets home from work and finds a message on her answering machine.

"Mahtab, it's me. Look, I know you don't want to talk. But I can't go to Iran without being sure. I thought of something that'll free you from doing me any favors. You said you hate your job, right? Well, what about this? You quit and I'll share my credit card." Listen, Khanom Omidi, this is a big offer. It means free money. "Check your mailbox. No one will know. You can use it for as long as you do me this one favor, even after we graduate. How's that sound? Call me back."

Mahtab laughs. She erases the message and goes to bed, shaking her head at his arrogance, his lack of remorse. She tries hard to hate him. Why doesn't he say anything about their lost love, about the future she imagined for them? Why doesn't he admit that he loves her back? It's two in the morning and she has to be at the theater at eight to sort receipts, but she can't fall asleep. She spreads herself across the mattress, her limbs reaching out to the edges of the bed like the top half of a starfish, and she tells herself that what Cameron told her is not true—that she can find a way to hold on to him. As she buries her face in her pillow, she thinks that she would never accept such an offer.

It's a funny thing about manly reputation. They are willing to give all their wealth for it. Do you think it's wrong to take it, Khanom Omidi? One day my money will come from this same source. The fates of twins are tied together, after all. At least Mahtab experienced a one-sided love. She was allowed to lie on top of Cameron and listen to his heart, to touch her lips to his and make him laugh, to run her fingers across his very white Harvard teeth. I wonder what it's like to have an afternoon's access to such a man. To want him and be allowed so near. To touch him and find him moved by me. Sometimes I don't care if such a man is my husband or a stranger tied to me only by our shared illegal desires. I hate Abbas for being old, for denying me even the smallest knowledge of such things, the slightest bit of pleasure. The feeling that I might be partly human, even with one half of me missing as it is. Sometimes I hate him more for *that* than for the violent thing he did to me.

Maybe I am an immigrant too, wandering through marriage like Cameron and Mahtab wander through America toward a fantasy that used to exist. I want to be my natural self, whole without Mahtab, and wild with uncovered hair. Maybe I could dance around a bonfire like women used to do during Norooz celebrations before the revolution. Black hair flying. Wives kissing husbands and lovers. Running off to bedrooms to do who knows what. Then I wouldn't want Reza to be like James or Abbas to be like Cameron. I wouldn't long to be in Mahtab's place. I would only want to be my most ordinary self, without books or refinement—just a wild, hungry thing running barefoot somewhere.

The world has changed, Khanom Omidi, and now we are *all* impotent.

"Oh, what strange times you children have to face." Khanom Omidi sighs. "We all wish for the old days, Saba jan, but we have to settle for the small joys. . . . Maybe we should eat something, have some tea. Then you must tell me what that man did to you."

Yes, maybe later . . . But now it's my sister's turn. The next day Mahtab finds the credit card in her mailbox. It even has her name on it. She puts it in a separate corner of her purse, away from her own money. She doesn't call Cameron or tell her friends or mother. She's too busy to correct his mistakes. She will handle it in the morning. But the next day her boss needs Mahtab to work more shifts and she has no time to send back the credit card. Besides, a part of her likes this connection to Cameron. He may be gone, but he is still tied to her by this tiny piece of plastic. This is something of his that she can hold on to—like a T-shirt or a book left in her room. This means that he's thinking about her. She ignores it, telling herself that doing so isn't a concession. Besides, in a month he will have forgotten that she even has this doorway to his family's wealth.

One afternoon, hands shaking, she uses the card to buy herself a cup of coffee. To see what will happen. To see if this is real or just another game. The payment goes through without a problem and the card falls heavy in her hand. She has accepted the unearned money and rubbed a thick coat of yogurt over it so no one can see. Two days later she tests the card again. She buys a book, which she returns twenty minutes later. The music of the credit-card machine confirms that someone has accepted her tacit consent.

"How, though, Saba? What machine?"

A week later, when confronted with a sleepless weekend, two deadlines, and an exam, Mahtab quits her job at the ticket office.

Does Mahtab feel guilty? Does anyone know what she has done? Does she soak her pillow at night, and blame that guilty piece of Hermès silk for her poor homeward-bound Aryan with his big dreams and hidden fears?

"So she accepts the money, then?" Khanom Omidi says. "Maybe it's wise."

It seems that she does. But credit cards are nothing more than plastic until you use them. That is how they work, each purchase a new bargain. And, as you say, love is an uncut watermelon. You might slice it open and find you've bought the wrong fruit.

And by the way, Khanom Omidi, even though you're nodding at the wisdom of it all, you should know that in English that's a damn good joke at Cameron's expense.

Even though she isn't sure if she will use the credit card again— Mahtab says good-bye to one of her biggest Immigrant Worries. She has vanquished many others so far: she no longer frets about her otherness. She doesn't worry about success. And now she stops think- ing about money too, not because of the access she has to the poor Aryan's wealth, but because she realizes how easily money can be obtained. Maybe I should learn from my sister. My wiser, stronger, worldlier sister. Maybe I should stop categorizing all the different types of money in the world; stop differentiating between old money, new money, Muslim-Widow Money, and Yogurt Money, judging and separating them into categories when really they are all the same. I've left so much sitting on the table unused. Maybe I should be braver, protect myself against the evils of weak-hearted men. Maybe I should stop waiting for my own inheritance to come through.

A Humble Word
(Khanom Omidi—
The Sweet One)

After Saba's story, I tried to tell her without telling her, because, of course, I cannot encourage bad behavior. But trust me when I say that I know what she is missing. I have been Saba's truest mother for all these years. I have tended to her wounds, whispered a thousand defenses and sympathies into every willing ear, followed behind her as she left a trail of fibs and blunders, and I rubbed a subtle coat of yogurt over it all so that no one would judge her. Who else would do this, especially after we lost Khanom Mansoori? My dear friend . . . God rest her soul, she was right that Saba's stories are good for her. Yesterday when the lady doctor, Zohreh Khanom, called and Saba wasn't home, I praised the girl's imagination and the doctor sounded worried, which is ridiculous.

What did Abbas do to her? I wish I knew. After her story, I began to wonder: is her sadness really about being married to the wrong man or is it something else? It is my personal belief that every woman should have her own private sums, a small bundle she has saved up that is safe from any man and that she can use to take herself out of bad situations. You know, I predict that if one day all the women in Iran woke up and they had their own money, there would be no more marriage. The giving and taking of daughters would come to a quick end. Maybe the whole country would fall. If it *does* fall, I will be safe because I have savings hidden in my chador.

Please do not tell anyone that I am of this opinion, because I will deny it.

I believe that no man will ever be enough for Saba. She lusts for independence and until she has it, there will be no end to the Mahtab stories. But that's not the *only* thing she lusts for, which brings me to the second thing I noticed.

The poor girl is aching to grow up, to become a woman, to experience a real and true awakening, which she obviously does not have with the old corpse she married. Now here is where I must be careful not to encourage bad behavior, but I tried to hint that there are things she should not miss in life. I said to her, "You are a clever girl. You read the old poetry?" She said yes, and so I said, "Rumi is my favorite. The aching and the hunger. There is a line about a thirsty fish inside that can never get enough of what it thirsts for." Saba just stared at me and shrugged. I recited more poems about new passion and human need. Such words! *I reach out*, Rumi says, *wanting you to tear me open.*

Does Saba understand it? I hope one day she will, even if for one night. One hour. Has the girl not suffered enough? Maybe she should have a lover, just to experience this precious part of life. And before you think I have a sinful mind, let me tell you that it is no sin to be human. When I was young, pleasures were plenty and lovers were like balls of opium at the bottom of a spice jar—if you felt around enough, there was always another to be found.

Don't give me rules about keeping chaste. Those rules are made up by someone other than God. Don't give me sentiment about the call of true love and the meeting of souls. Those sentiments are for storytellers. Life is no more than the small joys of many moments added up like coins in a chador. Probably in this world there is no love, only good sense and attraction—the matching of stature and age and smells to make a good fit. In my old eyes, that is what it means to go well together—no more magic to it than two legs, two arms, and, if you're lucky, a young and beautiful face.

Journal Notes
(Dr. Zohreh)

I don't blame Saba's father for asking me to stay away when she was growing up. The dangers to the family were real enough. And I suppose now she has no need of me, though I would love to give her a fuller understanding of her mother to balance out the undoubtedly hostile picture that the village women will have painted.

But I will not push too hard. That would be a mistake, I think.

Next time, if I find an opportunity, perhaps I will tell her that she is very much like her mother. The other day I called Saba and a housekeeper, a woman named Omidi, told me about her current "story‹ telling." Naturally I was worried. I've read the case studies of chil‹ dren who, in order to live with a tragedy or loss, use misinterpreted memories to create permanent other realities for themselves. Interest‹ ingly, the tragedy is often one in which they had a hand—like the subjects of the Milgram experiment who, when told what they had done, convinced themselves that they had argued or fought back when, in fact, they had been compliant. But why would Saba exhibit such symptoms? I wish I could speak to her, or that I had done so as she was growing up.

After the phone call, I recalled that Bahareh used to do some-thing similar. When we were in college, I became involved with a young man who later broke our engagement to study in London— a feeble excuse since I had also won a place in an English university for a term. Bahareh came to my room and sat with me all night inventing stories about his foolish antics there. She made a list. Num-ber one: he will use the wrong fork. Number two: he will try to kiss a man on the cheek. Number three: he will make rubbishy speeches to the queen. She was so amusing. The next day she brought me a wedding cake to throw in the river as a symbol of . . . well, I forget of what.

Chapter Eleven

AUTUMN–WINTER 1990

I n the last two weeks Dr. Zohreh has called twice. She has assured Saba each time, in her husky, chain-smoker's voice, that she is available if Saba should need her. Saba hasn't returned her calls, afraid of what the doctor might have to say about her mother. Her letters to Evin Prison have so far been met with a long silence, and she has been unable to find any new clues. The doctor's message might be a last hope, and she isn't ready for closure. What if the information brings back the old, buried anger against her mother for leaving? What if it confirms that her mother is dead or wasting away in Evin? Still, in an effort to recruit Saba, Dr. Zohreh has sent, via Ponneh, books to read, pictures to examine, stories to consider. Though exhilarated by the attention of her mother's friend, Saba can't imagine throwing herself into such danger and uncertainty. She flips through newspapers from all over the world, the ones that contain pictures taken by the members of Dr. Zohreh's group. These women come from all backgrounds, from cities all around Tehran and Shomal. They are Christian, Baha'i, Zoroastrian. Some are even

Muslim. Dr. Zohreh is Zoroastrian—a worshipper of fire. *My mother is made of fire*, Saba thinks, engrossed by the image of her mother the activist burning through chadors with nothing more than her rage. She wishes she had seen this part of her, the part that wasn't so sensible. Does Saba too have a little of that in her blood?

Abbas knocks on her door to say he's leaving for the day. "Saba? Saba jan? I'm leaving now. Do you want to come out and say goodbye?" She has ignored his every pleading look, all his miserable mumbling and shuffling about the house day and night for months. She says nothing and hopes her silence is painful to his dying ears. When the house is empty, she will do some research about America, maybe about taking a trip there . . . *for later.* She needs to create a tangible next step for herself because that is what a sensible girl would do. Maybe it's time to visit Dr. Zohreh just once, only to retrieve whatever information might exist—to stop being afraid and listen to her mother's distant voice. What could the doctor possibly say that would hurt her now? Maybe she will find an answer, something to cling to while she decides how to live out her life here.

⁞⊙⊙⁞

When she has summoned the courage and made a plan, Saba holds a pencil-drawn map in one hand and the steering wheel of her father's car in another, weaving through snowy streets. Soon the road joins the mountainous highway that so many Iranians take to escape to lush, green woods and dewy seaside villas in summer and to reach the ski slopes in winter. She eyes the map, which instructs her to abandon the Qazvin–Rasht road, itself curvy and dangerous, for a road even more prone to avalanche deaths. She pushes back the chador she wears out of town, rolls down the window, now foggy from her breath, and accelerates over a patch of old snow. Driving to the mountain shack on her own has been easier than she thought. Her father is spending the day walking through his spotty white fields and doing paperwork in the offices of his friend and bookkeeper, and he won't miss the car. So far, the roads have been empty and unmenacing. Saba relaxes, watching the changing landscape—tan and orange dunes and rocks, slightly snow-covered—rolling across the horizon followed by frosty white trees leading up the mountain. When she was a child, Saba used to think that all distances could be measured with a teaspoon. Today she measured the distance using the gas in her father's tank. Maybe after this she can travel even greater distances alone—distances measured by seas and oceans instead of teaspoons and gas tanks. In a few months spring will reach the top of the mountain and Saba is glad she has made this trip to witness the winter season.

She stops the car in a flat area on the side of a hill, just beneath the plateau where Dr. Zohreh promised the shack would be. Getting out of the car, she spots it right away, a small, cubelike wooden house hidden by the colors of the mountain. Unpainted brown logs in a blanket of white and evergreen. This part of the mountain is close to the sea. She can smell it, though the trees block the view. A woman is making tea on the other side of a window. She looks up and waves at Saba before disappearing to open the door.

"Saba jan," she says in her tobacco rasp as she holds the door open and waves her inside. "Welcome. You look so grown up." Dr. Zohreh is tall and slender with a dark face and a black, uncovered bob. She is wearing stylish tan slacks, and her ivory sweater looks like it came from America.

"Thanks," says Saba. "I'm twenty." Then she feels foolish, worries she's made an inane first impression. The air inside is warmed by battery-powered space heaters and kerosene lamps. The house consists of one main room, a tiny kitchen, and an outdoor toilet beyond the back wall. Saba takes a seat at a large table covered with white lace and gives Dr. Zohreh her chador, which the doctor stuffs unceremoniously behind a box—strange, Saba thinks, and grows curious about the contents of the box. Pamphlets? Letters? When the teakettle whistles, the doctor rushes to the kitchen. Saba runs her cold hand through her hair, working her fingers through a tangled strand.

Dr. Zohreh's voice wafts in along with the smell of warm honey pastries. "I'm so happy you came." Already Saba is enthralled by the shack.

"Me too," she says. She stares out the window, relishing the quiet all around. When Dr. Zohreh brings the tea, it almost feels like a luxury, like meeting a new friend in an unfamiliar café for a frivolous hour. No loud mothers gossiping and giving advice. No Ponneh and Reza with their unspoken dialogue seeping through thick clouds of hashish smoke. No history at all, which is the very essence of peace.

"Tell me about your husband," Dr. Zohreh asks in a detached, psychoanalytical tone. She takes a bite of *ghotab* bread and pushes the plate toward Saba. This very un-Iranian gesture—serving herself first—somehow makes Saba trust her more. There is no *tarof* here, and Saba hates pretend generosity, which is a lie, after all. She takes a piece and realizes that it's the same bread that Ponneh has been bringing to the pantry lately.

"He's very old," Saba responds. Then she adds, "I hate him."

Dr. Zohreh stops chewing and narrows her eyes. "Does he hurt you?" she asks, skipping any kind of polite hesitation. "If so, I think you should tell me."

"Why?" Saba tries to fix her face into an ironic smile. But it seems that she succeeds only in looking sad, because Dr. Zohreh reaches over and touches her hand. Right away Saba fears that she has said too much, because it is vital to her future that no one probe into the workings of her marriage. So she says, "He's a coward. He stays out of my way when I want him to." And since the Dallak Day, this has been true.

"Do you know what your mother said to me once . . . after the accident?" Dr. Zohreh offers. "She told me, if anything ever happened to her, to make sure you don't grow up to be too safe and sensible." She shakes her head and sips her tea. "What a funny thing to tell a daughter in this day and age."

Yes, what a funny thing, Saba muses. Certainly her mother would be disappointed to hear of her choices. Marrying an old man for money. Putting aside college to tend to a man who can barely read a word of English. There is a frightening possibility that Saba has made a lifetime of foolish choices. But is Bahareh Hafezi in any position to judge? Whether she left or was arrested for her activities, didn't she abandon Saba one way or another? Didn't she leave her daughter to fend for herself? And this is how Saba has chosen to protect herself—it's the way her surrogate mothers have taught her, and Khanom Hafezi has no right to interject her opinion through this stranger. The mothers who raised her instructed her to follow the old ways, and that is what Saba has done. There was no one around to push her to do otherwise. "That's all she said?" Saba asks. "Tell me more about her. When did you talk to her?"

Now Dr. Zohreh looks surprised. "Talk to her?" she says. "Well, same as anyone else, of course . . . years ago, before she was . . . taken." She examines Saba with her inquisitive doctorly gaze and adds, "I think she means you should have some purpose. Something that's worth being reckless for. She cared so much about your potential."

Saba nods, sips her tea.

"You know," the doctor says as she straightens the tea tray, "our work is your mother's legacy in a way. You should visit one day when we have a meeting—"

Saba cuts her off. "Can you tell me anything about what happened to her?"

When Dr. Zohreh gets up and starts lighting a lamp and two candles, Saba thinks she is just creating work for her hands. Soon the frosty windows shine yellow and Dr. Zohreh sighs, pleased. "Isn't that lovely?" She warms the bread over a hand stove, but Saba is well aware of this trick. Her mother used it to avoid her father's questions in the weeks—or was it months or a different year entirely?—before her disappearance. Saba sits back and refuses to say a word, determined to wait out the game.

Finally Dr. Zohreh breathes out again and says, "If you don't hear from someone after they're taken to Evin Prison . . . Well, you know."

"I don't," says Saba, as she considers the reasons for the arrest. Maybe her mother passed out Dr. Zohreh's leaflets or played too much Gospel Radio Iran for the field-workers.

"Here's how I see it," the doctor says. "Somebody told your father they saw her at the prison, correct? That's why he began to look for her there." Saba nods. "But did you know that there was never any paperwork?"

Saba's fingers are working through a piece of *ghotab* bread, breaking it into crumbs on the table. She wishes the doctor would just get to it. "I don't understand."

Dr. Zohreh nods. "The prison claims that she was never there, and of course, I have to be very honest with you, this is what they often say when something unexpected has happened to the prisoner. . . ." She trails off and cleans up some of Saba's crumbs. "I think it's easier for your father to believe that she died there. She was so brave, you know. . . . And it really *is* the most logical explanation, Saba jan."

Saba conjures the vision of her mother at the airport. She refuses to believe Dr. Zohreh. Who is she to say definitively that her mother is dead? She takes a deep breath and tries not to touch her throat, because surely the doctor will judge her weakness.

"But," Dr. Zohreh continues, "who is to decide that the person claiming to have seen your mother is any more reliable than the prison guards? I say that the lack of paperwork gives us two possibilities." Saba can see a glimmer of excitement in the doctor's face, and her mind wanders through the jumbled memories of the day at the airport. Did she see the *pasdars* take her mother away? In that last moment—before her mother disappeared into the crowd headed for America—did they see each other in the terminal lounge, at the gate, in the security line? Was Mahtab wearing a coat in summer?

She tries to focus on the possibility that her mother's best friend is now offering. "She might have died," Saba begins, "or . . ." She stops there, considering what this other, more hopeful option means.

"She might never have been arrested at all," says Dr. Zohreh.

"Yes," Saba mumbles. *She might have abandoned Cheshmeh and her family.*

Since seeing the letter to Evin, Saba has tried so many times to piece together the sequence of events from that day. How could Mahtab have gotten on a plane with a mother who had just been arrested? But now, with this new possibility, her airport memories could very well be true. *Baba might have been wrong about Evin.* Now her elegant mother returns, wearing a blue manteau, holding Mahtab's hand, boarding a plane—a picture that's suddenly lifelike again, as if someone had turned the knobs on a TV and cleared up all the static and white lines.

Saba exhales, letting a pleasant calm wash over her.

It makes sense. After all, how could her father have been distracted enough to lose his wife to the *pasdars*? Is he too ashamed to admit that she *did* abandon him? That she did run away without a word? Why isn't he angrier? Why does he never curse the wife who brought such plagues into his life? Maybe that is a part of his private suffering. Maybe he helped her run away and refuses to tell Saba, because she too might leave him.

In the early evening, when the candles and lamps have grown dim and the sun is lost behind acres of frosted mountains, when the bread is dry and the windows have lost their warm yellow glow and returned to their gray coat of wet glaze, Saba excuses herself. She doesn't like to be near the sea at night. "I have to be home before Abbas."

"What do you think about coming to our next meeting?" Dr. Zohreh asks again as she looks for Saba's chador behind the boxes. Glancing out into the black, Saba imagines her younger self, playing with Mahtab that day in the water.

"Today was nice," Saba says. "I'm glad I came. But I'm sorry, this isn't for me."

Dr. Zohreh seems surprised. "Are you sure? Your mother—"

"I'm sure," says Saba. There is far too much at stake. Her entire future for what? The thrill of broadcasting the country's collective misery to the world? Shaming hordes of oblivious Iranian men who may never even know that they have been punished? She has no need for that. There is a real man, a flesh-and-blood sinner to punish all she wants, waiting in her own house. "Besides, this is Ponneh's project. I think I'll let her have it."

Dr. Zohreh smiles, as if she knows this is just an excuse. "Take this then," she says, and reaches for something in her pocket. She gives Saba an old key on a thick string. "Come to this house anytime you need a place to think."

The two part ways—each with a few nostalgic words about Saba's mother—donning their black-and-gray coverings and disappearing in their cars into the night. All the way back home, Saba pictures the sea just beyond the tree cover. The frightful rocks. The creaking, unsteady pier. The boats tossed by waves. Such misty winter days have a strange effect on the Caspian, giving it the murky, gloomy quality of an unhappy dream. Saba longs for summer. She rubs the key to the shack between her fingers and thinks of the knife-wielding *pasdar* from her nightmares, the one who says, "On your life, where is Mahtab?" *Across the sea,* she whispers to him in her mind, certain again after so long.

Revolution Music
(Khanom Basir)

In 1979, when the girls were nine, the Hafezis put them through some bad things for the sake of their religion. Before that, the family had lived peacefully in Tehran and Cheshmeh, just the four of them, with their doors mostly closed. Once in a while I saw their Christ-worshipping friends come and go, and a few of us helped Bahareh in the house, but that was all. After the revolution, they had to live differently—in more ways than just tossing out the short shorts and doing without foreign chocolate squares. Now the secrets of the house became a point of trouble. Their heads began to smell like lamb stew, as they say, tempting for predators. But Agha Hafezi wasn't the kind of Christ worshipper who advertised, and he soon realized that the best way to hide was out in the open. Unlike cowards in big cities who shut themselves up in their houses, thinking they were safe, he welcomed villagers into his sitting room. If he was ever accused, an entire village could honestly say, "I've dined in his home. He has a Koran and Muslim friends. If he was Christian, *I'd*

know it." It was a clever thing, oiling the bread of the neighbors, turning them from spies and informants into friends.

During the revolution, there weren't any street riots or protests in
Cheshmeh, only radio broadcasts and new rules for living—no foreign logos, no more non-Muslim music. Soon, in the bigger cities,
*pasdar*s began to appear everywhere in their olive uniforms, piled
four by four into camel-colored jeeps, taking people to the offices of
the *komiteh*—the police force that sprang from the mosques in 1979
and started telling people that everything was a sin. It got worse
and worse over the years. Your ankle is showing? Sin! Your nails are
red? Sin. You have a tan? You must have been naked in sunlight. Sin!
Sin! Sin! If you have your sunglasses on top of your head, you are
posing too much. If your jeans are inside your boots, you are too
exposed. Imagine that. I joked that if they made nose jobs a sin and
levied a fine, there would be big money from Tehran. Bahareh fumed
against all this. Most of us were too afraid to speak and were glad to
be living in a quiet village with fewer *pasdar*s. Gradually, over several
years, women felt the chafe of the mandatory headscarf and long,
dark manteaus. Even here, where hair coverings are part of our traditional dress, and we still wear colors without trouble, there is a feeling of loss for not having chosen our modesty. I sense this even from
the very religious. For the most part, we villagers are noticed only
when we travel to the cities or sell straw handicrafts in box stands by
roads near the seaside. In big cities, anything can happen. Once, when
Ponneh was only thirteen, she was stopped in Rasht because her manteau was buttoned on the side—more fashionable even though it
covered everything. Nothing was ever enough for them. They wanted
to turn us to dust.

If you ask someone from the North, someone whose life moves
with the sea, they will tell you that one of the worst new rules was
about the beach. Before the revolution, we used to go with our families to the sea, eat together, swim together. Women wore shamefully

small swimming costumes and changed in beach huts that smelled like wet bamboo and reed mats. Then they began putting huge curtains, old pieces of dirty cloth full of holes and tears, across the beach to separate men and women, husbands and wives, daughters and fathers. Sometimes they divided the beach by the time of day— mornings for men, afternoons for women. Either way, no more swimming with family. No more fun. Women had to swim fully clothed. They were told not to draw attention to themselves. Little girls watched longingly as boys played in the water in shorts, never taking care to be quiet. Maybe that's why on the day Mahtab was lost, the Hafezi twins thought they would have a better time swimming at night.

Between 1979 and 1981, we heard about riots from friends in Tehran. We heard about tortures and executions and shootings into crowds. People disappeared sometimes, never to return. The Shah fled. The clerics took over, hanging pictures of Ayatollah Khomeini everywhere, filling the streets with posters of bloody fists and "Death to America." In the early days of the revolution, schools were closed and the Hafezi girls were locked in their room, reading their books and listening to their foreign music.

During that first month of not knowing, when the world outside was changing and the girls were shut up in their big, big bedroom, mullahs from Cheshmeh and Rasht started visiting the Hafezi house. Agha Hafezi felt the need to invite them, these new cleric kings, to keep them close and happy. Mullah Ali was one of them, but he was different because he had known Agha Hafezi for years. He lived in Cheshmeh and made himself the grease that kept Agha Hafezi's sharp edges from grinding against the mullahs' ears. He offered up loud jokes, laughing at his own stupid wit and telling long-winded stories from the Koran. It worked because none of the mullahs asked extra questions, and after a while, only one or two of them ever came back. If they had discovered the family's secret, Agha Hafezi would have been jailed or killed because the family weren't born Christians like the Armenians or Assyrians. They were converts from Islam. If a Muslim killed them, it would be no sin. Of course Mullah Ali knew. So did I. But wise old storytellers like us know that it would be bad for everyone if that were made public.

Hidden in their fancy prison, the girls made up their own revolution songs and war slogans. For months, the jinns and *paris* from another time gave way to martyrs and heroes and blood and rifles. One day, at the dinner *sofreh*, Mahtab said that the lamb had been martyred for our sake, and Bahareh told her to stop talking nonsense and eat. If you ask me, the loss of good stories in favor of all that war and revolution garbage was the worst part of it. To Bahareh, the worst was the loss of her house, no longer private, no longer hers at all. She became angry. She lost her temper more often with the girls.

There is a rumor that Agha Hafezi spent two weeks in prison in those days. Maybe it's true. He was gone once for that long and came back with his hair shorn off. When he returned, he listened to all of Saba's music and let her keep only one English-language tape of children's songs. He made a show of the new rule in front of the mullahs and other guests, even though he had never been strict with the girls before. But you know what they say, he who has been bitten by a snake is afraid of black and white.

Ei vai, the trouble this American music caused! I don't see why those girls were so crazy for it—and once it was banned, they craved it more. That day in her room, I heard Saba crying in her mother's lap, and Bahareh told the girl that the revolutionaries were wrong. Every beautiful or fun thing isn't a sin and God loves all people's music. Jesus loves women's loose hair, she said, and foreign books, and especially artistic talent. True art, she said, is God's greatest creation. Then she told Saba she might as well throw away the tape of children's songs too, because if no one cares about it, then it is pointless, with no power or meaning. She sounded sad, like she wanted to run away.

Later Saba managed to dig up some of her tapes from the garbage outside.

"Nothing's gonna change my world," she hummed a hundred times that year, so we all learned its meaning—and later too, as she rode in her baba's car, on a bad, bad day full of green scarves and blue manteaus and brown hats that separated her from her sister.

Mark my words, God will never forgive Bahareh for her impractical ways, for teaching her daughter to search for meaning in illegal nothings.

Chapter Twelve

SUMMER 1991

According to the customs of women from the North, it is bad luck to cut fabric on a Tuesday. Traveling on Mondays brings ill omens, and if you sweep on a Wednesday, you will have jinns in your house. It is not advisable to clip your nails on Fridays or in the evenings, and when you do, the clippings should be wrapped in news-paper and hidden in the cracks of the walls. Since being married, Saba has found a new place among the women of Cheshmeh, sharing their bawdiness and their tales, their sweets and their superstitions, in an entirely new way. They live by a thousand unexplained rules. But now that Saba has learned to listen, she can hear reason behind every one.

"I can't sweep, Agha jan," Saba's neighbor says to her husband as she reclines with a book of poems. "Do you want to invite jinns?"

"I can't mend your clothes today," the Mansooris' granddaughter, Niloo, says to Reza's older brother, Peyman, as she points to the calen-dar on their wall. "Tuesday."

It seems that in the old days the men of Rasht struggled to comprehend the need for a day of rest. "The wives are at home all day," they would say. "They have too much rest." But the women soon discovered that even though their husbands did not understand fatigue and moderation, they did understand jinns, omens, and bad luck. And so a series of fortuitous discoveries were made. The laziest women made the most astonishing finds: if a person sneezes once, she must drop everything she is doing and wait for the second sneeze— even if it takes all day. Otherwise . . . jinns. And the jealous wives discovered that if a man leaves the house in the morning and he sees a woman in his path, he must go back into the house and start over.

Saba sits in her front yard and reads about these rules in an old book she found in her mother's collection. She loves Abbas's front yard. The high walls painted white. The small fountain with goldfish. The low benches tucked beneath the roofs of Spanish-style covered walkways. Along the rough walls pocked by jutting straw and clumping paint, massive jars of ten-year-old pickled garlic, each tall enough to reach Saba's thighs, are lined up like sentries. They have been prepared and left there by Abbas's first wife. Beside them hangs a massive portrait of a long-dead family patriarch. A colorful *ghali*, a small rug sometimes used on the backs of donkeys, cushions Saba's favorite bench where she likes to read or watch the fish in the fountain. She imagines that Abbas's first wife was a superstitious woman.

After a while she meanders back to her room where her latest books and newspapers await. She has been reading more foreign news lately. The publications are usually out of date, but she is interested to know what *The New York Times* and *The Economist* have to say about her country. She picks up an article from an April *New York Times*, brought to her by her faithful Tehrani. A reporter named Judith Miller quotes a diplomatic source: "The revolution is finally over." Saba snorts and reads on. The article talks about the *komiteh* officers and their recent merge with the regular police. It talks about how women no longer wear the unfashionable *maghnaeh*, the triangular academic Super Scarf required (along with a manteau) for school. It says the *pasdar*s are pulling back and there are no more photos of Khomeini in the streets. "Well, that's good of you to tell us," she says aloud—certain that there are still more than enough photos; even one in her father's office—and envies the female reporter whose name is the only clue about her. Probably she is like Mahtab, head‹ strong and ambitious. A real journalist.

Later someone knocks on the door. She ignores it at first. But the banging grows louder, and Saba puts down the book she is skim‹ ming—a highly illegal political one about American government called *Electing a President* that Dr. Zohreh lent to Ponneh and that Ponneh, too embarrassed to admit that she could barely read high school Farsi, let alone English, asked Saba to read and summarize. She creeps down the steps leading from the front door of Abbas's house into the yard and wraps herself in a speckled shawl.

She opens the gate to find Ponneh in a travel chador, struggling with two large bags. Saba takes one and shuts the gate behind her. "What's going on?" she asks.

Ponneh's face is paler than usual and she looks frightened— or shocked. She doesn't say hello, and her eyes are wide and dull. She moves mechanically, feverishly, rummaging through the two black bags as soon as they are inside. "We have to hurry," she says, and digs to the bottom of the bag. "Is your car here? You'll have to drive us."

"Have you gone crazy?" says Saba. "Where do you think we're going?" When Ponneh doesn't answer, she presses. "Does your mother know you're going somewhere?"

Ponneh still lives in Khanom Alborz's house. Her mother rants, raves, and grieves daily by her ailing daughter's bed. She maintains that if her precious eldest child must suffer like this, then the least Ponneh can do is bear a fraction of her pain and wait her turn to marry. Ponneh's voice is resolute. "We're going to stop something bad from happening." She pulls out a video camera from the bag, and then an old photo camera.

To Saba's ears, her friend sounds so deranged that she wonders if she shouldn't just take her arm and force her into the house. Ponneh finds a roll of film. She loads the camera and avoids Saba's worried stare.

"They're hanging someone today," she says. "And we're going to document it."

"What?" A nervous laugh escapes Saba. She shakes her head and starts toward the house because now she is sure that Ponneh has lost all reason. "You're insane."

"Saba, please," Ponneh begs. "Please, I *have* to do this."

"I thought you weren't involved with them," says Saba. "You said you didn't join Dr. Zohreh's group. I've told you that it's dangerous."

Though Saba refuses to join the group, she has visited the shack by herself many times now, to be alone, to think of her mother and Mahtab. It is hidden by acres of forest, and in warmer months, it smells like fresh fish and garlic—seaside aromas that no longer frighten her like they did when she was a child but provide an almost sweet sort of ache. From the window on a clear day, she can make out the outline of the sea through the trees. Sometimes she drives down to the seaside. She walks up the boardwalk to a tiny fish house perched precariously on a rocky pier, orders the catch of the day with garlic pickle, and watches the wooden houses hovering above the waves on their tall, slender stilts, like women lifting their skirts as they stand in the surf. The terns fly close to the mountain house and Saba has seen them, with their sinful red mouths, their defiant white feathers against that shock of black on their head. She has even touched one, fed it with her hand until it was scared away by the sound of a car. Saba likes being alone there, in a secret shack in the mountains, sometimes walking toward the sea, eyeing it like a mysterious lost love . . . humming about a dock and a bay.

Ponneh tries to thrust the camera into Saba's hands. "Look, I need your help."

"I don't want to be involved in these things, Ponneh," Saba protests. She suspects that ever since the beating, Ponneh has allowed Dr. Zohreh's pamphlets and the photos and other illicit documents into her house. Her behavior, her allegiance to this unknown cause, is almost cultish; she follows the group's news clips with the loyalty of a teenage movie fan. Saba wonders if she feels cleansed each time she reads their essays, if she imagines herself lurking in a corner somewhere, catching a member of the moral police in some brutal act. Saba feels none of this longing to save the world. Because what will happen after? Will it change anything? Will it be enough to erase the thought that she, Saba Hafezi, wealthy-widow-in-waiting, is not a good person? That she is a disobedient child, an unfaithful soul, a cruel wife to a feeble man? Can it take away those paranoid flashes, when she's alone in a smoky stupor, that she might be a girl who was so greedy for her own life that she let go of her sister's hand in the water? Saba imagines herself crouching behind a wall or in a deserted alley, waiting for evidence to send abroad, getting caught and paying for her crimes. Enduring blows like Ponneh did and becoming one of the beautiful things *pasdar*s despise. *No,* she thinks. She has already paid.

Now Ponneh is staring at the camera in her hands, and all Saba can see is the top of her face and the bridge of her nose. Ponneh begins to shake. "I have to," she whispers.

Saba takes a step toward her friend. "Ponneh jan, how can you possibly stop this from happening just by taking pictures? Can't you see that you're being crazy?" She wants to help, to show Ponneh the importance of being careful. Hundreds of executions happen every year in Iran—maybe even thousands—either in prisons or in public. Though there has never been one around Cheshmeh, and though she has never seen one, Saba knows from her father that when judges choose to hold an execution out in the open, it is often for a moral crime, a weak soul the crowds can judge while bearing witness to what can happen to those who want too much. No one at this event will feel Ponneh's pain. No one will be her friend. It is best to stay away from such spectacles.

"No," Ponneh snaps. "No, I didn't say I would stop the hanging. I said I'm going to stop *something bad* from happening. And that's letting my friend die for no reason."

Saba tries to swallow, but there is something lodged in her throat. She starts to speak, but doesn't want to ask. "What friend do you mean?" she says finally.

"Farnaz," whispers Ponneh. As soon as the name is out, her shoulders begin to shake. She fumbles with the camera, then stops and wipes her nose on her jacket sleeve. "They're murdering Farnaz in public today, for being indecent. For . . ." She trails off, past whispers and on to sickly gasps. "They say she slept with many men and that they had four witnesses. How can that even *be*? And they said she had enough opium and cocaine to count as trafficking. She doesn't even smoke cigarettes, let alone— Anyway, it happened so fast and Dr. Zohreh has been trying to get her out, but they made up so many charges. They want to hang her because of her work—" Her knees give way and she reaches for something. "Oh God, it's my fault . . . maybe they know things."

Saba puts an arm around Ponneh's waist and leads her to a bench in a corner behind the flower beds, next to a tree and the guest-room window.

"Was there anything else . . . Did they ever see *you* with her?" Saba tries to be rational, but there is a tightening in her chest, like wringing out a wet cloth. The familiar sour taste of fear fills her mouth.

Ponneh shakes her head. "I think they only noticed her after she refused a marriage. The man became obsessed, like Mustafa, and started following her everywhere. . . . But she only likes women." She scratches her thumbnail and mumbles, "I thought you could give the pictures to your video man . . . You know, to show to Americans."

Saba stares wide-eyed at the two bags. She tries to find comforting words, but she can't think of a single thing to say. She only has questions. When was this decided? How long has Ponneh known her friend was in trouble? "What's in the other bag, then?"

"More cameras," says Ponneh, her face flushed. "I went around collecting them. The first one I borrowed was broken. The next one was old and took bad pictures. I had to go to Rasht to develop them and they came out all black. So I borrowed all these because maybe you know which one is best. You're always playing with movies and this and that . . ."

Saba squats in the middle of the yard beside the other bag. She rummages through the contents and chooses a camera that looks functional. "I don't know. It's hard to tell. I only push a button on my VCR. You know I'm no photographer. Besides, you're not going."

"It's two hours away, in a *deh* closer to Tehran. We should leave soon."

"Ponneh, do you hear what I'm saying?"

Ponneh sniffles, shakes her head. "What about the video camera? Does it work?"

"Video? You want to get video of an execution? Are you suicidal? There will be *pasdar*s everywhere."

"I can hide it. Look." Ponneh slips the discarded video camera under her chador, balancing it so that only the lens is exposed through a slit under her arm. "These rags are good for something."

Saba lifts herself up. "You can't save her," she says.

"It's not about saving her," Ponneh snaps, her voice shrill. "It's about making her death count! What do *you* know about it, anyway? Even if I couldn't tape it, I have to be with her. Do you know what it's like to have her die—*die!*—for the sake of something I saw as just playing around? *That's* the real reason they hate her so much. I *have* to go."

There is no arguing with Ponneh. Saba already knows what her friend is thinking. If Ponneh could find some way to dignify the bruises on her own back, to make the experience of being beaten for red shoes mean more, she would happily do it. A silence follows. Ponneh seems to drift into her own private place, Saba thinks of all the ways this day could end—a lashing? One of them in prison, or worse, vanishing from a prison? Maybe Evin, with its ever-silent stone walls that swallow up letters and phone calls from those left behind. Who knows what Ponneh is thinking. Her stare is catatonic, and she whispers Farnaz's name the way Saba imagined she would do when her sick sister finally left the world.

"It's all my fault," Ponneh says, glassy-eyed, her tone cold, prophetic. "She'll die because of me."

And now Saba isn't thinking about Farnaz. She can only hear Ponneh's words—the grief for the loss of a sort of sister. Soon her mind fills with Mahtab and she knows that Ponneh is right. *Why should this be so difficult?* she asks herself, trying to trick her body into being braver. She has seen death again and again. She's the bad twin, the one with the thousand jinns. She can handle the most brutal things, and there is no way she is letting Ponneh do this alone.

⁌⊚⊙⊱

When they reach the village, a dusty little town with a police station, town hall, and thatch-roofed store on the same unpaved street, there is no need to ask directions. Every detail of today's event was carefully arranged, the location chosen to attract just the right number of visitors from Tehran, Rasht, and the girl's hometown, the square chosen to fit many spectators. Even the air is full of a breathless doom that seems to have been purposely planted there. Dozens of men in loose, rural clothing, jeans, or business suits, and women in black chadors, stand around a crane as it inches back and forth into position in the center of the town square. "Oh, dear God," Saba whispers when she sees the crane, its clawlike hook swaying back and forth weightlessly, ready to hoist its victim into the air. Saba has never seen a hanging or any kind of execution before. Such things aren't done in bucolic mountain towns or *shalizar* villages like Cheshmeh. Saba has no wish to see this now, though so many have come from all over to witness it. On catching sight of the crane, Ponneh, who is lying in the backseat to calm her nerves, lets out a guttural, almost animal sound. They sit for ten minutes so she can compose herself, then leave the car several meters outside the town square, its ground now muddied by the crane and dozens of spectators' cars.

Both women have donned dark chadors, and Ponneh wears a second layer despite the warmth. They each take a camera, tucking it under their arms. They allow their great robes to billow, so their figures appear large and amorphous—able to contain many secrets without drawing attention. Ponneh has an ordinary photo camera and Saba carries the video camera, having finally figured out how to use it. She grips it in her right hand as her left holds tight to the fabric at her neck. For just a second Ponneh lets go of the folds and takes Saba's hand. She starts to say something when a dirty green Paykan screeches angrily past them, splashing mud and dingy water on their clothes.

The Paykan comes to an abrupt stop, blocking their way to the square. Saba, shrouded in too much unwieldy fabric, jumps back and clutches the camera. But Ponneh makes no effort to hide the contents of her robe. She knows this car—the one Reza shares with his brother and a friend. She steps out of the way as Reza bursts out, nearly tearing the door from its hinges as he slams it shut.

"*Toro khoda*, what's this?" he shouts. "What the hell are you two doing here?"

Some passersby size up the young, clean-shaven boy with dark eyes and continue walking. "What are *you* doing here?" Ponneh demands. "How did you even know—"

"I saw Farnaz's name in the paper. No one knew where you went. And look at this, I was right. You've come to throw yourself on the fire." Trying to shame her, he adds, "Very wise, Khanom."

Saba breathes out, relieved at the possibility that Reza will talk Ponneh out of this.

"Look, I'm taking you both home before anyone gets jailed or lashed . . . or a lot worse." His eyes dart past Ponneh as he mumbles the last words. Then he glances at her camera.

"I'm staying." Ponneh pushes past him. "You know why. Let's go. We'll be late."

Reza rushes after her. "Ponneh, please. If they catch you . . . with a *camera?*"

"It's nothing!" Ponneh starts to walk away. "People take pictures all the time."

"Not like this, with the big cameras." He follows her, always a step or two behind, out of a habit developed in their adolescence when it became dangerous to walk together in public. "This is going to look so suspicious. No one knows you here. You're two strange women on your own."

Saba doesn't wait for Ponneh to answer. Maybe the safest thing is to get Ponneh through this event and leave as quickly as possible. No sense in making a scene. "We're fine, Reza jan. It's a public event. The only danger here is being seen with you."

Ponneh tucks the camera farther into her clothes.

The lines on Reza's brow deepen. He rests both hands on his head and interlaces his fingers like a nervous player waiting for his teammate to score. He paces near his Paykan, glancing toward the square for signs of the moral police. The crane has stopped moving and the dangling hook is lowered toward the ground. "Okay," he says. "Okay, here's what we'll do. You give me that camera. I'll do it instead."

"No, no," says Ponneh. "This is *my* friend. I'll do it."

"For God's sake, Ponneh," he says, "please let me help you." He takes a deep breath and whispers, "I may be a man, but I'm still your friend." He waits a moment until Ponneh's face falls. "Saba, give me your camera." He forces a smile and holds out his hand. His face is ragged with worry, no longer the hashish-smoking boy she once knew, the football-obsessed youth who obeys his mother and sits in the pantry, drinking and choosing which girl to torment with his fickle love today.

"Thanks, but I'm fine," Saba responds, thinking that she *would* feel safer if he stayed. "I can't exactly show you how the thing works out here in the open, can I?" In truth Saba doesn't want to let go of the camera. What would her brave sister do now? The Mahtab who clawed her way into Harvard, the Mahtab who wanted to be a journalist, the one who was always the best at things—that Mahtab would never let Reza take over. She would hold on to this camera and capture every detail of today. She would hand deliver the film to the front door of *The New York Times* and say to Judith Miller, lady reporter, "See? Things aren't as simple as that, are they, Miss Foreign Correspondent who spent maybe two days in Iran, and both of them in some *gherty-perty* hotel in Tehran?"

Reza wipes his palms on his thighs. He takes Saba's hand through the chador. "I'll be a few steps behind you. I'll be able to see you the entire time."

Saba pushes his hand away, takes Ponneh by the arm, and they walk toward the square.

She tries not to lose track of Reza behind her in the crowd. They face the long stretch of road where the prisoner is expected to emerge.

From her position on this side of the makeshift scaffold, Saba can see the faces of the curious onlookers. Some of them nod and make room for her, and she hopes they can't see the camera lens—such a small part of the black, billowing mass of her body, like the gleaming, beady eye of a blackbird overhead. Can anyone be expected to remember the small shapes or colors in the midst of so much eye-catching sameness? Still, the thought of being discovered sends waves of fear through her and makes her pull the camera tight under her arm.

A dirty white van pulls up near the square moments after Saba has settled into place. The crowd of men and women stretches all the way from the crane to the parking lot where the van emerges. They shift and make way, leaning their heads toward an open path where the prisoner will arrive. Saba reaches under her robes and turns on the camera. The red record light shines hot on her forearm, and Saba is certain the whole world can see it, a big red dot coloring her entire body. Still, in these fearful moments, she is a journalist in charge of creating this last gruesome memento for the world. The van doors open and two *pasdars* pull a screaming girl out of the back. She is handcuffed to a female officer of the moral police, who yanks at her chains and tells her to shut up. The crowd, roused by curiosity and awe, grows louder. Do they feel sympathy for the girl? Maybe they are too full of moral outrage at her crimes. Saba notices that the girl is exceptionally beautiful. Like a *pari*. Like Ponneh. She feels her heart jump at the sight of the officer, a lumbering black-clad crow of a woman, exactly like the two peasants in her bedroom. Women always do these kinds of jobs—cleansing each other of filth and sin. It is a way of showing the world that it is not by the standards of men that they are judged and found lacking. Saba spots the officer's hand pretending to soothe the condemned soul. A Basiji hand, a former *dallak* hand.

Ponneh's chest rises and falls in such deep, fitful arcs that surely her footage is ruined.

"Don't worry, friends." A scratchy voice behind them reassures. "They won't do it." An old woman leans on her metal cane. She speaks with certainty.

Ponneh turns, hungry for a different story. "Excuse me?" she says.

"They won't kill her," says the old woman. "They'll teach her a lesson she'll never forget and then we'll all go home."

Ponneh swallows and wipes the corners of her mouth with two fingers, nails bitten to the quick. "Do you think so?" she says. She tries to link her arm through Saba's, then gives up, hampered by the layers between them. "Did you hear that?" she whispers to Saba.

The old lady continues. "I saw the exact same thing happen outside Tehran. They read her crimes. They ask her if she's sorry. And then, you see the mullah standing over there. . . . He will step forward and say that Allah grants her another chance."

Though Saba knows the impossibility of this, though she knows how much it costs to bring a crane to this remote village, and how widely the news of this event has spread, and how much the mullah standing by the crane scratching his dirty beard must thirst for some righteous purpose, she allows the old woman's comment to give her hope. Ponneh too must know all the concrete facts that make this hope foolish. Though she doesn't read newspapers as Saba does, she has spent enough time with Dr. Zohreh to know. But Saba doesn't want to think about facts or probabilities now. This whispered possibility sprouts in her heart and grows in seconds, taking over her body so that her sole intention and belief is that today she will photograph nothing more than a public humiliation. She ignores the duty in the mullah's eye, the high calling—this girl is one of the beautiful things of this world, like the Warhols and Picassos and Riveras shut up in a dark place somewhere, like Ponneh's red high heels, or a schoolgirl with pink fingernails, or a song called "Fast Car." She draws the world's eyes to herself.

The mullah steps onto the platform and nods as the female officer puts a black hood over the girl's head. "It's a game," Saba whispers. Ponneh repeats it. "It's a game. Farnaz jan, it's just a game." The mullah lowers the noose around Farnaz's neck himself, making sure it is fastened tightly to the hook on the crane. With a wave of his hand, he silences the crowd and reads her crimes from a gray sheet. ". . . actions not in keeping with a chaste life and the laws of Islam, acting against national security, enmity against God, membership in a drug-smuggling organization . . ."

The crowd murmurs. Dozens of shrouded heads and bearded faces look up. Farnaz shivers, sucking the hood in and out of her mouth with each terrified breath.

"She did all that?" another onlooker asks the old woman. Saba strains to hear, every cell in her body screaming to run away or at least step back from the crowd. She can sense Reza listening too, and Ponneh has gone unnaturally still, her body stiffening like a corpse.

The old woman shrugs. "They say they found the drugs in her house. But if you ask me, she angered the wrong man." She points to the front, toward a bearded man with fiery eyes who watches with anticipation like a creditor watching the confiscation of his collateral. "She was supposed to go to the mullah's son, but she refused. I think she was friendly with the wrong type. Activists and Baha'is."

Ponneh bows her head and sucks the tears from her lips. She covers her face with her sleeve and leans on Saba, who can see what her friend is thinking now. *It's my fault.*

"It's all pretend," Saba says. She hears Ponneh's breath, shallow and strained, her camera hand shaking under her clothes. The mullah climbs into the crane operator's seat. He holds on to his white turban as he is helped up by the driver.

"What is he doing?" Ponneh asks, turning to the old woman again.

"He wants to do it himself," she says.

"But it's fake," Saba reminds her.

The woman seems bored. "He wants to be high up like Allah when he showers his mercy on her."

The slight sarcasm in the woman's voice calms Saba a little. Ponneh is shaking harder now, and then Saba hears a thud. Ponneh has dropped the camera. The old woman squints and points to the hem of Ponneh's chador just as Reza comes bounding toward them. "Excuse me, Khanom," he says to the old woman, "I thought I had lost my sisters." He leans down with the casual air of fetching a ball, picks up the camera, and wedges himself between Saba and Ponneh.

"Are you okay?" he whispers to Ponneh. "Let's go. This will be very bad."

Ponneh seems unable to take her eyes off the crane. How can a person not look at such a time? How can she not gawk, stifling each blink until her eyes water? She stares straight ahead, maybe thinking that the strength of her gaze is the only thing keeping the mullah from pulling the lever. Saba stands on her tiptoes and scans the crowd behind her for *pasdar*s, her video camera still fixed on the crane and the girl. Then she hears Ponneh gasp and it is done. The crane hoists the girl into the air mercifully quickly, with one hard motion, not slowly lifting and suffocating, the arc of death revealed by a flutter of small kicks, as in most crane hangings. The mullah places the control stick back into the driver's hand. Farnaz's body swings in the air, her neck unnaturally extended, her head bent to the right in a distorted, cartoonish sort of supplication, her sneakered feet twisted around each other in a childish demonstration of her fright.

For an instant the crowd is hushed and there is no thought of modesty or caution. Women cry openly. A man takes his wife's hand. A young girl's chador slips back and curly chestnut strands sweep her face as she watches death for the first time. Saba struggles to find breath. Did these onlookers hope for a pardon as she did? Did they come here thinking Farnaz would be spared? Some of them must have known, and yet they are all overcome with shock. Maybe some of them do hate her, or they expected the many scars in their hearts to protect them. Or maybe they came to show her she was loved. Reza reaches over and takes Ponneh's hand. Does he know? Has Ponneh told him, perhaps in a moment of teasing, about how she practices for the day they're married? He takes Saba's hand too and they stand in that silent half second, watching, unmoved by the danger to themselves. For the second time, Saba marvels with her friends at this cruel new Iran and takes an unseemly comfort in their threesome, a warming of her heart at the moment of deepest sorrow. This time they are just spectators, everything smells like death and gasoline, and there isn't a broken high heel to blame.

Though she wants to look away, Saba can't stop staring. She follows the easy swing of Farnaz's sneakers; the girlish pink stripe on the side of each shoe sends a wave of nausea through her body. Then she is transfixed by the broken neck, Farnaz's pretty throat tied off with rope. She takes a gulp of air and remembers what it felt like to almost drown, to swallow mouthfuls of water, to be desperate for breath. Mahtab was there, having the same water forced into her small body, unable to move or fight the sea the same way Farnaz can't fight the rope or the crane. She imagines Mahtab hanging in the sky—a flash before she is swallowed into the abyss. Now she sees her mother in Evin, marching in a doomed line, helpless in prison clothes, with her head down and hands tied, one of throngs executed en masse. Saba has seen the photos, the grisly lines of hanging bodies. Is her mother among them? *No*, she assures herself. *The Evin rumor was wrong. I saw Maman get on a plane with Mahtab.* The back of Saba's tongue swells and she reaches for her throat, moved by the urge to scratch. She swallows hard and looks at Farnaz's frail body again. The image of her sister giving up, dropping to the bottom, forces itself in and is just as quickly replaced by the fisherman's callused hands pulling them out. They are together again, letting go, then alternately disappearing into the black chasm below and being pulled into a boat.

Mahtab was there. She sang songs all the way back to shore. Where is she now?

Iran has grown a great many blemishes and stains that Mahtab has not seen. She was here just long enough to experience a child's version of Shomal, seaside games, Norooz bonfires, and wading in the *shalizars*; then she escaped. She took her bow and exited just in time. But here is something Saba has witnessed that even the Mahtab of Harvard hasn't seen—maybe the journalist in her would want to see it, and she is imagining the stories of Saba's life through newspaper clippings, as so often Saba has done for her.

I should leave this place soon, Saba thinks. *Or maybe one day it will kill me too.*

"No," Ponneh whispers. "No, no. It's supposed to be fake." Tears stream down her blotched, cracked cheeks, forming rivulets that foretell the coming end of Ponneh's beauty. She jerks away from Reza. She takes the camera from him and begins to snap photos, oblivious, her bare arms jutting out of her robes. Before Saba can react, Reza has pulled Ponneh away, taking the camera from her and motioning for Saba to follow. Across the square, Dr. Zohreh is heading toward her car. Probably she has come to do the same thing: to bear witness and document. As Reza tries to navigate through the crowds, Ponneh convulses. Big racking sobs seize her body and cause her to shudder and collapse into feverish, almost deranged spasms.

"Stop it," he whispers through clenched teeth. "Ponneh, stop it right now."

When they reach the cars, Saba notices that her face too is damp. But Ponneh has known about this event, suffered over it for months, without telling anyone. Despite her own scars, Saba knows she can never understand Ponneh's pain. She fixes her chador and helps Reza put their friend in her car.

Dr. Zohreh reaches the parking area. "Is she okay?"

Reza nods. "We're going home." He looks to Saba, who introduces them.

When Ponneh sees Dr. Zohreh, she starts to scramble out of Saba's car. "Dr. Zohreh," she says, her voice gravelly. "I'm going with you. We can print the pictures today."

"*What?*" demands Reza, but Ponneh ignores him.

"Of course." Dr. Zohreh glances around. "If you want—"

"No need to trouble the doctor," says Reza, "Saba will drive you and I'll follow."

"No!" Ponneh is becoming very loud now, and Saba eyes a *pasdar* watching them from across the street. She nudges Reza. Ponneh continues her rant. "It's my fault!" She takes a shallow breath. "She refused that man because she loved me. You know what's worse?" She swallows hard. "I'm not . . . I mean . . . I did love her, but I'm not—"

"Yes, I know." Dr. Zohreh doctor lifts Ponneh's face and whispers, "Farnaz wouldn't want you to feel guilty."

Ponneh laughs bitterly. "You know what Khanom Basir used to say? *Only die for someone who at least has a fever for you.* Someone should've told Farnaz that."

"What a thing," Reza whispers, "my poor girl." The words land hard on Saba's chest.

"No, no, Ponneh jan," Dr. Zohreh says. She strokes Ponneh's hair over her scarf. "You are wrong. She didn't die for you. Farnaz wanted to live her own way. She died for that. It was her calling and *that* is a very good reason to die."

A good reason to die. *What a stupid thing to say,* Saba thinks. How can Dr. Zohreh expect Ponneh not to feel guilty? Doesn't she realize that Ponneh's guilt isn't for anything she has done, but only for being alive? Saba has no clear memories of struggling to get out of the sea with Mahtab. She doesn't quite recall letting go of her hand. What she remembers most is Mahtab in the fisherman's boat. But sometimes in her nightmares, she watches her sister disappear and is consumed by the guilt of not letting herself drop into the depths beside her, of failing to leave the world the way she entered it, with Mahtab, and opening a chasm between them that all the teaspoons in Iran couldn't fill.

The *pasdar* is walking toward them. Ponneh is half inside the car, her feet scraping the gravel outside. Dr. Zohreh lifts Ponneh's legs into the car. Reza's eyes are already fixed on the approaching *pasdar* and he takes a step away from the women.

"*Salam alaikum*," the *pasdar* greets Reza. "Who are these women to you?"

Reza doesn't stoop as he used to in front of *pasdar*s. He does nothing to hide his height. In fact, Saba thinks she sees him pull back his shoulders.

"I saw they needed help," he says. "They're my neighbors. I'm parked just there."

"Papers," the *pasdar* barks at Dr. Zohreh.

Dr. Zohreh reaches into her purse for her identification. Saba prays the officer doesn't look into the cars, that he doesn't see the cameras. Dr. Zohreh shows her papers with perfect calm. "I'm a doctor," she says. "These girls are my patients."

The *pasdar* bends and glances in the backseat at Ponneh. Saba holds her breath, willing him not to spot the cameras. "I saw this girl in the square. . . . Why the hysterics?" He waits for an answer, but Ponneh just glares at him with red eyes and swollen cheeks. No matter how much she tries, it's hard to be threatening with a runny nose and bewildered eyes that have just witnessed death. He mutters, "We shouldn't allow women and children to these things. It's undignified." Then he straightens, and Saba thinks he will ask to look inside the car. But the officer nods and turns back toward the square. He says to Reza as he walks away, "Go to your own car. This isn't your business."

Without another word, they each fumble for keys and drift away. The gloom of dusk settles all around as Saba follows Dr. Zohreh's orange Jian and Reza's green Paykan north toward Cheshmeh.

Ponneh lies in the back of Saba's car and they ride silently for a while. Saba counts the passing seconds, willing her friend to come back to life. They drive out of the village, past the sloping dirt roads leading to the highway. As they pull onto the main road, flanked by the familiar rocky embankments that signal the way home, Saba struggles for something to say. She thinks of how small Farnaz looked, hanging in the air with her feet crossed one over the other like a lost child in a too-big chair, and she knows that Ponneh is thinking of her too. That Farnaz will haunt her for a long time.

The forest appears on the horizon. Ponneh is slumped, her body crumpled in a corner of the wide backseat, her eyes so bloodshot that the whites are gone. Saba glances from the road once or twice, reaches back and gropes for Ponneh's hand. Then she turns and blurts out, "Ponneh jan, I can't stand you thinking this is your fault." She thinks of a day when she too was in such a state. What did Saba need to hear then? Maybe Ponneh should open her eyes to how uncontrollable things are in this new world; that Farnaz's fate wasn't about one or two afternoons of experimentation, but about an unmarried girl who wanted to outwit her captors. "If this is your fault," she says, "then what happened to me has to be my fault too . . . and I don't believe that. It's tempting, but no . . ." Ponneh sits up. "It's about Abbas." Saba's hands move on their own down the wheel. The sun's rays jut past the felt visor and warm her skin. "I used to think it was my fault," she says, "because I should've annulled the marriage and let them disinherit me."

"What are you talking about?" Ponneh asks.

Saba exhales.. "He never slept with me. He's completely impotent."

Ponneh is wide-eyed. "That's good," she ventures. "Right?"

Saba laughs a little. She rubs her neck and tries to push the heavy feeling out with her fingers. "Maybe," she says. "Except he hired these women to attack me." She waits for her meaning to become clear. "You know . . . because of his reputation. Two *dehatis* . . . maybe Basiji, I'm not sure. He let them into our house and paid them to hurt me."

Ponneh's face grows more ashen. "Oh God, Saba," she whispers.

"I'm okay now," says Saba, deciding that there is no need to tell her about the bleeding. "But see what I mean? Is that *my* fault?"

"Of course not," says Ponneh. "But it's different."

"It's not different," she says to Ponneh. "None of us can prevent these things. This garbage happens all the time, and you and I can't change any of it. We can't even see it coming! Blaming yourself is crazy. You have to take care of yourself, Ponneh jan."

Ponneh leans in, her head between the two seats. "I hope you told your father," she says. "Those women should be in jail." Saba shakes her head. She doesn't want to reveal her hopes for the money or a future abroad—*when will it be time?* She has such an urge to run. "You haven't told him?" She grabs the headrest, her voice shrill. "You're going to let Abbas get away with it? Haven't you learned anything from Dr. Zohreh? You *have* to say something. It's not only about you. What if they do it again?"

The orange Jian disappears behind a mountainous curve ahead. The air is stifling and Saba rolls down the window. The smells and sounds of the road pour into the car. She turns and gives Ponneh a pleading look. "Just don't tell anyone, okay? Things are different for converted Christians. Baba and I can't have a legal battle with a devout Muslim. If they start digging around . . . Look, Ponneh jan, I've already waited so long . . ." Her face grows hot. "You can't tell Reza. Promise?"

"Fine," says Ponneh. "But I think it's wrong." Saba is glad to see the fire back in Ponneh's voice. "You should go right up to them and slap them across the face."

"Next time I see them," Saba mutters, and they drive silently through the trees.

That night, when Abbas knocks, she ignores him. She listens to "Fast Car" and decides she is finished here. Would it be so hard to try to leave? She falls asleep with images of suspended pink-striped sneakers and red high heels swimming through the foggy places that separate her from her dream universe. And she thanks God that he plucked Mahtab out of Cheshmeh just as the world was about to crumble down.

Soghra and Kobra
(Khanom Basir)

A year before the revolution, when the children were eight years old, Soghra and Kobra captured their attention for a full three months. It was all any of them talked about. Soghra and Kobra were sisters who lived in the next town—distant cousins of Ponneh's, who told everyone about Soghra's marriage plans. Soghra was twelve, but her parents were desperate people, stricken with poverty and old-world thinking. They said that she had already "become a woman" and so she was ready to marry. Shameful! They married her off to a man whose sister had come to a local hammam to examine Soghra's body, as was customary in my parents' time. And what was so fascinating about her marriage? What made the girls follow her in the streets and tell stories of her to their eager friends? Well, the man Soghra was engaged to marry was forty years old.

"Are you sure he's forty? Maybe he's fifty!" one of them said as they spied on the man's shop in the marketplace.

"It doesn't matter if he's forty or fifty," Mahtab announced. She was always sure of everything that she said. "Because you stop count-ing at thirty when you're officially old."

"It *does* matter, stupid," Saba said, "because fifty means he'll die ten years sooner." They had this same ridiculous conversation half a dozen times.

After her marriage, we adults watched Soghra for signs of what the man might have done to her. The girls could sense it too. "What do they do?" I heard Saba asking, and Ponneh said she had *some* idea. Apparently she and Reza whispered about it sometimes. Mahtab asked them a hundred dirty, dirty questions before I lost patience and separated them. Usually we laughed at the children's curious talk, but on that day, because of poor Soghra, my ladle hit the bottom of the pot, and I ran out of good humor.

The next time the children saw Soghra, they went on and on about how she didn't look different at all. I tried not to laugh at their shock. She didn't walk funny as Reza had said she would, and her face hadn't sprouted moles. Her feet hadn't swollen, and she didn't grow giant breasts. And—here's the part that's my fault—she didn't have blood coming out of her nose. Fine, so I had told them that married women get a lot of nosebleeds, and that is why a sheet is needed to catch the bride's first nosebleed on the wedding night. What do you want, that I tell them the truth at eight years old?

I did notice two small changes in the bride. As she paraded around the Cheshmeh food market, pulled from place to place by her thick-mustached husband, twelve-year-old Soghra seemed taller and damn disappointed with her fate. But then again, I could be mis-taken. Maybe it was just the high heels her husband forced her to wear because he had always wanted a sophisticated wife (and these were, after all, prerevolution days). And maybe it wasn't sadness clouding her eyes, but all that blue eye shadow.

"It's a shame. A real shame," Agha Hafezi said when he was

sipping tea with his wife and me and Khanom Omidi. "How can the law allow the rape of a *child*?"

I reminded him that in Iran rape is a very specific thing. *Too specific.*

But why dwell on sad things? Here is the reason I tell this story. Afterward, when the children were sitting in a circle with their feet touching, Saba said the strangest thing for a girl so young. She said that it was good for Soghra to have her own house to govern and no sister to share it with. A logical choice, she called it, since Kobra was such boring company. I wonder if she would still say that to Soghra if she ran into her today. Even though I can't imagine what goes on inside Saba's marriage, sometimes I see that same sad, haunted look, all covered in eye shadow, in the faraway gaze of poor Saba Hafezi.

Chapter Thirteen

SUMMER 1991

People say that twins feel the force of each other's movements from afar. Saba has read magazine stories about a miraculous few who have felt change overcome their twin while completely unaware that the other exists. In the frightening first days after witnessing death again, Saba tries to feel the forces in Mahtab's world. She gives herself up to dark thoughts of her sister sinking into the water, of a *pasdar* gripping her with his knife, forcing her to admit truths that she still doesn't know. When the images threaten to undo her, she fights them off by recalling better ones, Mahtab singing in the boat back to shore and holding her mother's hand in the airport. *Yes, there is a good chance.*

On quiet mornings she imagines her sister, her TV-quality life, and talks to her like one of her American friends would do. *What do I do now?* she asks Mahtab the day after Farnaz's hanging. Mahtab's voice swirls in her head, repeating the same command again and again: *Get out! Get out! Get out!* That night she begins to entertain an enticing possibility. What if she ran away to America *now*? She could try for a visa, forge Abbas's signature, tell them she's leaving behind a husband to make it easier. But the fear of *pasdar*s and border controls holds her here like it does so many others. One day soon—before she turns twenty-two, or twenty-four, or thirty at most—Abbas will be gone. When that day comes, what will keep her in Cheshmeh? If she is patient, she will be an independent widow in New York or California. Maybe she will go to journalism school. She did, after all, save herself for an American university. She digs up old travel guidebooks collected by her mother before the revolution, and even finds piles of papers from visa offices, passport agencies, and airlines—a treasure of information that her mother amassed just in case. There is comfort in knowing that this desire to run is inherited, a piece of her mother that can never be taken from her. One day soon her feet will loosen their hold on this sodden Gilaki soil and she will go.

Lately Khanom Omidi has developed a strange affection for *The Karate Kid*. She stumbled upon it when visiting Saba, who was reviewing her latest purchases from the Tehrani in her childhood bedroom. Khanom Omidi doesn't understand the dialogue, but manages to follow along from one sparring match or training montage to the next, stopping the tape to ask questions or offer opinions. "That Johnny *folani* is no good. He is wicked already at such a young age, and I think his snake-worshipping dojo has jinns."

Saba's favorite summer movie is *Dead Poets Society*. On a night when Abbas has gone to bed early and she is alone with Khanom Omidi, she lets the old woman prepare a pipe to soothe her nerves. They talk about love and death and Farnaz, watch the movie together, and sip tea. This season Mahtab will begin her fourth year at Harvard. She will have made friends with prep-school boys like the ones on screen. Look at them in their crested jackets and elegant ties, so confident, so poised. Entirely different from Iranian men shouting in their *pasdar* uniforms, or sitting in corners of the house in morose opium trances, or dancing like fools at illegal parties. Once at a late-night party without the mullahs or cousin Kasem, Saba saw Reza and his brother get up and dance with the full force of their hips and arms, hands twisting this way and that. That's the difference between men from here and there, she thought. Other than the occasional tuxedoed waltz, American movie men don't dance. Iranian men dance to impress. Maybe Western manners have eradicated their natural wildness. Iranians have *pasdar*s for that.

Halfway through the movie, the pipe begins to lull her to sleep. She drifts off on Khanom Omidi's lap, thoughts of her sister and dancing melding together in her memory.

Mahtab used to dance. As a child, she loved flailing raucously, being the sudden center of an attention vacuum. This is the one Persian thing she will likely retain. After all the hours spent twirling in pairs in dresses and tuxedos, Mahtab will crave center stage. In her stupor, Saba can see it, a scene good enough for a movie. Mahtab will cast aside her escort, and suddenly, out of nowhere, there will be *setar* music and Iranian lyrics. Maybe the "Sultan of Hearts" will play right in the middle of Harvard Square. A miracle!

One heart tells me to go, to go.

Another tells me to stay, to stay.

Except Mahtab has no such qualms about staying or going. She is already in the place she wants to be. She will dance alone in her elegant dress and no one will dare enter her spotlight. The beauty of being Mahtab is that you need no partner at all.

❧⊙☙

Come, Khanom Omidi, come and listen to a story about my sister. This year has been a dark, endless one for me, and I want to glimpse into her world tonight. This one is about the defeat of another

Immigrant Worry: *importance*—the one that my mother fretted over for as long as I knew her, even though she was no exile. My cousins in America are afflicted by something similar—nightmares of second-class invisibility, mediocrity, and anonymous death. Legacy-losing, taxi-driving, dry-cleaning worries. All those engineers and doctors cleaning floors and selling cigarettes in corner shops. Mahtab too loses sleep over it, because she knows that she has been lucky, that she owes something monumental to the world. She wants to do good things. But this too will pass, in 22.5 minutes. She will cast it off as she always has. This is the story of how Mahtab stops worrying about living an important enough life.

In the summer before her final year, Mahtab finds a full-time job: a position as a junior reporter for *The New York Times* that she will begin this June and continue after graduation. She will work for *khanom* reporter, Judith Miller, checking her facts and correcting her frequent spelling mistakes. She will ride in a big white news van and go hunting for stories and quotes. She will become an official a story-teller—only she isn't allowed to lie, not even backhandedly by choos-ing which details to tell. You see, these Americans have figured out our true-bending tricks. And that destroys all the fun. Lucky for us we have Iranian journalists who understand how to weave a good tale.

"Ai, Saba! Enough with the double-talk. Stop complaining and tell the story."

Fine. In the days before she leaves for her summer in New York, Mahtab carries a dull but constant ache for Cameron, whom she runs into often at the student gymnasium. She struggles daily with the decision to use or abandon his credit card. She changes her mind each time she runs into him or his waifish lover on campus. You see, realizing you are a secondary character in someone else's movie, it hurts to the bone. Sometimes Cameron looks sad to see her. Some-times he tries to say hello. Neither of them ever brings up the card and it becomes an awkward, unmentionable topic between them—the fact that she is linked to his family like some bizarre estranged relative. On angry days, Mahtab tries to torture him from afar. She carries a bag with bundles of towels hanging out, all white except for the thin layer of blue-and-violet-checkered silk peeking out from among the thick cotton. The scarf is faded, that guilty piece of silk she wore to the Aryanpurs' now relegated to wiping Mahtab's sweat. She makes sure it is in plain sight in order to make a statement of her power: I am above it, and above *you*.

"Hah! It's just what Khanom Basir tries to say with her fancy old scarf."

One day Cameron tries to say hello in the exercise room, and she finds herself unable to form words. She only walks past, rubbing her neck with the blue cloth.

He shouts after her, "Wiping your sweat with an Hermès scarf, Khanom Shahzadeh?"

She turns. "Don't talk Farsi to me," she snaps, because the language of her family and of their romance is sacred to her. "You're no longer my friend." I have wanted to say those words to Abbas so many times. He and I used to be friends in our own way. Each time he tries to talk to me now, I want to say: *You are no longer my friend.* But I do not have Mahtab's courage or her options. She can take his money and be free, as long as she keeps his secret, whereas I must keep the secret and continue to be imprisoned with him.

But Mahtab is kind, and as soon as the words are out, she regrets them, because what if she's hurt him? She searches his face. Is he unhappy too? She wishes she could reach inside him and wipe away this new, unfamiliar Cameron who pretends he can never love her. She wishes the old Cameron would come back.

How strange, she thinks, that he should have such a fear, such an intense feeling of dread surrounding his secret. Is it really so dangerous for him in Iran? Could he really be hanged? Mahtab can't fathom such things. For a future journalist, her mind is too pure, her eyes too unsullied. Is it really so important for Cameron to go back and try for change? How can anyone feel so strongly about an intangible thing? Just a blurry shadow of a concept that may never become truth. She envies him for having such a passion. She listens to the hum of the exercise equipment all around, feeling like the only dysfunctional cog in the engine of some great, success-powered machine. Cameron is making his way onward. He wants to go without her, to become one of the powerful men who rule us all, a changer of fates, and she is only falling further and further behind.

She decides that the only way to overcome Cameron's hold on her is to become bigger, better, more successful than he is. This was, after all, her mother's greatest teaching: You must live an important life. Tomorrow she will move to the big city to start her internship at *The New York Times* and take her place in the white news van. She will make the men and women in business suits—those crows in a line— marvel at her talent.

In New York she lives a movie life. She attends dances like the one in *Dead Poets Society*, where couples spin in circles over wooden floors. She plays golf in green shorts. She hides a tape recorder in the pocket of these shorts so that she can catch dirty businessmen admitting to things they should not have done.

"So, Agha Businessman," she will croon, "tell me what you did then." She will bat her Middle Eastern eyelashes and the fool will fall to his knees and admit to this embezzlement or that filthy-*bazi* and she will print it all on the front page of *The New York Times* under the byline "Mahtab Hafezi, Harvard Class of 1992."

"Are American businessmen really so stupid, Saba jan?"

Hush now, Khanom Omidi! I'm telling a story here. Stories are full of these wonderful alignings of coincidences that lead to smart men confessing their every sin. They are full of quick victories. Do you remember the part in *Karate Kid* where Daniel kicks horrible Johnny *folani* in the face, even though his leg is broken? When I watch that scene, I imagine Farnaz at her hanging, looking into the crowd like she has a plan, kicking the mullah in the face with her girlish sneakers and saving herself from the crane to a wave of hurrahs from an audience of onlookers who suddenly worship her.

Mahtab's life is filled with such unlikely triumphs.

She rises quickly in the ranks of the interns. She becomes a news-paper star.

She lives in a small apartment in New York that she shares with another girl. Each night when she turns her key, drops her pretty purse of real leather onto her couch, and plops down in front of the television, she knows that today she has done something important. Still, she wants more. This summer she must do something monu-mental, change the world like Cameron plans to do, and have her voice heard across oceans.

A few weeks later she exposes a series of sophisticated crimes in the government, some of them leading to people so high up that even I must refrain from mentioning them here. Please don't ask for details. I only know that they are big, big news. And with each ac-complishment, Mahtab comes closer to finding her true self, her nat-ural self.

One night, as she sits on her couch in her miniskirt, with the win-dows wide open and her music blaring, drinking a beer openly so the neighbors can see, the answer arrives among a pile of junk mail and bills. It is a tattered envelope from Iran, covered with a hundred stamps and postmarks, smelling of rice and addressed in a careful hand—a nervous one that hasn't finished school, reads no English, and seems to have traced the address over a printed copy. It is from a Miss Ponneh Alborz, Cheshmeh, Iran.

Is it true? Her childhood friend Ponneh has written to her? What tales can this long-lost friend have to tell? Will her letter be full of stories about Reza and his crazy mother, about her sister's health? What a lucky thing to have a letter from Cheshmeh.

She rips open the top of the crinkled white envelope and lets the contents spill out.

Suddenly all joy is gone as her table is flooded with photos, letters, a videotape, and some audio recordings. The photos are gruesome. They show a beautiful girl dragged from a van, then hanged by the neck from a crane. It is difficult even to touch the photo paper. A scrawled note reads: "My friend Farnaz: framed for activism and for preferring women."

Ah, but Khanom Omidi, do not despair. For Mahtab these pictures are an opportunity. She is savvy enough to know exactly what to do with them. Because, after all, our girl works at *The New York Times* now. She is our bare-legged champion, and she is armed with a videotape that I shot with my own hand.

She spends the next week watching the video, rewinding and watching it again. It is impossible not to lean closer to the television, to try to peer into the face of the beautiful Farnaz and touch her cheek before it is hooded. Did such a thing really take place? I ask myself that sometimes in the middle of the night when I view that grainy film to torture myself into feeling alive. Despite the shaking hand, the static, and the black chador covering the lens every few seconds, the image is undeniable. It happened. I was there.

Mahtab wipes her tears with a checkered scarf that no longer holds so much meaning in comparison. When she thinks of Cameron now, she no longer hates him. Not after witnessing the tragedy on the grainy tape. She understands now about the intangible things that must be done by people just like him. He is a good man, a man with all the virility in the world despite what his father might think, because he is willing to go back to this place that wants to kill him for his tastes; to risk *this* fate in order to live a life that is important. She thinks back to a time when she was the top half of a starfish and decides that it is better to cherish it, the beautiful memory, than to hate him for not desiring her.

Oh, but he *did* want you, Mahtab. There is more than one way to long for someone. And look at Cameron now, making use of his life. He is off repaying the universe for his good fortune. Mahtab will do the same.

She will live a courageous life, like Daniel LaRusso of *The Karate Kid* or Professor Keating of *Dead Poets Society*—both so brave in the face of a formidable evil. As she prepares her report based on all the evidence Ponneh has sent to her—Dr. Zohreh's testimonial, the pictures, and the video—she considers the Aryanpur credit card. It will not give her freedom from her desires, she realizes now. Secret unearned wealth never does. Deep down she knows that she will have such freedom only by living the kind of life Maman wanted, a significant life, a life noticed by the world.

And there you have it. Mahtab spends one summer in New York and conquers an Immigrant Worry that some people live with forever, because it takes an exceptional person to overcome it—the one about making a mark in a strange land. In two weeks' time, the front page of *The New York Times* will shout a bitter-tasting truth to the world:

THE REVOLUTION IS *NOT* OVER!
by Mahtab Hafezi, Harvard Class of 1992

Oh, Mahtab joon. You have done so well. So very well indeed. You have made me and our parents proud. Can you imagine what Maman would say if she were to see your name stamped thickly in finger-staining black ink and distributed across oceans?

To celebrate, Mahtab and her friends go dancing in a real New York City nightclub with flashing lights and flowing cocktails. They dance alone, no escorts. They jump up and down in short skirts and bejeweled tops, as in the best music videos, and Mahtab is the cause of their joy, the very center of it. She is finished with the poor Aryan for now. She doesn't need a partner. The room is full of men and women together, but it is unlike the clubs she used to walk past at Harvard, with boys appraising scantily clad women at the door— a white scarf transforming into a turban and frightening her away. Here she is in charge, and there are no *pasdar*s lurking in dark alleys.

When I imagine her there, I think of the scene in *Dead Poets Society* where the boys dance secretly at night in a way very different from their polite suit-and-tie functions. Their dancing is tribal, much like the men from Cheshmeh. They dance to release, to impress, to express ecstasy, madness, and a too-wild-for-daylight kind of glee. Mahtab is a wild thing now, a free creature. She can do as she wants, mullahs and *pasdar*s be damned.

She sends safe wishes to Cameron, her homeward-bound friend. Maybe one day she will love an American man instead. American men may not dance, but they are experts at understanding women like Mahtab. And it seems they pride themselves in not having their own needs. Do you think this is true of all of them, or just the movie men? Iranian men are brimming with their own raw, seething hopes. They call out to us to care for them, to save them—without so much as a name in the byline. I wish sometimes to have one of them say to me, "You, Saba Hafezi, impress me." They never would, not the least of them. We women have become too strong in that unshakable, garlic-fisted way, and we frighten them. But if one of them were to write a love song for me, it wouldn't be full of old-world dramas. It wouldn't be about dying or forever things. It would simply say this: "Saba joon, you've done so well."

Soon I will find enough courage to break free from this place, and maybe I will be brave enough to hide that videotape in my luggage. I asked the Tehrani to smuggle it out of Iran, to send it to someone important, a journalist or a professor, maybe one at Harvard. But he said it was too risky and refused. It is a frightening thing, to abandon a home.

One heart tells me to go.

Another tells me to stay.

But I will try. That much I promise . . . because you, dear sister, impress me.

Chapter Fourteen

SUMMER 1991

Saba sits in a chair by the window in the guest room where she now keeps all her belongings, listening to her tapes and watching the small television she has moved here. On her lap rests a glass with Abbas's medicine, which she mixes absentmindedly, stirring in sour cherry syrup. He has trouble swallowing pills, so this is how he takes his heart medication, though Saba finds it unwise. Each time after he drinks it, she fills the glass with water and gives him that too, to get every last molecule. Today she mixes the drink on a tray in her room instead of in the kitchen to avoid having to talk to him when he comes home. He has deteriorated in recent months, is almost blind now, and though she refuses to forgive him, she has softened toward him because of his obvious weakness. In a few minutes he will knock on his way to bed and ask her for the medicine. This is their routine.

Saba stares out into the yard, where the roses Ponneh and Reza planted for her in the spring are bathing the garden in fragrant yellow dust, and she becomes unaware of the work of her hands. She watches. Stirs. Watches. Stirs. In the background her favorite American drama replays a story she has nearly memorized—a couple begins their romance in an Italian restaurant. Soon she will need new videotapes, new dialogue, new words, new glimpses of American life. These days she relies on distractions for comfort.

She thrusts a few cherries into the cherry pitter, extracts the pits with a snap of her wrist, and drops them into her own medicine-free glass, remembering the days when she and Mahtab used to steal the cherry pitter, a rock, and a bowl of fruit, and hide in their bedroom pitting cherries, eating unripe almonds with salt, and smashing apricot pits for the nut. Sometimes their father would have procured a banana, a luxury after the revolution.

The *sharbat* is cold, and sweet, and splashes red against her teeth and tongue. The ice clinks in the glass as she empties it with three gulps, so she doesn't hear the knock on her door. Abbas enters tentatively, as he has done every night for months. He clutches something wrapped in a newspaper. It smells like meat and is soaking through the pages. Saba doesn't ask about it, because even the casual conversations of their first year are gone now. He reaches for the glass, thanks her, and takes a few distracted sips. He mumbles as he leaves, "Tomorrow, maybe *ab-goosht*." Lamb stew. Saba decides she would prefer chicken, and so that is what she will make.

"Let me see you drink it all," she says. He obeys. She takes back the glass and fills it again from a jug of water. He drains that too before he slips out.

Half an hour later she heads to the bathroom. In the hall she runs into Abbas, still gripping his glass. Is he aware of how much time he wastes shuffling around? She makes a disgusted face at his old age, at his feeble mind, at everything that is her husband.

She holds his gaze, watery, gray, flanked by intricate webs of worn skin, the hopeful look of a small child who wonders if his bad behavior has been forgotten. She frowns at this pathetic old man that she has married, small, bent, with folds of skin gathered up around his neck, as though the flesh were fleeing from his face. His paunchy stomach rises and falls in his white undershirt and enormous gray pajama pants. "Where are you going?" he asks, his breath raspy, his eyes pleading. "Are you going to read tonight?" She knows what he wants, that this wretched man wants her to forget, wants to hold her again, to feel the warmth of human company. He has tiptoed around the house since the Dallak Day, always hoping, silently begging. Somewhere inside she feels sympathy, like a lump of coal glowing with the first hint of orange and red, but her anger is torrential and it douses the tiny flame.

Abbas drops his gaze and clears his throat. She can see that what she does to him daily is so much worse than any court's judgment. Maybe he craves punishment so that this misery can end. But she can't give him release, this man who has cost her a real life. Saba responds coldly, "Go to bed, Abbas. I like to read alone."

He gives her the empty glass. "Yes . . . I should get some rest." He peeks at her face again. "Do you want me to buy more fruit tomorrow? I noticed you're eating a lot of fruit this summer . . . very healthy."

"I can buy my own fruit."

"Would you like some money? Maybe to buy some books."

"I have a bank account," she says, "remember?" Agha Hafezi has made certain of this provision for his daughter in her marriage contract.

Abbas nods. "Well, I thought maybe you would like to have some of your young friends for dinner. If you want that . . . um . . . I will be a good host. I know a good joke."

She stares into his cloudy eyes and thinks she is in danger of accepting his kindness. The sad way he can't decide if he is her husband or her father. She senses her resolve about to weaken and walks away. He is just an old man, like Agha Mansoori. . . . But no, Agha Mansoori loved his wife more than himself. How can she dishonor his memory by comparing that sweet, gentle man to the monster who lives in her house?

She takes the dirty glass to the kitchen. She washes it and replaces the medicines in Abbas's private cabinet. One of the bottles, which was half full with Abbas's blood thinners when she began her nightly routine, now falls with frightening lightness in her hand. A few remaining pills rattle around. She counts them, her heart fluttering with memories of Agha Mansoori and his last attempts at tricking fate and death. But she can't recall the right number of pills. Did Abbas realize that the medicine was in the drink? What if he forgot the routine and thought she was offering something to wash it down?

He couldn't have. This has been their routine from the start. Medicine *in* the drink. Besides, Abbas knows the dangers of taking more than the precise dose of the pills. He takes them to prevent clots and to aid blood flow to his heart. Too much can cause fatal bleeding and a stroke. *No,* she thinks. *He's the one who explained this to me.*

Later in the night Saba hears Abbas call for her. She crouches outside his door. He seems confused. He is saying nonsensical things, slurring the simple syllables of her name. There is a knock, like he has run into something. She waits behind the door, but does not go in. Instead she leans against the wall and pulls her knees to her chest, listening to her husband struggle. Then he is silent again for a few minutes before he begins snoring. Once or twice she falls asleep but is jolted awake by Abbas's pained voice and the pounding of her own heart. *How many pills were left in the bottle before tonight?*

She thinks about calling the doctor. In a moment of quiet, she opens the door and goes to Abbas. She leans over him and listens to his breathing, which seems normal.

"Should I call the doctor?" she whispers, uncertain that he can hear. Then he lets out a small moan and an unexplained panic rises inside her, exactly like the one she felt during the ten days of caring

for Agha Mansoori. Each morning that he hobbled to his door a minute late, she felt this same urgent dread.

She runs to the phone and dials the doctor's number, jamming
her fingers in the rotary holes and switching to a pencil because her
hands are shaking. No one answers. She wonders if she should go out
to find him. But he lives in the neighboring village and is only a gen-
eral practitioner. The clinic in the town center will be closed—and it
employs only family doctors, nurses, and midwives. She would have
to drive an hour to Rasht to find Abbas's heart specialist or a hospital.
Should she call an ambulance? It would probably take as long. Finally
she dials the number of Ponneh's neighbor, the one around the corner
who has a phone and can fetch her friend.

Since the hanging, Ponneh hasn't been as readily available to Saba
as she used to be. Saba suspects her friend has become more involved
with Dr. Zohreh. But Ponneh makes the time to visit a few times a
week, plants herbs in Sabas's garden and cooks with her.

The phone rings ten minutes later and a breathless Ponneh
demands to know what has happened, why her neighbor dragged her
from sleep to come to the phone. On hearing the explanation, she
only says, "I'm on my way," and hangs up.

Saba returns to check on Abbas. His moaning calms for a while,
and she assures herself that all is well until she sees the vomit in the
corner of the bed. She hurries to the kitchen to get him some water
and a towel, and considers this unexpected terror at the possibility of
his death. How could it be, when she has been dreaming of this day
for so long? She tries to get Abbas to drink the water, cleans him off,
then lies outside his door again. Through fits of sleep, she dreams of
a somber tune about an American fisherman on a boat called *Alexa*.
The song makes her think of Mahtab and the rough hands of the
fisherman who pulled her out of the Caspian. In her stupor, she hears
Abbas's voice and the unbearable sound makes her gulp for breath.

She wakes up to Ponneh shaking her shoulder. "How is the old devil?"

"*Shhh,*" Saba warns. "Don't say these things. What if he dies?"

"What if?" Ponneh looks shocked and amused. "Saba, this is a long time coming. He's so old. He's had much more time than he deserves. We'll just sit and wait."

Ponneh's icy expression jars her. Abbas calls out and Saba rushes to his side. A pleading look colors his uneven gaze, reminding her of all the little cruelties she heaped on him for what might be the last year of his life. Just a few hours ago he begged to buy her fruit, to watch her read or entertain her friends, and she brushed him aside like a market peddler. She touches the cold, slack skin of his hand. "I'm sorry," she whispers.

Ponneh is pacing behind them, her scarf already discarded. As soon as the apology leaves Saba's lips, Ponneh lets out a breathless snort. "Saba, you will regret this, I promise you. You'll hate yourself forever if you let your emotions get the better of you. Tell him what he did was unforgivable. You'll never get another chance."

"Stop it! I'm doing my best," Saba says. "The doctor wasn't answering his phone before. Please just try calling him again. Actually, call the ambulance too."

Ponneh exhales loudly in protest as she stomps into the living room to make the call. She returns a minute later and says, "He's coming soon."

"When?"

"I said soon!" Ponneh sounds angry, as if it were *her* life that's spiraling out of control. She taps her feet as Saba hunts for clues on Abbas's tongue, in his eyelids. How pale are they supposed to be? She remembers something the doctor said about his arms.

"Abbas jan, lift your arm," she shouts. "Lift your arm for me." No response.

Ponneh mumbles, "You'll regret it."

When she can find nothing else to occupy her, Saba sits on a chair next to Abbas's bed and watches him. Ponneh leans over the old man and listens to his heart, her hair falling over his chest. She looks like a young girl observing a sleeping grandfather. Maybe she expects that Abbas will die tonight. His eyes are cold, chilling to watch.

Did Saba do something wrong? She *always* puts the medicine in the drink. That was their agreement. But it's true that she has been preoccupied lately. Did she carry out one of her latent fantasies? Is it possible? No. She did nothing. Except this: for a moment, as she watched television and dreamed of her sister, she let someone else take over, some wild creature that lives inside and survives on crumbs. A monster that never has its own way. Sometimes during her cruelest daydreams, when Abbas is thrown into the Caspian or disemboweled, she fears she is no different from the Basiji women. That she too has a beast with a Cheshire grin waiting inside, and the only reason hers is safely caged is that she has wealth and family. An empty stomach is a powerful motivator, and maybe, swallowed up in her own desires and facing another lonely, hungry sundown, Saba let go and the banshee found a way to get free. Did *she* mix a bit more sour cherry into the drink than usual? Was she trying to cover up some foul taste?

"No," Saba says aloud. She did nothing. She counted a perfect dose.

She returns to the kitchen to inspect the glasses because she will never be able to live with such a mistake. But they are already washed. She comes back to the room and leans beside Abbas, takes his hand in both of hers. "Abbas, the doctor is coming. But you have to tell me, did you take medicine with the juice?" She searches his eyes. "Tell me."

He makes an incomprehensible noise. Then he seems to nod.

Relief and panic wash over her, followed immediately by disbelief.

"Don't you remember the routine? I put your pills *in* the glass!" He nods again and she wonders if he knows what he is saying.

Before she has a chance to think, Ponneh is beside her. "Tell him," she whispers. "Saba jan, tell him now."

There is too much pressure from all sides and she turns and screams at Ponneh, "What do you want me to say? What? You were supposed to come over and help me! What are you *doing*? And where the hell is the doctor?"

Ponneh doesn't raise her voice. She says, "I never called."

Saba is frozen. She feels around for her chair and drops into it.

"Have you forgotten that day?" Ponneh yells. "Remember the women and their tools and the way they threw you around like a rag?" Saba rests her face in her hands and pants into the air between her legs. She can't decide if she should get up to call the doctor or if it's too late. Has Abbas heard any of their conversation? Ponneh doesn't seem to register Abbas's presence. "I know you're emotional, and it's easy to forget when you look at how old he is . . . and how sad it is to be near death. And you know what else, Saba jan, I know you don't want to be alone. But you won't be. You have me, and a real family. And you have Reza." Ponneh sits on the ground beside her chair. She glances at Abbas, interlaces her fingers with Saba's, and says in a childish voice, "The three of us forever."

Saba shakes her head. No, she hasn't forgotten. The memories of the Dallak Day are as fresh as ever and there is no cleansing for her despite the many afternoons she spends washing herself in her hammam. The details of that day expand in her mind, swelling and pressing up against her skull until there is room for nothing else. There is simply this: her breath quickening. Her hand flying to her throat. Her body splayed out on her bed and the blood beneath her. It happened more than a year ago, yet it comes back to Saba daily, nightly. It is happening again now.

She gets up to try the doctor again, avoiding Ponneh's gaze. In the living room she picks up the receiver and starts to dial, thinking of her wasted life here in this house. She considers the cruel torture she has inflicted on this man, and the way Agha Mansoori begged to join his wife in heaven. She thinks of her first few nights with Abbas, his anecdotes about the warmth of his first wife. Maybe Ponneh is right that he has lived a complete and blessed life.

She dials a few numbers, her fingers heavy and shaking. What if Abbas heard her talking to Ponneh? He might be aware of the time it has taken her to decide his fate. He might even forget that he took the extra medicine himself. What brutal accusations will he make to all the medical and legal men who are bound to parade through here?

Then Saba thinks of how Abbas nodded when she asked him if he remembered the routine. It's possible that he took the extra medicine on purpose. The thought makes her chest constrict—the image of the old man reaching out for the company of his first wife the way Agha Mansoori did for his. Maybe this is a mercy. Maybe she should use the power she has been given and return this man to his true wife. Agha Mansoori tried so hard to die; he misplaced his pills and left ovens burning and begged Saba to help him. Like an angel of death, she held his hand as he moved on, and it was easy and timely and good. She can see that Abbas has been waiting to die, and that it is a kindness and a blessing to leave the world peacefully, without the sting of violence that accompanies so many deaths here. Abbas must realize this. She replaces the phone and returns to Abbas's room, where Ponneh is feeling his forehead. She must feel guilty too.

"I'm not calling the doctor," she says, her voice exhausted. She falls into Ponneh's arms. Ponneh strokes her hair and says that all will be well. If Saba talked to him, could Abbas hear her? She can't be certain because the light is leaving his eyes. Ponneh whispers into her hair, "Tell him."

Saba fumbles with her shirt. The room has grown hot. She runs her hand through her long hair. "I don't know what to say." She sits on the bed beside him.

Ponneh moves to the chair. "I'll start," she says, and shifts around. She begins to speak several times but reconsiders her words. Finally she says, "Good-bye, Abbas . . . Just repeat what I say, Saba jan. Go on . . . say good-bye to him."

"Good-bye," she groans, unable to get out more than the one word.

"May you find peace somewhere," Ponneh says, confident even though she's improvising.

"I hope in heaven you find peace—" Saba says. It feels like a prayer, repeating Ponneh's words. When she was a little girl, her mother explained the rules of prayer. She said that each person must have her own individual words. "That's the difference between Christian prayer and Muslim prayer," she told Saba and Mahtab. "We don't chant. We tell God what's in our hearts." Now something inside stirs and she can feel all the words she wants to say bubbling up, rising to the surface from the mouth of the injured beast that lies there. She swallows hard and listens to Ponneh try to continue.

"But what you did . . . God, that was . . . evil." The steely quality of Ponneh's voice is gone and she seems unsure, shaky, maybe too young for it all. But this is a poison that must be expelled. Saba doesn't want any more help. She waves her hand for Ponneh to stop.

She takes a breath and says, "That's enough now," then licks her lips. "Abbas . . ." She stops and considers the possibility that Abbas did this on purpose. Does he believe in heaven as Agha Mansoori did? If so, he too will need someone to bear witness that he didn't commit the ultimate sin. "You made a mistake with the medicine. It was only a mistake, but I can't fix it for you. I gave you plenty of time, and we were friends at first, remember? But that day—" She stops. There is no use in rehashing it. "I can't help you now. You're no longer my friend." When she is finished, she lifts herself up, unable to recall her own words, though she can feel by their absence how heavy they must have been. She touches Abbas's withered face, now grown cold, and adds, "I hope you find your wife." With that she leaves the room, consumed by thoughts of what it means to be a Christian, and how disappointed her mother would be that Saba has chosen to drop her cross and walk away. But maybe the world doesn't need so many martyrs and cross-bearers. Or maybe Saba just doesn't believe.

Ponneh shuts the door behind them. They wait outside, Saba stroking her neck because the tickle inside her throat has become unbearable. She takes a few gulps of air and tries not to hear his breathing. Ponneh runs to the kitchen to get tea and tissues. Saba doesn't notice when she comes back. When the noises stop, she falls asleep in the hall outside Abbas's room and doesn't wake again until daylight.

The next morning Abbas is dead and Saba is a rich widow, a fierce tern in crow's clothing, dark eyes downcast, red mouth stained and shining like blood, mourning alongside a line of her black-crow sisters. The women around her touch her head and kiss her cheeks, some of them whispering that she has a very prosperous life ahead. But behind her black layers, she holds on to her lifelong wish to fly away, toward her mother in America. To explain her sins in person.

Abbas's death is pronounced accidental—a stroke that, given the number of pills left over, may have been caused by too much blood thinner. Though dazed and unsure of herself, Saba tells the doctor that he administered his own medicine that night. Maybe he took too much. She has learned to rub yogurt like an expert storyteller, and so has come into her very own Yogurt Money. She has become a grandmaster of *maast-mali*.

An overdose is unfortunate, the doctors say, but he was an old man. In the end, no one thinks about it much. It isn't such a strange thing, and uninteresting as far as scandals are concerned. Abbas had a full life and there is no mother-in-law to make a fuss.

᪥᪥᪥

That's the trouble with being old. No mother to make a fuss for you when you are sick or dying, or just drowning in an imaginary sea. *I feel so old.* Five days after her last period, again she leans over the porcelain hole in the ground, her feet firmly planted on the ridged footrests on each side, and packs herself with cotton. Her bleeding is erratic and she wonders just how damaged she is inside, in the places she cannot see.

On her first night alone she has nightmares—about her mother, Abbas, Mahtab. She turns on the lights and reads books to protect herself from what she has done—letting Abbas die, letting Mahtab get on a plane or drop to the bottom of the sea. Either way, Saba was there. Could she have prevented the loss of Mahtab one way or another? And is it possible to love someone who spent so many months torturing her own husband?

Sometimes she shocks herself by missing him and realizes that her guilt doesn't come from letting him die but for having made his last year a sort of purgatory. Was that her right as a wife? Or as the victim of the Dallak Day? She attends Abbas's funeral in black and faces the men who eye her, some suspicious, some sympathetic. There is something rejuvenating in the process. A slow clarity comes with hours of watching people pass by and pay their respects—the knowledge that none of them can take away what is hers. No one can stand in the way of a life that is now in her name, fully and independently.

At the burial, she sees Reza. Though she does not speak to him—it is forbidden for a mourning widow—twice he holds her gaze with the tenderness of their years of friendship. He nods sadly and goes to pay respects to her father. Ponneh stays constantly by Saba's side. In

311

four months her mourning period will be over and she will be allowed to marry again, though she has no such inclinations now. She will go to America.

But first there is this: four months in crow's clothing.

Saba counts the friends of Abbas and her father as they say their prayers, and she takes stock of the people around her—those in her husband's debt, in her father's debt. Agha Hafezi takes her hand to reassure her, and Saba realizes that these bowed heads are now also in her debt. So much that belonged to Abbas and her father now belongs to her. Not only fortunes. But a name, a reputation, a power to change things.

Maybe now she will be like Mahtab, the journalist. Maybe Saba can do even more than that. She remembers her mother's words at the airport, about not crying, about being a giant in the face of trouble. What was it that her mother used to say?

I'm no Match Girl, she thinks, and says aloud so that Ponneh can hear. Not because of her father's unbreakable contract, but because of her own plans and suffering and patience. These truths become clear to Saba, so she accepts the mourners' words of comfort, one by one, and she is transformed.

Part 3

MOTHERS, FATHERS

Baby, Grandma understands
That you really love that man.

—*Bill Withers*

Chapter Fifteen

AUTUMN 1991

Three months later Saba sits with her father in a mullah's office in Rasht. The mullah speaks to Agha Hafez while Saba examines the soft lines of his face. He has kind eyes, though he doesn't look at her, but nods in her direction every now and then as he explains that marriage contracts are still subject to Shari'a law. "I see that all funeral expenses and debts have been paid off," he says, looking at a thin pile on his desk, "and other than this very *informal* marriage agreement, Agha Abbas left no will."

Saba holds her breath. This is absurd. The contract was as tight as could possibly be made and, in fact, much of the property and money was put under Saba's own name. *What if it was all for nothing? No,* she thinks. Mullah Ali, who is an expert in Shari'a law, assured her father that there were no impediments to her inheritance.

"If no entitled descendants exist—and I believe Agha Abbas had no children by any previous wives—then the wife is entitled to one-fourth of his estate automatically. That is God's law. We do not dispute that your daughter deserves that much."

Saba breathes out, somewhat relieved. She can feel her father beside her thrumming with anger, struggling to control himself. She fidgets in an itchy black chador.

"Yes, but the contract we negotiated was very solid," her father says. "It was in keeping with Islamic law and agreed upon by Abbas and myself. There were witnesses. Come now, Hajj Agha, do you see any other claimants here with us?"

The mullah puts his hand up, feigning impatience, though he obviously respects her father's education and standing. He continues. "The issue isn't your knowledge of the law. It is whether any heirs escaped your notice. There are no other *primary* heirs in this case, since the man had no other living wives, no children, and so on. But we felt it necessary to do our duty toward Allah and the deceased to find any *secondary* beneficiaries. These would be residuaries who would be entitled to the rest of the estate."

"The *rest?*" Saba blurts out. Her father grabs her arm and tells her to hush. This seems to satisfy the mullah, who smiles patiently, ready to continue his speech. But Agha Hafezi, still holding Saba's arm, jumps in.

"*Looking* for secondary beneficiaries seems excessive. Agha, our family has looked already. Not to mention that secondary heirs will always appear if you advertise for them! Show me a dead man with money and I'll show you forty Arab cousins crawling out of nowhere. Who are you looking for exactly?"

The mullah sighs and adjusts his glasses as he reads from his notes. "Brothers, sisters, nephews, nieces. Clearly there is no possibility of living uncles or grandparents."

"Why?" Saba whispers, shocked that such a small, underfunded office with plastic chairs and a draft seeping in through the floor cracks would go to so much trouble to search all of Iran for the long-lost relatives of a dead recluse.

The mullah raises both eyebrows. "Would you not have us do the right thing?"

"Did you find any?" Her father sighs. When he becomes impatient, his voice takes on a condescending quality that he is now trying to control. He forces a smile and says, "It seems that if no one has come forward, this is a very simple case."

"Yes, I do see your concern," says the mullah. "But we have found a brother."

Her father shakes his head, disbelieving. Saba hasn't studied Shari'a law, but she does know one thing: a brother's share is much bigger than a wife's—never mind the fact that she was bruised and mutilated for Abbas's sake, and that this man probably didn't even know of Abbas's existence until a few days ago. A cynical part of her congratulates the men of the world for a first-rate win.

"Don't worry, Agha Hafezi," says the mullah. "He is only a *uterine* brother. He only shared a mother with Agha Abbas, and since that poor woman died recently, he is all that's left. The man lives in the South and is near death himself, but alive enough to inherit. We have already contacted him. The law dictates that he receive one-sixth."

"And the rest?" asks her father.

"In the absence of any other claimants, we divide the residue *proportionally* between you and the half brother." He looks at Saba and slowly explains the logic, skipping over the parts with math for her benefit. "That means you will get the most, my child."

Sixty percent, Saba calculates in her head, just before her father says it aloud for the record. The mullah waits a moment. When Saba shows no gratitude, he says, "I discussed this with my colleagues. They wished to continue searching for male heirs. They were concerned . . . it's so much money for a young woman, and this isn't Tehran. I myself travel to Tehran often, and I know that many good Muslim widows manage their own money without scandal. But others aren't so modern-thinking. You are very lucky, indeed. Women are not meant to shoulder such heavy responsibilities."

Agha Hafezi nods politely for the mullah. He pinches Saba's arm as he used to do when she was small and they had an inside joke between them. "I will watch over her," he assures the cleric. "I'll make sure she buys a book and pencils once in a while, and not just fabrics and kitchen supplies."

Saba bites the inside of her cheeks. Her father used to joke that if she was let loose in a foreign bookstore without supervision, she would blow the entire family fortune. And she knows her father well enough to realize that the part about the kitchen supplies is his subtle message to her—that he has watched over her from their separate houses, that he hasn't stopped at knowing her hobbies, but has cataloged all the daily things she considers worthless and mundane, a list very similar to her mother's.

"Good," says the mullah. "Before we turn over the deeds, bank accounts, and other papers, I have to go over a few fine points, technicalities. You see, there are only two rules of eligibility to inherit. And since we know that your daughter didn't *kill* her husband," he chuckles, "we just need to have her testament that she is a true Muslim."

She considers all that she has lost, the high price she has already paid. The bleeding. "Yes," she breathes, without looking at the mullah. "Yes, of course I am a Muslim." *This is just one more thing. One more lie to add to it all.* This is simply the inevitable whitening that comes with secret stashes of undeserved money.

Her father stares at the floor. There is sadness in his eyes and for an instant Agha Hafezi, savvy businessman, student of religion and wit, looks like a simple Gilaki farmer.

When all the papers are signed, father and daughter get up to leave. "There is just one more thing I should tell you," says the mullah, tentatively. He purses his lips and flares his nostrils in a way that Saba has noticed is his habit when he is trying to find the right words.

"You see, Abbas's relations had no idea about the money. Abbas lived in a village, after all. How much could he have? It's very much a windfall to them." Agha Hafezi doesn't comment, since he too is rich and living in a village. "The head and tail of it is that the family is *trying* to prove that the man is a full brother. You should be aware of the possibility that they might succeed, in which case they will inherit the majority." He shakes his head. "It's a shame. . . . Man is a greedy beast."

Moments later they cross the busy streets of Rasht, Agha Hafezi grasping the crook of Saba's arm through her chador. Usually Saba finds the sharp sounds and pungent smells of the big city wonderfully overwhelming—the gasoline and car exhaust, fresh market fish and grilled kebab, perfume and body odor. Usually she relishes the sounds of the street vendors and traffic; the flashes of color displayed by brazen passersby, a scarf here, a bright collar there. But not today. Today it is all a dim yellow and dusty-blue haze, the color of faded fabric and low-budget movies. Saba can see that her father is angry. She can see that he feels cheated for her. Yes, she has more money now than any other woman she knows—enough to live on for the rest of her life—but the look on her father's face makes Saba want to enumerate all the precious things she lost in that one transaction. Over and over she tries to forgive herself for the lie she uttered in the mullah's office and begs God not to allow Abbas's relations to create a legal frenzy and ransack all that she has earned. There are so many secrets that could lead to the loss of her fortune: the unconsummated marriage, the circumstances of Abbas's death, her Christianity, and this man who claims to be Abbas's full brother. . . . *What if he really is?*

"We can still celebrate," her father offers before they reach the bus stop. "How about lunch at one of these kebab places? I know a good one not far from here."

Saba smiles—because her father is choosing not to dwell on the battles to come. She tries to push away the awful realization that her sacrifices, the scars she has suffered, guarantee her nothing. Like her father, she tries to ignore the sins of today. She reasons that all possessions are fleeting in the new Iran—all of life is a trick—and that she should enjoy her fickle reward while she still has it. A free pass for the girl with the thousand jinns, before she finds her way out of here.

"Good idea," she says. "I'm so hungry."

"You look thin," her father jokes. He always teases her when he wants to make her happy, in those rare moments when he is himself and not consumed with work or the hookah or his lost wife and daughter. Maybe this is a new start for Saba and Agha Hafezi, not just an awkward father and child, but a pair of equals—in their hopes, in their wealth, in their grief for all that they have lost. "Time to start making you a fat, happy widow."

ᔰᘏᘖᘏᔒ

Heiress—*a person (f) who lawfully receives the property of one deceased.*
Hermit—*a person who chooses to live alone, apart from others.*
Hermes—*Greek messenger of the gods. Also a store with orange boxes.*

Later in the evening she makes a new list of English words and considers her two options: staying with her father or looking for a ticket to America. She could do it now. She could finally try to get on that plane she missed when she was eleven. The resources are available and, after much research, she knows exactly what needs to be done. But somehow each time she begins counting the steps, she loses track of her thoughts and finds herself sinking into the warmth of village life. Maybe things will be better now.

She wonders what Mahtab would do. She would probably choose America. If her mother were here, Saba would show her the piles of word lists she has amassed and ask if her English is good enough to make a respectable life there.

She sorts through sheets of visa and passport instructions, her mother's travel guides, and her bank statements, wondering how long it will all take. One day soon she will have to tell her father about her plans—but not yet. She cooks herself a lamb-and-eggplant stew for dinner. Overcome with gloom and desperate for distraction, she spends an hour skinning, stabbing, salting, and draining the eggplants. She fries them in olive oil and lays them on top of the meat—so tender after two hours that you can eat it with a spoon. When she is done, she realizes that she has made too much eggplant for the stew and so she roasts some tomatoes, adds them to the leftovers, and cooks the mixture with eggs, turmeric, and garlic. This dish, *mirza ghasemi*, is one of her favorite foods, yet she makes it now only as a way to rid herself of unwanted extra ingredients. When it is ready, she eats it standing up, not as an appetizer but as a part of cleaning up, with old bread, because that too should not be wasted.

When the food is ready, she makes herself a plate, skins an entire clove of pickled garlic from the giant jars lined up outside, drops the pungent copper morsels onto her stew, and takes it all into the sitting room, where she arranges six pillows and leans back, preparing for an evening of solitary smoking and outdated American television.

She has already achieved an impressive stupor, far more powerful than any herb or television or despair alone could provide, when there is a knock at the door. She rubs her garlic-and-vinegar-stained fingers on her jeans. No point in washing her hands—pickled garlic, with its skin-penetrating smell, is a long-term guest, invited in only by a certain type of unmarried woman, the kind who is no longer looking.

Hopeless. Housebound. Hermit.

She rolls herself off the rug and ambles toward the door. Her feet have fallen asleep and so takes her time crossing the front yard and unlatching the tall gate.

Reza is waiting outside with his arms crossed over his brown jacket, his eyes darting from one side of the street to the other, check-ing for nosy neighbors or roaming *pasdar*s.

As Reza slides past her and into the front yard, Saba's first thought is, *Why has he come?* There is no reason, now that she has no husband to receive him.

"I meant to come see you earlier," he says.

"Why?" she asks. The fact that she smells like a house cook makes her want to be cruel, but the best she can do is a vague stab at indifference.

Reza shrugs. He looks a little sad and tries to cover it with an uncertain half-smile. "I thought we could spend some time together. I've decided that we should."

"You've 'decided'?" she teases. "And why have you decided now?"

He fidgets. She thinks she understands why he is here, yet neither of them knows how to be anything but the two friends who used to smoke together and talk about American music. "I'm sorry I took so long to visit," he says. He looks down as if trying to remember a pre-pared speech. "It's not easy avoiding gossip around here, you know. But I'm not going to leave you alone twice. You're unprotected now . . . maybe you need someone to check on you once in a while. To fix things for you."

Saba chews on her thumbnail. It tastes like vinegar and oil. Surely he can smell it too. She feels the need to explain the way she looks. "I made a big dinner."

Reza looks confused, worried about losing his place in the speech.

"You can have some, if you want," she says, as she leads him inside. "But anyway . . . I didn't know you were coming."

"Or you wouldn't have cooked?" Reza jokes, and momentarily her old friend is back. She has the urge to take him to her father's pantry and show him her new songs.

Saba smiles. "Yes, actually, I wouldn't have," she says. She gives him a defiant look—a world-weary widow look. When the door is closed, she holds out her hand toward his back, motioning for him to come inside, but he takes it and kisses her palm, pulls her close to him, kisses her lips.

She glances over his shoulder at the door, but now he has his hands in her hair and she forgets about doors or roaming *pasdar*s or nosy neighbors or the garlic. She thinks of his feet in the pantry— the two of them barefoot and slightly drunk in the dark, daring only to feel each other's toes. "I'm happy you came," she says.

"You taste like eggplant *khoresht*," he jokes.

She pushes against his chest and tries to pull away, but he doesn't let go. "In that case," she says, "you can't have any of it."

They spend the evening in blissful seclusion, sampling the many private pleasures in Saba's house. They have never been alone together for an entire evening. Never had a meal without the families. They eat at the kitchen table at first, but decide to move the food to a *sofreh* in the living room instead, to sit on a pile of cushions together, lie back, and feed each other morsels of lamb and stew-soaked bread. "Too bad we're not back in your father's pantry," says Reza, and Saba is reminded of her bag of herbs. Reza rolls a joint in a blank back page he rips out of one of her books, and they lie back on the cushions, smoke, and pick at the dinner with their fingers, heads pressed together, Saba's Walkman stretched taut over both of their ears. They listen to Janis Joplin, Madonna, the Beatles, Michael Jackson, and a series of artists Saba thinks the Tehrani has mislabeled. When the honey-rich conch-shell voice of Tracy Chapman murmurs the first notes of "Fast Car," neither sighs or mentions the last time they heard it. They listen and quietly hum along. Then Saba switches the tape to her favorite songs about the sea. She saves the best for last, "Sittin' on the Dock of the Bay" and "Downeaster Alexa."

When Reza grabs her by the waist and pulls her to him, she won-ders if it's a mistake becoming involved with him in *this* way. Did she not suffer to remove him from her heart? Did she not find him weak when she needed him? But Reza was so young when he let her be mar-ried. What could he do? And he has since apologized. He has been brave and kind, a true friend. She thinks of the day of Farnaz's hang-ing, when he came to find them. Certainly Reza has changed, as she has done. And he is choosing her now, despite the predictions of his mother and all of Cheshmeh. Maybe he is using her because Ponneh is still not allowed to marry. But then again, maybe Saba is using *him*. Why not?

One day she might be far from this place, and she will think of him—her beautiful friend who used to show off for her, kicking his football with sandaled feet outside her house. If she lets this chance go, she would wonder what his skin and hair would have felt like, what it would have been like to lie across him once or twice.

"Let's not do this here," she says, suddenly afraid of what she might experience, her first time with a man. What about all the dam-age that waits unseen inside her? Should she tell him her secrets? She rests her cheek against his neck. "The neighbors will know."

He reaches for her hand. "Then how do we see each other in this small town?"

"I know a place we can go. Dr. Zohreh gave me a key."

⁂

Twice a week at dusk, Saba sits alone in her father's car and drives to the shack by the sea. If she is going to lose Abbas's fortune and end up wandering the earth looking for entry into a new country, she might as well enjoy the here and now. Why should she sit in a pantry

dreaming of things she can reach out and take? She remembers pining over happy memories of the Caspian of her childhood. Of Friday
trips to the beach in summer. Of the cold sea leaving salt on her bare
skin. Of bare skin. Of fish cooked over open fire. The family car
climbing a small, flat, rocky hill on a winter day, barely hanging on to
the now dusty, now icy, unpaved road chiseled into the side of the
mountain. The sea, gray and foggy, then hills, mountains, and rock.
And then in the spring, the bursting green forest, the terns, and the
never-ending water. Now seaside trips are tedious. No more breezy
picnics. A tattered curtain dividing the beach. The heat of eyes
always watching.

For weeks Reza has visited Saba in the mountain shack, sometimes in the green Paykan he shares or, when he has less time to
spend, speeding to her on a borrowed motorcycle, sometimes hitchhiking in the backs of overloaded Jeeps full of day laborers. They
have had many afternoons and nights there, in Saba's secret house.
They make love relentlessly, though she was afraid at first. She wondered if she should do this, if it would hurt as much as the Dallak
Day. But then, on their first visit, Reza touched her cheek like someone holding a baby bird, and things were no longer awkward between
them. He mistook the fear in her eyes for memories of Abbas. What
did he make her do? She laughed and they spent the evening talking
instead, about music and the old days. Later in the night she discovered that it hurt only a little. And the second and third time didn't
hurt at all. She had expected something searing—like that other day.
But always afterward the skin of her fingers hums—a beautiful surprise. How can skin be capable of humming? It seems there are uses
for her body that she has overlooked.

Sometimes she has a hard time getting up right away, and Reza
makes jokes—using a vulgar phrase translating roughly to "fucked
stupid," which, in the mouths of villagers, used to shock her, but now
makes her laugh. Sometimes he growls, his stubble running over her

stomach as if he is trying to whisper to the banshee, the wild hungry thing running barefoot inside, or maybe their future children. It is an animal part of him—and exquisite. But other times, when it is dark, she imagines the shadows on the wall pulling together, coalescing into the silhouettes of the two fleshy women from another lifetime. They are here in the cabin, hovering over her. But they never stay for very long. She pushes them away, stores them in a different compartment of her memory, in an attic or cellar, a place for boxing away items no longer needed for the day-to-day.

She reads "The Sin" by Forough Farrokhzad, a poem she finally understands.

I sinned a sin full of pleasure . . . Oh God, I know not what I did.

Despite the thrill of her new secret, she feels guilty about Ponneh and unbalancing their trio. Even in their teenage days, when Saba mentioned Reza, Ponneh grew quiet, afraid of losing them both.

As autumn winds down, she stops wishing she could run away. She stops looking for her mother, but she doesn't discard any of her research. The passport forms, visa guidelines, and California leaflets remain her paper security blanket, though since her romance with Reza, they are no longer an obsession. She begins to consider an alternate future, imagining herself a wife again, but this time one who is beloved, sexy like the actress Azar Shiva, full of life, worshipped by her husband. Maybe one day she can be a mother, a strong, principled one like her own. Secretly she pictures Reza's chin, his nose, his mouth on the faces of her future children. It is an easier daydream now that her plans for America are tainted by the fear of taking a first step. There is no longer anything stopping her from trying for a visa. Why hasn't she?

She tells herself to wait a little longer. When she goes to America, everything will be strange and unfamiliar; she will want to have experienced this time with Reza, to take it with her as a comfort.

On their fourth visit to the shack, late in the afternoon when the air is heavy and the walls seem to drip with seawater that has traveled in through a window and settled on their bodies, when Reza is tangled up in her arms, her legs, her hair, a discarded Walkman in a corner whispering about a lonely town and a lonely street, she feels a sharp sting below her belly. She asks if he wants her to change position, but Reza, thinking she is worried about pleasing him, kisses her and continues. A minute later he looks down at their legs, naked on a thin sheet on the floor, and says, "What's this?"

Saba sits up on her elbows and pushes back her hair. "What?"

"You're bleeding," he says. "I thought today wasn't one of those days . . ."

Saba feels herself flush from her temples all the way down to her shoulders. Will she have to tell him now? She takes a deep breath and collects the sheet around her body. "I don't know what it is," she mutters. "Maybe it came from you."

Reza scans her face, then the bloody sheet. "Don't be crazy," he says. "Tell me."

Saba takes a deep breath. What is the harm? He might as well know this last intimate detail. After she has finished explaining, there is a long silence. Reza looks away and whispers to himself. Maybe he's trying to figure out what is expected of him—what a man might do in those times when a boy would be forgiven for running away.

Then he reaches over and pulls Saba into his arms—a hard, jerky motion because he is overwhelmed. But to Saba, this is a release, a shock of cold and warm. She rests her head on his shoulder; he strokes her hair. Somehow it reminds her of the day Ponneh was beaten, when she watched Reza comfort her with children's songs and tell her the bruises would take nothing from her beauty. That day she watched Reza's too-long hair mingle with Ponneh's as they whispered to each other. And now, as he holds her in their shack, she thinks that maybe he feels the same about her, that they might have the same intimate ways. Maybe she's no longer Saba Khanom, but someone equal to him.

"I'm sorry I didn't do more," Reza whispers. He chews the corner of his upper lip. "I should have said something. But don't cry, Saba jan. I'll take care of everything." He looks into her face again, pushes back a sweaty strand of hair, and says, "Let's get married."

She looks up at her dirty-haired lover, this careless boy from another world, a peasant world that is in many ways more removed from hers than the ones on television. He is asking for her, though he has nothing to offer, no education or family. The romance of it makes her want to say yes. She hesitates, wondering, does he love her or does he feel sorry for her? Is he attracted to the wounded part of her that needs protecting? When he was a child, he used to think she and Mahtab were princesses. Maybe he still wants to be a storybook hero. And what about America? Can she wait a little longer? He studies her hand and he says, "We could even have a baby, to make you forget all your troubles." Her heart leaps at this. It seems her body at least wants a child more than an American life. This could be her destiny, finally to blend into the comfortable, protective tapestry of Cheshmeh. If she has children with Reza, she might never leave. It would tie her to Iran forever, because one thing is certain: Saba would never leave a child as her mother did. So if she stays in the safety and warmth of Reza's arms, if she forms a new kind of bond with him, one that even Ponneh doesn't have, what will happen to her other dreams? When she remains silent for too long, Reza seems to falter. "I'll take care of you," he says. "I know you don't need money . . . but it's not all about money. This is what I should have done from the beginning," Reza whispers. "We're already family."

For the rest of the night, he wraps himself around her like a winter coat. He darts this way and that, looking for ways to ease her every burden, making her tea, bringing her pillows and aspirin though she assures him she has no pain, softening the cold edges of the shack with the warmth of his concern. It seems that he is desperate to help her heal, to marry her not out of pity but because he wants to protect her from the world and make her whole again. She studies him and thinks he would make a good husband. How beautiful their children would be. A baby might fill the empty space in her heart—someone tied to her by blood, like Mahtab, like her mother. If she were to take on a new role, have a daughter and name her Mahtab, she might never again wonder about the airport day or wake up in a sweat, convinced she is drowning. Reza has brought his *setar* with him. He toys with the strings and hums "Mara Beboos," the haunting melody about good-bye as he leans against the wall, his voice revealing a trace of sadness that she has come to love. Saba lies between his legs, her head against his chest, and stares out at the black night beyond the small window.

Yes, she thinks, the sorrows of the past are dwarfed by the happiness of this moment. *This is the best thing.* It is a strange and welcome feeling, being part of a pair again. Two people devoted only to each other. No extra lovers or other configurations. She will wake up every morning from this day on knowing that she is safe, secure, and loved by the person she has wanted most since she was seven. Can America give her that? When she agrees to his proposal, Reza beams. He kisses her and holds her closer to him. As they begin to fall asleep, he whispers, "You should see a doctor soon."

***

In the pantry, they tell Ponneh their plans. She kisses them both, wishing them a happy life. Later Saba gives her father the news over tea in his kitchen. He looks at her with sullen eyes. "Saba jan, you're almost there. Just a bit more waiting and you will have your own undisputed wealth. Look, I'm not saying to abandon your friends . . . you're a kind girl. And I'm past caring about the differences between our families. They are good, hardworking people. But you've had a lot of sad times. You're finally starting to be happy and you want to cage yourself *again*?"

"Baba!" Saba looks at him wide-eyed. It warms her to know that he has noticed her small day-to-day burdens, the loneliness and confusion and boredom. "Reza is the *reason* I've been happy."

"But are you sure you want to marry a poor villager?" he says matter-of-factly. "You won't be able to take him to Tehran. People will talk. You know how they are."

"I don't care," Saba says. "I never go to Tehran. I barely know our friends there."

He starts to object and seems to change his mind. "If you're happy, I'm happy," he says. "I'm sure your mother and Mahtab are happy too . . . up in heaven."

She moves her chair beside him. "Up in heaven," she whispers back because she doesn't want to argue now. Neither of them has mentioned the faded possibilities in a while.

She thinks of making a joke to lighten the mood but decides against it. Her jokes always misfire with her father. They are either inappropriate or too close to the truth.

But then her father pats her hand and whispers into her ear, "Or America."

She lets out a shocked laugh. "Or America," she says, unable to hide her disbelief.

He sighs and touches her cheek. "Oh, to be so certain of things. To *know* is half the battle, and my Saba always wins."

My Saba always wins. Her father has never been unkind to her. He has never withheld anything from her, but somehow this seems like a new triumph—like something she has toiled and longed for, because Iranian men are so rarely impressed. *Saba jan, you've done so well,* she imagines him saying. Funny, she thinks, how a person can wait her entire life for something and it can be a hundred times sweeter when it comes than the farthest boundary of her imagination.

Islamic Education
(Khanom Basir)

Let us be honest, Saba would make a bad mother. Her own mother had so many jinns. Though, I admit, she wasn't *all* crazy until the revolution. Then in 1980 the Iraq war started. In those days the Tehran bombings and such horrors hadn't begun yet—only news of young people killed in border battles. But funny enough, the thing that drove Bahareh Hafezi into a deep, deep depression was Khomeini's rule that all universities must become Islamic. The news made her hysterical and selfish. It put such dirt on her head, made her rant, sent her to her bed. She stacked up illegal books and buried them in the yard. She thought people didn't see, but I did. She flitted around the big house, looking for something to do, to protect her girls against what was to come. She gave them long speeches about the new government and the way things would be now, and told them to keep reading banned books—that's how crazy she became. When she was finished ranting, she would look for something to do again, and when she didn't find it, she would repeat the advice she had already given, word for word, like the crazy beggars on the street who repeat the same thing over and over like an *ayah* from the Koran.

One day I brought over a ragged old chador for the girls to play with. They were trying it on in front of the mirror, posing and finding ways to tuck it behind their ears, waving the long fabric around, making it into wings. It was such a sight, little girls playing with a colorful thing. Then Bahareh walked in, and when she saw Mahtab with the chador wrapped around her body, her eyes filled with rage. She screamed. She ripped the chador away, making her own daughter stumble to one side, and tore it in two with her bare hands so that her palms turned red. She took the pieces of fabric and put them in a garbage bag outside. "Not inside the house," she said, as if that means anything to small girls.

Chapter Sixteen

WINTER–SPRING 1992

Two days before her second wedding, Saba wakes to the sound of the telephone. She reaches inside her underwear, as she does every morning. No blood; she breathes out. She hasn't bled for fifty-one days. Khanom Omidi, who never uses a phone, screams into the mouthpiece the way people do in old movies, "You have to come now."

"What for?" says Saba, alarmed. "What's wrong?"

"Poor child . . . The poor Alborz girl has died. I made the halva."

The room is quiet. She lets the seconds slip through her fingers. Her best friend has lost her sister. What pain she must be suffering now. Saba must go to her house. She will be a placeholder for Ponneh's sister, just as Ponneh has been for hers. She feels foolish for once believing that Ponneh was waiting for the freedom to marry, waiting for her own sister to die. How could she have thought this when her own greatest obsession has been the loss of Mahtab? She touches her belly, where a baby might be forming even now, and thinks she should take some food for Ponneh's mother.

Despite this, as she runs to her bedroom, a selfish part of her wonders, *What will happen now?* Reza is technically unmarried. Will he cancel everything and marry Ponneh? Since their engagement, his mother has refused to speak to her—making excuses and broadcasting her disapproval through friends. *Why wasn't there a proper* khastegari? *Why no chance for his family to negotiate the marriage terms? Are we too low to follow the customs?* If only she knew about Saba's baby plans.

Saba dresses carelessly, barely stopping to brush her hair before throwing on her manteau and scarf and rushing to the Alborz home. The house is loud with wailing. People spill out into the tiny yard and the floor is covered with plates of halva. The women gather inside with the family, while the men linger outside, talking softly about practical things. They loiter around the old wash pool in front that is filled with rainwater and leaves, useless since the arrival of plumbing (except to rinse dusty hands or feet under the faucet, or to drape clothes on the thick outer edge). In the dead girl's room, Khanom Alborz tears at her hair and buries her face in her daughter's empty blankets. She pounds the bed mat with her fists and curses God and all the people lined up against the wall, who are silently observing but refusing to leave. *So ugly,* Saba thinks, *losing a child.* Ponneh and her two older sisters cry together in one corner of the room. A young man in a white medical coat stands a short distance away, watching the girls. His hands are folded, and he wears an embarrassed expression. Saba finds Khanom Omidi just inside the main entrance of the packed home next to two piles of visitors' shoes and sandals.

"It's so sad," says the old woman. "So sad. But I'm telling you, Saba, this was the will of God. Those girls need to live." Saba gives some kind of assent and remembers her own first days without Mahtab. Does Ponneh feel like she is drowning? Does she want to wander the streets, trying to decide which way to turn now that her sister is gone?

"See?" says Khanom Omidi. "It was good that no one made them brother-sister."

"Huh?" Saba is watching her friend. Reza is nowhere to be seen.

"I'm talking about the doctor, Saba jan." Khanom Omidi's beady gaze roams as she pulls Saba closer to hide her lazy eye. "Remember Mullah Ali's scheme about the milk and . . . uh, Saba, don't make me say it. It's not good to talk of funny things now."

"Fine, I remember," says Saba. "So what?"

"Well, it's obvious, isn't it? He can marry one of the girls now." Khanom Omidi nods happily three or four times and quickly clears the smile from her face.

"Is Reza here?" Saba asks.

"Oh, my dear," shrieks the old woman, as if she has just remembered that Saba is about to be married. "I'm so sorry this happened during your *aghd*. This is not good. Not good at all, poor girl."

Just then there is a noise from outside. A high-pitched shriek followed by a flurry of male voices. She rushes outside, old Khanom Omidi waddling slowly behind.

"Let go of me. Let go, you useless donkeys. Let go, I have a right to be here." Khanom Basir is screaming as Ponneh's uncle and a bewildered man in a patched gray suit and black Gilaki skullcap try to silence her. When she sees Saba, her rants take on a new pitch. "You," she spits at Saba. Her eyes are wild and Saba grows frightened, thinking that maybe Khanom Basir has taken a bad drug. "You scheming girl. You tried to manipulate my innocent son. . . . Evil little *jadoogar*. You can't marry my son now." She waves a finger at Saba as Ponneh's uncle begs her to stop. "Let go of me. I only came to talk to my friend. She will have no objection to giving up her daughter now. She will want to see me. Let me go."

Saba's stomach turns and she thinks she might vomit right here. *Does she really hate me so much? Am I so awful a person?* Strangely, in the face of Khanom Basir's taunts, she wishes for Ponneh.

She tells herself that Khanom Basir suffers from wounded family pride. That she regards herself as important in this village and that Agha Hafezi has insulted her and her son. The contract with Reza is even tighter than the one with Abbas. Reza has nothing of his own, and when it was time to negotiate, her father asked him to sign twenty pages of text before he was satisfied. He made Saba promise never to combine finances, never to share her bank details, to name him, not Reza, as her closest male relative in every transaction.

The men hold back Reza's mother, looking over their shoulders every so often to make sure the mourners inside cannot hear. Someone runs to close the front door. "It's not time for this, Khanom," says Ponneh's uncle. "Please, control yourself. Come back tomorrow."

Khanom Basir drops her shoulders. She breathes heavily and tries to calm herself. "There is no time," she says in a hoarse whisper. "My son will marry the witch in two days. There is no time." Saba is numb with disbelief and fear that this insanity might succeed. Should she speak up? Maybe stand up for herself or for the respect owed to Ponneh's dead sister?

Ponneh's uncle whispers to Khanom Basir; Saba imagines he is trying to reason with her. Reza's mother shakes her head so violently that her headscarf slips onto her shoulders. Her hair is a mess, her eyes desperate. There is nothing left now of the vibrant storyteller or the sensible mother figure who stood with her in a smelly toilet and told her she was lucky to be a girl. Saba hates this vile stranger.

She doesn't notice the eyes on her until Khanom Omidi tries to lead her inside. But she wants to stay. She is overcome by the fear that Reza *would* want a choice.

He arrives moments later, quietly greeting the men gathered around the front steps until he sees his mother in hysterics and charges past them. He pulls her away, tries to comfort her as the men whisper the details of her errand into his ear.

Reza listens, his face growing more and more impassive as the picture becomes clearer. The men watch Saba, a few of them wearing amused grins, the older ones, those who know her father, lowering their heads in sympathy. She wants to run away. But then maybe she should walk over and slap one of them like Ponneh might do. Then the door opens and Ponneh stands there, sent by the women to see what has happened. She sees Reza and turns to go back inside, but Khanom Basir calls out to her, begins pleading again. Ponneh freezes, her face pale. Does she think Reza will change his mind? She doesn't look at Saba, her good friend. But she is bold enough to lock eyes with Saba's fiancé, right there in front of their friends and neighbors. Reza waits. He seems confused. He waits too long.

What is that on Ponneh's face? Expectation? Accusation? Hope? Maybe it's just annoyance at the scene his mother has created. Reza seems to wither under her glare, and though neither of them speaks, what passes between them feels like the worst betrayal.

Someone whispers. Saba catches fragments: ". . . He's only a man . . . couldn't wait forever." And then someone says a bit louder, "It's easier with a widow, no waiting."

"Just in time, though," says one man. "Unless she's caught him with a pregnancy."

She tries to push away the overwhelming fear of going home alone, of canceling the wedding, of having to attend Ponneh and Reza's marriage ceremony disgraced—maybe pregnant. What if Reza chooses Ponneh and she has to care for their child alone?

At least a dozen people are loitering on the grass in front, watching or whispering. Khanom Basir sits on the edge of the wash pool, wetting the seat of her tunic with rainwater. Every eye is on the trio, an electric triangle, staring at each other, dumbstruck. Saba counts the seconds. *One more*, she thinks, *and he will choose her. He's considering it now. Just one more second, and I've lost him.*

The seconds tick away, and Saba, desperate for a moment alone, turns to leave. As if awakened from hypnosis, Reza tears his gaze from Ponneh and hurries to Saba's side. He takes her hand, kisses it deliberately. His awareness of the audience is tangible, like a thick, airborne vapor slowing his movements and keeping her from feeling his lips on her hand. A strange unease takes hold, as if she has escaped disaster but come out missing a limb. What was it that just passed between them? A part of her still wants to run, because she heard every unspoken word between her best friends. She felt the tension as they looked at each other, so different from the meaningful glances she and Reza shared across *sofreh*s and bazaar stalls—those giddy, mischievous looks meant to remind the other of everything they had done and would do again. Reza looked at Ponneh with grief and longing. He looked at her with something other than concern.

Ponneh rolled her eyes and went back inside, receding into the house like a tired matron behind familiar hand-sewn curtains.

As Reza collects his mother and they leave the Alborz house with its baby blue windowsills and modest flowerpots, Saba recalls that in the past weeks, whenever Reza entered a room, Ponneh did her best to leave it; and Reza developed a habit of asking after Ponneh's mother.

What has happened between Ponneh and Reza? Why are they no longer friends?

Is Ponneh angry with him for his choice? Is she confused by the new Reza who isn't scared or impressionable, no longer a boy she can control? Probably she's just sad for her sister and wishes to have her best friends back. What if the three of them could return to the old days when they sat in a pantry unburdened by marriage or romance? Just three friends in danger of getting caught.

She wants to wash away the stench of this day. She knows now that despite all that she and Reza feel for each other, he loves Ponneh also.

After the funeral, the Gilaki marriage machine works quickly, and within the next day, the two older Alborz girls are visited by eager *khastegars*—men in such a rush that they flout custom and ignore the mourning period. Probably secret lovers, the town whispers. The older daughter is promised to the doctor, and her sister to another close family relation. Both men strut about the town elated, their chests pushed out, as if they are some great divine example of dignified patience to the world. Lovers not to be outdone. Modern-day Rumis and Saadis. No one comes for Ponneh, whom they have long called the Virgin of Cheshmeh, cursing her mother for letting such a beautiful girl become pickled. Ponneh, it seems, has not had a *khastegar* marinating behind the scenes. She busies herself with the preparations for her sister's burial, receives well-wishers for her older sisters, and pulls back from the Basir-Hafezi wedding arrangements. At times Saba wonders why her friend does not come. And then she admonishes herself for her stupidity. Maybe this one time Ponneh needs to be selfish.

On the first day of the new year, Norooz, which marks the spring equinox, Saba and Reza are married in a traditional *aghd* in Saba's own house, the one she once shared with Abbas. They sit under a canopy and read Hafez and Nezami instead of the Koran to show off their youthful rebellion, while two women thought to be lucky rub giant cones of sugar over their heads to protect them and symbolize a sweet life. Saba tries to ignore the erratic pacing of her mother-in-law. "The first thing you must do is learn to laugh," says Khanom Omidi. "Be amused by her wickedness and you will always be happy."

"It's a mother-in-law's job to do *jadoo* to sabotage the bride," says her aunt, Agha Hafezi's sister. "All the tricks of burning hair and soaking this or that in vinegar. Replacing sugar with salt. It is to show that without evil there can be no good."

Saba decides to accept this. Rashtis have a way of making everything seem less serious, less grave and worrisome. *Life is life.* They coat bad things in layers of sugar. They cover ugly truths with yogurt. *I can laugh at the small things,* she tells herself.

She starts with the ceremony—tittering with Reza at the old Zoroastrian custom in which the cleric asks the couple to promise not to "cooperate with fools" or "cause pain to their mothers." And a tradition from farther west that has a female relative—Saba's Azerbaijani cousin—sew a cloth in the corner and say loudly so everyone can hear, "I am sewing the mother-in-law's mouth shut. I am sewing the sister-in-law's mouth shut."

She only flouts one of the old Persian rules. When the cleric asks if she wants to be married, she is supposed to stay quiet the first time. The ladies in the room know to say things like "The bride has gone to pick flowers." The cleric asks again, and again the bride must be silent. The guests then cluck, "The bride is off to the mosque to pray." Finally, on the third attempt, the bride must say yes so softly, so coyly, that she is barely heard. Then all the guests scream and claim they heard it first. But today Saba answers clearly the first time, and when the guests pretend to be shocked and the cleric looks up with raised eyebrows, she shrugs sweetly and eyes Reza, and their friends whistle and hoot instead.

Later, when the guests are lulled with food and wine and good gossip, Saba's father finds her alone and takes her outside to greet two of his oldest friends. One of them, a tall, oddly shaped man with sunken cheeks, a concave stomach, and long spindly legs, holds a golden basket with metal handles—an *esfandoon*—in one hand. The sides of the *esfandoon* are ornately decorated in old Persian style and it is half filled with hot coals. Saba recognizes it, the same one that was used on neighborhood children years ago to ward off evil and the jealous eye.

"Are you becoming superstitious?" Saba teases her father.

But his expression is serious. "After the Alborz girl and that out-rage by Khanom Basir. My poor daughter. The jealous eye has been on you for a long time. I want to give you this extra protection." Then he adds, his speech slurring a little, "These Zoroastrian practices belong to everyone. It's not a Muslim practice, you know."

Another one of the men, a shorter one with a full head of black hair and a thick black mustache that comes down over his lower lip, takes a bag of *esfand* seeds from his pocket. He tosses the chocolate-colored seeds onto the hot coals. They crackle, making loud popping sounds and emitting tufts of aromatic smoke. Saba breathes deeply. It is this rich smoky smell that is said to ward off the jealous eye. Her father takes the basket and moves it in a circular motion over Saba's head—as he did when she was a little child, as will be done again and again tonight with Reza beside her—reciting an ancient incantation to a long-dead Persian king. When he is done, he gives the basket to his friend and leans over and kisses his daughter on both cheeks.

"You always said not to believe in nonsense," Saba says.

Her father nods. He looks at her with solemn, watery eyes. "I've reconsidered things . . . ever since I got a teacup full of salt at your engagement party."

Saba starts to say something, but there is little point. Of course Khanom Basir replaced the sugar with salt—a standard trick for cursing an event. Her father laughs his deep, throaty laugh. He waves the *esfandoon* a few more times ("One more for your mother-in-law") and ushers his friends away. Saba stands in her courtyard next to the little fountain, examining her hennaed hands and savoring the possi-bility that her father wouldn't have gone to this extra trouble for Mahtab. She remembers competing with her sister over which of them had their father's love—one kind act versus another.

She finds Reza again, and for the rest of the evening, scarves are flung aside. Sugar cones are ground down to nubs, and Reza and Saba exchange a glance as guests remind them of their sordid beginnings—that day cousin Kasem caught them kissing behind the house. The party drifts into the front yard, where the roses and hyacinths are beginning to bloom. Some early petals have escaped the grassy lawn and are scattered on the concrete walkway and in the fountain. Fragrant blossoms trickle down from the orange trees, showering the guests with undeniable spring.

Later when the sun goes down and Norooz, the first day of the year, is fully upon them, they pluck stringed instruments in the yard, Reza no doubt thinking of his absent father, who first taught him to love music, and showed him how to play the *setar* and *dutar* and *saz*. Because Saba loves Suri Wednesday, a celebration that passed a few days ago while she was busy with wedding preparations, she has insisted that they build the traditional bonfire on her wedding day instead. She jumps hand in hand with Reza over a flame inside a ring of rocks and singes her dress at the hem, but no one notices except the boy who puts it out with his sneakers. They clap and sing loudly, and fall exhausted on the benches along the outdoor walkway. All down the street, windows glow orange and dot the dark sky as other families welcome the New Year with songs and dancing. For one night it is safe to celebrate, and for one night Saba doesn't dream of where her mother and sister might be.

Norooz
(Khanom Basir)

This is the injustice that breaks my heart, because I know love when I see it.

Nineteen eighty was the year Reza kissed Ponneh in an alley behind the Hafezi house. The twins saw it. Everyone did. It was Suri Wednesday, celebrated all over Iran on the Tuesday night before the start of spring. On this night people build big bonfires and jump over them in the old Zoroastrian way. They chant to the fire, "Your red to me, my yellow to you," and so they pour their illness and frailty into the flames, and take from it strength, passion, and renewal. It is well known that during this ceremony, charms and magic spells are extra effective. That night, with all the celebration, my Reza must have thought that no one would notice him kissing Ponneh over and over behind the house. But we saw.

For the rest of the time, those cruel sisters refused to play with Ponneh. They took blankets and pillows outside under a mosquito net and, though it was cold, stayed up talking evil about her. Did Reza love her? Did she love him? What would this mean for them (selfish girls), for Saba's marriage to Reza, for Mahtab's friendship with Ponneh?

"She didn't jump over the fire," said Mahtab. "Maybe she'll get sick."

"Maman says that's all rubbish," responded Saba. "Stop believing every superstition people say."

"Stop believing everything Maman says," Mahtab shot back. "I think you should just find someone else. Reza's not worth it."

On the day of Norooz, the first day of the New Year, all the families were gathered for a party at the Hafezi house. A still-depressed Bahareh was wandering around with her new dress and the two girls both in new dresses with their hair back in fancy clips. Ponneh's family didn't have money for new clothes. No one else did. But that didn't matter to the Hafezis with their fancy-*bazi*. And if you ask me, it didn't matter for Ponneh either. She had the so-so-white face, and the extra-red lips, and eyes that every week someone compared to a different kind of nut. "Oh, those almond eyes are made for early marriage." "No, no. They are like hazelnuts, so round."

During the party, the girls spied on Reza and Ponneh to see if the kiss was just a one-time thing or if they were engaged. And, yes, my Reza did play with Ponneh that day. And here's the part where Saba and Mahtab got the best of me. They heard Ponneh complain of a tomato spot on the rim of her dress, and when Reza took a red marker and put matching spots all over the hem of the skirt so that people would think it was a pattern, the jealous little girls told on him. And I dragged him away and scolded him for ruining the poor girl's best dress. If I had only known what he was trying to do . . . such a good heart. Later he played with the Hafezi girls too, because Reza is a caring boy. It was the same game all the boys liked to play: trying to tell them apart, closing their eyes and asking them to switch places.

I spied him once more with Ponneh. They were sitting across from each other in the yard, feet touching, so that the space between them was a diamond made of skinned knees and marker-stained skirts tucked under downy thighs. And when she asked him to tell her a story, he did, and he put her name in all the best parts. Then he played football until Mahtab pretended to faint and he came running to play rescue because my Reza has a fascination with rescuing people. The boys built a pretend hospital out of throw pillows and Reza played the doctor and brought her back to life. Suddenly Saba called out that she was dying and needed all the attention, and Reza was conquered for the afternoon by twin witches and their thousand jinns.

Chapter Seventeen

SUMMER 1992

What is Mahtab doing now? Is she married? Is she dreaming about being a mother? Probably not. Most likely she is too busy with her career. The bleeding has returned. On her free days Saba visits the university in Rasht where a friend of her father's, a professor, allows her to browse his medical books and journals full of jargon—phrases that she looks up in his frayed, pencil-marked Latin, English, and Farsi dictionaries. He doesn't ask her what she's researching. He offers tea and closes the door behind him so she can be alone. She sits on the floor and reads about pregnancy and unscheduled blood, obscure disorders and medical opinions. She reads other women's stories in journals. After a while, their collective suffering takes its toll and she moves on.

She spends much time thinking about her legacy. What if she never has one?

They live in Abbas's house. It is the first time Reza has slept in a Western bed. He fits it nicely, she thinks each time she wakes up and stretches herself across him as she once dreamed of doing. When he opens his eyes, smiling with the first realization of where he now lives, she feels happy to be able to give him so much—something of her own, as in childhood days when she offered him her music tapes.

No, she thinks. *Money will never come between us. It never has.*

In the mornings Reza brings tea for them and he studies his farming textbooks while she listens to her Walkman and reads or writes. They sit in bed for hours while Reza studies for the college exams he should have taken years ago and only now has the means to pursue. He no longer does odd jobs, but he still sells his mother's handiworks to please her. If accepted, he will study agricultural engineering at Gilan University in Rasht. He will become a man like Saba's father, and he will do this because of Saba. How wonderful it feels. Sometimes in her daydreams of Mahtab and James and Cameron, she wonders if her sister knows this feeling of helping someone so beloved.

Mahtab will never feel this small pleasure because the men around her can make their own way. But Mahtab will also never have to wonder how it might suit her to be a journalist darting around an office in a pencil skirt, collecting passport stamps, boarding planes to shadowy places to find stories that interest Western readers.

On most days she visits the bathroom before Reza wakes. Some days the bleeding won't stop. It's become more erratic since she started sleeping with Reza, who frets about it and brings her herbal remedies and concoctions he claims should be inserted inside her. He begs her to see a doctor, but she is afraid. Sometimes she snaps at him, tells him she will go when she's ready. He gives annoyed shrugs and moves on. It is the first bud of a deep gloom that he hides from her the way newlyweds do.

"Saba, come and help clean the fish." Khanom Basir's voice floats in from the kitchen. She lives with them now, in Abbas's old room, because Saba cannot stand to sleep there. Allowing her mother-in-law to live here has been part of the slow process of winning back Khanom Basir's love by relinquishing the position of matriarch in all but name. Saba thinks it's going well. She likes the way Reza worships her generosity with his kind eyes and never says anything to invite the lingering memory of Abbas's death here. His thankfulness is a source of contentment in their young marriage.

Saba finds her mother-in-law bent over two buckets full of Caspian bream. "Caught an hour ago," she says, delighted. "Some are still bouncing around in there." She picks up each shiny gray fish by its tail and chops off its head with a swift motion of her wood-handled chopping knife. She wraps them in paper from a pile near the sink and throws them in a clean bucket. "For the freezer." She points with her chin and continues her work. "I already started. Young brides should have rest."

Each time Khanom Basir utters something remotely kind, Saba's desire to find her own mother in America returns with a new vigor. Now that she is older, twice married with her own home and family, she considers all the mothers she has been offered, each good for a handful of things: Khanom Basir for household tricks, Khanom Mansoori for mischief, Dr. Zohreh for educated advice, Khanom Omidi for wisdom. Together they have failed to replace her mother, who was good at none of these things.

Khanom Basir has mellowed since the wedding. She is often confused, and each time she has a meltdown, Saba's anger and hurt are dulled by the nascent suspicion that her mother-in-law may be losing her grip on reason, that she might be legitimately ill.

Sometimes when the older woman thinks she is alone, Saba catches her sobbing into her tea. "Oh, blessed Mohammed. I don't know . . . I don't even know anymore." Sometimes she brings her hands down on her own head in the unconscious way people do when trapped under falling debris, and Saba thinks that maybe Khanom Basir really doesn't know what to do, or what is right, or even true.

When she sees Saba, she usually apologizes and shuffles off. She mutters, "I'm very tired, I think," and leaves Saba to ponder this odd new emptiness all around.

Now Saba watches her wrap fish with discarded papers and recognizes a page from an old travel guide. "Don't use that one," she says, and takes it from her mother-in-law.

"Why?" asks Khanom Basir. She reaches for another sheet in the pile.

"It's California," says Saba. "Who knows, we might want to go one day."

If Khanom Basir knew about her former plans for America . . . Saba can only imagine what she would do. How she would try to sabotage her—the overly educated girl with her fancy-*bazi* who one day might run off to a life of Western debauchery like her mother has done. Saba can almost hear her mother-in-law making one of her epic declarations: *I will keep her where she belongs and protect my name even if it causes me to lose every last fingernail and all my hairs go gray and I am bald with grief!* But Reza's mother only laughs, mumbles, "Crazy-*bazi*," and continues with her work.

⁕

Her doctor's office in Rasht has not changed in the past ten years. Green shag carpet. Bright red plastic swivel chairs that squeak at the slightest touch. Cheap wood paneling in an unnatural shade of toffee curling near the floor and ceiling. Bulky fluorescent lamps that are too dark and too harsh at the same time. A rotary phone next to a relatively new IBM computer that sits tentatively at the edge of a desk, trying to belong.

"Khanom Hafezi," the stout nurse in a white manteau and black headscarf calls. It takes Saba a moment to realize that her name has been called. She follows the nurse into a small room with a flat bed covered in sterile-looking white sheets. She has been in this room before. In fact, she has been called back twice in the past two weeks, because her doctor, a very young woman, probably a recent graduate, with Trotsky glasses and a slight mustache, likes to double-check "every small thing." These are the doctor's own words, delivered in a voice that belies her lack of enthusiasm for the profession.

In Iran, medicine is the most respectable career choice. If Saba had gone to college, she might have become a doctor, but she was saving herself for American journalism. Maybe she still is. *My path and yours in this world are so long*, says a memorable line from the old song "Sultan of Hearts."

When the doctor enters, Saba notices that her mustache is gone. *She must be engaged now*, Saba thinks, *or in love*. Then she notices the doctor's nervous expression and roaming eyes and her thoughts turn to her own health.

"Should I change into a gown?" Saba asks.

"No need," says the doctor. "But thank you. Very kind."

What strange politeness, Saba thinks, and begins to worry. Like the monstrous love child of *tarof* and *maast-mali*. A sort of hybrid fake generosity and fake innocence that has no name and appears when people use over-the-top manners to mask their discomfort at knowing something they shouldn't.

"I have your results. I called you only so we can talk." She rubs the reddish spot where her mustache used to be. Then suddenly her eyes stop roaming and fix on Saba and she blurts out in what sounds like one long word: "What have you done to yourself?"

Her tone and eyes are accusing, the way only the young can be. She must be twenty-five at the most, only a few years older than Saba, who sometimes feels a hundred. She fixes the doctor with what she hopes is an authoritative stare.

The young doctor consults her notes, flips a page in her chart. "You said last time that your cycle is irregular, sometimes painful." Saba nods. The doctor scowls again, and when Saba doesn't flinch, she adjusts her white coat and looks away. "Do you ever bleed outside your cycle?"

Saba tries not to snap. "How would I know that, if my cycle is irregular?" She breathes out. "Yes, yes, I do." She begins to add, *I had an accident once,* but doesn't.

The doctor clears her throat and launches into one-breath attack. "Have you ever tried an abortion, Khanom?"

"Excuse me?" Saba almost laughs. She reaches for her neck, feels an old tickle coming back out from deep hiding. She tries to look natural as she massages her throat.

"An abortion. Have you tried removing a child illegally?"

"Is there a legal way? No, no. I'm trying to get pregnant. You know that."

Saba shakes her head and exhales, fighting back embarrassing tears. She already knows what's coming; has always known it, every morning when she checked her body for blood, and each time she and Reza tried to make a baby—a child that would be her new Mahtab, her tie to Iran, her reason to stay. Now the black-clad women are back, hovering above her and in the shadows cast by the equipment across the doctor's floor and walls.

"Well, Khanom," the young doctor says, "the chances of a baby aren't very good. You have an infection that has gone undetected for a long time. It can be cleared up with antibiotics so you might conceive, but your uterus is very damaged, full of scars. I don't think it will hold a pregnancy for very long, even with surgery."

Saba begins to drift. She stops listening, allows the dark figures to carry her to places she hasn't dared to go in many months, back to the spring day almost two years ago, struggling on the bed, the crude instruments, the weeks of bleeding followed by short respites. Then that day in the shack when Reza first saw the blood—that was the day she began to hope for a baby, despite all the signs, because she wanted so badly to stay. Something inside rages. Floating beside her, the young doctor continues to ask questions. How heavy is the bleeding? How often? Does she have fevers? Is she certain that she has never attempted an abortion? What has she been doing? Has she slept with dirty men? Maybe some more testing is in order, though, to be honest, maybe not.

"I'm putting you on birth control," she says. "And Khanom Hafezi, you should never stop taking these."

"Why?" asks Saba. Now she sounds young and naive, and the doctor takes her hand. She has the faintest remains of baby-pink polish on her thumb and Saba wonders about this woman's life away from the office. Though, if she thinks hard enough, Saba already knows. The young doctor is here because she has no choice. A brilliant female student can get away with only so much excellence before she gets coerced into becoming an ob-gyn. This girl looks more like a research scientist, or a business owner, or a frustrated poet.

"Because, Khanom," says the doctor, her voice soft like a teenager's, "you don't want to bring dead babies into the world. It isn't right."

ↁↂↁ

"Can we go to Baba's house?" Saba asks one day when Reza is almost asleep and she is examining the lines of his back with red polished fingertips. "Let's invite Ponneh."

Last week when a distraught Saba called Reza from her doctor's office in Rasht, he told her not to drive. He took a bus and arrived two hours later to bring her home. The girlish ob-gyn sat with her in a teahouse near her office and they shared stories and talked about their favorite books. When the doctor offered Saba her home number, Saba shook her head, and only later realized she had been rude. The girl wasn't offering her services, but her friendship. In the car

Saba told herself that it's just as well. She may not be here next month, or next year. Reza kissed her cheek, said he didn't care about babies. He promised that happier days were ahead.

Now in her father's pantry with Ponneh, they push back the scattered boxes of useless items—flyswatters, batteries, items that were required shopping during the war years, along with milk and eggs—and make room around the drain. They shed their outer clothes and sit cross-legged in a triangle, knees touching, heads close, whispering like teenage fugitives from a party of adults who don't realize that their children have grown.

It is a miracle how this small cupboard alters the very air between them. Now they are back in another time, before marriages and hangings, babies and widowhood, before any of them had witnessed death—when they were just three children playing.

Eighteen years old, smoking in the pantry, hidden from the world.

Seven years old, tumbling in a pile of arms and legs in the open air.

Now, at twenty-two, they gulp from a bottle of *aragh* quickly but carelessly, with their backs toward the door. Within an hour the bottle is empty and they have forgotten their strange history. They have forgotten about many things and nothing is unmentionable.

They talk about the day Ponneh was beaten. They discuss Saba's first marriage without reserve or embarrassment. It is just a fact now, and none of them cares. Once they even talk about Reza's schooling and his good fortune in having a rich wife. In their drunken state, none of them finds it awkward and they laugh at the idea of Saba the benefactress. And then they arrive at the day Reza visited Saba in her home. That is the moment in the conversation that Saba remembers most clearly, the instant when she catches something pass between her friends—a signal that, despite their touching knees, bypasses her and goes directly to Ponneh. A glimpse like an apology.

Though it is only a moment, Saba will always recall that this was the time when she felt most like the other woman. It isn't a vague feeling, but something clear and tangible and devastating. *She*, not Ponneh, is the third, the far corner of the triangle, the one who doesn't belong, a character in *their* movie. And in the gloom of trying to find her place, she feels decades older, because she realizes that she does have a role, that Reza and Ponneh are tied and she is the matron. The provider. The mother.

What is her purpose here, now that she can't even have children with Reza?

She thinks back to her father's warning that she should use her independence well. Has she done that? She might have already made it to America, or even found her mother. She could have searched among their exiled relatives or dug for prison records to make sure her mother was never there. There is so much she didn't try.

They hear a noise coming from a far corner of the house, and Ponneh gets up to leave. She sighs and pulls on her scarf. Before slipping out, she says, "This was nice."

But Saba is already in another place. Already on a flight to America. So much becomes clear when you are drunk and really able to see. She remembers that day in the alley near the post office in Rasht, when she was eleven and she offered Reza a music tape. Ponneh told him that he couldn't accept such a gift from her. It was part of their pride, their shared village ways. The two of them were rooted in a place to which Saba would never belong, whether or not she shared the bond of parenthood with Reza. How could she have believed that money or class wouldn't come between them? How could she believe that she could build a life with someone based only on a love of foreign music? As she follows her husband's gaze to her best friend, Saba licks her dry lips, certain that she has made a lifetime of mistakes.

Yes, she has managed to become part of a pair again, but is it the right pair or just a substitute for them both? Though Reza has proven that he loves her, is devoted to her and determined to be happy, he still pines for Ponneh the way Saba pines for Mahtab.

She lies in bed all of the next day, thinking about what she has done. She thinks of her damaged body, of the Basiji women, of her father's advice, and curses herself for being so foolish, so cowardly, to mistake what she experienced with Reza as the kind of love she saw over and over in her books and movies. How can she compare it with *Casablanca*, or *Romeo and Juliet*, or even the couples in thirty-minute comedies who fall in love over pasta in Italian restaurants? Reza can't even share these tales with her. Worse yet, if she ever writes her own stories in English, he will never be able to read them.

But maybe this is the end of her bad luck. Doesn't it have to be true that bad fortune is finite, and that one unlucky streak can use up an entire lifetime's allowance?

Reza enters, tentatively, to ask again what has happened, what is wrong.

"Go away," she says, hoping that he will become angry, that he will pull her out of this. But Reza simply nods and closes the door.

Overwhelmed by dark thoughts, she finds herself drifting in and out of sleep until she gives up and reaches for her headphones. She puts on an old favorite by Melanie, letting the lyrics soothe the spot of guilt deep in her chest. She hums the words to herself and revels in the fact that no one has confiscated this song. With Melanie's little-girl voice and the *pasdars'* cursory grasp of English, it has slipped past them wearing the mask of a harmless children's song about skating. She sings along and mocks the audience of ill wishers she keeps in her head for occasions like this.

> *For somebody who don't drive,*
> *I've been all around the world,*
> *Some people say I've done alright for a girl.*

She dreams of her father and mother, standing next to a child Mahtab. They are together, though her mother's face is from ten years ago and her father's is an older version. He is offering Mahtab dried sour berries from his pockets. That was the gift he always bought for them, for the less tangible milestones of their childhood—heartbreaks, disappointments, mistakes, successes. Even now he brings dried berries every time he visits Saba. He sends them along with the mail carrier, puts them on reserve with the fruit seller, prepaid and waiting for her. He always remembers to send this small, almost daily gift, though sometimes he forgets her birthday.

The next scene is a real moment that occurred a few days before her wedding—the only time Khanom Basir tried to confront her father. She knocked on his door on an evening when Saba had made dinner for him. From the main room Saba saw her father straighten up, tuck in his paunch of a belly, and roar through the alcohol and opium that ran thick and sluggish in his blood, "No more of this!" Khanom Basir drew a breath and stepped back. "You are speaking about my *only* daughter!"

My only daughter. In that instant Saba didn't think of Mahtab. She didn't conjure memories of her mother holding her sister's hand at the airport. There is something crucial about fathers at weddings and in that regard she had much to be thankful for.

She wakes and reaches for a stack of papers. English words and half-written stories. If her mother heard Saba's stories now, she would be proud of all the words that she knows. But which of her real-life friends can be trusted with Saba's last story—the one about Mahtab and her husband and her Big Lie? Maybe one day she will tell Khanom Omidi. But for now she lies back in her bed and weaves the story for her mother, the mother who lives in her memory and with whom she converses from time to time. No one else can be trusted to listen and understand. This one is too raw a sore, too close a connection, Saba's own secret storeroom.

⁓⊙⊙⊙⁓

These are the people Mahtab has put behind her:

Khanom Judith Miller—because Mahtab is now a journalist in her own right.

Cameron the poor Aryan—because he lied, and because the card in her purse is nothing more to her than a trinket, a keepsake.

Babies—because I may not be able to have them, but she doesn't even want them.

Baba Harvard—because he has no arms, no smile, no fatherly knobs in his shoulders. He is cruel despite his deep pockets and erudition. He stares into and beyond your tear-soaked eyes with academic nonchalance, perfect poise, total control, and then he moves on to the next eager scholarly face in the line. He has too many children who vie for him, and no dried sour berries in his deep pockets, no blood in his heart. He never smokes too much, or drinks too often. He never forgets birthdays; he has secretaries who send packages on his behalf. He has no need for you. Good fathers have need.

Yes, there are *some* things in my life that Mahtab envies. I have witnessed things she wishes to see with her journalistic eyes, and I have a father made of flesh and blood.

Nothing else, though, because I have been a coward. I know that later in life, long after Mahtab is beyond the reach of my imagination, I will pick up the phone, wanting to discuss the remarkable coincidences in our lives, all those tricks of blood and fate that forced us to live the same life across so much earth and sea. I will wish that I had been strong enough, secure enough, to live life the way she did, not so pragmatically, not so afraid of risks. I will lament my choices,

358

having married Reza because I was afraid to run, to follow my twin and our shared dreams away from this new Iran. I will think about my lost sister, put the receiver to my ear, and have a pretend conversation with her instead.

On that day, as I hold the phone to my ear, ignoring the frantic *beep-beep-beep* of the disconnected line, I will realize too late that I shouldn't have wasted the time I had with Mahtab, my other self. I should have been braver. Mahtab is brave. She doesn't care what the world tells her to want. Are young brides supposed to want babies? *Pfff!* Mahtab doesn't care. She has her own plans. This is the story of how she rids herself of the last and most important Immigrant Worry so that she is no longer a foreigner. This one is about children and lovers.

No, that is untrue. . . . This story is about fathers and daughters.

I think Mahtab is probably married now because, after all, I am married and she is my twin. Who has she chosen? Cameron? James? Someone else? She can't have retuned to Cameron. He has a secret and has moved to Iran—committed a sort of suicide and left her with Yogurt Money. As for James, isn't he the one she always wanted? A pale American princeling? I think that she can forgive him his one failing, as I forgave. She can forget that he was once a coward, too weak to stand by her after a series of events involving a broken high heel. Her road back to James happens like this:

It is May 1992 and she is about to graduate from Harvard. She visits an Italian restaurant in Harvard Square—run by a cousin of the Tehrani; but she doesn't know this detail that connects her to me. She reads the menu and tries to choose a pizza to take back to her room, where she plans to spend the evening packing.

James Scarret passes by the door just as she looks up from her menu, and for the first time since the incident at the bar, they both smile and he doesn't rush past. He enters reluctantly and she remembers all the parts of him that she found so foreign and enticing. His wide jaw covered with sandy stubble, his matching hair, longish, with a touch of russet. That almost-white baby fuzz on his arms. The very opposite of Cameron with his black hair and his soft comedian's features and too much confidence in every expression.

"Are you eating alone?" he asks. She says that she is. He pauses, then says, "Why not stay?" He looks for signs of refusal in her face. "We should eat here one last time."

Before she can think of a reason not to, they are seated.

It is May and Cambridge is reborn. Maman jan, have you ever seen Harvard Square in springtime? Have you visited it on your adventures abroad? There are details I know I can't imagine just by looking through the famous bird's-eye movie shots or at the photos of an emerald dome overlooking the river. I can tell you that afternoons are longer now, and that restaurateurs have set up tables and chairs outside, tentatively at first, looking up at the sky, then shedding all caution and gliding from table to table with white wine and red wine and sangria, until droves of warm-weather customers spill out of their establishments and onto the street like popcorn kernels exploding out of bags on the stovetop. I imagine that it looks very much like certain parts of Tehran or Istanbul.

James asks what she is doing next year, and over two plates of pasta, she tells him about *The New York Times*. She is very proud of it. James watches her eat, reaches over and dips a piece of bread into the last of her sauce. "We'll need to stop for something in an hour," he says. "Right? Since it didn't have rice? What was the word? . . . *Domsiah!*"

Mahtab looks up, surprised that he remembers the name of the rice and that he is willing to mention things she told him about Persians and their bizarre eating habits. She examines his captivated expression and thinks maybe she doesn't need another wandering Iranian man like Cameron if she has someone like James. Someone who doesn't know about Farsi letters or the rules for Persian authenticity,

but who *wants* to know. Someone without Immigrant Worries or a
longing for a home that may no longer exist. Someone who isn't an
exile, isn't lost in the search for a country, but worships her for her
exotic troubles—her beautiful melancholy; almond-eyed turmoil that
knocks men in the heart. Maybe the Persian-cat, Persian-carpet brand
of curiosity isn't so bad. At least she's not in a village where she is
mundane.

You see, Maman, I have learned some things. When I go to
America, I may fall in love again, and if I do, it will be with an American man. Do you know why? Because Mahtab has taught me that I
don't need someone who is tied to me by blood, a childhood friend,
or someone from my own part of the world. Yes, there is comfort in
such pairings, but I have lived without it before. Maybe I can manage
without a baby and Reza and every other stand-in for Mahtab. Why
should my life be an echo of someone else's? I am done with invisible
strings and tethers to a dying homeland. I don't want to be a lost
immigrant with worries and longings that keep me from fitting in.
I need someone who thinks I am unique on this earth, though he
knows that I am half of a broken pair.

American men understand uniqueness much more than blood
ties. They find no romance in the familiar, in village bonds. They are
raised to be adventurous and brave. My nameless American may not
fit into a grainy old Iranian movie, he may never play me "Sultan of
Hearts," with its mesmerizing anguish, on a badly tuned guitar. In
that way he is like Reza, who can't read my books. But at least he
won't be in love with someone else. It seems to me that Persian men
are *always* in love with someone else. They eye every dish except the
one in front of them. They have too much hunger for their own
good—poetic lunacy not worth passing on to the next generation.

For all his past faults, James has a wide-eyed fascination for no one
but Mahtab. He speaks of her background as if he believes all Iranian men have curly black beards, smear kohl around their eyes, and

spend their afternoons fighting Greeks in iron loincloths; as if all Iranian women have heavy-lidded gazes and pomegranate picnics like in the old paintings, wrapping their huge soft thighs around *setar*s and leaning back into the embrace of mustachioed lovers. She likes these clichés. They're not the ones about *hijab* and turban bombs.

Suddenly he seems impossibly young and Mahtab wonders why she was so harsh with him. They order drinks and settle into conversation, quickly discovering that formerly bitter memories are now funny. Soon they stumble onto the realization that this dinner is a milestone—that Mahtab is giving him another chance. He moves to her side of the table and they share dessert. He plays with his spoon for a few minutes, but Mahtab isn't uncomfortable. He is very good at being quiet. Why didn't she notice that about him before? "I'm sorry," he says, "about what happened."

She touches the soft blond hairs on James's forearm and says, in the nonchalant start-over way Americans do, "I don't care about that anymore."

Two weeks after graduation, they elope and move to New York City, a rash decision fueled by the unfortunate combination of a Dutch beer, a whiskey sour, an old-fashioned, a sidecar, and a martini. Yes, she is reckless. She can be, because American divorces are easy. And American divorcées are considered seductive and brave.

These are the things she remembers about her elopement: throwing away the guilty Hermès scarf. Trying to throw away the credit card and failing because Yogurt Money is sticky stuff. The ache of missing a father she hasn't seen in more than a decade, because, for all his books and philosophies, Baba Harvard can't walk her down the aisle.

Months pass. Soon after her wedding, Mahtab too has to face motherhood, because a baby with James is inevitable. Her father-in-law mentions it every day. At first he suggested it in passing, joking and laughing about his future grandchildren. But recently he has been grumbling about it, taking James aside and waving his hands in his face.

She realizes now that motherhood is the fate that will take her . . . eventually.

A baby will end your childhood says her old friend, the *pari* that used to perch on her mailbox in California. It will tie you to this man, this city.

Yes, it *could* mean the end says Mahtab's logical other self.

Certainly it *will* mean the end says a new voice, a bitter old lady with bad breath and spindly fingers who Mahtab fears might be *her* . . . someday. The banshee in old age.

No, a baby is not worth her journalistic dreams. So much could happen if a child enters her world. There will be no more freedom of movement. Her own mother had to sacrifice an entire life, her whole history, for her daughters. She had to leave one of her babies behind. What if Mahtab has to abandon a child? What if *she* has to sacrifice everything? What if Cameron comes back with news of Iran, with adventures she can write about for *The New York Times*, and the landscape of her world changes?

Never, she thinks. She will not have a baby. Not ever. Not for anyone. She has a career to tend to, worlds to discover and unveil for the world's best newspaper.

See? Mahtab doesn't need a child, or anyone at all. That is her greatest strength.

In the days after the wedding, Mahtab and James have frequent dinners with the Scarrets in Connecticut. There is something uncomfortable about the Scarret home. Have you ever seen American houses like this on television? I can tell you exactly what it looks like, with its untouchable furniture and decanter of scotch waiting between the cream couch and the deep-cherry grand piano. One night at dinner, over the rim of his whiskey glass, James's father asks if they're having problems conceiving.

"We'll have kids when the time is right." James squeezes Mahtab's hand.

"The time's right *now*," Mr. Scarret slurs. Mahtab wishes she had the authority to take the glass away from him and send him off to bed. "I'm almost sixty."

Mahtab feels the calm rushing out of her, abandoning her body and running down the street. She is beginning to hate James's father. But despite her fury, she doesn't lose control. She knows that, in a free world, the decision to have a baby is hers only.

A few hours later she and Mrs. Scarret get up to do the dishes. Mahtab returns to the dining room for the last plate and overhears her father-in-law mumbling to James in the living room. "Not ready?" he says in his whiskey-coarse voice. "What's the holdup? Back in Iran, she'd have four babies strapped to her back."

Maybe James expresses all the shock and fury that is owed to the world just then. Maybe he only drops his head and sighs, mumbles something conciliatory. Or maybe in that moment he musters up all the bravery and movie heroism he didn't have when he was a scared college boy in a bar. Maybe all of those things happen in another universe, and in this one Mahtab just storms into the dining room, grabs her handbag and James's keys, and blows out of the house, leaving ajar the thick wooden door of the Scarrets' home.

All night long she tosses and turns. She can't shake the image her father-in-law has created—the image of herself as a village girl. Did Baba Harvard lie? Maybe it's true that orphaned children can never be adopted into better worlds, an immigrant will always look like she belongs back in the village, and fatherless girls will remain fatherless.

She holds on to these thoughts and rolls them around protectively, maternally, in the warm space between her chest and her pillow. And so something with its own life does develop and grow inside her that night. Not a baby, but the first whispers of an epic misstep, an idea that she will later remember simply as the Lie—almost inevitable in both its ease and its potential to solve so much in one go—exactly the kind of thing that has caused so many people to mis-understand Mahtab over the long years out of Iran.

When the night is almost over and sleep doesn't come, her thoughts turn to her parents. Outside a few scattered memories and the many conversations she has invented over the years, she has no evidence of Baba's temperament or beliefs. She tells herself that Baba would defend her against Mr. Scarret and his baby-obsessing, igno-rant-about-Iran ways. Despite all the fathers she has coveted through-out her immigrant life, the fatherly shoulders she has admired and inanimate protectors she has created, Mr. Scarret has never tempted the lonely daughter inside her, and that is quite a statement from a girl who watched longingly as Jose did dishes and Mr. Arganpur drank tea.

She wonders what her mother would say and picks up the phone, because this is a privilege that Mahtab still has—calling her mother instead of trying to imagine.

"Why so sad, Mahtab jan?" Maman croons. "Be thankful. You are a girl from Gilan! Look at where you are now. You can do any-thing you want, and a baby is the best thing. A baby will make you immortal." When Mahtab is silent, she adds, "Leave it in God's hands. Try. If you are not able, that is your answer."

And there it is, the moment the idea emerges and takes form. *If you're not able, that is your answer.* In this vague appeal to a higher power Mahtab finds her solution things, this directive given by a mother who believes in the power of simple answers. She dreams up the big Lie now, but you mustn't hate her for it. She does it only for the most Iranian of reasons—to satisfy everyone and give them what they need, a cool sip of yogurt. She may be educated by Baba Har-vard, but she is still a wild creature. It isn't her fault. It is written in her Caspian blood.

"Okay," says Mahtab, before hanging up the phone. "Love you. Miss you. *Zoolbia.*" They laugh at the old joke, because *zoolbia* is a syrupy pastry, a word we used to say as toddlers instead of *zood-bia*, which means "Come soon."

୧⊙⊙୨

It is a Sunday when Mahtab first utters the words out loud. *I can't have children*—it's so easy. Done. Finished. Free. Now it is up to James and his family to accept it or decide blatantly to violate every pos sible Eastern and Western rule of goodness and decency. Because who can blame a woman who is willing but unable? She doesn't feel guilty over what she is doing. She is escaping the way her mother escaped from Iran. She feels heroic, virtuous, noble. Also maybe a little less scared. She breathes deeply once or twice. It's the freedom of abandoning her twenties and being fourteen again. The freedom of having—not becoming—a guardian. It feels good. When James smiles sympathetically and takes her hand, a wave of relief and affec tion washes over her.

Now she is released from this conversation. She can go back to documenting the injustices in the world, back to impressing Baba Harvard with her post graduation talent.

What power she has! That is the thing about Mahtab. She chooses all that happens to her. She doesn't want babies and so she doesn't have them, and in doing so she gives me such hope. A legacy can be so many things besides children. I will have a legacy one day that has nothing to do with Cheshmeh or Reza or Ponneh. It will be some thing entirely from within me. A piece of Saba Hafezi left in the world.

Mahtab is a skilled journalist, so naturally she has plenty of re search to back her story. Last week, as she rifled through facts and figures and the language of disease, she realized something: that she could create any fiction and wrap it in a cloak of verisimilitude, using the world's collective knowledge. These moments of authorial power have given Mahtab a thrill ever since we were young and she made up stories about the Sun and Moon Man. Her story is flawless: Infec‚ tions. Scars. Damage and more damage. She is getting into some bad business now—Mahtab the taker of risks, controller of her own des‚ tiny. Mahtab the dreamer, the sleeper, the abandoner of lonely sisters.

"Don't worry," James whispers. "We'll just adopt. We'll adopt a little girl. Maybe one from Iran." He cuts a piece of his own breakfast pastry and places it on her plate, as one would do for a sad child. Mahtab picks at the bread and makes room in her heart for the tor‚ rent of guilt that will remain with her from this instant, for the rest of her life.

She tries to make out the expressions on her in‚laws' faces. Mrs. Scarret is sympathetic, obviously looking for something positive to say. Finally she settles on the noncommittal. "There are always options, dear, in this day and age."

Mr. Scarret looks at the table, pokes his bacon with his fork. His jowls hang in a gray, deflated sort of way that clashes with the care‚ free pastel pattern on his sweater. "Can't they operate?" he asks so loudly that the couple at the next table looks up. "I'll research it," he breathes. "You kids can have whatever resources you need."

Now Mahtab throws herself into her work as a reporter. She is good at it, a star. For months she lives with the daily expectation that something will happen, and one day it does. She picks up the phone and it is Dr. Vernon, her ob‚gyn, asking that she come in. ("Yes, it is urgent. Yes, today, please.") She enters his office, situated in the center of a cul‚de‚sac of private offices in an upscale neighborhood, with all the trepidation of a child being summoned to a special convention of a dozen furious principals. She sits in the waiting room for ten min‚ utes before giving her name. When her turn arrives, the doctor him‚

self comes to get her. He is a kind-looking man in his late thirties, blond and gray-eyed, quick and petite in his crisp slacks and white coat.

"Mrs. Scarret," he begins, without asking her to sit or change into a gown or fill out papers. The sound of her new name briefly distracts her. "This is a bit delicate."

"Is something wrong?" Her barely audible voice seems to confirm his suspicions.

"It's just that . . . my wife is in the So-and-So Women's Club. . . . Do you know it?"

"Yes," she whispers again, "my mother-in-law is chair of—"

Dr. Vernon interrupts with three forceful nods. "My wife ran into her there. And they got to talking, and . . . I'm sorry to interfere, Mrs. Scarret, but is everything okay with you? Why have you told your family that you can't have children?"

Mahtab breathes out, because Dr. Vernon's voice isn't the condemning, hateful one she expected. "I . . ." she begins, unaware that she is crying now, ruining her lady-journalist makeup.

"It really isn't any of my business," Dr. Vernon assures her. "I wouldn't even be prying, if—and by the way, when Katie told me how bad she felt for you, I didn't tell her that it wasn't true. Patient-doctor confidentiality—but I'm worried, Mrs. Scarret, because if you said something like that . . . well, you know that it's not even a good story, right? I mean, besides the obvious fact that you are totally normal, the disease you cited does not cause definite infertility. A simple medical journal will tell you that."

"I know," says Mahtab, almost silently.

The doctor leads Mahtab to a chair, hands her a Kleenex. He lowers himself into a swivel chair and blurts out the rest of his prepared speech. "Mrs. Scarret. May. Can I call you May? You aren't doing anything more drastic, are you? According to my records, you are not on birth control because, well, you said you were trying to start a family. So I just need to make sure. It is my *job* to make sure."

"What would I be doing?"

Dr. Vernon shrugs. "Pills that haven't gone through me, home remedies, and such. It's the nineties, but you wouldn't believe the things that go on." He coughs and adds, "Mostly with teenagers of course . . ." He clears his throat, waiting for Mahtab to release him from this chore.

"Thanks, Dr. Vernon," she says, and gets up, "but you don't have to worry."

The lobby is empty. The doctor shakes her hand with both of his and tells her to "be well and please do call if you need us," before disappearing into his private offices. *Who's "us"?* she wonders as she surveys the room. She decides to sit for a minute, just to get her thoughts together. Her hands are shaking. She doesn't trust herself to drive. Outside the sky is turning gray and the cul-de-sac looks dismal and ordinary. Women's magazines are fanned out on the generic wooden tables that sit on ugly shag carpeting. Then Mahtab begins to weep loudly into her sleeve. She knows it's unseemly, that it makes her pathetic and weak, but she finds that she can't help herself.

She doesn't notice the receptionist running over to hold her hand or Dr. Vernon rushing back out and picking up the phone. She doesn't register his lame attempt at lifting her mood by changing the CD from classical to jazz, the only two options in the office. She sees only the wet blur of brown and pink and white where the tables and the magazines and the carpet used to be. She recognizes the feeling of not knowing what to do and of things unraveling, a caravan overturn-ing and crushing her chest; the vague lonely notion that if she called Cameron right now, he would explain away all her failures with a mas-terful quip about poetic license and lunacy. *Where is Cameron? Where is my friend? Another outsider to look in on the world?* And then, minutes later, she spots the Scarrets' royal-blue minivan slicing through all that endless gray concrete outside.

James and his father burst into the office. Mr. Scarret shakes hands with Dr. Vernon. Through the window, Mahtab spies Mrs. Scarret waiting in the car, tapping her long fingers on the dashboard and probably chewing the lipstick off her lips. She feels sorry for her mother-in-law, for all the trouble she has brought into this peaceful American family, a family that has probably never seen a day's worth of real drama.

"What's the matter?" she hears her father-in-law whisper. His voice is coarse and sympathetic, and she resents him for empathizing with the inconvenienced doctor.

"I'm sorry to have called," Dr. Vernon stammers. He is intimidated by James's father, a much older, more prominent man. "She just . . . she needed some help." He lowers his voice to a whisper. "Um . . . look, sir, about the fertility problems . . ."

But James's father cuts him off. He puts a hand on the doctor's forearm and shushes him like a subordinate. "We already know," he says sadly, and Mahtab realizes that James has found her research. Maybe his father has done his own, as he said he would do when she told the Big Lie. He jokes awkwardly, "Kids and that damn research library, like giving a pistol to a monkey," and laughs twice—up and down.

Mahtab shuts off her mind, turns her attention to the kind receptionist, as James and his father and Dr. Vernon discuss her in a far corner of the room. She notices James avoiding her and tries hard to hate them for their hushed whispers, tries to imagine them wearing turbans and passing cruel judgments, but she fails. She tries several times.

Then, as she rests her head on the receptionist's shoulder, Mr. Scarret comes over and kneels down beside her. The way he does that, the way he squats down so they can be face-to-face—like fathers do to their children on the first day of school—draws the tears out of Mahtab again. Beneath the salty droplets dripping over her lips, her skin feels thin and cracked, like rice paper or brittle seaweed. She tries to say "I'm sorry," but Mr. Scarret shakes his head. He puts an arm around her shoulder and helps her up. When she tries again, he says in a tired voice, "It's okay now, sweetheart." In the background, Otis Redding sings a song that he sang at her wedding, and Mahtab walks in step with her father-in-law, thinking what a funny way to dance.

But it's nice, letting go of the last and the worst of the Immigrant Worries, that pesky fear that when you enter a new country, you will be forever alone.

No, she is not frightened now—of being an outsider, or a failure, or poor, or unimportant. Her refugee skin is shed and gone. Her father-in-law says, "It's not all that bad, now, is it?" and she shakes her head, unafraid of being alone. I too am no longer terrified of loneliness in strange lands. How nice, Mahtab thinks, to shed the skin of an immigrant. To do wrong and be forgiven like a true daughter, to be adopted into a new country with its own flesh-and-blood fathers. And to relive all the moments she missed.

Seaside Pilgrimage
(Khanom Basir)

The whole town knows the story—the real one—though no one talks about it, because that's our way. We prefer pretty lies to ugly truths. But we remember it every time Agha Hafezi sighs, and we replay it in our minds every time Saba mentions Mahtab.

In 1981, when the girls were eleven, the family went for a week to a beach house on the Caspian Sea. It was only a short drive from Cheshmeh, but in those days Agha Hafezi didn't want to go far from his own house. "If you pretend it's a long journey," he told the girls, "it will feel that way. Pretend it's a pilgrimage, like in your stories."

"A pilgrimage to Mecca?" Saba asked, wiping summer dew from her face.

"No," Bahareh snapped, because she hated all mention of Muslim things.

"Hush," said Agha Hafezi. "No more of this talk." They fought a lot in those days, though the girls never noticed. They probably went back to making up jokes, eating raisins and smoked chickpeas, and pretending they were going to see the mismatched carpet-weaving

girls in Nain. Oh, these Hafezis and their trips! To the sea for fresh-
caught fish, to Qamsar to smell the rosewater from the highway, to
Isfahan, the center of the world, to Persepolis for culture, to Tehran
for visiting family.

I envy them, riding in a car in the early morning, especially into
the mountains! Watching the thick forest appear out of nowhere.
Strapping a full, steaming meal in thermoses and towel-covered pots
to their backs and climbing a peak for breakfast.

Before they left, I remember telling the girls that seaside villas
have Western toilets, a foreign devil's work that rises up out of the
ground like a throne. They squealed and fell on top of each other,
laughing at the impossibility of it, daring each other to go first.

How I wish I had asked to go along on that trip. In those days the
Hafezis neglected the girls and, yes, I'm not afraid to say I blame
Bahareh a little. They might have paid me for my services and I did
love the Caspian villas, the dewy beachside towns reserved for the
rich, with their pretty tributes to village life all around—houses on
stilts and tiny wooden shops sprouting every kilometer or two, with
their wicker baskets hanging outside, jars of preserves, brined garlic,
and orange-flower jam stacked by the door. And, best of all, huge
branches that jutted out from the walls covered with olives and garlic
cloves. In the spring the north of Iran smells like orange flower. In the
summer it smells of newly caught fish. Shomal is a sort of heaven.

That summer the Hafezi villa was close enough to the water so
they could fry fish while wading in the sea, and share their meals with
the gulls, and stumble back nearly blind through the fog and humid-
ity and still find the house in minutes. Bad omen, being so close to
the sea. That night they ate a dinner of local specialties, olives beaten
with hogweed powder, pomegranates, garlic, fresh herbs, and walnuts.
Kebabs on skewers. Green tomatoes and cucumbers dipped in herbal
chutney. When a beggar knocked, a cheerful Agha Hafezi gave her a
pot of kebab because he said that vagrants are often angels coming to

test the faithful, like the ones that visited Lot. If you ask me, that was another bad omen, because Agha Hafezi was tempting Allah with his homage to Christian prophets.

Later, after dark, the girls ruined everything by taking a swim in the black waters.

Chapter Eighteen

LATE AUTUMN 1992

The months pass in a frenzy, lost in the urgent hours and days that fill them. Getting a passport. Knocking on embassy doors and paying off bureaucrats. Buying a seat on six different flights spread out over four months, just in case. She doesn't tell anyone that she plans to leave. Not yet. Why should she? Better to be cautious, to once again make a habit of guarding her secrets and schemes. Goodbye to the sweet abandon of those first days of marriage, when no secret seemed too big to whisper to each other.

Enough of this. Though she looked for one, she has no excuse for staying in Iran, for never having tried to get out despite marrying Abbas based purely on that hope. She isn't trapped. She hates herself for thinking that she was, for always walking a step behind, for accepting lesser roles and playing them gratefully. Enough of the salty and the sweet of this seaside life. No more Khanom Basir, but also no more Reza. No more time spent as a village wife, but also no more time with her father.

No more Islamic Republic of Iran. But also no more Iran. No more foggy Caspian afternoons. No more thick soups eaten directly out of a cauldron on top of a roof in Masouleh. No more drives through tree-covered mountains toward the beach. No more fragrant rice fields or garlic strung up in batches around wooden doorposts.

No more of many things, but most important: no more fuzzy sketches of Mahtab through stories. Time to move on to something tangible, to discover the fuller story. To live out all the moments she gave to her sister for fear of living them herself.

She is very careful now to hide all signs of her impending departure until the last moment. She visits Rasht and Tehran on days when Reza is in class and Khanom Basir is playing backgammon, shopping, or cooking with Khanom Alborz and Khanom Omidi. She pays a friendly office worker to expedite the processing of her passport and to avoid questions about her husband and her planned travels. ("I've always wanted to visit Istanbul and Dubai," she tells him, and he smiles and says that Istanbul is very nice.) When the passport arrives, she hides it with her music tapes and her six plane tickets. Slowly she begins to empty out her bank accounts. She thinks of Reza, and the amount he will need to finish his studies, to buy a small plot, maybe even to take care of Ponneh.

With fearful disbelief she scans the list of steps required to apply for an American visa. *Really so many?* She remembers an article in an old copy of *The New York Times*, in which a wealthy Iranian man asks an American the desperate question that so many others have asked: "Why won't your government let me go to the U.S.A.?" Maybe it's hopeless. She is reading one of these visa applications, slowly becoming disheartened, when the phone rings. She ignores it and returns to her work, discreetly putting the items she will take in one corner of the closet, stacking all her scattered notes and stories into her journal. Fifteen minutes later the phone rings again. She picks up the receiver and waits.

"Allo? Allo?" the man on the other end shouts into the phone. *"Khanom Abbas?"*

This was never Saba's name. Even strangers haven't called her that for more than a year.

In the background she can hear a woman panting instructions. *Tell her now,* she says, and when the man hesitates, *It should be a simple thing, very simple.*

Another man hushes the woman as the caller tries to speak. He introduces himself, an Arab name that Saba immediately forgets, and tells her that he is a lawyer. His accent is distinctly rural and she imagines him as a frail, balding man. This image calms her. The man tells her that he is representing some members of her family, and as such, he is at her service, but he cannot fail to inform her of his research, findings, and proposed changes on their behalf. Saba waits for him to continue, though with each word spoken and implied she comes nearer to understanding. "My client is a close family relation. And so he will take care of you, his brother's widow."

"That is too kind," she says, "but not necessary, really."

"No, no. It is only right now that it has been proven that he and Abbas shared not only a mother but also a father." She recalls the uterine brother who took a small portion of her inheritance. The mullah told her that he would try to prove himself a full brother. A primary heir. The last remark hangs between them and Saba wonders if she can ignore it. But of course he repeats himself.

How has it been proven? Saba asks. What evidence does he have? Has he contacted anyone? What does he want from her at this time?

The panic that hits Saba just then—the knowledge that everything she chooses to say and do now will affect her entire future—is overwhelming. She presses the cold telephone receiver so hard to her ear that it leaves a reddish mark. When it is time for her to reply   a moment so fraught with expectation that the silence on the other side almost buzzes with energy—she gives the usual pleasantries, conveys her desire to work things out, and suggests a date several weeks away for them to meet in Rasht. The lawyer is reluctant but agrees, repeating twice that Abbas's brother prefers to move faster.

Afterward, despite the urgent feeling that engulfs Saba as she hangs up the phone, despite the fact that she allows survival and self-interest to rule her actions, she can't ignore the painful conviction that this man really does deserve the money because did she not let his brother die?

❧◗◉◖❧

"Baba, I need your help," Saba whispers into the phone not ten minutes after she has hung up with the *dehati* lawyer. "Who will buy my land for cash? Dollars."

"Oh God, Saba jan. What now? Are you in trouble?" Her father sounds like he was sleeping. More likely, he has been spending time with the pipe.

Saba explains about the uterine brother and the new claims. She hears her father cursing on the other end, and she can almost see him shaking his head, getting up, sitting down again. "You can't sell the land."

"Why not?" says Saba.

"Because no one is that stupid. If you try to sell it, even if you offer a price at half the value, the buyer will know that your ownership is suspect."

"But I have the papers."

"Wouldn't you wonder," her father says, "if someone wanted to sell you all that land for cheap and then demanded fast cash? Wouldn't you worry that the government would take it tomorrow and you would be out all that money?"

"What can I do?" she asks, wondering if she will have to leave it all behind.

Her father switches to a sort of telephone code, like the one he uses when trying to arrange alcohol for a party. "Leave it, Saba jan. The courts will decide fairly. You know, I just found your Victorian doll. Remember the one with the big skirt and lots of pockets? Maybe it's time to clean it out." He is telling her to empty her bank accounts.

"What if I send the doll to America?" she says.

There is a moment when he must be thinking, or pretending not to hear.

Then she says, not caring who is listening, "I want to go to America."

Her father breathes heavily. "Don't say foolish things. I have the name of a man who can turn milk to butter without question. Butter is good anywhere and doesn't spoil like milk." He means that she should change her tomans to dollars.

Over the next few weeks Saba makes so many mistakes. She goes to empty her accounts completely before realizing that the consular officers who grant visas will need to see that she has wealth in Iran and plans to return. She has settled on trying for a tourist visa at first, then finding a way to stay—perhaps by enrolling at a university. At the bank her hands shake as she tears up the withdrawal forms knowing that she almost wrecked it all. She wonders how much money in a bank will convince the officers. Can she withdraw more after they grant her a visa? Should she put back the sums she has already withdrawn? No, she decides. She will call that her travel money. She asks the banker for a statement of her accounts instead. What will the consulate people want to hear? They are so vague and mysterious about their criteria, presumably so people won't lie. It seems callous, but she is thankful she never gave Reza access to her larger finances. He doesn't care enough to ask and Khanom Basir is at least too ashamed to insist.

She asks her father to do all he can to delay the proceedings with

Abbas's family—to keep her money safe during this time when she can't withdraw it.

On a quiet night she scrolls through Hafezi after Hafezi in an old family address book—a gray handwritten one she took from under her father's bed. She has relatives in Scotland, Holland, and America. Is her mother one of them? She finds only one *B. Hafezi*, but when she calls just to see, an unfamiliar woman answers and claims not to know a Bahareh.

Sometimes Saba daydreams about hearing her mother's voice on the other end of a phone line. Her voice will be older and she will answer in an informal American way. Saba will speak in English, and her heart will leap at the thought that her mother is hearing her perfect Western greeting. She will ask a series of stupid questions, because this is, after all, her one-and-only mother, who, until their separation, heard all her most mundane thoughts. *What do you look like now? Are you happy to hear from me? Do I sound very old? Do you want me to say something else in English?*

They will spend hours mixing two languages, laughing at the few favorite topics they still share, stories from television and Saba's English books. Before they hang up, her mother will promise to send an official invitation letter. "I miss you, my Saba," she will say. *"Zoolbia."* And they will laugh that she still remembers that old joke.

Barely an hour has passed when the doorbell rings. Khanom Basir and Reza are both away for the day, and Saba pulls on her headscarf before entering the high-walled front garden. Lost in worries about invitation letters and visa interviews, she unlatches the big white gate, almost cutting her finger on the metal, and sees her father trembling in his house shoes and a ragged winter coat.

He doesn't have to say why he's come. He looks at her as though she were a foreign thing, ungrateful and cruel and selfish, like a *shali-zar* worker caught stealing rice or the shepherd who informed the moral police about the men listening to Gospel Radio Iran on the hillside. "What are you doing?" he asks. "Why did you call Behrooz in California?"

"What?" Saba had expected nothing more than his typical angry response to her earlier comment about America. "Who's Behrooz?"

"My cousin in California. You called his house an hour ago, asking for your mother . . . which, by the way, really scared his superstitious wife. He guessed it might have been someone in Cheshmeh and he called me."

"I'm sorry." She takes his arm and ushers him in. "I tried to tell you."

"Look, this Abbas thing can be fixed," he says. "You're being rash."

"No," she says. "It's just time for me to leave. I want to find out what happened."

"Your mother is not in America," he says. He sounds tired, frustrated. He follows her inside and closes the door. "I wish I could tell you exactly what happened, Saba jan."

They sit down in the kitchen. "I know," she says. "But that's not the reason I want to go. The phone call was just a whim . . . because I saw the name in the book. I want to have my own life. I'm not happy here." She hopes that will be enough.

It isn't. Fathers too have selfish needs. "It's because you don't have babies."

She decides to tell the truth. "I can't have babies." Briefly she feels the cool, quenching freedom of it. Then the rest comes out. The entire story of Abbas and their wedding night. Of the black-clad women in her bedroom and the inheritance she thought she deserved. Of the first days with Reza, that look in his eyes that she mistook for love but now recognizes as his attempt at love, a sort of theater mixed with boyish heroism and pity for all damaged women, for her ruined body—her reward for it all.

The way her father puts his head in his hands, the way he rubs his thinning hair in a circle on both sides of his head and looks up to her with big, piteous eyes, reminds her of Reza's reaction that day in the shack. That ashen look. Those fidgety hands. That immediate response to reach for her hands or her hair. Why do men show so much grief when a woman is harmed by someone other than *them*? Why so much pity now? Does he think she is less of a person? Is he angry that she has let herself be tarnished?

Her father recovers his voice. "You always loved Reza. Everyone knew it."

"And he never really loved me back," she responds. "Everyone knew that too."

"Have you told him? He won't let you leave."

"It's not up to him. Baba jan, don't you want me to get one thing that I want?"

"Don't be ungrateful." She can hear him trying not to snap.

She stares dumbly at her father. Talking to him is like trying to control a car on ice. Sometimes the way it goes has nothing to do with the way you turn the wheel. Maybe she should stop trying and just say something true. "Aren't you proud of me for not giving up?" she asks, her voice childlike. She clears her throat because she wants to be taken seriously. "I sometimes think she's out there with Mahtab, maybe not in the States, but somewhere. Yes, I'm an adult and my brain says one thing, but I . . ." She wants to mention the day at the airport but doesn't. "I just want to go and see."

Her father's sad, faraway gaze reminds her of Agha Mansoori when his wife died. Finally it settles on her face. Just as it does, Saba gives a too-big smile as she did when she was the child he didn't have time to know, and his eyes cloud over in a pool of gray. Is he going to chastise her? She fixes her face in what she thinks is a neutral glare.

"Saba jan, I wish you could look her up in a phone book or find her in America somewhere. You have a good heart to keep hoping when your father has stopped believing in everything." He trembles as if trying to shake out a painful memory. He speaks in spurts between thoughtful pauses. "What would Bahareh say, do you think, about what I've done? If a man talks like a Muslim, and eats and drinks with Muslims, and allows his own daughter to marry them, can he call himself a Christian? Does it matter what's in his heart if it's all covered up by cowardice?" Saba doesn't want to move; he has never told her so much. She wishes she knew what to say to preserve the moment, but each time they tiptoe toward each other like this, she manages to do something that causes the small light into her father's world to flicker off again. He sighs. "But never mind that. We must accept the truth no matter how much it hurts."

She sighs. Again he is failing her, refusing to understand. "Why is it so awful to keep hope? Maybe that's just what we both need." She gets up to refill their tea, but her father takes her hand. She stops but doesn't sit back down, just stands over him, letting him take her small hand in both of his like a firefly that might flutter away.

He pauses for a long time and she can see he is looking for the right words—that he is struggling to say them. "That particular hope is good, yes. But there are better ones. Remember what your mother and I used to tell you girls?" he asks. "That you were destined to be great. That it's in your blood to be powerful and strong and do big things?"

Saba nods. They were going to be twin titans, taking all their English words and piles of books and weaving a new history for the world, or a city, or a family. She hasn't done any of that.

Her father continues, all the while refusing to let go of her hand, as if he thinks she will run away, or that his meaning will soak through his sweaty palms into her veins. "Saba jan, accepting the truth doesn't dishonor your maman and Mahtab. But it's keeping you from becoming that woman. You're holding your hope so tight, using up all your power to hang on to it, that it's become like a big stone weighing you down. You see? Now you have no power left. And even if you try, you can't fly off and do all the things you were destined to do." When she doesn't respond, her father says, "I'm sorry if that comes across all wrong. I am not a twin. That part I probably can't understand."

She sits beside him, slips her other hand into the clamshell of her father's heavy palms, and says, "I think you understand." She rests her head on his shoulder. It's been a long time since she felt the twists and knobs of a fatherly shoulder against her cheek. "As for America, give me time. I'll figure it out."

"If you go," he says, a little sadly, "I will miss you."

"Only for a while." She smiles, then, when her father begins to dis-agree, she adds, "Because I'm not Mahtab, and it won't be forever."

✺

It takes months for the visa to come through. There are interviews and trips to Rasht, phone calls to the house at inopportune times, and dozens of made-up stories about doctor visits to investigate her condi-tion and shopping trips with Ponneh, who always quickly agrees to corroborate her story before rushing to hang up and most likely for-getting immediately. Ponneh never asks what Saba is doing, and Saba suspects that her involvement with Dr. Zohreh is not only deepening but also becoming much more dangerous. But Saba is far too busy to investigate.

The date of her meeting with Abbas's brother arrives, and she calls to plead illness. The lawyer becomes angry and threatens to demand that the courts intervene. But her father is friends with a well-respected mullah of his own, and though Saba has always despised him, Mullah Ali delays the proceedings by muddying up the issue, making sure his colleagues in Rasht are too busy to respond, and sweetening their plates with treasures from Agha Hafezi's pantry.

He paints an angelic picture of Saba the widow, who has only ever used the money to advance the cause of Islam.

For weeks at a time, the courts are placated and the case delayed.

Soon Saba begins to crave impossible things. Can she take Reza with her? Can they begin a new life in America? Can she convince him to go? On the other hand, Reza wouldn't be happy in America. He would miss his family and their traditional ways. He would become a wandering thing, an immigrant, always searching for someone with a familiar scent. She remembers all the Iranian men, welleducated ones, who end up driving taxis in New York or California. Where would someone like Reza end up? In Cheshmeh he could have his own lands. He could be like her father.

During the wait for her visa application to be processed, two of her tickets expire.

When the paperwork is in place, Saba comes to the most difficult part of her campaign, which is getting to an American embassy. There are none in Iran, and she has to find a way to travel to Dubai unnoticed. She has acquired visas to leave Iran and enter Dubai with the help of her father's friend who owns a factory there, and she has forged travel permissions from Reza, thinking that soon she will tell him. She plans to drive to Tehran from Cheshmeh and from there fly to Dubai, where she will hire a car to take her to the embassy. The entire trip, including her appointment at the embassy, will take two days. For this she begs her father's help. She is surprised when he agrees to something so risky. If she has to leave, he says, he would rather she had his help. He will hide her absence from the family. He will tell them there is a sick relative in Tehran.

The trip to Dubai proves tiring and dusty, but nothing extraordinary for a wealthy Iranian.

She sits in the lobby of the American embassy, terrified and desperate for some clue as to what the officer will want to hear. She has her story memorized, has practiced it, but there is no way to know the right answers. She has decided to downplay her English, her education, her resources, and to make this seem like a necessary once-in-a-lifetime trip, instead of a luxury. Luxuries lead to whims and expired visas and illegal migrations.

When her name is called, she inches out of her chair. What if she says the wrong thing? How did her mother behave when she was in this situation so many years ago?

"Why do you want to travel to the United States?" asks the officer, a middle-aged woman with a too-short haircut and a slim build.

"To visit relatives and to get treatment for my condition." She takes out a letter from her doctor, photocopies from books about medical procedures available in Iran and abroad. She shows the officer the name and address of a surgeon in California. The officer gives the papers a cursory glance, studying Saba's face instead. Saba tries to sound lighthearted, optimistic. "In Iran we have the best doctors, but I feel safer seeking the help of this man. He's an expert in this. My husband will stay and wait for me."

"And this must happen now because . . . ?" the officer asks.

"It will allow us to have babies. My husband and I. We've been in love since we were seven." Suddenly she wishes she hadn't added that last part. It seems sentimental. And it is a lie. Can the officer see through her act? She pulls out her bank statements. "Here is a record of our assets here. And of course my husband will stay." Why did she repeat that? It sounds suspicious even to her.

In the car to the airport she chastises herself a dozen times. She goes over every word and gesture in the interview, and tries to guess when she will know their decision. Back in Cheshmeh no one asks questions. When she arrives loaded with colorful fabrics, new shoes, and illegal tapes of Iranian dance music, they are all convinced she has been to Tehran. For weeks she waits for word from the embassy.

She becomes anxious, begins to chew her nails, develops another nervous tic of always checking the ground behind her.

Another ticket expires. She grows thin with worry.

One more week passes. Then two. And then one day the wait is over. A phone call in the middle of the afternoon and everything is arranged—magic. She can pick up her visa in Dubai, and from there she is free to travel to America—to California, New York, or Massachusetts. An entire continent is open to her now. It seems that her weeks of sleepless research and her strategy of not seeking permanent asylum worked after all.

Saba spends nearly four hours on hold with airlines, trying to change her flight itinerary from one that includes a stopover in Istanbul to one with a stop in Dubai. Despite her three remaining unused tickets, she is forced to purchase a new one, a flight from Tehran to Dubai, from Dubai to Istanbul, connecting with one of her other tickets. When she hangs up the phone, she is dizzy with the reality of it. She is leaving. And now what is left to do? She has an overwhelming sense of being unfinished. Can she take out her money now? Will anyone check? How should she transport it? Should she try to sell her properties again or maybe sign them over to her father? What about Reza?

At the bank she struggles for breath. Is anyone watching? She tells herself to stop being paranoid and drains her accounts, leaving a respectable but modest sum in each so that they don't close and trigger some sort of alarm to Abbas's family. She changes her fortune into dollars at a preposterous exchange rate, half of it in a grungy office in a quiet part of Rasht through a black-market dealer whose name she got from her father and who seems to smell urgency. The other half she changes through a contact of the Tehrani's, who accompanies her to his friend's office and shakes his head dramatically. "So we're losing you, Saba Khanom. Who will buy all the videotapes now?" Saba smiles and says good-bye, even promises to tape a few programs for him in America.

Her fortune, the part she manages to liquidate at least, amounts to forty-eight thousand dollars, a small bag of Pahlavi gold coins, and an armful of precious jewelry.

One morning she receives a phone call regarding her exit visa. "I need to tell you, Khanom," the man mutters, "that your passport is in order. Everything looks good. You only need your permission let-ter, one specifically for this trip, to show at the airport."

"I'm sorry?" she says, though she knows. She has avoided this detail until now.

"Your husband," he says. "He must give permission each time you leave Iran."

Saba spends the morning considering her options. Should she tell Reza now? Should she forge another letter like the one she used for Dubai? No, she decides. She will find the courage. She will sort out all her paperwork and when he comes home, she will tell him her plans. She will say good-bye, tell her most faithful friend that he has given her some of her best days and convince him to let her go. Maybe he will struggle, but in the end he will understand. He may be old-fashioned, but he has a musical soul, a rebellious heart. He is the one who plays the guitar for her when she dances. He hates *pas-dar*s in Jeeps, black chadors, and curtains at the beach, and he loves the Beatles.

She digs through Reza's drawers, looking for their marriage cer-tificate. As she is closing the top drawer, her gaze falls on an unfamil-iar tape. Is it one of hers? She slips it into her Walkman and presses play. Reza's silky voice wafts from the headset. He laughs boyishly as he tries to figure out how to record. Then he starts to sing. It's the good-bye song, "Mara Beboos." *Kiss me for the last time.* He strums his *setar* the way he did for her in the shack. Saba turns the plastic cover in her hand. It is dated autumn 1991, a few days before Reza began their romance. When his song is over, Reza speaks through the crack‑ling in the background, pausing between words. "My beautiful friend, I see now that you'll never marry me, so rather than dying for you, let's call this good‑bye."

The Caspian Day
(Khanom Basir)

After dark, when their parents had already gone to bed, Saba and Mahtab sneaked off to swim in the Caspian. They were eleven then and good swimmers, but the sea is much too strong for little girls. At night jinns come to bathe and drag away all life that dares enter the black water. From what I heard, they played for an hour before one of them noticed they had drifted too far. They tried to swim back and made it a long way too. Apparently Mahtab pulled Saba for part of the way and then got tired, so they both started floating on their backs, trying to avoid the waves.

They floated on their backs for two hours. That's the tragedy of it, because a normal eleven-year-old could never do that in the middle of the night when she's tired and scared and certain she can't beat the sea. Any other girl would have given up. But they had each other, and they lasted for two hours against all those water jinns. They told stories and held each other's hand. They whispered about the trouble they would get into once they were rescued. That is how Saba described it to me. When I imagine that night, I don't see it as so peaceful. I imagine them struggling for air, kicking the murky water with their tiny feet, trying to breathe while the terns circle overhead. That is the scene that comes to me when I see Saba alone now, poring over her Mahtab writings, grabbing her throat like she's struggling for air. She doesn't think I see it, but it's obvious that she is in the Caspian again. The body remembers much that the mind forgets.

Agha and Khanom Hafezi had been looking for them for some time. They had searched the entire town and had only just begun to consider that their daughters might have gone for a swim. By some coincidence of timing and fate and the tie between mothers and daughters, Bahareh chose that critical final moment, when the girls were just about to lose hope and let the jinns carry them off, to demand a search of the sea.

The local police ignored them at first. They refused to listen to Bahareh because she was a woman in hysterics, letting her headscarf slip, becoming indecent, cursing and insulting them. Then, when they finally answered the pleas of Agha Hafezi, or rather his wallet, they said they had no boat and had to wake a fisherman and take his. The old boatman was quick to the task, but when they were ready to set off, the officers refused to let Bahareh on the boat with the men. Bahareh, now overcome by absolute madness, threw aside her *hijab* and ran into the water. She started to swim fully clothed into the sea, and the men cried sin and indecency. They pulled her out and chastised her before allowing the old fisherman to set off with Agha Hafezi to find the girls.

The girls couldn't have been asleep for more than a minute or two when the men in the boat spotted them in the water. Saba was still floating on her back when she was plucked out of the water by the callused, briny hands of the town's fishmonger. Her father spent an hour more diving after his other daughter. At some point the coast guard joined the search. I don't know if Saba was awake, if she saw her father trying desperately to recover Mahtab during those sixty minutes of panic in the belly of the Caspian. Probably she didn't, because she used to tell us that Mahtab was with her in the boat, singing songs or some other crazy, impossible thing.

When the search for Mahtab was over, the boat came back to shore and Agha Hafezi never stopped blaming himself. *I wish I had done things differently,* he said, thinking that he might have reached the girls sooner, or he might have stopped them from sneaking away in the first place. But he didn't have much time for self-pity—because at that moment his wife was being questioned by the police, who already knew that they would need an excuse. Soon people would ask questions. Why didn't the search for the girls begin sooner? Why the delay? They blamed Bahareh for indecency. And later for bringing harm to her own daughters by impeding a police search.

✤

You've heard the saying "His donkey passed over the bridge," which is to say that when a person is in trouble—his donkey wobbling over a shaky bridge—he behaves one way. But when his troubles are over—his donkey having passed over safely—he is back to acting superior, as if he doesn't need anyone at all. This is how most people behave. But not Agha Hafezi. After the Caspian day, when all of Cheshmeh came together to nurse his daughter back to health, he opened his doors to us all and never once did he close them again. Some people think he did it only to *maast-mali* his secret religion and, yes, there was that reason. I don't think his soul cries out for the friendship of some old mullah, or that he yearns to spend every night with old women. No . . . but there is more to it than safety. He has a Gilaki heart, a soft heart. I see genuine welcome in his eyes, though he and I have had many reasons to disagree over the years, even after his wife left. No matter what, he didn't cast me off. He never told me to stop talking or get out of his house.

For the Hafezis that was the beginning of a long hell. A hundred black years rolled into a few days. When they came back from that Caspian trip, everything changed. Saba had a high fever for weeks and was delirious. She stayed in bed most of the time, asking for Mahtab, but we told her that her sister was sick and contagious.

Bahareh, in all her selfishness, had been planning her escape from Iran for months before, but after that trip, she had to be *sneaked* out of the country. Her husband paid every bureaucrat and paper pusher in town to get her unflagged documents, to sneak her away before the investigation into her crimes could continue. It was lucky the police had let her out, put her in the custody of her husband and Mullah Ali. Every day after that, during the time when she should have been tending to Saba, Bahareh was in some embassy or office or giving piles of cash to this document forger or that passport checker. She had planned to go to America with the girls even before all this. I don't know how her husband could have allowed her to take his daughters away, but the whole family was obsessed with the Western world. Agha Hafezi couldn't leave his lands and money behind; he would stay, but Bahareh was stubborn about her plans. One day as I was nursing Saba back to health, I heard her screaming at her husband, "I'm leaving this place. How can you expect me to raise Saba here?"

Mullah Ali was either too dazed or too wise to interfere. He saw and didn't see the Hafezis' scheming to get Bahareh out of the country. He saw camel, he didn't see camel, as they say. Later, when there were *pasdars* and interviews and too many questions, Mullah Ali said that women are capable of great evil without the knowledge of their husbands. And so Agha Hafezi was spared. Funny what the old mullah will do for well-hidden alcohol, something to fill his pipe, and a free *sofreh*.

And then, suddenly, after days of blurriness and visions and tidbits of information fed to her along with bowls of barley soup, the day came when Saba was clear-headed enough to travel. Soon after, the documents were ready so they could sneak Bahareh the fugitive out of the country. I don't know how Mullah Ali kept the police and *pasdars* away for so long. It must have been a number of things: the war with Iraq, bureaucracy, the influence of the old cleric, and, most of all, Agha Hafezi's streams of money.

"Where is Mahtab?" Saba kept asking her parents as they buttoned her up and tucked her favorite books and sweaters into a little suitcase. They had kept Mahtab away for so long by then that Saba was beginning to doubt the excuse that her sister was contagious. Wasn't Mahtab going with them? Didn't they need to sit together on the plane? "Hush, child," Khanom Omidi said, as she brushed Saba's hair. "Hush, you poor thing." And she started muttering prayers to Allah.

The family drove to the airport in a car they had borrowed from Bahareh's friend Dr. Zohreh, that same troublemaker activist who has sucked in Ponneh and tried to get her hands on Saba. They left their own car behind in case *pasdars* were spying on the house.

"Where is Mahtab?" Saba asked again. "Isn't she coming too?"

What a moment it must have been. I heard it all later from each of them, in pieces.

Bahareh cried quietly. "She's meeting us there," she told her daughter.

"Who is driving her?" Saba asked.

"Khanom Basir will drive her," she answered. What bad luck to bring me into the family's curse!

Then Agha Hafezi gave his wife a list of instructions: people to call when she arrived in California, how to behave in front of the *pasdars*, which documents to have ready in her purse, and so on. His wife continued to cry so he put on some music and they drove to the airport in silence, each of them heading toward a different imagined future. None of them guessing that the little girl in the backseat might ruin everything. That you can't lie to a girl with a thousand jinns. But it wasn't their fault. They were just trying to give simple answers, short answers, to life's too-big, too-confusing questions.

Anyway, to bring head and tail to it all: at the airport Saba saw Mahtab.

Chapter Nineteen

Even before Saba is finished listening to the tape, a strange, unexpected calm washes over her. She has always known this. Nothing has changed. Her decision is made and there is no future for her in Cheshmeh. Oh, but to be a nothing player in someone else's love story. It hurts—has always hurt—to the bone. She drops the Walkman on the floor and meanders to her private hammam, remembering that in America baths lack a certain indulgence. She sheds her clothes and wraps herself in a towel, turning on both showerheads in the far corners and watching from the bench by the wall as the room fills with steam. Her thoughts drift back to the tape. It is dated shortly before Reza came to see her, and it was obviously intended for Ponneh. But he never gave her the tape. Or maybe Ponneh sent it back. Did he ask her to marry him first? Clearly he did. This must be why they behaved so strangely before the wedding. But instead of anger, Saba feels pity for her husband. Why did Ponneh refuse? Because she didn't love him? Because she wanted to keep the security of their threesome? Or because of her mother's rule? Ponneh's sister was still alive then. As the steam relaxes her, she lets her mind wander down these many paths, but then she finds herself asking, Does it matter? No, she answers, it doesn't—a comforting revelation now that she is sure of it.

She thinks of all that happened between the date on the tape and now. Before the wedding, in Khanom Alborz's yard, she knew from the way Reza stared at Ponneh. He loved her then. And yet he turned away and continued with his marriage to Saba. What a bizarre notion of fidelity. If only he could understand that Saba didn't need protecting, that he has harmed and caged her with his love, given her a reason to be a coward.

The three of us forever, they have said to each other since childhood, and it has been true. Ponneh was there when Saba first married, when Abbas died, and for every milestone in between. Reza asked after her daily in the town square and at her father's house, and came to see her whenever he could. To him this is a natural ending to years of devoted friendship—that he should marry one or the other—like the *Zanerooz* story they read with Khanom Mansoori when they were fourteen.

But who is Saba to judge Reza's choice, his ideas about loyalty? She was raised by the same mothers and longed to be a part of his world before realizing she belonged in Mahtab's. Briefly she considers the money. Was he motivated by it? She remembers the day she told Reza and Ponneh a Mahtab story in an alley behind the post office. She offered Reza a tape of songs and he refused to take it without paying. She is confident that he would behave exactly the same today. He is an honorable man. It was never class or money that came between them; she is finally certain of this. Now another memory from that day comes to her, when she told her friends the difference between old, inherited money and new, earned money. She smiles at her childish logic, because isn't it all the same? She should let them have it. What use is money if not to clear the road for cherished friends. They will need it after she is gone.

She lies back on the bench and closes her eyes as she drips hot water on her belly with a sponge. She considers one of her father's favorite verses from Khayyam's *Rubaiyat* and says it aloud as she douses herself with a cup of hot water.

Ah Love! Could thou and I with Fate conspire
To grasp this sorry Scheme of Things entire,
Would not we shatter it to bits—and then
Re-mould it nearer to the Heart's Desire!

A few minutes later Reza enters with the battered guitar her father used to keep in the sitting room closet, the one Reza once plucked, comparing the notes with his *setar*. The guitar is old and out of tune now, and it has become their habit to take it into the hammam. One day they know the steam will end its life, warping the wood and rusting the strings, but they take pleasure in using it up in this indulgent way. Reza takes off his clothes and joins her on the bench, bringing the guitar and a plate of sweet lemon wedges. He puts the plate beside her and looks at her expectantly.

"I saw the tape on the floor," he whispers. She shakes her head to make him stop.

He strums a few notes, the beginning of one of her favorite songs, as she gets up from the bench. He watches her drop her long hair down her back, the fog enveloping her sinful, overindulged widow's body. He has an old-style way with the guitar, playing with just two fingers so that the notes drone pure and uncluttered like *setar* music and echo through the hammam one at a time. He plays "Fast Car" beautifully now, so that it sounds like a twangy Iranian version of itself, and recently he learned "Stairway to Heaven" because she mentioned it once and left a mix tape cued up to it. Through the steam and the water, she catches him looking at her and wonders if he is thinking about how damaged she is. Can he see all that she can still do, her coming legacy?

She thinks of their best days, all those early mornings when they started the day in this hammam, when he put away the guitar and pulled her to the bench and they wasted the early hours—the time when only jinns come to bathe—covered in fog, reliving those first uncertain wood-shack visits when they decided to forget about dead husbands and Basijis and Ponneh and meddling mothers and discover something illegal and exquisite. At thier best, they might spend hours like this before some buried sorrow surfaces and Saba forces him out of her world. Can they have one more of those days now, a sort of good-bye? There are things that are impossible to let go. But a hammam at the skirt of a mountain, with its softening light and shad-owy half figures moving through steam like ghosts, is a place for cures, for good memories. Sometimes the light from a small window catches a watery patch of air above the bathers, revealing the particles of dirt settling around them like clouds. Then you can begin to see the harsher, less beautiful angles.

"I don't think we did so bad at marriage," she says, "considering..."

She tells him she wants to go, but not because of the tape or any-thing else he has done. He tells her that he never lied about loving her, that he is sorry it wasn't enough, in that hand-of-fate way from her books. He pulls her to him, her hair dripping against his chest. "My overlooked beauty," he whispers, because now they both know what will become of them. "I'll keep your every detail in my memory, like a painting."

Later she watches Reza disappear toward the entrance, letting in a cold gust of air as he opens the door. Now that he is slipping away, she recalls the way he brought her tea when she was angry, his guitar songs and village-hero dreams. Soon he will be gone and she will have to bottle up her memories of hammam music and days spent pretending. As he is about to shut the door, she shouts after him. "I need permission to leave Iran," she says, holding a small hope that he will object or ask to go along.

But he only says, "Whatever you need," and Saba's briny Rashti heart, the part of her that belongs to Cheshmeh and is terrified of the strange and unknown, struggles to find its momentum again.

ഉ—©©—ഉ

He let me go. She drives through the mountains alone, early in the evening. It stings a little. But it wasn't all false. Reza tried to love her. He tried with every song and every showy kick of the ball outside her window. He wanted to save her, to keep her for himself. The lines from Khayyam meander back to her; maybe now she can love Reza in a new way. It is possible to shatter the old and remold her fate to her own heart's desire.

It isn't Reza's fault, she thinks, or Ponneh's. The Reza she married was as much a creation, as much a distortion of reality, as the Mahtab of her stories. She made him up to help her live her life here. He is a falsehood, a phantom, a magic shadow show. We are all invented beings, she thinks, built this way or that to suit each other's needs.

The drive to the mountain shack is a blur. She doesn't even know why she is going there, only that now she is too somber to do anything else and she needs a mother. She surprises herself with the realization that her sadness isn't about Ponneh and Reza. They have been building up to this since childhood. Rather, she is angry at herself for waiting, for never making the brave leaps she imagined for Mahtab. For believing so many lies. How many lies has she told herself over the years?

The car winds around the mountain and slowly the winter chill seeps in. She parks near the precipice and glances at the landscape before getting out. But as soon as she approaches the shack, she realizes it was a mistake, a step backward, coming here to this familiar place. Every detail reminds her of the life she is abandoning. The smell of woods and a fire and winter cold. The sound of the nocturnal sea rushing toward the shore. The cold grainy doorknob in her hand. This is the place where she first found romance, where she and Reza had their first nights alone. A flood of memories overtakes her. She turns back to her car and is about to climb in when the front door of the house opens.

Dr. Zohreh calls out to her, "Saba jan, what's happened?"

The concern in the voice of her mother's old friend makes Saba feel foolish. When the doctor approaches, Saba breathes in, summoning strength. "Nothing," she says. "I was just feeling sentimental." She smiles for the doctor's sake, so that she won't worry, and says good-bye before Dr. Zohreh can invite her inside. She drives down the hill toward the water, remembering long-gone days when she and her family drove down these mountain roads to swim in the Caspian. How long has it been since she dipped her foot in the sea? For years she has crept closer and closer, but has been too afraid to touch. Now who knows when she will see it again?

She parks near a beach and makes her way toward the stilted houses in the water and the fish shack perched on the pier. Patches of snow dot the darkening horizon. There are no seagulls in sight, but something birdlike calls from afar. She walks along the now calm, now raging sea. The light spray of water on her face reminds her of that day in the summer when she and her sister took a midnight swim. But that was long ago. Everything is decided now, so what is this sudden unease?

Halfway down the beach, she hears a voice calling her name. She turns to find Dr. Zohreh rushing toward her, trying to keep her scarf from flying away in the wind.

"Saba, wait for me!" she calls. Saba stops and waits for Dr. Zohreh to catch up. The doctor's face is red and she is panting as if she hasn't run in years.

"You didn't have to come!" Stunned, Saba takes the doctor's arm. "I'm fine."

"No, you're not," says the doctor, as if delivering a diagnosis. She clears her throat and reaches for Saba's hand. "What's wrong, Saba jan? You don't have to pretend to be so in control all the time. . . . Just tell me."

Saba shrugs, searches for an answer. *Nothing is wrong.* Cheshmeh is no longer hers. So many people she loved have disappeared from her life, and yet she is still here with her feet on the sand and the rocks. No wave has come to sweep her away. She has handled it all with some grace, she hopes. And now the spray on her skin feels like the old days. She licks the water from her hand—that unique, half-salty Caspian taste.

Dr. Zohreh touches Saba's cheek, setting off an unexpected trembling in her chin. "Is it something to do with Reza?" she asks. Saba shakes her head.

Then an answer appears on its own. It surprises even Saba, because she has tried so hard not to know. "Maman is dead," she blurts out. A cluster of words lodges in her throat; she forces them out with a new kind of strength. "And Mahtab is dead. I saw her die in the water."

Maast *and* Doogh
(*Khanom Basir*)

At the airport Saba saw her.

She had been complaining of dizziness and headaches from her illness, but through the grogginess and the commotion of the airport, she said she spotted her holding the hand of a woman in a blue manteau. The woman was walking away with Mahtab, so Saba screamed her name. "Mahtab! We're here!" Right away Bahareh swept her up in her arms and told her to be quiet. "But what about Mahtab?" Saba asked.

Isn't it funny about memory? Her own mother picked her up and told her not to bother the strange woman, and yet, when she remembers, she confuses the two of them so that she can place her mother on a plane. The mind does these things to make life go on.

I can't imagine what I would have said to the girl in that state. Bahareh chose to say "Mahtab will meet us. Now, please, Saba jan, behave."

They stood in several lines, having their bags checked, having their papers checked. *Pasdar* after *pasdar* asked Khanom and Agha

Hafezi questions. *Where are you going? Why? For how long? Is the whole family traveling? Where do you live?*

"My wife and daughter are going alone," Agha Hafezi said. "For a short time, on vacation to see relatives. And I'll stay here to wait for them."

The *pasdar* nodded, but then Saba jumped in. "Mahtab's going too!"

The *pasdar* looked down at the girl and furrowed his brow. Saba smiled and tried to find Mahtab in the crowd. "Who is Mahtab?" he barked at the parents.

Bahareh laughed uncomfortably. "That is the name of her doll."

Before Saba could make a fuss, her father picked her up and said that she could have all the cream puffs she wanted if she could go all day without saying another word. Saba nodded and pretended to zip her lips. Thinking back on the years since, I'd swear that was the last day Saba asked for cream puffs. That was the last day for a lot of things.

When they were through the final line, Bahareh muttered something about how much trouble children are—which is probably why Saba didn't say anything when she saw Mahtab again, this time in the arms of a middle-aged man with a brown hat. She pulled on her father's arm and pointed, but he ignored her. The family was waiting now in the room right before boarding, and Saba could see the planes outside. She knew that once they went through that door, they would be on the plane and Mahtab would be left behind—which frightened her since Mahtab was *right over there*. Didn't anyone see that Mahtab was standing there with the wrong baba?

She pulled her hand out of her father's hand and ran as fast as she could, because the man and Mahtab were getting away. Her baba was chasing her and screaming for her to come back, and the man and Mahtab were going through the security line in the other direction, and before Saba knew it, she was no longer in the room next to the airplanes, but in a huge room with thousands of people all around. When she saw her father looking for her, running this way and that, wild with fear, Saba hid behind a chair and waited. She was not leaving this country without her sister, no matter what they said.

We heard later that Agha Hafezi looked for Saba for two hours while she hid under the chairs.

During that time, Saba must have seen the strange woman again, because when her father finally found her, her story had changed and the man with the brown hat had been transformed back into the woman with the blue manteau. Saba had seen them with her own eyes and was convinced the woman was her mother—that she and Mahtab had boarded a plane without her. Funny, because Agha Hafezi told me that the little girl she kept pointing to didn't even look like Mahtab. She was just a waif in a green scarf. Or maybe she was just Saba's own reflection in a window.

Probably the man with the brown hat, the woman in blue, and the ghost girl in the green scarf were real, a family that looked vaguely like her own. I doubt Saba made them up out of nothing. Whoever they were, they caused Agha Hafezi to lose his wife forever.

We heard through rumors that Bahareh Hafezi was arrested. An officer of the moral police spotted her, probably with fake or incomplete documents. Maybe one of them recognized her from the arrest on the day of the accident, or maybe they found out she was a Christian and an activist. Either way, they had to blame someone for causing a girl to die, and here was the mother escaping the country. Though even I know that they were trying to cover up their own guilt for Mahtab's death—all those delays they caused. Later someone said they saw Bahareh in Evin Prison. But no one at the prison ever admitted to this, which is a bad sign. Some people said that she must have gotten on that plane and abandoned her family out of grief. I suppose that is why Saba clung to the memory of the woman and the girl boarding a plane without her. But how can she believe such a thing? A mother leaving her daughter behind because she has too much sorrow of her own? Doesn't she know that a mother's curse is to grieve for the rest of her days?

Bahareh didn't make it onto the plane—of that I'm certain. All her forged papers must have been discovered. She was a criminal, so who knows what they did to her while her husband was searching for Saba. He never saw her again, and at the airport those sons of dogs shoot to kill. Saba rode home in her father's car, tears covering her face, and accused him of leaving Mahtab at the airport. He put on a song called "Across the Universe," because that was where Mahtab had gone. Saba played it many times in the years after, when she was contemplating all the things that had changed her world.

Now you have your answer. The proof that Saba is a broken and cursed thing. The reason I have never accepted her into my son's life. I like to think of it as a storyteller's riddle: Now that there is so much earth and water between the sisters, how many scoops of a teaspoon would it take for Saba to reach Mahtab? Well, let me tell you: It wouldn't take very long to cover the earth between them—but you'd have to empty the sea.

Khanom Mansoori used to sit under the *korsi* blanket and say that there are forces joining sisters together, no matter how far apart they drift and how many kilometers separate them, even if one of them leaves this world altogether. I can see that, like her, you wanted it to be true. But a story is by nature a lie and *korsi*s are the place where all lies begin. Sitting with a hookah, all eyes upon you, how can you possibly not be tempted by wild stories? So you should know what comes next, and what should have come out of Saba's mouth at the end of every tale about Mahtab.

Up we went and there was maast,
Down we came and there was doogh,
And Mahtab's story was doroogh *(a lie).*

Chapter Twenty

LATE AUTUMN 1992

Later they sit together in the shack, drinking cups of hot chocolate imported from Switzerland by one of Dr. Zohreh's many
scattered friends. Saba looks out the frosted window and tries to
make out the water below. "It's true, isn't it? Everyone believes it. She
was taken to prison from the airport and then they said she had
never been there."

Dr. Zohreh nods. "Yes, that's usually a sign—"

Saba isn't listening. "And then we never heard from her again."

"Another sign," says the doctor matter-of-factly.

Saba takes a sip and taps the window. The far-off outline of the
sea in summer used to remind her of her favorite song, the one about
the dock and the bay. In winter it used to be a frightful thing, a cavernous black mouth swallowing up her sister. But now the sea is nothing more than many droplets, rocks, algae, and shells.

"I thought I saw her getting on a plane with Mahtab," she says.
"I saw a woman in a blue manteau with a girl my age."

"You were so young," says Dr. Zohreh. "Children invent things in order to cope."

"It's just such a strange thing. Both of them *lost*. . . . No bodies, no funeral." Those words, *no bodies*, sound morbid, like a betrayal. "And within days of each other."

"It took weeks for your mother," Dr. Zohreh corrects. "But yes, it's a beautiful mystery. And I guess you're right. It doesn't help that there are no graves, no closure."

"I wonder where she is exactly," Saba muses. "Where in the water."

"Do you want to talk about that day?" says Dr. Zohreh.

Saba shakes her head. She is consumed with another idea. Yes, she will go to America, but it will be different. She will build a new life for herself and stop searching for some hazy past. And while there is sorrow in knowing that she will never find her mother, that knowledge is also a burden lifted. "I have to go now," she says.

The drive to Cheshmeh is black and slick, and she is distracted from her thoughts by the condition of the road. Pulling up to her house an hour later, she thinks of Abbas's funeral, that feeling of power and possibility. The way she took stock of the people around her, the people in her debt, and realized that everything that had been her father's and husband's was now hers. On that day she was sure that her patience and suffering had redeemed her, and she was transformed. She longs for that certainty again. She wants to reach for it, grasp that rush of being powerful, no longer just a girl slapped around by the wind. She will do this, she decides, a little each day.

On the day before her departure, while Reza is in Rasht, Saba shuts herself in her room and sorts through her hidden wealth. She puts a third of it in an envelope with the deeds to her properties. Then she and Khanom Omidi sew the other two-thirds of the cash and jewels into the lining of every jacket, every pair of pants, even the suitcase itself, while her father keeps Khanom Basir busy with a suddenly dire level of household incompetence. He is trying so hard for her, Saba notices. He always has.

On her last night walking in her house, sleeping in her bed, looking out onto the garden Reza and Ponneh planted for her, Saba listens to all the music she can't take with her. She speeds mournfully through all the books that she knows she can buy again in America. She sits up in the bed she still shares with Reza and, for the first time, realizes that this is the very bed on which she was so viciously attacked. Why did she never think to change it? To give it to one of her father's workers and buy a new one? Maybe it was Reza, the thought of him, the idea that this bed, the knowledge of what happened here, was what held them together. A poor, damaged girl and her childhood friend with his mixed-up sense of chivalry and a weakness for broken things.

Watching Reza sleeping in a tight ball at the edge of her bed, Saba remembers all her favorite times with him. The nights in the mountain shack. Reza with the rusty old guitar in the hammam. But in the end, she decides, the very best times were shared with Ponneh when they were young—the three of them hiding in her father's pantry, passing stolen joints, hitchhiking to Rasht to search for letters from Mahtab.

She kisses him good night—good-bye—then places all her paperwork in a folder on top of her suitcase and climbs into bed. She falls asleep with her headphones still on, her favorite music playing over and over, because she cannot bear to throw it all away.

Shortly after dawn her father knocks on the door, whispers a greeting, and says he will wait in the sitting room while she gets ready. "I will make you breakfast," he says, holding up a bulging plastic bag that smells strongly of *lavash* bread and cheese. John Lennon is singing about rain in a paper cup, dying love, a changing universe, his voice faint and muffled out of her fallen headphones. Soon the frenzy of her last shower in her hammam, her last cup of tea, her last good-bye to all the objects around her overpower him and the music fades away. Around her father's clumsily prepared breakfast *sofreh*, she finds him having tea with Reza and Khanom Basir. The air above them is full of tension and *tarof* and unspoken truths. Khanom Basir shakes her head in mourning and clutches something covered in yesterday's stew. Saba recognizes the blue edges, the glossy paper—one of the expired plane tickets that she had sunk to the bottom of the trash as she was sorting through the remains of her old life.

"Maybe my brain is finally old, but I'm confused," Reza's mother huffs. "It's a plane ticket. I should have known when I saw that book with foreign pictures."

"Calm down, Khanom," says Saba's father. "She was going to tell you before she left. Now we're all here and you know everything that's happening."

But Khanom Basir isn't listening. She sinks into a cushion like a lost thing and puts her head in her hands. "You're leaving him," she says softly. "I knew you would."

Reza reaches to help his mother, but she shrugs him away. Her reaction is surprising, because didn't she *want* Saba out of her life? The others are silent as Khanom Basir unburdens herself. "After everything my son has gone through, you're leaving him? I thought things were good now." She isn't hysterical. Only curious and sad.

"I'm taking your advice," Saba says, and sits beside her mother-in-law on the rug and the cushions, their legs tucked beneath their haunches, while the men bring them fresh cups of tea. She takes Khanom Basir's hand.

Khanom Basir looks up, glassy-eyed. It's a strange look, and Saba thinks that maybe she is just afraid of being left behind. "What advice?" she asks.

"Only die for someone who at least has a fever for you," she says.

Khanom Basir gives a resigned laugh. She nods a few times. "You kids have made such a mess. Such a mess." She sighs and squeezes Saba's hand. "I want some of the special tea." The storyteller lifts herself off the floor. She seems to be convincing herself of things. "No need to make a *fatwa* out of family misunderstandings. My special tea from India would be nice now," she mutters, leaving unspoken the words *before you go* and Saba baffled about why they went through such trouble to keep this a secret from her.

They drink the Indian tea in silence, each of them sipping and remembering, interrupting the hush of the early morning only when there is a particularly important memory to share. Khanom Basir conjures up the day seven-year-old Saba proposed to Reza. Reza, in his infinite kindness and penitence—or maybe just his inherited penchant for beautiful lies—talks about their kiss in the yard and how in that moment he was thinking of no one else—what man could? Her father mentions the day she and Mahtab stayed up all night, reading their first shipment of English storybooks, and he realized that these wide-eyed, hungry creatures were never his to keep.

When it is time to go, they reluctantly get up from the *sofreh*, and Saba puts on her manteau and scarf. Reza loiters by the gate, pretending to check on the garden. He takes her hand, touches her cheek. "Now who will sing the lyrics when I play?"

She pulls out the envelope with a third of her liquid assets and the ownership papers for Abbas's properties. She weighs it in her hand, turns it over one more time, before holding it out to Reza. "This is for Dr. Zohreh and Ponneh. I want you to use it to help their group. And I want you to finish school."

Reza opens his mouth but doesn't say anything.

"I want you to hide the money, okay? I've rescued it for you."

Reza begins to shake his head. "No," he says. She can see his pride is wounded. "I didn't marry you for this. I would marry you even if you had nothing but your stories."

"I know," she says, thinking that this is the best thing he has ever said to her and that she will remember it always. She closes his hand around the envelope and adds, "I've always had plenty . . . maybe too much. Let me share it with you. I found out that Abbas's family still has a claim to the money. They might take away everything you have here, so just hide it, and after it all settles down, you'll have something." She notices him looking at the land deeds bewildered. "I haven't had time to figure out what you should do with the property papers. Maybe nothing. But maybe you can claim it or find a way to sell some before they come for it. But Baba can't be the one to do this. He's going to say he knew nothing about my plan to leave."

"Okay, but—" Reza begins.

"You can't let Abbas's brother get the money. You know what I went through." Reza is looking at his feet now and nodding, and Saba can tell that he is still unsure. "A lot of people sacrificed for this money," she says. "How much did you and Ponneh go through to protect me? She was there when Abbas died. And you . . . you've made me happy since we were children. Now I want you to be happy."

Reza flips through the stacks of bills and Saba feels a strange unanchored sensation, watching him reluctantly accept her blessing. It feels good to finally give something to Reza. She has wanted to ever since the day they were eleven and he held out all his coins to her in exchange for a music tape. But in all these years and for all her money, she has never found a way.

Before they leave, Saba calls Ponneh's neighbor and asks her friend to go to Khanom Omidi's house—quietly, no questions. In a sleepy rush, her father drives her into the wooded area higher on the mountain. When they arrive, the door is cracked open; Saba and Agha Hafezi slip inside. Khanom Omidi is flitting in every direction, heaving Saba's suitcase toward the door despite her extreme old age.

Ponneh appears from another room, separated from the main sitting area by a hanging canopy. "What's happening?" she whispers. "You're really leaving?"

"I just wanted to say good-bye. And say good-bye to Dr. Zohreh for me too, okay?"

"But why?" Ponneh is dumbfounded.

Saba reaches for her friend, hugs her, kisses her cheeks. "I love you, Ponneh jan," she says. "You were my best friend since Mahtab."

"What about Reza?" Ponneh's voice is muffled by Saba's scarf. "Is he going?"

"He loves you," says Saba, pulling back to look at her friend. She shrugs as if to say it's no big deal, that Ponneh shouldn't worry. "I'm going to make my own life. And one day, when you've done all your activist work and things are better, you should marry him. And then you should both visit me."

"I promise about the visiting part . . . not sure about the marrying part." Ponneh's face melts into a smile, as it did when they were small and she and the twins made elaborate plans to steal leftover pastries or get Reza or Kasem into trouble. "Say hello to Shahzadeh Nixon for me," she says, and Saba can see that all is well between them.

"If you promise to be careful," she says, "you can send me your photos anytime . . . for the newspapers. I'll call you with my address."

She kisses Ponneh good-bye again. It's over, not as hard as she imagined. Another sister left behind, not so monumental a thing to do when there is a life waiting to be lived. Moments later Saba drops into Khanom Omidi's arms and inhales her unique scent— a mix of jasmine, turmeric, coins, and dried mulberries—knowing that *this* friend she will likely never see again. She kisses the old woman's soft hand, streaked with brown freckles, blue veins, and yel-low saffron stains, and thinks of a song the Tehrani gave her once, calling it his favorite. *Grandma's hands used to ache sometimes and swell,* a voice like a warm palm to the chest, like a winter *korsi,* crooned. Will Saba find another such person in New York or California or Texas?

With each good-bye Saba sheds tears, but her hands aren't desperate to clutch her throat. There is no sense of drowning or being buried alive. Nothing is closing in around her.

Saba and her father spend the day in the bustling Tehran airport. Agha Hafezi paces by the benches in the waiting area as Saba goes through each step that leads to boarding the plane. After she has endured the agony of watching airport security paw through her suitcase—praying with every breath that they don't search the bottom layers of clothing too carefully—they say good-bye quickly, awkwardly.

"Losing another daughter," Agha Hafezi sighs.

"Except I can come back anytime I want," she says, trying to sound cheerful. She wants to apologize for all that she has put him through. For all the nights she ran off to buy illegal tapes or sneaked alcohol into his pantry. Most of all she wants to tell him that she is sorry for all the times she pushed him away when he tried, in his own uncomfortable way, to create a bond. How can she say that she has seen him worrying about her; that she knows he has gone to great pains to help her finally catch her plane to America; that she has seen his shadow running ahead of her and clearing her path for twenty-two years? Before Mahtab's death, he used to say, "My daughters, I will take you to the sea and dry you with hundred-dollar bills." Lately she has had a recurring dream in which her father holds a towel made of American bills, arms stretched out, calling out to her. In the dream she is only a little girl, and she turns her back and runs into the sea instead. For so many years she has treated him like the dead parent and chased after her mother. Somehow she managed to miss them both.

But she can't say these things outright because she has chosen to leave him, has chosen an independent life, the possibility of college and a legacy, over staying close by him. Maybe she will write it all in a letter. Or maybe she will live the rest of her life the way he wanted, grandly, powerfully, secure and unafraid of life's biggest risks. It won't be so hard. It's the way Mahtab lived in all those immigrant stories. And wasn't the girl in those stories really Saba, after all? Saba Hafezi as she would have been if the world wasn't so full of rules and punishments and missed flights.

"Remember our father-daughter song?" he asks. He clears his throat, and it seems to Saba that he doesn't know how to say goodbye.

"I'll come back one day," she says. "This isn't a last goodbye for us."

"Yes." Her father nods morosely. Then he takes her face in his rough, sun-chafed farmer's hands and adds, "I've been lucky to have you here for this long."

Epilogue

Years have passed. Today the world outside learns to live with all that is new and unnavigated, and Saba rushes to her apartment in California, pops a roll of film into a heavy camera, and packs a suitcase. A few days ago a group of Arab men struck her new country. The twin towers of New York have been attacked twice in the years she has lived here. Every American statesman, bureaucrat, journalist, and right-wing pundit is calling for stricter immigration policies. But Saba has a green card now, is almost an American citizen. It has been three years since she graduated with a degree in journalism from a college where she was four years older than her classmates. She works for a newspaper. She is a reporter—the real kind, a storyteller without a license to lie, but with the freedom to tell the entire truth.

On this September morning Saba prepares for a road trip to New York—the place where her plane first landed, and where she began her own immigrant life. She scans the streets on the television, the cameras venturing south where more and more of the roads are soiled by smog and debris. The streets look eerie during those first days. A quietness seems to have fallen over this indestructible American city. When she sees a newspaper cover photo of a jubilant Palestinian woman, a *dehati*, hands in the air, mouth open in rejoicing, Saba feels sick at her own connection with her.

Finding plane tickets has been impossible, so she grabs her laptop and her camera, puts on a pair of travel jeans, and prepares for a long drive to New York. When she walks the streets, with her hidden Persianness, no one blames her. She isn't accused of anything—just another American participating in the shock. But she wants to stop the passersby and tell them that she is innocent. *I'm a Christian, a well-read woman. I will be an American citizen very soon.* She wants to say these things in a loud, confident voice, in her overeducated accent with its fake British undertones, to some anonymous assailant.

She has Immigrant Worries now.

Despite the peace of all the years gone by, sometimes in crowded rooms she scans the faces for her mother's. Once a year she indulges in a letter to former Evin prisoners.

When she returns to California, her camera filled with photos and her notebook with stories, Dr. Zohreh calls. Ever since her move, Saba has slowly acquiesced to Dr. Zohreh's requests to help her secret group. The two have talked often—when Saba first arrived and later when she felt alone and needed a mother to listen to her fears. "Is everything okay? I've been trying to get through for days."

"It's bad," says Saba. "I can't stop thinking how hard it will be now for you or Baba to visit. Or for me to go back." She misses her father the most. She calls him often.

"I'm sorry," says Dr. Zohreh. "Maybe this is a sign to look forward."

"Yes," she agrees, though she thinks of Reza too much on lonely days. Sometimes she goes for drinks with her friends, in dirty bars with shots of tequila for three dollars or three-dollars-twenty for the better kind, and she imagines that Reza will walk in any minute. That he will have changed. Maybe he will be something like Mahtab's Cameron, an amalgam now, a third something, as she is. They will be free to kiss or touch because people do that here, but they won't, because of the time and the distance, maybe a little because of their friendship and the ghosts of past *pasdar*s always watching. For the sake of the rest of the party, she will pretend he is a cousin—as lovers sometimes do in Tehran streets—smile coyly and say, "How is Uncle So-and-So?" He will like this game and fire back with something irreverent like "Still full of cancer" or "Still in love with his house-cleaner." The others will leave them alone to discuss their shared roots, while whispering open-minded American things, pretending to understand. "Look at that," they will say, heads shaking knowingly. "That's blood." The two will leave the bar together. Maybe it will take a block, maybe three, before he takes her hand and kisses her palm, his beard tickling her skin. Maybe they will dance in the street to no music, like men and women in movies. Then America will recede for a while, and Iran and Reza and her family, all the smoky smells and *setar* sounds and watery-green details of home will come rushing back and she will be herself again—not a fancy American reporter who knows thousands of English words and arranges them in elegant passages for her readers but a Gilaki girl dancing in a street to the music of her village lover's easy humming.

But Reza would wither here, and each day Saba lets him go. She is an expert at it. She makes a pot of tea for her neighbor—a Spanish artist who spends her days painting badly and applying for grants—and imagines a closing for Mahtab's story.

⌘

Another year passes and Mahtab feels a pain in her heart, an immor-tal longing—she doesn't belong here. You know this. I know it too.

But I've kept her alive for so many years, and now she has begun to feel the artificiality of it. It's time I let her go. This is not where Mahtab wishes to be. Not Iran. Not America.

When we were children, she once asked Maman, "Do you ever wonder what it's like to be immortal? To die and still live forever?"

"Everyone wonders," said Maman. I remember her speech almost word for word. "Some people think that children will make them immortal. Others say it is a lifetime's work, or that it comes from what others remember of them. Some people, like the Mansooris, are just tired and want to join their friends. But we know that it's all about making a mark. Not just a lifetime of work, but *important* work."

Mahtab is tired now, stretched thin from her time in limbo, and she has already lived an extraordinary life. All that's left now is to sleep.

Good-bye, Mahtab jan. Rest in peace and know that you are a better woman than I.

I may never be able to shed the skin of the immigrant, put away the dreams of an old Iran that no longer exists, and start belonging somewhere. But my sister can.

Who knows if one day I will make a true legacy for myself. But I once promised myself this: In exile I will be a different kind of person—not the Saba of two failed marriages, not the damaged Saba, the one who ushered two old men to the grave. I will no longer be the other half of my dead sister. So I have written her story and the jinns have run away from me just as easily as they arrived. I have banished these immigrant fears through my sister's bite-sized television epiphanies so that I could wander the streets as if they were my own. And in the end, I will put Mahtab back in the water, many thousands of scoops of a teaspoon away—where she belongs.

Now I walk to the market in my new city and I . . . wait . . . who was it that just passed? That woman with short gray hair, the one wearing a blue manteau. Who was she? Would she have held on to that same old overcoat for all these years?

I must stop telling myself stories, but it is too much in my nature.

Up we went and there was maast . . .

AUTHOR'S NOTE

I am an Iranian exile. This story is my dream of Iran, created from a distance just as Saba invents a dreamed-up America for her sister. Saba longs to visit the America on television as I long to visit an Iran that has now disappeared. This book is my own Mahtab dream.

Cheshmeh, a fictional village in Shomal (northern Iran), is an amalgam of several villages that were part of my childhood memories of my home country. Some details I have taken from one village, some I have blended from several towns and provinces, and some I have imagined. As is the norm in fiction, when a detail did not suit the story, I made the story my priority, sometimes ignoring confusing or irrelevant facts or customs. Specific organizations named in the novel, such as Sheerzan and Gospel Radio Iran, are fictional. Post-revolutionary Iran is a place of contrasts. In my research I discovered that so much of what we Westerners characterize as modern Iran varies from day to day, and from city to city, and family to family. Even in a small region like Gilan, people live vastly different lives. I have tried to be true to the spirit of the region and the time, though there are details I have chosen to ignore (e.g., the many varieties of *hijab*/chador and the rarity of a *korsi* so far north—though I have seen it set up to show children). Some aspects of Saba's story are unique—a prominent Christian family living mostly unbothered in a village; a well-read Iranian girl who is fluent in English yet chooses to delay college. (Iranian girls tend to be studious and ambitious. The most gifted, if they have the means, often find their way to foreign universities.) These are the uncommon nuances of Saba's life. I am indebted to the people named below who helped me research this book from the United States, France, and Holland.

I would like to thank those who read my novel, those who gave hours of their time to be interviewed or help me locate books, videos, photos, and other documents (particularly those who sent their personal albums or located volumes available only in Iran). Due to the dangers to those who travel to Iran, I had to leave out some surnames. A big thanks to my primary readers: Anna Heldring, Chris Saxe, Eric Asp, Tori Egherman, Andrea Marshall Webb, Jonathan Webb, Pierre Dufour, Clara Matthieu Gotch (who read this twice!), Julia Fierro, Catherine Gillespie (for therapy and one hell of a twenty-page critique letter), Natalie Dupuis, and Caroline Upcher. For special research help, thanks to: Azadeh Ghaemi, Sussan Moinfar, Donna Esrail (wow, a reader sent by God!), Mahasti Vafa, Maryam Khorrami, Maryam S., Nicky and her aunt in Iran, and my own aunt Sepi Peckover and her family, and of course my mother and father, who shared their memories. To all the people who passed through the Mezrab critique groups and the Amsterdam novelists' group over the years and left their mark on my novel in so many ways. Friends, you have been a lifeline. I regret that I've almost certainly forgotten some acknowledgments, and some of you didn't even tell me your last name as we tore into one another's work over many bottles of bad wine (and *jenever* in canal boats), but I will at least thank those who gave me key ideas: Amal Chatterjee, Nina Siegal, Ute Klehe, Barbara Austin, and David Lee. *Proost!*

To Christian Bromberger, renowned Gilan scholar from France whose willingness to help was a beautiful surprise, and to my unlikely Iranian educators: Cyrus (for talk of home, reading, inspiring, and "Persian men dance to impress"), Arturo (for finding the old songs, the poems), Kian ("Love you, miss you, *zoolbia!*"), Sahand (for Mezrab, where I learned much about our crazy people), and Pooyan (a wealth of knowledge and hope. Thanks for including me in your Iran-loving world).

Thanks to my first Dutch editor, Pieter Swinkels, who offered much perspective, and to Sam Chang and all the wonderful people at the Iowa Writers' Workshop, who will be properly and individually thanked in my next novel. Thanks most of all to my amazing agent, Kathleen Anderson, her team at Anderson Literary, and her partner agents around the world; my brilliant, tireless editor, Sarah McGrath, who made the book so much better with her vision and talent, as well as Sarah Stein and everyone at Riverhead Books. Finally, thanks to Philip Viergutz, for cheerfully eating cereal for so many dinners, making three a.m. tea, and encouraging some truly spectacular whims, starting with "To hell with these business school loans, I want to write novels."